I0818316

Printed in the United States of America

ISBN 978-0-9981676-1-9

Visit www.appalachianstorms.com

If y
aware that
and destr
publis

THE P

Appalachian Stor

B

Dianna

Table of Contents

Chapter 1
Camp Fire Tales

"NO! I WON'T GO!"

"I WANT TO STAY WITH YOU!" The little girl arched her back, her arms stretching towards a woman sitting near the fire. "I WANT TO STAY WITH YOU, MOMMY!" she yelled.

The young mother gently but firmly pushed the crying child away into the arms of her father. "When you're older, you can stay."

The girl started screaming, as her father quickly walked towards the parking lot. Seeing her cries were being ignored, the child went into full-fledged tantrum mode. The piercing scream made everyone within hearing range wince. The young mother gave everyone around the fire a rueful smile as a low chuckle emanated throughout the crowd.

"It looks like we have another Katie Johnson on our hands," someone said in a low voice.

Katie quickly glanced in the direction of the voice, trying to discern who had said it. Looking around, she could see everyone's eyes in the group looking towards her. They all had varying degrees of smiles on their faces. She could feel her face getting warm, despite the cold wind rushing through the empty branches of the trees. A few leaves took flight, and whirled around the fire, only to settle on the empty hard ground once again.

Katie shielded herself from the wind as she automatically moved long strands of black hair away from her face. She couldn't help glancing towards the parking lot. The little girl's piercing scream could still be heard as the young father struggled to put her in a car seat. She couldn't help grinning, thinking everyone in the group was probably right. As far back as she could remember, she had pleaded and begged. If she was to be totally honest, she'd had several tantrums exactly like that. Her mother always gently, but firmly sent her home with the younger children. She told her when she was older, she could stay.

The next morning curiosity would literally drive her crazy. Katie would pester her mother with questions about what she and the others did around the campfire. Her mother would always give her a secret smile, and tell her when she was old enough, she could attend and find out. This year was different. She was old enough to stay. Finally, she was going to be able to know what happened, at these secret campfire sessions.

Hardly able to contain her excitement, she slapped her hands on her dark jeans. The sound made her two best friends, Lizzy and Samantha, turn and exchange a smile. They'd had endless discussions on what the women did during these campfire sessions. Katie looked around the campfire. Her mother was sitting next to Lizzy's mom. The mood was relaxed and festive. Everyone was having a good time, laughing and talking.

As darkness descended like a cloak in the Appalachian Mountains, long shadows darkened the wooded area, making everything around them black. Fire was the only light, as it flickered and danced on familiar faces. Portable seats were jumbled together as close to the large fire as possible, its occupant's intent on keeping warm.

Katie, Lizzy, and Sam sat close together on a fallen log, allowing the older women to take advantage of the heat. Katie had scoped out the ideal spot earlier that day and immediately laid claim. It was close enough to see and hear everything going on around the camp fire, but far enough away to not attract unwanted attention. Of course, that was before the young girl started her tantrum, and all eyes found her anyway.

Lizzy's grandmother slowly stood up, her wrinkles more pronounced in the firelight. Her withered hands rose slowly as if she were offering a silent prayer. A respectful hush immediately descended around the fire. The old woman turned and sat down again, the chair creaking under her weight. Her voice was raspy but firm as she started to speak.

"This story I speak to you today has been handed down from mother to daughter since the Sugaree first walked these mountains. I am getting old, and soon my spirit will join the spirits of my mother and her mother. All mothers, or soon-to-be mothers of the Sugaree, must hear this story so they will tell it to the next generation."

She paused, looking into each face. Katie felt the old woman's eyes on her for just a moment, before it passed onto Lizzy's face beside her. "You must make a solemn promise in your hearts today, that the story of the Sugaree be told and not die out." The old women leaned back into her chair, obviously intent on being as comfortable as possible.

Her voice, soft and raspy, rang with authority. "When the earth was young, it was covered in water. No land touched the face of the earth. A water beetle worked under the water and pushed mud to the top of the water, forming the first land. Then a black bird came down from the spirit world. It landed on the mud, resting its wings. When it flapped its wings, great mountains were created. These mountains around you were the first mountains formed on this earth. Because they were the first, they hold the strongest magic of the spirit world. Every living thing in these mountains holds this magic. As time has passed, the magic has grown less. The magic was diluted by the number of living creatures who lived and died in this ancient and sacred forest.

"When these mountains were young, great animals that no longer live roamed and called them home—the great wolf, saber tooth tiger, the mammoth, the sloth and many more we do not have names for."

The old woman paused and took a deep breath. "The Sugaree, looking for food, found these mountains full of game. They settled in one of the valleys. Soon other tribes came and settled —the Saprini, Elno, Yuchi, Occanechew, Congaree, the Cherokee, and others. Through time, we have lost the names of great tribes who lived, loved, and died. The memory of those who lived before are now forgotten.

"It was a happy time for the Sugaree. There was plenty of game, and the women planted gardens. They grew corn, squash, gourds, and other items. The clay in the earth was made into pottery. The men soon grew tired of hunting and started warring with other tribes. Warriors replaced hunters. Women were the driving force in keeping the tribe and family units together. The kinship descended through the women's line. We have always been, and always will be, a matriarchal people."

Lizzy's grandmother paused again. The firelight flickered across her wrinkled features, making her look haggard. "The great animals of the forest started dying off and became no more. The last of The Great White Tigers came upon a Sugaree woman and her child. Hungry and too tired to hunt, the tiger decided to eat the child. When the Tiger approached, the young woman came between it and the child.

"With only a rock as a weapon, the woman faced the great tiger. The Tiger could have easily killed the mother and her child. The animal was surprised by the courage the woman showed in defending her young, impressed with her determination to save her child, despite the odds. The tiger backed away and turned into the woods. Curious of these creatures, the great tiger quietly followed them to their dwelling. She watched the villagers closely, learning their ways. She became a silent protector of the courageous woman and her child.

"One day the tiger grew careless and was seen by a warrior in the village. Misunderstanding the tiger's intent, the warrior got other warriors to track her. Eventually, they killed the great tiger. The spirit of the tiger knew she was the last of her kind, and did not want to leave this world or the woman she protected. Instead of entering into the spirit world, the tiger's spirit joined the young woman's spirit. All the magic the old tiger and her kind possessed entered into the woman. They became one.

"The magic of the tiger was passed down, from mother to daughter. The descendants of the woman became protectors of the Sugaree. When danger arose, a young woman would take the shape of the tiger. She would destroy, whatever threatened them. The tiger could only be in one young woman at a time, but the old magic made her very strong. She could run for miles, without resting. When she was hurt, her wounds would heal quickly. She could sense danger, and have the ability to be where she was needed to protect her people.

"Many generations passed, and the people of the Sugaree lived in peace. The old ones stopped telling their young, the tale of The Great White Tiger. The courageous gift, that was given the woman was forgotten. The tale was lost to the Sugaree. There was a time when a great evil entered these mountains, and the great tiger again returned to a descendant of the courageous woman.

"Strange people with strange animals entered the village. They wore metal on their breasts and heads. They had pale faces and eyes the color of grass and sky. The sleeping tiger spirit recognized danger and turned a young woman into a tiger. Not knowing what was happening, the young woman named 'Running Deer' was frightened. She ran into the woods and did not protect the village.

"The strange pale men in the village demanded to know where gold was in these mountains. They were cruel to the Sugaree, often killing or maiming members of the village to set an example. When Running Deer realized her destiny was to fight this evil, she returned to the village, ready to fight. By then, the pale faces had left. A sickness entered the village, killing the old, and then the young. The spirit tiger could not fight this new evil the way it could fight a foe. Running Deer watched helplessly, as all her people died of the white man's sickness.

"Desolated by what she saw, she wandered through the forest. She found other tribes, like the Yuchi, Saprini, Elno, and the Congaree. All the tribes became no more, as the white man's sickness spread through the mountains and the valleys of Appalachia. Running Deer, was afraid to turn human. She did not know if the sickness would also take her, as it had taken her family. She stayed as a tiger, for many moons. Eventually, she climbed the highest mountain and found a tribe not touched by the white man's sickness. Turning back into human form, Running Deer joined the tribe. She was counted and lived among the Cherokee.

"Running Deer never forgot she was a Sugaree. She made sure her children, and her children's children, knew about the spirit tiger that possessed and protected the Sugaree." The old women raised her arms and gestured to all the women surrounding the fire. "All of you, are descendants of Running Deer. When there is a great evil that threatens the Sugaree, the spirit tiger will possess and change your form into a great white tiger.

"The magic of The Great White Tiger within these mountains will help you to survive, and, will help you protect the Sugaree. The mistake Running Deer made, must never happen again. If your human form changes into a tiger, remember a great evil is close, threatening the Sugaree. You must stay, and protect your people."

The old woman stopped talking. Her gasping breath could be heard above the wind and the crackling fire. Katie watched the labored breathing, pondering the story she had learned. She casually looked around the campfire to try and gauge everyone's reactions. Some of the women sat looking into the fire, while others were intently watching the old woman. A tingling sensation was raising the hairs on her neck and arms before resting, in her chest. She could feel something in the air. A feeling, or an emotion she couldn't place. It was a feeling of unity, a bond that touched her heart and burned.

Sitting in this setting with the cold mountain air touching her face, the warm crackling fire, the tale touched her imagination. She couldn't help but imagine what life would have been like for Running Deer. Whom had been able to change into a great white tiger, and run through the forest. As Katie pictured herself becoming a changeling or were-animal. She wasn't sure of the term. Suddenly, another tingling sensation went through her body. The heat in her chest magnified into a force that would have scared her if it didn't seem right. Heat rippled from the pit of her stomach like a soft glow, from the inside out. She looked over at Sam and Lizzy, to gauge their reaction. Sam was watching the old woman, while Lizzy was looking down at her shoes. Neither one of them noticed her glance.

Lizzy's grandmother started to speak again, her voice now sounding very tired. "If and when you turn into The Great White Tiger, there are certain dangers you must be aware of. Seekers are out there..." She broke off, her head bowing down as if weighted by a great stone.

Katie kept staring at the top of the old woman's head, wondering if this was part of the story.

Lizzy's mom got up and moved towards her mother.

"Mom, are you Okay?" She knelt down, and lifted the old lady's head and looked into her eyes. She turned her head, towards the group. "I'm sorry, but Mom is just too tired to go on. We are going to have to cut this short." She gestured for Lizzy, to come over.

Katie watched Lizzy hurriedly get up, and help her mother slowly move the old lady towards the parking lot. Disappointment weighed heavily in her chest. She knew there was much more to the story. In previous years, her mother had not come home for hours. She tipped her arm towards the firelight, looking at her watch. Barely an hour had gone by since the men and young children left. She bumped Sam's arm and stood up. Sam quickly got up and followed her away from the fire.

"What did you think about..." She paused, not sure how to continue. "about the tale?" she ended lamely.

Sam looked around checking to see if anyone was in hearing distance, her shape barely discernible in the darkness. "I don't know. You would think it was just a bedtime story, if it didn't seem so serious. There has to be a lot more to this than what we heard." She shook her head, making a soft rustling sound. "I mean, why all the secrecy?"

Katie heard someone approaching them. Turning, she could make out Lizzy coming back to the campfire.

"Can you stay? You're supposed to be able to sleep over, at my house tonight."

Lizzy shook her head. "I'm sorry, guys, my mom is taking Grandma to the hospital. She wants me with her."

Sam patted Lizzy's arm, "Hey, don't sweat it. I hope everything goes okay."

Katie shrugged, trying to keep the disappointment out of her voice. "Yeah, your grandmother's more important, than a sleepover." She paused, her thoughts returning to the evening events. "What did you think, of the story?" she asked quickly.

Lizzy looked down at her feet, kicked an unseen pebble in frustration. "Actually, I was disappointed. Grandma has told me this story, many times. It used to be, my favorite bedtime story. If this was all it was about, why all the secrecy?"

Katie blew out her breath, her frustration evident. "Yeah... There's has to be something else, right? What else was going to happen?"

No one spoke. Each girl contemplated what they had heard and learned so far.

Katie couldn't help it; she just had to say it. "Did you guys feel a little funny, when she started talking about the white tiger?"

Sam looked towards Katie, trying to see her in the dark. "What do you mean, by 'funny'?"

Katie shrugged, liking the idea that her two friends couldn't actually see her face in the darkness. "I don't know," she said, wishing she hadn't said anything, "kind of warm and tingly?"

Sam giggled softly. "Yeah, I had a little too many hot dogs myself. I really need to burp." She patted her stomach as if she was in pain.

"That spicy sausage I ate is keeping me a little warm," Lizzy said with a half laugh. "I don't know why I kept eating it."

Katie stepped closer, trying to see their expressions. "No... No, I mean I felt something. You didn't feel anything?"

Lizzy reached out and gave her a soft punch in the arm. "Come on, Katie. Everything we heard so far my grandmother has told me many times before."

"Lizzy, come on; we need to go." An impatient voice came from the direction of the parking lot.

Lizzy immediately looked towards the sound of her mother's voice.

"Sorry," she yelled. She turned back to face her friends. "I'll call you tomorrow." Without waiting for a reply, she ran back in the direction she'd come from.

Sam watched Lizzy walk away, her dark figure disappearing quickly in the blackness around them. She turned towards Katie. "Do you mind if I cancel tonight also? I have to get up early for dance practice. Since this turned into a blowout, I'd rather get a good night's sleep."

Katie was so frustrated, she felt like throwing the same type of tantrum she had witnessed earlier. Knowing it would make her look as if she was three instead of sixteen, she quickly agreed and made her goodbyes.

Sitting in the passenger seat on the way home, Katie decided it was time her mother gave her a few answers. "Mom, what was that all about? I don't understand, all the secrecy. Was this story about a tiger, the only thing we were going to hear?" The questions came out in a rush, all jumbled together. Katie wasn't sure the words were even decipherable in her rush to get some answers.

Her mom gave her a quick glance, before returning her eyes to the narrow road. "I know, honey, you have been looking forward to this. I'm sure it's a big disappointment. I was disappointed, when I was your age. The biggest thing you need to remember is, Elizabeth Hawk senior is the matriarch over all of us and deserves our respect."

"What do you mean?" Katie interrupted. "Are you saying there really isn't anymore?"

"Well, there's a little more." Her mother began, before shaking her head. "It's along the same lines of the story you just heard."

"You mean that's it?" Her voice went up an octave in her frustration. Disappointment warred in her chest, as heat welled up inside her. Her face was flushed. "It's not real?"

Exasperation in her voice, her mother replied. "You tell me; is it possible for a young woman to turn into a tiger? Is that what you are asking?"

Katie felt foolish, slumping in her seat. She stared out her window, not seeing anything. "No, I just..." She paused. *What did she think?* She was very much aware that she was sounding like an idiot.

"Katie," her mother began. "Elizabeth Hawk has done a lot of good, and has helped each person around that campfire, even you."

Her mother paused, as she drove through a windy patch in the road. "When I got a divorce from your father, I was at my wit's end. How was I going to get by? She babysat you for free, so I could work. Believe it or not, that was a very big help. I will never forget her kindness."

She paused again, trying to articulate her words. "Elizabeth Hawk firmly believes in the story. I don't know if she has entrenched herself so much in the old ways, she actually believes them or what." Trying to stress this even further, she repeated herself. "She firmly believes in the story, and feels it is her duty to tell all the descendants of Running Deer." She shrugged. "Who am I, to try and dissuade her? She is the one who demanded the secrecy. Each of us solemnly promised not only to keep it secret but sacred." She paused again, turning into their driveway. "Because I respect and love her, I did exactly as she asked, and so did everyone else."

Having nothing else to say on the subject, Katie got out of the car and slowly walked into the house. She was so disheartened about the night, she could hardly stand it. There was no use talking anymore. She studiously avoided her mother's eyes and headed for her bedroom.

Chapter 2
Facing Tigers

Katie stepped out of the woods, looking around her. Her eyes were automatically drawn to the sound of a cascading waterfall. The torrent fell about thirty feet into a pool. The clear pond looked cool and inviting. The edges were over fifty feet in diameter. It looked like there was very little shallow water, as the color immediately became a deeper blue. She could see the rocks in the bottom ripple in, and out of focus.

It looked like an ideal swimming hole. Green ferns and other plants surrounded the edges, except for a trail, leading to the edge. The trail followed a small creek, as it emptied still further down into the valley. The familiar scent of earth, wildflowers, and evergreens reached her senses. She took a deep breath, of the clean, thin air. She sensed, rather than knew, she was far away from any kind of civilization.

Katie glanced around and caught sight of a toddler playing in the shallow edge. Frowning, she automatically looked around for the child's guardians. She didn't see anyone close. She stepped closer, realizing just how deep and dangerous the pool was to the child. The naked little girl, had short black hair sticking out in several angles. Her black eyes danced, as she picked up rocks and threw them in the water. Each time the rock hit the surface, she let out a giggle. Her soft pudgy cheeks, upturned in a smile. Before the rock could sink to the depths of the pool, she quickly stooped down to grab another.

Laughing at the antics of the little girl, Katie ignored a movement she saw in her peripheral vision. A small sound made her turn her head, her laughter dying on her lips her eyes widening. Just a few feet away, approached the largest tiger Katie had ever seen.

IT.....WAS......HUGE!!!

The head stood over six feet. Its fur was almost all white, with barely discernible gray stripes. Its eyes were green, as it gave the baby a deadly stare. Its massive feet made very little sound, as it slowly moved towards the child.

Katie stood frozen, as she watched the tiger step closer, its intent clear. She felt a protective instinct, rush through her system. She closed her eyes, seeing the outcome in her head if she did nothing. Without thinking about the consequences of her actions, Katie quickly looked down. Seeing a rock twice the size of her hand, she reached for it. As the rough texture bit into her hand, she lunged herself between the tiger and the baby.

The tiger paused, staring at her with its cold green eyes. It stepped towards her and made a low growl making her hair stand on end. Katie shifted the rock in her hand, sweat pooling from every pour. Her mind froze, as the tiger took another step towards her, the growl in its throat getting louder. Somewhere behind her, the child started whining as if sensing danger.

Hearing the sound, Katie straightened her shoulders. She knew she was going to be dead in seconds. The baby's death would soon follow.

“If you want the baby, you are going to have to go through me,” she said, with false bravado. The rock shaking in her hand, she lifted it ready for the attack.

“Well? Come on! Let’s get this over with!” Her voice sounded shaky, despite her determination to sound stronger than she felt.

To her surprise, the tiger took a step away from her. Not believing, what she was seeing, she watched the tiger slowly back away, turn, and leap into the woods. Not believing her luck, Katie dropped the rock in her hand. She barely registered the soft thump it made, as it fell onto the mossy forest floor. In one quick movement, she turned and grabbed the little girl and started running as fast as she could.

The toddler was crying in earnest. Katie tried to shush the baby, afraid her cries would bring the tiger back. She stumbled over a limb and almost fell. Grasping the toddler tighter, she slowed down to a quick walk. Her breathing ragged with exertion. She clutched the baby close to her body. The trees and underbrush around her looked menacing. Sounds magnified and bounced around the undergrowth. Her eyes darted to each bush, expecting the massive tiger to emerge once again.

Stumbling into a small clearing, she saw a young man leaning against a tree. Relief welled up inside her chest, as she rushed towards him.

“There’s a tiger! **A GREAT BIG TIGER!** Back there!” She pointed behind her. “In the woods! It wanted to eat this baby!" Her body twisted as she immediately looked behind. Her eyes darting around, still expecting the tiger to return. “Please, you have to help us get out of here.”

The guy looked down at her, his eyes, unreadable. “What baby?” he asked quietly.

Frustrated, Katie hitched her arms, lifting the baby higher on her hip. "A TIGER IS GOING TO EAT ME, AND THIS BABY IN MY ARMS, YOU IDIOT!"

She looked down at her arms, which were stretched around... nothing, holding absolutely, nothing. "I… What the….?"

Exasperated, she turned and glanced around. "What happened to the baby?" she said in bewilderment. She couldn't help looking down at her arms. At that very moment, she had felt the baby's weight on her hip.

A low chuckle came from the direction of the young man, standing in front of her.

Katie stopped and studied him a little closer. He was drop dead gorgeous, she decided. He was tall, almost six feet. He stood with a natural, athletic stance. He wasn't large like a football player, but he obviously worked out. His lean muscles rippled under his white t-shirt. His high cheekbones and strong chin resembled a Native American. His skin was white, and his hair blond. His eyes were sky blue, so blue they didn't look real. It was as if, he was in a magazine ad and was air-brushed. He looked around her age, maybe older, but his eyes, which never left her face, seemed to look much older.

Another chuckle escaped the lips of the stranger.

Hearing the sound her eyes narrowed. She didn't like being the brunt of a horrible joke. She folded her arms. "Okay, who are you?"

The stranger gave her a tight smile. "Jackson."

"Jackson… Who?"

He shrugged his shoulders. "Just... Jackson."

"Well, Jackson with no last name, do you have any idea where we are?"

Jackson looked around. "If I had to guess, I'd say we are in the Smokey Mountains. Since this is not my dream, I believe you would know more about it than I would."

"I'm dreaming?" Katie said with surprise. "I'm dreaming," she said softly to herself.

Realization dawning, the last hour was finally making sense. Katie could not remember a dream seeming so real. She looked at the guy, standing in front of her. It made total sense now. There was no way, anyone was that beautiful in real life.

"So, you're not real."

It was Jackson's turn to narrow his eyes. "What makes you think I'm not real?"

"Because you're in my dream," Katie said. "What are you doing in my dream?"

"I was..." Jackson gave a pause. "Curious."

Intrigued, Katie folded her arms. "What are you curious about?"

"You"

Jackson took a small step towards her, when a low growl sounded in the clearing. Jackson paused, his eyes focusing on something just over Katie's right shoulder. She did not want to look. Doing so would make it real. Katie kept staring into Jackson's eyes, fascinated as they turned into a pale icy blue. Another low growl, much closer this time. Katie's hair stood on the back of her neck. She closed her eyes, squared her shoulders, and slowly turned to see The Great White Tiger. The tiger was so close to her, she could smell its breath. The tiger was ignoring Katie. It was looking straight at Jackson, with deadly intent.

Jackson's arms made a slight movement, as he reached towards Katie. The tiger snarled so loudly, Katie thought her eardrums might puncture. Jackson slowly lowered his arms, and stepped away from Katie. That resulted in a low growl in the tiger's throat. He slowly backed away from her, his arms raised in surrender. With every step backward Jackson took, the tiger took a step forward.

Eventually, the tiger stood between Katie and Jackson. When Jackson was far enough away to appease the tiger, it turned towards Katie. Very slowly and methodically, the tiger walked towards her. She started to push Katie to the other side of the clearing, with her head and shoulders.

At first, Katie was terrified, but her emotions quickly turned into frustration as the tiger kept pushing against her.

"What do you want me to do?" She said in irritation. As the tiger's head bumped against her chest, causing her to take another step back.

The cat was relentless, as it kept pushing her until she tripped over a rock jutting from the ground. Immediately, she rolled over to get back on her feet, she felt the hot breath of the tiger on her back.

She froze, "*This is it,*" she thought, "*She's going to eat me.*"

She felt the teeth scrape on her back, as the tiger picked her up by her belt with its teeth. She dangled like a rag doll, with her butt in the air. Katie's feet and arms were dangling uselessly, several feet above the ground. As the tiger launched into the woods, her thoughts were, *I'm glad this is only a dream. Otherwise, this would be humiliating.*

Katie woke feeling so hot she could hardly breathe. Her sheets were soaked in her sweat, making her feel sticky. Getting up, she walked over to the window, trying to catch some cool air. She decided to take a cold shower. With her hair damp, she sat in front of a fan. She slowly relived every detail of the dream. *Did this dream have a meaning?* She wondered.

She thought about the guy in her dream, Jackson. The name could be first or last. She remembered his face, the long lashes that framed those beautiful blue eyes. He seemed so real... The dream was so vivid. Everything about it felt real. Usually, a dream started to fade, until the details got drowned out in reality. This dream felt so real, it was like an actual memory she had lived through.

She couldn't help shuddering when she remembered the size of the white tiger. It effortlessly picked her up and carried her away. *At least I know that wasn't real, s*he thought distractedly. *There is no way, there's a tiger that large anywhere on this planet.*

Katie's mom walked into the kitchen. "You're up early," she stated. "On a weekday, I can't get you up for school. On the weekend you're up much earlier, then on a school day."

Katie grimaced. "I had a really weird dream last night."

"Oh, yeah? What did you dream about?"

Katie almost hated to say it. "A great big white tiger."

Laughing, her mother looked over at Katie. "I've had a few dreams like that myself."

Katie jerked up, alert. "What were your dreams like?"

"Oh, I don't know, it's been so long since I've had one, I don't think I remember anymore."

Katie watched her mother pour a cup of coffee, and sit down across the table from her. She wondered if her mother would have faced a great white tiger, with just a rock for a weapon. Watching her mom closely, she realized her mother had already faced a tiger.

For as long as she could remember, it had been just Katie and her mom. When she was younger, she pestered her mother with questions about her dad. All she got was a resounding silence she could never penetrate. Frustrated, she eventually went to Old Elizabeth Hawk.

She remembered Lizzy's grandmother sitting there for a long time, not saying anything. Katie thought she had reached another dead end. She then spoke so softly, Katie had to lean forward to hear.

"I've never seen a young girl, so much in love. Your mom loved that boy, with all her heart. When your mom married your dad, they appeared very happy. When you came along, your mother just glowed. Suddenly, things started to change. Sometimes, men get bored with their lives. They look around, want something different. Some wonder about the choices they made. They think they're missing out on something, out there in the world."

The old lady paused. Katie didn't say a word. She waited patiently for her to continue.

"He never cheated on her, so get that out of your mind right away. He was just unhappy with his life. He loved your mom, but somehow he felt trapped. So... he started drinking. Your mom put on a brave face for a while. She got a job as a waitress at the diner in town. She was willing to do anything for him.

"One day she went to work and left you with him. I don't know if he drank while babysitting before, but that day he was drinking rather heavily. He ran out of alcohol and decided to run to the store. I don't know if he forgot you were in the house, or just didn't want to take you. I know he only intended to be gone for about ten minutes. He ended up getting a DWI, with the county sheriff. By the time he was booked and got his one phone call, he had been gone from the house for hours. He called your mom and told her he was in jail. He wanted her to bail him out.

"Your mom called me, frantic, and didn't know where her baby was. She was on her way to the house. Since I was closer, she asked if I could run over to make sure you were okay. I got to the house, just before she did. Your pants were messy, and you had been wandering around the house screaming for, I don't know how long. I will never forget the look on your mother's face when she rushed into the house. Tears were running down her face, as she picked you up and took care of your needs. She just held you close and cried and cried. There was nothing I could do but sit there. I tried to let her know she wasn't alone.

"When there seemed to be no tears left, your mother asked if she could live with me for a while. I told her it would be tight, but we'd manage. She then packed everything she could and left. She never bailed out your dad. After a while, he came around asking for another chance. He didn't know what he had until it was gone. He promised never to drink again. Your mother never said a word to him. She just listened for a while, and then walked away.

"Eventually, your dad stopped coming around. I would see him around town, every once in a while. When he received the divorce papers, he packed up and left. We never saw him again. I know he's alive because your mom receives child support."

Katie watched her mother, with admiring eyes. She never thought her mother pretty. She was just Mom. She had heard enough comments from friends and strangers to know her mother was considered beautiful. She was tall and willowy, with jet black hair. Her high cheekbones had a classic shape, and long lashes enhanced her large black eyes. Through the years, Katie had watched men approach her. They always had been politely but firmly turned away.

Yes, Katie thought, "*my mom already faced a tiger for her child.*

The phone rang, disrupting her thoughts. Her mother reached for the phone. Katie got up and started fixing herself a bowl of cereal. She sat down at the table, before glancing up. Her mother's face was white.

"Yes, we'll be right there," her mother said into the phone.

"What's wrong?"

With a shaky voice, her mother explained. "Elizabeth Hawk had a stroke. They're not sure if she's going to make it. She's in some kind of coma, and unresponsive."

"Is that what happened, at the campfire?"

"I don't know, maybe. Come on; let's get going."

Chapter 3
Old Elizabeth Hawk

The hospital, like any other hospital in the country, was filled with the smells of cleaning supplies and antiseptics. The waiting room was filled with empty chairs. In the corner, Katie saw Lizzy had placed two chairs together. Her legs were outstretched on one, and she was hunched over, asleep. *She must be completely exhausted to sleep in that position*, Katie thought. Her mom must have thought the same thing because she hesitated before walking towards the nurse's station.

"We're here for Elizabeth Hawk," her mom said in a soft voice.

"Are you family?" the nurse immediately asked.

Katie could see the indecision in her mother's face. "Ah, yes." Her mom was a terrible liar.

The nurse paused, before pointing down the hall. "Room 316."

Katie didn't know what to expect when she entered Old Elizabeth Hawk's room, but she hadn't expected a crowded room. With the crush of bodies, it was hard to decipher who was there. It was surprising how quiet it was, with that many people in the room.

Old Elizabeth Hawk, was lying on the bed. Her long gray hair, resting on her chest. She looked as if she was sleeping. The room was empty of monitors and equipment. Feeling uneasy, Katie reached for the door behind her and slipped out.

Katie went to find Lizzy. Entering the waiting room, she was glad to see Lizzy awake and talking to Sam. They both smiled when they saw her.

"It's really crowded in there," Katie said softly.

"Yeah, people have been coming, and going all night," Lizzy said, sleep making her voice sound scratchy.

"Soooo," Sam said in a hesitant whisper, "she's really not going to make it?"

"No," Lizzy said quietly "You should have seen Mom when they tried to hook her up to a respirator. She completely lost it. She started screaming the place down. She told them if her mother was going to die, it was going to be with dignity."

All three girls looked up, as another group of people came into view. They purposely walked to the nurse's station. "Elizabeth Hawk's room please?"

"Are you family?" came the repeated question.

A pause. "Yes. Yes, we're family."

The nurse pointed down the hall. "Room 316."

"Do you know those people?" Sam asked in a whisper.

"Never seen them before in my life," Lizzy whispered back.

Unable to help themselves, all three girls started giggling. Katie looked over at Lizzy. Her shoulder length hair was tangled. Her long legs were still stretched out over the chair. The most remarkable thing about Lizzy was her eyes. They were such a light blue, they looked gray. She sometimes wondered how her friend had such beautiful eyes. Her mom and dad, both had black eyes. It didn't make any sense.

Sam was shorter than Katie and Lizzy. She used to tease them and say she was average height; she just had two very tall friends. She was always smiling, and her disposition was to laugh at everything. She came from a very religious family. She didn't cuss, smoke, or drink, and she didn't like being around people who did. A couple of times, when Katie had tried to get Sam to do something against her beliefs, Sam just walked away, leaving Katie feeling stupid. Apologizing was something Katie didn't like doing. She eventually came to this conclusion: if Sam did things totally differently than everyone else, that was okay with her.

"How many more people, can fit in that room?" Lizzy said, as another group came down the hall asking for Elizabeth Hawk's room.

Katie smiled. "Yup. They need a bigger room."

The funeral was a couple of days later. It turned out, Elizabeth Hawk was loved and respected by a great many people. Lizzy's mom set up the funeral, with an open microphone. People could randomly get up and talk about their experiences with Elizabeth. There were so many people wanting to tell stories of how Elizabeth Hawk had helped them, it took hours for everyone to be done. Instead of being bored, Katie was fascinated by all the stories. How could one person, have helped so many people?

At the informal family luncheon, more people felt they needed to get up and tell their stories. Elizabeth had helped them all at particular times in their lives when they really needed someone.

"You have some big shoes to fill," Sam told Lizzy softly.

"Yeah, I know," Lizzy replied.

Eating their meals in silence, all three girls looked up when a loud blustery voice called out. "You have got to be related to Forrest. Are you his daughter?"

A surprised Katie looked up to see a large burly man standing in front of them. He was staring straight at Lizzy.

"Excuse me?" Lizzy asked in surprise.

"FORREST, you know, 'Forrest,'" he said, as if that was really supposed to mean something. The big stranger stared expectantly at Lizzy.

"My mom and dad's names, are Mike and Mary Hawk," Lizzy said in a clear slow voice. Her eyes were watching the stranger intently.

"Ahhh," said the stranger. He looked hard at Lizzy. "Well, ah, I need to get going. It was nice meeting you." He nodded, at Katie and Sam. He then turned and ducked into a crowd of people so quickly, it was hard to see where he went.

Katie looked questioningly at Lizzy. "What was that all about?"

Lizzy's beautiful eyes were narrowed and transfixed to the spot where the stranger had disappeared. "I have no idea, but I'm going to find out."

Chapter 4

Chess

Katie looked around. She didn't seem to be anywhere she recognized. The room was not very large, and almost bare of furniture. An old couch was in the corner. Two chairs and a table sat across from the couch. The walls, once white, were stained yellow. There were no curtains or furnishings in the windows.

"Hello."

She turned towards the sound, realizing she wasn't alone. She had a hard time containing her excitement, when she saw Jackson leaning on the door frame. She smiled and took a couple of steps towards him. "Hi!"

Jackson straightened and put his hands in his pockets. "I thought this would be easier for us to talk. He gestured, around the empty room. "See, no tigers."

Katie laughed a soft tinkling sound. "Yes, it would be hard to imagine a great big tiger in here."

Jackson chuckled, then caught himself, as though he wasn't used to the sound. "I'm pretty proud of myself for coming up with this."

"Why would you do that?" Katie asked, taking another step towards him.

"I told you, I was curious."

Baffled, Katie cocked her head to one side. "Curious about what?"

"You."

The words sent a warm glow, throughout her body. She beamed. "I'm really not that interesting," she said in a shy voice, her head dipping down.

Jackson cocked his head. "Really? Who else has a great white tiger as a guardian?"

Katie gave him a small frown "A guardian?"

"You didn't notice. The tiger only wanted to take you away from me."

"Yeah, I noticed," she said with a shrug. "I didn't think she was protecting me." She paused, giving Jackson a questioning look. "Do I need protection, from you?"

Jackson simply shrugged. "Yes."

"Why?"

"Because, I'm the bad guy," he said with a grin.

"Bad guy, huh?" No one could be that gorgeous, and be a bad guy. "How are you the bad guy?"

"Oh, you know, total world dominion, sacrificing of small children, slavery of the minions, power, money, that sort of thing." He took a step towards her. He was close enough to touch her. He slowly reached out to touch her hair and froze.

Katie stood, mesmerized by his closeness. Seeing him freeze, she gave him a puzzled frown. A shocked expression came into Jackson's face. A familiar growl echoed in the room behind her. Once again, she closed her eyes, squared her shoulders, and turned slowly to face what she knew was behind her. The tiger took up the entire room. It really had no place to move. It must have appeared, out of thin air. The growling increased echoing off the walls, making the sound all the more menacing. Jackson raised his hands in surrender. This seemed to appease the tiger a little, because the growling slowed down, becoming softer.

"I just want to talk," he said to the tiger in a soft, not-so-steady voice.

"Is that going to work?" Katie whispered.

"I don't know. I'm willing to try anything at the moment," he said not taking his eyes off the tiger.

He did something completely surprising. He knelt down, in what could only be described as a complete submissive posture. The tiger stepped forward and grasped Katie's shirt with its teeth, tugging her away from Jackson.

Jackson sat back on his haunches with his arms outstretched in submission. "I just wanted to talk; that's all."

The tiger stared at Jackson, before slowly getting down on the floor. Katie, not knowing what she should do, studied the scene in front of her.

Jackson took a quick glance towards her. "Why don't you sit down too?"

Keeping her eyes on the tiger, she cautiously sat down in front of Jackson. "Now what do we do?" she whispered, keeping her eyes steady on the enormous beast.

Jackson shrugged. "It appears your guardian has agreed we can talk."

"My guardian?" she repeated, stupidly.

"Yeah, you know, the humongous tiger sitting behind you."

Jackson's voice halted as the tiger got up, walked between Jackson and Katie, and lay down between them. The tiger's backside was touching her leg, while its head was facing Jackson. The tiger's face was so close to Jackson, he immediately scooted backward till his back was against the wall. She tentatively reached out touching the tiger. Its fur was springy and very soft.

Jackson sat, watching her inquisitively. "You're not very afraid of it, are you?"

Katie looked up, realizing he was right. "No... it feels like we've been friends for a long time."

"Apparently." Jackson gave another pause. It looked as if he decided to ignore the tiger between them. "So, tell me about yourself."

Since this was a dream, and the boy sitting on the other side of the tiger wasn't real, Katie felt completely relaxed around him. She told him everything she could possibly think of. She talked about her two best friends, Lizzy and Sam, and what she liked best about them. He didn't seem surprised, when she told him she liked playing every sport her school had to offer. He liked the same things she did. She loved to watch his eyes light up when she told him a funny story about herself.

He was open about sports and activities he did in school but became reserved when she asked about his personal life. Katie didn't mind. She just thought he didn't really know her. When he knew her better, he would open up to her more. After a while, Jackson reluctantly stood up.

"Are you leaving?" Katie asked surprised.

Jackson smiled, still cautious of the tiger between them. "No, you are."

"I'm leaving?" Confused, Katie glanced around.

"Yes, it's time for you to wake up."

The alarm sounded, and Katie woke up, startled. Sweat was streaming down her face. She felt so hot, she thought she was going to combust. The cold shower did not cool her down. She dressed for school and ran to Lizzy's car when the horn blared outside.

"Are you crazy? Lizzy asked as she climbed into the car.

"What?" Katie asked, looking at the dumbfounded faces of both her friends.

"It's November," Sam said in an exasperated tone.

"Yeah, I know," Katie said, not getting their point.

"Normal people wear jackets when it's cold outside," Lizzy said in a slow exaggerated voice.

Katie saw for the first time that her friends were bundled up in warm jackets. She, on the other hand, was wearing a t-shirt and shorts. "I'm hot," she stated. "I'm not going to change, so let's go."

Katie endured several snide comments, from teachers and friends about her attire. By lunch time she was so cold, she didn't think she would ever get warm again. She went to the nurse's office, asking if she could go home. The nurse huffed about what she was wearing, but eventually called her mom.

The next couple of weeks, Katie was in a constant state of confusion. She randomly became so hot, she could hardly breathe. The next minute she was so cold, she thought icicles would hang off her nose. Her first thought was maybe it was the flu, but nobody else seemed to have her same symptoms. She started toting around a backpack, so she could change into shorts or warm clothes on demand.

Her emotions were all over the place. Basketball practice helped her get rid of a lot of steam. Several times she had to bite her tongue and not lash out at her coach.

She didn't tell her friends, about Jackson. It was the first time, she had kept anything from them. Her relationship with him wasn't exactly real. Was it? How do you say, "Hey, guess what, I met this really cute guy, and I see him every night in my dreams"? They would think she was crazy. Maybe she was, she wondered to herself.

Her only sanctuary was when she fell asleep, and could see Jackson. Every night, she looked forward to going to sleep, so she could see him again. Sometimes, he wasn't there. Later, she would ask him, where he was.

His reply was always, "You're the one who didn't show up."

Since she didn't know how they were able to see each other in the first place, she had no idea how to change the situation. The tiger was always there. She got so comfortable with the tiger, she would stroke her till she purred. A couple of times Jackson reached out to stroke her, and almost got his hand bitten off.

Katie had pointed out, since they were both in some kind of dream world, maybe he wouldn't get physically hurt. He gave her a twisted smile, and told her he wasn't about to test her theory.

One night, Jackson pulled out a chess board, and started setting up the pieces on the small table in the room.

"Where did you get that?" she asked.

Jackson looked up, surprised. "This is a dream," he said, as if that explained it.

"Soooo," Katie said in a drawn-out voice, trying to get more information.

"Soooo, "Jackson mimicked her, "you can have anything you want."

Katie lifted her arms and gestured around her. "Are you telling me, we don't have to be in this cramped ugly room?"

Jackson's eyebrows rose. "You don't like my room?"

"You live here?" Katie gave the room, a closer look. "I don't want to hurt your feelings or anything, but your place needs some serious help."

Jackson gave her a questioning look. "If you were the decorator, what would you do?" he asked quietly.

"Oh, I don't know... paint, hang pictures, maybe some curtains." Katie started ticking off changes with her fingers.

"What color paint?" Jackson asked.

"White, with a little touch of blue," Katie said without hesitation. "Ahhhh!" she said in surprise, as the walls instantly had a fresh coat of paint. She turned and stared at Jackson, a look of surprise on her face. "How did you do that?"

Jackson shrugged. "Like I said, this is a dream world; you can do anything you want. Well... within reason," he said looking at the tiger.

"Blue curtains," she said in a rush. Light blue curtains, appeared on the windows. "No, not that color blue," she said with a laugh.

"Do you have any idea, how many shades of blue there are?" Jackson said dryly. "Why don't you try the decorating so I don't have to read your mind?"

"Okay." Katie rubbed her hands together. "How do I do it?"

"You just picture in your head what you want. Then you just make it happen," Jackson said with a flourish.

It was much harder than Jackson's explanation. Katie had to really concentrate. A few times, Jackson had to jump in to help her. Soon, she got the hang of it. By the time they sat down to play chess, the curtains were a navy blue. A new hardwood floor gleamed in the glow of new light fixtures. Her mother's painted artwork was on the walls. She was rather pleased with herself.

"I never knew it could look like this," Jackson said grudgingly. "It has..." He paused, a strange catch in his voice. "It has a real homey feel." He smiled and turned to her. "Thank you."

Katie couldn't stop smiling. "You're welcome," she said.

"Checkmate," Jackson said.

"What? No way!" Katie said, trying to find a way out. Finally conceding, she laid down her king. "Drat, I never win at this game."

"You would play better if you were willing to sacrifice a man," Jackson said dryly.

"Hey, everyone is important."

"No," he said slowly, as if talking to a child. "Pawns are not very important and can be sacrificed. If for example, your queen is in danger, you sacrifice a pawn to save the queen."

"I don't agree. Don't you think the pawn's feelings would be hurt, if he knew he was expendable?" Katie tried to explain her reasoning.

Jackson couldn't help himself. He started chuckling. "Pawns are pieces of wood, they don't have feelings."

"I know that," she said in exasperated. "I'm just saying they're important too."

"You can't try and save everyone, or nothing gets done." He gestured towards the board. "If no one dies, there is actually no room to move."

"A pawn," Katie said with dignity "is just as important as any other man on the board. It has a job, and that job is not always to be sacrificed for some fancy pants."

Jackson was laughing so hard, tears were coming out of his eyes. "Fancy pants?" he repeated.

Katie couldn't help the smile creeping into her face. "Yes, f-a-n-c-y p-a-n-t-s." She spelled it out slowly, grinning when Jackson roared with laughter.

A buzzing started sounding in her ears. "What's that?" Katie opened her eyes and reached over to turn off the alarm. Once again, her sheets were wet with sweat. Going to the shower, she wondered if she was truly going insane.

Chapter 5
The Big Day

"So, tomorrow's the big day."

Katie glanced up puzzled, "big day?"

"Yes, you have only been looking forward to it, for months." Sam was sitting on her bed, her legs stretched out. Katie was in her usual spot, on the floor up against the door. The room looked as if it had a split personality, surrounded by two twin beds, each side determined to outshine the other.

Sam's little sister Norah, owned the side of the room with the little princess theme. The walls were painted pink and white, with little flowers on the border. Sam's side of the room was painted lavender, with dark purple borders. The dark purple was the same shade as Sam's bed spread.

Katie wouldn't dream of entering the princess side of the bedroom. Over the years, she had watched the drama of the two sisters. If Katie was seen by Norah to have entered her domain, this gave Norah every right to get into Sam's possessions. An argument always ensued. Sam would start yelling at Norah to stay away from her things. Norah would state, "Since Katie was in my things, then I can get into your things."

Sam had a large family. She was the middle child, in a household of five children. Sam's oldest brother, Robbie, was in college out west somewhere. Her second oldest brother, David, was a senior in high school. Sam's younger two siblings were Ben fourteen, and Norah twelve.

The house was always in an uproar. There seemed to always be, some kind of crisis. The first-time Katie entered the Black home, she was taken aback by all the commotion. Now she enjoyed it. Her most favorite place to be was with Sam's family. She used to spend all her time there.

Since she was eleven years old, she'd had a secret crush on David. Recently, she had been mortified to find out that her "secret" crush on David Black, wasn't a secret. Even Norah had known about it. Katie stopped coming around for a while. Finally, Sam told her to get over it. Her family loved and missed her, and to stop being such a dope.

So, now she went to Sam's house, but still felt uneasy around David. She tried to avoid him as much as possible. Today, David was at some scout camp, probably freezing to death. Katie was enjoying the day, with Sam.

Katie watched Sam with a preoccupied look on her face. "What are you talking about?"

"You've forgotten? You really have forgotten," Sam repeated stunned.

Katie's mind started racing. *Did I forget someone's birthday?* Her mind was a total blank, as to what Sam was referring to. "Okay, I give up. What's tomorrow?"

"Tomorrow is the day you play basketball against Central High," Sam said it very slowly, and as dramatically as possible.

Realizing the significance of Sam's statement, heat immediately went through Katie's body. How could she have forgotten about tomorrow? She loved playing against Central High. She paused in her musing and thought she needed to change her statement. She loved, playing against Candace Franklin.

Every sport Katie played, Candace played against her. They were both the best players, on their respective teams. When they played against each other, they were almost a perfect match. Last year in track, she barely beat Candace in the 880-yard dash. Candace had beaten her in the 440. Katie didn't even want to think, about volleyball. The match went to game point repeatedly. Each player was determined to win. When one of her teammates missed the ball, they lost.

Sweat pooled on her forehead. She felt so hot, she thought she was going to combust. "I need some air," Katie whispered. She got up from the floor and went to grab the door handle to leave the room. She heard a voice she recognized, immediately just outside the door.

"Mom, where are the towels?" David yelled.

"There in the linen closet," came the reply from downstairs.

"No, they're not, I looked!"

Katie froze—literally— as cold immediately enveloped her body. Her sweat now felt like cold drops of ice. Her body started to shake with each breath, and her teeth began chattering. She stood there on the other side of the door, waiting for David to find the towels. Hoping she could find a way to leave, before he could see her.

"You don't have to leave, Katie," Sam told her softly, so only she could hear.

"No, I, I need to go. I don't feel very well." Katie mumbled. She opened the door slightly, and peeked into the small hallway. Seeing the coast was clear, she darted into the hallway, ran down the stairs, and headed for home.

Arriving home, Katie was surprised to see men carting out their old living room furniture. Katie stepped out of their way, before entering the house. Her mother was taking down the last couple of pictures on the walls. Except for a couple of cushions, and a box full of pictures, the room was completely empty. Looking around, the room looked much larger.

"Mom, what's going on?"

"Oh, Katie shut the door; it's freezing out there," her mother said in an offhand manner. Her mother turned around, and set the last pictures in the box. As she straightened up, she glanced around the room, with a satisfied look on her face. "I sold some pieces," she said, as if that explained everything.

"And that gave you the idea we now could sit on the floor?" Katie suggested.

Her mother smiled and laughed infectiously. "No... You have no idea, how long I wanted to have a nice living room set. For years, I just took hand-me-downs from everyone who was willing to give what they had to me. I couldn't afford, to be picky. Now, I'm going to finally have it."

Katie couldn't help smile with her mom. "Wow, Mom, congratulations."

"Thanks." Her mom beamed, rocking back on her heels.

"Do you need any help?" Katie asked.

"Absolutely," said her mom. "We need to have these walls completely painted before tomorrow morning when the new furniture arrives."

Katie actually had a good time helping her mom. It was nice, seeing her mom so happy. Over the years, they had really struggled to make ends meet. Her mother had worked as a waitress at the local diner for years. On the side, she painted landscapes of Appalachia. She also made pottery, using old Cherokee techniques. Lately, she started sculpting animals and people, using the clay from an old river bed. She placed her artwork in local consignment shops.

When Katie was twelve, her mother was able to quit the diner, and become a full-time artist, but things were still lean. They lived in a small two-bedroom, one-bathroom home. She didn't mind the small home. She always felt close to her mother, as if it was the two of them against the world.

"Katie, I need to talk to you about something important."

Katie glanced up, from the pizza she was eating. Her mother was sitting in the middle of the floor, careful not to touch the wet paint. "What?" she said, with a mouthful of pizza.

"I've been invited to go to Chicago," her mother said in a rush.

"Chicago?" Katie asked, surprised, and then choked on her pizza.

"Yes... Chicago," her mother repeated. Her eyes sparkled with excitement. The sound of awe echoed in her voice. "The woman who bought those pictures from me thinks I will be able to sell them in a gallery she works in. She has already shown the pieces she bought to her boss, and they are really excited about my work." Her mother could barely contain her enthusiasm. "They want me to go immediately."

Katie was grinning so hard at her mother, she was at a total loss for words.

"Well… Say something," said her mother, exasperated.

"I really don't know what to say," said Katie. "Ah…. Congratulations again, Mom."

Her mother got up off the floor and began pacing in the small room. "I thought about it for a while, and I think it would work." She paused, looking down at Katie. "There are two ideas I have, and I've decided you can pick one of the two."

Katie had no idea where her mother was going with this. She sat quietly, waiting for her mother to continue.

"I'm going to be gone about two weeks. I have talked to both Lizzy's and Sam's moms, about your staying with them. Lizzy's mom has too much going on, so Lizzy's is out. Sam's mom will be happy to have you," her mother finished with a flourish.

The cold feeling began creeping in on Katie. The thought of staying with Sam's family, would just be absolutely the most horrible experience in her life. She would rather die than face David. "No way! I can't do that!"

Her mother looked a little confused. "You can't do what?"

"I cannot stay at Sam's house. No way." Katie flew her arms in the air, as if to ward off an imaginary foe. "That is not an option."

Her mother stopped her pacing, and faced Katie with her hands on her hips. "I thought you loved, being at Sam's house."

"I do... I did... I don't want to talk about it." She could feel heat, rising into her cheeks.

"Is there something, you need to tell me?" her mother asked.

"No, I just don't want to stay over there. Okay?"

Her mother acted as if she wanted to pursue the conversation. Katie was relieved when her mother finally dropped the subject. "I'm not sure you should stay here by yourself for two weeks," her mother stated.

"Sure I can," Katie burst in.

"You think you can get yourself up, go to school, and all your activities without parental supervision?" her mother asked dubiously.

"Mom, I go to school without your help every day," Katie said in an exasperated voice.

Her mother shook her head. "Not always."

"Mom," Katie said, realizing her voice had gone up an octave, and somehow ended in a whine. She paused a moment. "I can get up for school… I promise." She said it slowly, trying to sound as grown up as possible.

"I do <u>not</u> want a phone call from the school that you were excessively tardy, or absent while I'm gone," her mother said.

"You don't have to worry about it, Mom. Everything will be fine."

Her mother frowned. "I'll have to make sure you have enough money to live on."

Katie was so happy she had convinced her mom. She made a quick exit before she could change her mind.

Katie opened the back door of her old Honda, and shoved her gym bag inside. She slammed the door so hard, the vehicle actually swayed with the force. She was so angry, she could spit bullets.

"I cannot believe, I lost again to that albino." She said in disgust. She wrenched the driver's side door open.

"Katie, what exactly did we just witness?"

Katie turned to see Sam standing behind her. Lizzy came running up out of breath.

"What!" Katie shot back at her.

"I'm talking about that spectacle of a basketball game we just saw," Sam said with indignation.

"I know exactly what you mean." Katie tossed her head, trying to get rid of the frustration vibrating throughout her body. "That ref was completely out of line!"

"No," Sam pointed her finger at Katie's chest "You, were completely out of line!"

"WHAT?" Katie was stunned. All she could do was glance back and forth, between her two best friends. Lizzy bobbed her head in ascent, agreeing to everything Sam was saying.

Sam took in a deep breath. "Katie, I love you. You know that, right?"

Katie stood silent. Whenever she heard those words coming from Sam, she knew Sam was going to give her an honest evaluation of what she thought. Through past experiences, Katie always braced herself for what usually came next.

Sam seemed to take Katie's silence, as a go ahead. "I know, you are competitive. I have always enjoyed, watching you play. Today, though, you were way past competitive. You were downright... I don't know what else to call it, but *aggressive*. I do not mean aggressive, in a good way." Sam raised her voice, when she saw Katie was going to interrupt.

"You could have really hurt that girl," Lizzy said in a soft voice.

"Hey, it was not my fault. She was in the way," Katie said defensively.

"Yes, it was your fault," Sam interrupted, "and don't think that just because the ref didn't see you push number fourteen, didn't mean the rest of us didn't see it."

Katie started to speak.

"I know *why* you did it... It was obvious... You were angry, because she stole the ball from you. So in retaliation, you knocked her flat, when the refs were not looking... Very big of you!" Sam said sarcastically.

"Candace Franklin," Katie started to say.

"Candace Franklin was playing fair, while YOU-" Sam emphasized it again, pointing her finger into Katie's chest "YOU, were out to win at all cost, including trying to completely take out the opposite team. Your actions were the best example of ***poor*** sportsmanship I have ever seen."

"The ref didn't have to kick me out of the game," Katie said defensively.

"ARE YOU LISTENING TO US?" Sam yelled. "I would have kicked you out, when you elbowed number twelve in the first quarter. That ref gave you so many chances, I wondered if someone was going to have to go to the hospital!"

At every jab of Sam's finger in Katie's chest, the anger she had been feeling for the last two hours evaporated. In its place was a hurt so deep, it cut through her.

"I can't believe you're saying this to me," she said, obviously on the verge of tears.

Sam paused in her tirade, to look at her friend in astonishment. "Are you crying?"

Katie's eyes started to well up, even more at Sam's questions.

"What is going on with you?" Sam yelled, her frustration evident in every syllable. She raised her hand's palms up. "I haven't seen you cry since you broke your arm falling out of our tree house."

Katie shook her head, trying to stop the tears from spilling onto her cheeks.

"Is it PMS?" Lizzy asked.

"Oh, yeah, let's blame it on PMS. It's only been going on for several weeks," Sam stated. "Look, just go home, and get some rest."

"I'm not taking you home?" Katie asked, surprised.

"No, we're both going home with David." Sam gestured behind her.

For the first time, Katie looked over Sam's shoulder, and saw David Black leaning up against his jeep. His arms were crossed, his gaze locked on the scene in front of him. He was far enough away, not to have heard every word, but close enough to get the gist of what was going on.

Katie was mortified. *"Please, let there be a hole, where I can crawl into and die,"* she thought quietly to herself. How many times could she make a fool of herself in front of this guy? She looked down, trying to hide her face. The tears were now rolling off her cheeks. "I'll see you later," she mumbled.

"Katie?"

She heard Sam, but decided to act as though she didn't. She jumped into the car, started the engine, and left. Cold penetrated her body, her tears flowing freely. She just wanted to go home, and tell her mother everything that happened. She knew her mom would give her the support she so desperately needed.

She turned into the drive, and got out of the car. She practically ran into the house. She turned on the lights, and she called for her mom.

The house was dark, and silent. She realized she was alone. How could she have forgotten? Her mom was somewhere in Chicago. She sat down on the brand-new leather couch her mother had purchased, and cried herself to sleep.

Chapter 6
Changes

Katie stepped out of the forest, her eyes automatically drawn to the sound of the waterfall. She recognized the beautiful scene in front of her. The pool of water still looked cool clear and inviting. The scent in the air was exactly as she remembered. She couldn't help glancing around, to see if the toddler was playing next to the pool. The sun was hot on her face, and she looked longingly at the clear water. She cautiously stepped around the pool, until she reached the trail. Getting on her knees, she took a drink of cold water. She heard a rustling in the trees. She glanced up, expecting to see The Great White Tiger.

Instead, a beautiful woman stepped out of the forest, and into the sun. The woman stepped towards her, with a friendly smile on her face. Katie smiled back. She looked at the woman curiously. She was dressed in traditional clothing, with a leather dress decorated in beads. She was barefoot. Her feet didn't seem to be bothered by the hard ground. The woman looked strangely familiar.

"You don't recognize me, do you child?" the woman asked. She shook her head, giving Katie a rueful grin. "Of course you don't. You've only seen me, when I was old and feeble."

Katie recognized the style and tone of the voice, as well as the gestured hand movements. “Elizabeth Hawk?” She stumbled a little. She almost put the word "old" in front of the name.

“Yep. I knew you would eventually, come up with it.” Elizabeth Hawk laughed. “You really didn’t think I’d have stayed old and feeble in the spirit world, now did you?”

Since Katie had never really thought about it, she had no idea what to say. “Ah… What are you doing here?”

“That’s good. That’s good; let’s get right to the point.” Elizabeth stepped closer to Katie, “You’re in danger, girl.”

Dumbfounded, Katie could only stare at Elizabeth. “I’m what?”

Elizabeth continued, as if Katie hadn’t said anything. “You have been chosen, child.” Elizabeth laid a hand, on Katie’s shoulder.

“The Great White Tiger has chosen you. You must watch out for the great evil that’s about to come. You and your friends did not go through the sacred ceremony that will help you on your way. You must ask your mothers to perform the ceremony in my place, so you will be prepared.”

Elizabeth’s face darkened. “It will be hard to convince them to perform the ceremony, because they do not believe.”

Katie looked up, into Elizabeth Hawk’s face. “Isn’t this just a dream, like all the others?”

Elizabeth gave her a startled look. “What other dreams, have you been having, child?” She was watching Katie very closely. An edge had crept into her voice.

“Oh, I don’t know.” Once again, she was reluctant to talk about Jackson. “I dreamed about this place before. I tried to fight a tiger, with a rock.”

Elizabeth gave her a relieved smile. "Yes, I have had that dream, many times." She turned to the woods, as if she could hear something Katie could not. "Listen, I must go soon, but I feel I need to warn you about the Seekers."

"What?" Katie asked uncertainly.

"Seekers will try to convert you to their side. They are evil. Stay away from all of them." Elizabeth grabbed Katie by the shoulders, and shook her intensely. "Never trust them. Promise me you will not trust them."

"Okay, sure, I promise." Katie had no idea what she was promising, but trusted Old Elizabeth Hawk to know more about these things than she did.

Katie woke up, freezing. She rolled off the couch, getting slowly to her feet. She took a hot shower and felt much better if, not completely warm. She noticed how late it was. She walked around the house locking the doors, and turning off lights. She lay down in bed, wondering about what Old Elizabeth Hawk had told her in the dream. "*Seeker*" was a weird name. Laying her head on the pillow it didn't take her long to drift off to sleep.

"Are you Okay?"

Katie looked around. Once again, she was near the waterfall. She turned to see Jackson in the clearing, in almost the exact spot where Elizabeth Hawk stood.

She smiled a greeting and walked towards him. "Hi! Of course, I'm okay. Why wouldn't I be?"

Jackson paused for a moment, and gave her a relieved smile, the concern fading from his face. "I lost you for a while."

"Lost me… "Katie repeated. "What does that mean?"

Jackson was watching her closely, a small frown marring his features. "You disappeared from my mind. I couldn't reach you."

"I was here," Katie said, gesturing around her.

Jackson's frown deepened. "What do you mean 'here'?"

"I was in this exact spot, talking to Old Elizabeth Hawk," Katie said.

Jackson paused, taking in his surroundings. "Old Elizabeth Hawk?" he repeated quietly.

"Lizzy's grandmother. She passed away not that long ago."

Jackson frowned. His eyes had a watchful intensity about them.

Katie shrugged, trying to lighten his mood. "Actually, she passed away just a few days after we met." Her words slowed down to a crawl when Jackson's features contorted in dismay, a mask, forming on his features.

Jackson stepped closer. It looked as if he was not only listening intently to every word she said, but also memorizing her features.

"How did she die?" he asked quietly.

"She had a stroke."

He nodded, his features still set into a mask, "When?"

"The first time, we met in my dreams."

Jackson's features lit up. "Are you sure? The exact day we met?"

Katie started feeling uneasy. "Yes, we were at a..." She paused, not sure how to describe the campfire scene. "A ceremony. She started to tell us about The Great White Tiger, and how it ties to our family. She never finished. She sort of collapsed, and then we all went home. Later that night, I had a dream about the tiger and I met you."

Jackson stepped closer. "What did she tell you today?" The question came out calmly, but his voice belied the intensity in his eyes.

"She told me I was in danger."

Jackson closed his eyes immediately, rubbing his hands through his hair in agitation. "Did she say anything else?"

"I needed to stay away from S*eekers,* whatever that means." Katie stepped away from Jackson. She had just about enough of answering his questions. "Look, I seem to always be giving you answers you need. While you, remain *Mystery Boy".* She raised her hands, doing the quotation mark with her fingers. Her voice dropped into a mocking whisper. "I think it's time you start giving me some answers. For example, you obviously know more about what's going on here. Why don't you let me in on the big secret?"

Jackson grabbed Katie shoulders with both hands, his hands slightly shaking her shoulder. "Listen, I don't have much time. I need you to trust me," he said in a desperate voice. "Okay? Please, trust me."

Katie looked up into his face. His clear blue eyes looked scared. She couldn't deny him anything, she decided. Before she could say so, a growl erupted through the clearing. Katie looked over and saw The Great White Tiger. Her eyes locked on Jackson.

Jackson slowly raised his hands in surrender, backing away. He gave Katie one last look. "Remember your promise," he whispered.

Katie woke up startled and rolled off the bed. She was so hot, she felt physically ill. She stumbled to the bathroom, retching in the toilet. She crawled into the tub, turning the shower on cold. She lay in the tub with cold water cascading down, soaking her pajamas. She was still too hot. Unable to find relief, she got out of the tub opening her bedroom windows. Cold winter air filled the room.

"What is wrong with me?" she cried. At that moment, heat burst from her body. She stumbled back, into the bathroom. Her hands were braced on the sink, as she glanced into the mirror.

TOO MUCH INFORMATION! was her last thought, before falling to the floor.

"*Katie, are you okay?"* the voice paused. *"Katie, come on, wake up."*

Katie opened her eyes, looking around the bathroom. Water was still running in the tub, from the shower. Ice was starting to crystallize the water on the floor. Looking around, she could see she was the only one in the room.

"Katie I'm so glad, I thought you were never going to wake up."

Katie did a double take, and looked around the room again. Nope, nobody in the room.

"Are you going to talk to me? Maybe you can't hear me. Damn, I really thought this would work."

"What is happening?" Katie thought to herself.

"Oh, there you are!"

"No one is in the room, and yet I hear someone," Katie thought.

A low chuckle entered her mind. *"You're right, I'm not in the room with you, and yes you can hear me."*

"What is going on?" Katie thought she sounded like a broken record.

"If I had to guess, I would say you have turned into a beautiful large cat."

Katie remembered the image she seen in the mirror, before she passed out. "*Yeah, I'm not going crazy. The ship has already arrived. I am stark raving mad."* she thought.

"Oh, come on, you had to have known something was happening. All those dreams, about The Great White Tiger. Old Elizabeth Hawk coming to you," came the voice in her head.

"Who are you?" she said to the voice.

There was a pause. *"You don't know who I am?"*

"NO! I don't know who you are, and I don't know how I am talking to you. I don't know what's going on..." Katie glanced down at her feet and shuttered. *"This truly is not happening."*

"I'm sorry. I know a little about, what you are going through." There was a slight pause. *"I'm Jackson."*

Katie didn't respond, she sat staring at her feet.

"Katie? Are you there?"

There was a long pause, before Katie quietly said *"Yes,"* in a small voice.

"I know you're having a hard time. Trust me, it's going to be okay. You just need to get used to the new you." Jackson's voice seemed to vibrate, in her mind.

"You're not really here, are you?" Katie said softly, her voice was quite lost by the sound of the shower.

Jackson heard her anyway. *"No, I'm not."*

"How are you able to communicate with me?" Katie asked.

"It's a form of telekinesis. I don't exactly understand, how it works."

"You can read my mind?" Katie asked.

"No."

"What does no mean, exactly?"

"I can't read your mind, but if you allow me. I can see what you see, feel what you feel, that sort of thing." There was a slight pause. *"I have to concentrate really hard to communicate with you from my location. I'm still in the learning process."*

Katie closed her eyes, resting her head on the floor.

"Katie, are you there?"

"I'm having a real hard time, digesting all of this," she replied.

"Why don't you let me see what you look like?" Jackson asked persuasively.

"No, I'm ugly."

A soft chuckle rippled through her mind. *"You will never be ugly. Please let me see you."*

Katie sat there for a long time, trying to digest all the information. She was thankful Jackson stayed quiet as she struggled with her emotions. Finally, she became resigned. *"You asked for it."* Katie slowly got up. She was so big, she could hardly move in the small bathroom. In fact, she had to duck her head, to look into the mirror. What she saw, completely horrified her.

"Are you looking in the mirror?" Jackson asked.

"Yes," Katie said, dejected.

"Will you let me see?" Jackson asked.

Frustrated, she said, *"I don't know how to make you see."*

"Do you trust me, Katie?"

"Yes," Katie said to her reflection, in the mirror.

"Just relax and let me into your mind," Jackson replied.

Katie had no idea how to relax, and let him in. She closed her eyes, and took a couple of breaths. She opened her eyes again. Her reflection remained the same.

"I'm a little confused." Jackson's voice could be heard a little stronger in her head.

"Oh, well, as long as you're the only one."

"I thought..." Jackson paused, clearly at a loss for words.

"What's the matter, the cat's got your tongue?" Katie replied sarcastically.

"I just assumed..." Jackson again paused.

"That's what you get, for assuming," Katie thought, staring at her big white head in the shape of a wolf.

Chapter 7
Adjusting

It took several hours, before Katie could turn back into human form. Jackson had repeatedly told her she would eventually be able to control the changes being made to her body. Regardless of what he said, an overwhelming feeling of relief washed over her when she turned back into a human form. She had been unable to turn the water off in the shower, or close the windows in her bedroom. In wolf form she was so large, she couldn't turn around in the bathroom. She actually had to back out, to get out of the bathroom. When she lay down on her bed, it collapsed under her weight. Just exactly, what every teenage girl needed.

Jackson was her lifeline to reality, or rather her lifeline to the twilight zone; she hadn't decided which one. After all, she met him in her dreams, and now she'd turned into a huge white wolf. She'd heard a voice in her head. She followed his instructions to the letter, because he seemed to know what the heck was going on. She could hear him chuckling now, in her thoughts.

"I'm glad you're enjoying this," she told him irritably.

His chuckle kept ringing in her ears, as she drifted off to sleep.

The next morning was Friday. She thought about the two tests, she was supposed to take that day. The thought made her cringe. Going to school, was not an option. She would just have to make them up another time. Now, she had to control the inner beast, raging inside of her—no pun intended.

Jackson tried to explain to her the mechanics of changing. When she felt the heat rising from her belly, she was on the verge of turning into a wolf. Her emotions helped the process along. If she was angry, the heat would come quickly. On the flip side, when she felt the cold seeping into her pores, she would change into human form. Emotions were tied to the cold as well, he explained. Sadness or hurt was a human emotion. Therefore, it would help her turn into human form.

From Katie's perspective, there was absolutely no control. She started feeling hot, and before she could even register the heat... Bam! She changed into a wolf. As a wolf, she concentrated so hard on the word ***cold*** and her body temperature actually increased. To her frustration, she was a wolf longer than she was human. Jackson seemed to think, it was because she hadn't "accepted" being a wolf. Her only thought to that was, "WHO IN HER RIGHT MIND, WOULD ACCEPT BEING A WOLF?"

The phone began ringing around 4:30 pm. Each time it would ring, Katie would listen to the messages of her two friends. They knew she was in the house and not picking up. *They probably think I'm sulking,* she mused. She knew eventually she would call them back, but for now, the only person she needed was Jackson.

Katie's mother's itinerary, was posted in great detail on a scratchpad held by a magnet on the refrigerator door. When she called her mother, Katie always made sure her mom couldn't actually answer the phone. She would leave messages, telling her mother everything was fine. She made sure to mention she was feeling ill, to try and explain her absence from school.

"Do you realize, I still know nothing about you?" Katie asked, relaxing on the couch in the living room, its new leather smell filling the room. It was a Friday night. A whole week had passed, since she had first turned into a wolf. She did not return to school, but eventually answered Sam's call. Her friend had started calling every hour. With each call, her voice sounded more frantic than the last. Katie was afraid if she didn't call back, she would call the police, or worse, her mother. She explained, she wasn't feeling very well. When Sam started asking questions, she quickly ended the call.

She was on the verge of falling asleep, when Jackson finally answered.

"You know me well enough."

"No," she responded. *"I don't know, who you are... Where you're from"* Her thoughts drifted off expectantly.

Jackson took so long in responding, she thought he had left her. *"I don't want you to know, who I am,"* came the soft reply.

"Why?"

Jackson sighed, *"I would just like to prolong, the inevitable."*

"What is inevitable?" Katie questioned.

"You... hating me."

"Jackson, I will never hate you," Katie thought firmly.

Jackson's sighed again. *"You will, Katherine Johnson. You will."*

"Don't you know, how much you've helped me?" Katie's voice rang through the empty room, as she gave voice to the thoughts in her head. *"I will never forget the kindness, you have shown me. Never!"*

Jackson was silent, for several moments, *"Katie."*

A knock sounded on the door. Distracted, Katie turned to see Sam's face in the window peering into the room. "I know you're in there, Katie Johnson, I can see you. Open this door!"

"Don't let them in," came Jackson's swift reply in her thoughts.

"I can't pretend I don't see them, or they me," she replied.

"You're right I just..." Jackson paused in mid-sentence. "I would just like to keep the world, at bay for a little longer."

"I know." Katie got up, to let her friends in. She opened the door, with a flourish smile pasted on her face. "Hi, guys."

Sam and Lizzy, barged into the room.

"We brought peace offerings," Sam said with a smile. She was holding a big box of pizza, and Lizzy held up a stack of DVD movies. "Pepperoni pizza and about ten hours of chick flicks."

"We are spending the night," Lizzy announced. "If you don't like it, well, too bad."

Katie heard Jackson's soft groan in her head, and couldn't help smiling.

"Hey, I like the new look," Sam said referring to the living room. "Your mom really knows how to blend colors."

Katie slowly began relaxing with her friends, as they caught her up on everything she missed in school. She was aware Jackson was listening in to the conversation, and was glad he didn't make any comments to distract her. The only question he asked was, "Which one of your friends is directly related to Elizabeth Hawk?" This seemed rather odd. Everyone knew Lizzy was related to Old Elizabeth, so she passed on the information.

She laughed good-naturedly, as Sam described her new crusade. Since Sam was one of the best dancers on the dance team, she believed she had enough clout to push her "skimpy outfits" idea. The team needed to wear more appropriate clothing than they had worn in previous years. There were some really nice dance outfits, more "appropriate" to wear. She described the dance coach's reaction, to her views.

Sam brought from her bag, three hot pink t-shirts that had "Modest is Hottest" emblazoned on the front. Katie good-naturedly put on the t-shirt. She carefully averted her eyes from Sam and Lizzy changing, aware Jackson was still watching through her eyes.

Stuffed with pizza, they were still laughing over the comedy romance they just watched, when Sam made a point to turn off the TV. "What's going on Katie?"

Just because she wasn't surprised, didn't mean she had a ready answer. Katie looked down at her hands, as quiet descended into the living room.

Sam sat down beside Katie and put an arm around her shoulders. "Sometimes I put my foot in my mouth. I'm sorry, if I was too hard on you after the basketball game."

Katie looked at her best friend, tears welling into her eyes. Yet, she still couldn't put into words her plight.

"Don't tell them."

Jackson had been so quiet, Katie had almost forgotten he was there. *Why?*

Jackson's pause was weighted. "Just don't tell them, please."

"These are my friends. I have never kept anything from them," she replied back with her thoughts.

Katie's attention was brought back into the room, when she heard Sam apologize again. "David told me I was too harsh. I should have taken his advice and come right over. Instead, I waited a few days. I just thought it would be better, if I waited till both of us cooled down."

"Oh great," Katie thought. "*David was close enough to hear.*"

"Who's David?" the question came immediately from Jackson.

Katie rubbed her temple, getting a little mixed up with two conversations going on at the same time. "Let's not go there, Okay?" was her abrupt thought. She was grateful when Jackson didn't reply. She made a quick glance towards Sam, who was watching her expectantly.

"Look, this has nothing to do with the stupid basketball game." She got up on her feet and started pacing the small room. "I have always valued your opinion, Sam, and I always want you to tell me straight if I'm acting like a jerk." She amended for Sam's sake. "The thing is,..." She paused. How the heck was she supposed to tell them? She looked at her two friends. They were sitting silently waiting for her to continue.

"Do not tell them," Jackson pressed firmly into her thoughts.

Katie decided, to ignore Jackson altogether. "I… Lizzy, your grandmother's story is true," Katie said it in such a rush, she wasn't sure if it sounded correctly.

Katie felt Jackson leave. She felt the loss immediately. She had never felt so alone, as she did at that moment. She looked over at her friends, hoping they would help fill the void left behind. Her friends stood staring at her, as if they didn't quite understand what she'd just blurted out.

"You heard me, right?" Katie looked from one face to the other. Finally, unable to stand it, she added, "Say something! I'm dying here!"

Lizzy and Sam exchanged puzzled glances. "I'm not sure, what you're saying," Lizzy explained hesitantly.

Katie blew out an exasperated breath. "You know... the story about the tiger that was going to eat the baby. The mother of the baby tried to fight the tiger off with a rock..." Katie trailed off, staring at her friends. "You were there sitting right next to me, when Old Elizabeth Hawk recited it around the fire."

"Yeah, we know the story," Lizzy answered wearily.

"It's true! The story is true."

Katie kept switching her head back and forth between her two friends, trying to gauge their reaction. She became frustrated when there didn't seem to be any. They were both looking at her, waiting for her to go on.

"Look, I know it sounds crazy, but I can turn into a great big white wolf. Not a tiger. I was quite surprised about that, but maybe the story isn't completely true. Or, the story changed, through the generations... except for the fact that when I dreamed about it, it was a tiger." She knew she was rambling, but didn't know how to stop herself.

"Katie can turn into a wolf," Sam said to Lizzy in a voice Katie knew well. She didn't believe what was said, but was willing to go along with it to smooth things over.

Frustrated, Katie started to feel the heat rise from her belly, and for the first time, she didn't fight the sensation. She just let it flow into her limbs. In a split second, she changed. Her eyes never leaving Sam's face.

Sam first had a concerned look, then shock followed immediately by horror. Her mouth looked as if she was saying oh, except the sound never left her lips.

"AAAHHH!"

Katie turned towards the sound. She wasn't sure if Lizzy had jumped off the couch or fell. She was on the other side of the couch, only her forehead and eyes were visible. Katie's massive body took up the whole living room. She knew her friends, were having heart attacks. She was quite surprised when she could just as calmly turn back into human form.

Of course, she was naked, and her clothes were completely destroyed. She left them to go to her room and get some fresh clothing. She took her time, to let them get over their initial shock. Dressed, she waited as long as she could before slowly walking back into the living room. Both girls had not moved. She decided to give them a little more time. She walked over to her clothes, picking them up.

"Oh gosh, I'm sorry I ruined your T-shirt." Katie lifted the hot pink shirt. It was shredded so badly, it was hard to tell what the words said anymore. She casually walked to the kitchen, and dumped the clothes in the trash bin. "If this keeps up, I'm going to have to get a whole new wardrobe," she said conversationally.

Still, not a sound was made in the living room. She walked back and sat down on the couch, patiently waiting.

The questions from her two friends were very hesitant at first. Katie told them how she had turned that first night, and how she was unable to control it. Sam and Lizzy both agreed it would have been mortifying, to go to school like that. As the shock wore off, the girls discussed everything they could possibly remember, about the story Old Elizabeth Hawk told. They had all come to the conclusion that they didn't know much at all, except the basic details.

Katie told them about her dreams, excluding Jackson. She didn't know why she kept it from her friends. She felt her friendship with

Jackson was kind of, well... special. She didn't think her friends would understand.

The three girls talked well into the night. They all came to the conclusion that they needed to do more research on the subject. Sam was a little concerned about the "great evil," that was supposed to threaten the Sugaree people. Since that seemed to encompass an infinite number of possibilities, there didn't seem to be anything they could do about it now.

Lizzy and Sam stayed the whole weekend. Once Katie embraced being a wolf, she could control her "changing" much easier. She couldn't imagine, staying away from school any more than she already had. She knew the amount of homework, was going to be staggering. She also had missed a whole week of practice, and a game. She shuddered at the thought, of how her coach was going to react.

Jackson continued to stay away. He didn't appear, in her dreams either. Although her friends were there supporting her, she missed him. A couple of times, she tried to reach out in her mind to contact him. All she received for her trouble, was a resounding silence. It reminded her just how much she didn't know about him.

She didn't even know, if Jackson was his first or last name. She had no idea, where he lived. She was pretty sure he was real, but then she only spoke to him in her dreams or her mind.

Chapter 8
Back to School

Monday morning, Katie woke up with a happy smile on her face. She was ready to get back to school and her life. Today was December 12th, her seventeenth birthday. As she got dressed, she hummed a happy tune to herself. Before Lizzy and Sam picked her up, she sat down and wrote an excuse letter signing her mother's name with a flourish. The sound of a car horn had Katie bouncing out of the house into the car.

"Don't worry, I have complete control." She blurted out before they could say anything.

"If not, you can hide in the woods for the rest of your life," Sam quipped with a smile.

"You can count on us to say we have absolutely no idea what happened or where you are," Lizzy returned.

Katie couldn't help grinning. "You know, I love you guys. I could never have done this without you." She felt a twinge of guilt thinking of Jackson and decided to ignore it for the time being.

"Yeah, well better you than me," Lizzy laughed. "By the way… Happy Birthday!"

"Is your mom planning anything special? She always goes way out for her one and only child." Sam said in a dramatic voice.

"Last year was such a big bang for my sweet sixteenth birthday, I don't know, how she could top that," Katie answered, ignoring the dramatic sarcasm.

"I am sure it's going to be Big!" Lizzy said.

Katie waved her friend's good-bye, and headed for the school office. She handed the excuse note, to the secretary. Instead of writing out the excuse for her teachers, the secretary asked her to wait in a chair. Surprised, Katie sat down, wondering a little about the lady's behavior. Principal Davis immediately came out of his office. The secretary handed him Katie's note. He looked down, studying the note.

Not good, she thought. Butterflies started fluttering in her stomach, but she still wasn't worried. She believed she would be able to talk herself out of any situation.

"Miss Johnson, will you come with me?" Principal Davis stretched his arm indicating his office.

Katie steadied her nerves, got up smoothly, and walked confidently into the office. She curbed the impulse to immediately start talking or explaining. She sat down on the hard chair and waited for him to begin.

Principal Davis sat down behind his desk. His balding head reflected the light in the room. "Katherine, this note seems to indicate your mother knew you were sick all last week. When I talked to her this morning, she had no idea you missed any school at all," he said in a smug voice. He had a small smile on his face, which didn't reach his eyes.

"My mom," something was lodged in her throat, she had to clear it before she could continue. "My mom is out of town. I have been unable to talk to her directly, but I told her on her voice mail I was sick." Katie wasn't sure, all the words came out clearly.

"As I have just explained, I was concerned about the number of days you missed school. I called your mother. She indicated to me, as far as she was concerned you were not sick at all. AND, she has been out of town, the very length of time you have missed." He paused. When Katie didn't respond, he continued. "You have obviously, decided to take advantage of your mother's absence and skip school."

Davis raised a hand for quiet when Katie tried to interrupt. "Your mother has graciously left it up to me, to punish you. School policy is: if you do not have a proper excuse for an absence, you will not get any credit for that day. In other words, you will receive a zero for everything that was due." He paused again, watching her.

Katie knew he wanted some kind of reaction from her. She didn't know what it was but decided to give him nothing. She thought her stomach was going to jump out the window, but her face was void of all emotion.

Disappointment crossed Davis' face before he masked it and continued. "You were given a copy of the handbook at the beginning of school, which you and your mother have signed, saying you have read it. Do you still have your copy?

Katie shook her head. *Who EVER reads that?"* she thought in disgust.

"Since I'm sure you don't have your copy around, I will give you another one. I have highlighted the places, which affect you." Davis reached over his desk, with the pamphlet opened. Katie automatically reached out for it. "You will also have after school detention for six days, this includes every day you decided to skip."

"I have basketball practice," Katie interjected.

"Sports are a privilege, Miss Johnson, one you no longer have. I will inform Coach Tanner, you will not be on the girls' basketball team."

Katie sat listening, while heat filled her stomach. She started taking slow breaths, to calm herself down. She didn't want to change there. She had never been in trouble before. The injustice of it made her furious. The rest of her meeting with Principal Davis didn't last very long. He droned on about "consequences for actions," till she thought she wanted to bite him.

She walked out of the office, dazed. "Six days," she kept repeating to herself, "Six days of zeroes." She was a solid B student. She had no idea what six days of zeroes, would do to her GPA. She might not pass any of her classes. The thought made her sick to her stomach.

The bell had already rung. Taking her time she walked slowly to her locker. She dreaded walking into first hour. It would make it all real, when she handed the teacher her note from the office. She stood outside the door, still not wanting to go in. Taking a deep breath, she forced herself to open the door and walk in. All eyes turned to her. Mr. Thompson paused in mid-sentence, as she walked up and handed him the note. His eyebrows raised in surprise, as he quickly glanced through its contents. He told her to go ahead and sit down. She sat frozen as Mr. Thompson went through his lecture.

Ten minutes before class was over, Mr. Thompson asked Katie to come with him for a moment. Not knowing what more she could take, she got up and followed him. They walked, into the hall. He turned, and shut the door behind him.

Mr. Thompson informed her, that there was nothing he could do about the unexcused absences, but, he could give her some extra credit to help her out. He would have the list of things she needed to do, by the next morning. The extra credit would be due Wednesday, December 21st, before the term was over. Relieved, Katie couldn't thank him enough for giving her a break. He smiled at her and told her not to worry about it.

Her second-hour teacher reacted the same way as Mr. Thompson. She was to receive her extra credit the next day, and it would be due by December 21st. By the third hour, it was obvious teachers gossiped just as much as students. Her third-hour teacher had already put together her extra credit homework with the same due date. Katie was beginning to relax, until she walked into English class.

Miss Smith looked to be around 75 years old. She was standing by her desk. Her pinched face, always looked like she smelled something bad. She automatically reached for the note. She gave it a quick glance, to confirm what she already knew. She informed Katie in a loud voice, so everyone in China could hear, "There are reasons for rules. School policy dictates you are to get a zero for those six days, which included a test and a paper." She had already figured Katie's grades. As of right now, she was receiving an F, for the class. If she were to do all of her work from now until the end of term, she might get a D minus.

Katie started to turn away, but was informed in a still clear voice not to expect any leniency, because she was popular and a jock. Miss Smith paused, to make her point clear. Katie stood stone-faced, keeping all emotion from her face. She patiently, waited for the teacher to finish. Finally, Katie turned and sat down, looking straight ahead. She ignored the stares of the other students and Lizzy's shocked face.

Lunch was a nightmare. Sam and Lizzy, showed their outrage. The rest of the school seemed to revel in her dilemma. She tried to talk to coach Tanner, but before she could explain, he turned and walked away.

She followed him, with her eyes, every step he took, her respect for him vanishing.

Her last hour was Algebra 2. She had been on such a roller coaster all day, she didn't know what to expect. Mr. Kelly told her she was behind, and there would only be one way for her to catch up. He would meet with her during lunch, and tutor her. He was positive he could get her up to speed by the end of term. He then did something that was completely unexpected. He told her she probably needed time, to finish all her homework. He had already cleared it with the librarian. During his class, she could go to the library and work on other homework. She gave him a hug, her eyes filling with tears. He got a little embarrassed, patting her back awkwardly.

By the time Katie got home, she was exhausted. Darkness descended quickly, leaving cold shadows to welcome her home. The phone immediately began ringing in the empty house. Ignoring it, she put her book bag on the table. She paused, recognizing her mother's voice on the answering machine demanding her to pick up the phone. Reminding herself her mother usually was reasonable, she reached over and picked up the receiver. Ten minutes later she hung up, her mother's voice still ringing in her ears.

It was too much. The heat in her belly was simmering into a rolling boil. She turned off the light, took off her clothes, opened the front door, and allowed herself to change. Heat soared through her veins. The need to run was overwhelming. She took off into the woods, letting her instincts take over. It felt good to let go. The miles faded away, as she ran. She hardly noticed anything but the cold wind, which felt good against her heated body. She didn't know where she was going and didn't care.

Again, she heard her mother telling her what a *disappointment* she was, how she was *untrustworthy*. She deserved the punishment Mr. Davis had inflicted. Her mother never stopped to listen to her explanation. She just rolled over it as if she hadn't even said anything. The real kicker was when her mother said her grades had better not drop a single decimal. How, exactly, could she accomplish that with only two weeks left until end of term?

Happy Birthday, to me! Katie thought. Her mother had always made a big production about her birthday. Even when she didn't have anything to spend, her mother tried to make it "*her day special.*" Last year was a huge sweet sixteen party, with most of the school invited. This year, her mother never even mentioned it, which meant her mom had probably forgotten. That hurt more than any other humiliating thing that happened that day.

Katie started following, a well-marked trail. She was surprised, when she realized she could see just as well in the dark, as broad daylight, another feature she could get used to in this crazy situation. She followed the trail until it came to a large two story cabin. Instinctively, Katie sniffed the air. The place had a deserted smell. Nobody had been here for some time, she deduced. Walking on the tall grass, Katie was able to read a sign on the door.

If you're lost and need a place, you're welcome to stay.
Just clean it when you're done, fill the pantry for the next lost soul.

Forrest

The name "Forrest" seemed to trigger something in her head, but she couldn't remember where or what exactly. The sight of the cabin and the welcoming words seemed to erase the frustration she was feeling. She had been shown some unexpected kindness from people she didn't expect. She was going to remember who gave it to her, and try to pay them back somehow. She lay down in the tall dead grass. A feeling of calmness pervaded her senses. She closed her eyes, breathing deeply.

"Ah! Where are you, and how come I can't see anything?" came the thought.

"Jackson?" Katie raised her head in surprise.

"Who else talks to you, in your head?"

"Where have you been?" Katie demanded.

"Uuuhhhh."

"I decide to tell my friends about what I'm going through. YOU VANISH?" Katie went on before Jackson could say anything.

"That wasn't my fault," Jackson said defensively. *"Why? What's happened? You are okay, aren't you?"* he said in a rush. *"Your friends didn't betray you?"* He sounded worried.

"NO! I'm just...I didn't know how to get a hold of you. I thought you were mad and left me for good," Katie thought with a sigh.

"So, you missed me," Jackson came back, a little too smug for Katie's taste.

"Don't change the subject." Katie bristled. "*Where were you?"*

A long pause.

"I'm waiting for an answer," Katie thought impatiently.

"I'm thinking," Jackson replied.

"Wow, look at that. You get to think in private, while I am open for you to see my every thought?" Katie flashed.

"That's not how it works," Jackson laughed.

"Oh... Really? How does it work then?" Katie responded.

"I can communicate with you, but I cannot tell what you are thinking. You have trusted me, and have allowed me access to what you see. I can also feel your emotions," Jackson explained.

"I'm not sure, I like the emotions part," Katie thought.

"Believe me, I don't like it either. Your emotions, take me on a complete roller coaster ride. No wonder, girls cry a lot. If I was going through that regularly, I'd want to kill myself," Jackson responded.

"Oh, you poor baby," Katie thought irritably. "*Wait a minute; we got off subject. Where have you been?"*

"Damn, you don't get distracted very easily, do you?"

"Don't you dare go silent on me, mystery man," Katie thought quickly. *"I don't want a half-cocked story either."*

"Half-cocked story?" Jackson chortled.

"You know what I mean," Katie's thoughts responded.

"Okay... Okay... Well, it goes like this.......ahhhhh...Okay, this is kind of hard..." He paused a moment *"Okay, have you noticed the moon?"* Jackson stumbled.

"The moon?" Katie looked up. It was big and bright in the evening sky. "*No... Am I supposed to notice it?"*

"She doesn't notice the moon." Jackson's thoughts sounded like a mumble.

"I'm waiting," Katie thought, trying to bring him back on track.

"I'm trying," Jackson's thoughts almost shouted at her. *"Okay... When you look at the moon, what do you see?"*

Confused, Katie looked into the night's sky again. *"I see that it's round and big."*

"Not completely round," Jackson thoughts corrected. *"It was completely round, a couple of days ago. Let's say... about the time, I disappeared."*

"You can't talk to me, when the moon is full?" Katie guessed.

"Something like that," Jackson answered.

"Why didn't you say so?" Katie thought back. "*That's no big deal. Really, guys are sometimes so worried about such stupid things,"* she mumbled.

"Other things happened, besides not being able to talk." Jackson's thought came back defensively.

"Whatever, look; I need to get home. I've got long days ahead of me, till term ends. Katie thought "*I'll ketch you later, okay?"*

"Wait, you never told me where you are?" Jackson replied.

"I don't know, some cabin in the woods."

"There's a cabin, in the middle of the woods?" Jackson asked.

"Yeah, owned by someone named Forrest", Katie responded.

Dead silence followed Katie's answer. Shrugging and muttering about all guys in general, she got up and headed for home. She was looking forward to a good night's sleep.

Chapter 9
Homework, Homework, Homework

The next morning, Katie woke up very hungry. Getting up out of bed, all she could think about was, *I need food. NOW!*

She entered the kitchen, stuffing anything edible in her mouth. She ate so fast, she hardly chewed. She made an omelet and decided to use all ten eggs. While it was cooking, she went through a box of cereal, and started in on the bread. While the omelet was still cooking, she reached for a box of cookies. The cookies were eaten before the omelet was completed.

She finished the eggs and began digging in the refrigerator for more food. She found a frozen fruit cake in the freezer. Not wanting to wait to warm it in the microwave, she broke it into pieces and ate the whole thing frozen. Finally full, Katie glanced around. The kitchen was completely trashed. Dishes were strung out and disregarded. In her mad dash for food, trash littered every surface. The cupboards were all open, including the refrigerator door.

With her back against the wall, she slowly slid down onto the floor. She placed her head on her knees, taking in slow deep breaths, trying to calm down.

"I'm not sure I can handle this," she said softly in the empty room.

She closed her eyes, trying to stop tears from spilling. Her mind immediately drifted, to the beautiful pool with the waterfall. Turning her head, she saw The Great White Tiger, her eyes watching Katie intently. It slowly walked towards her, its massive head level with hers. Her eyes never left the tiger, as it slowly placed its forehead against hers. As she heard the gentle purring from the great beast, she felt her emotions begin to calm.

When the tiger lifted its head away from her, she stepped back and glanced around. To her surprise, a saber-toothed tiger was standing next to the tiger. A few paces away a great white wolf stood. Katie slowly turned around, as she saw hundreds, perhaps thousands of animals. Some species she recognized, others she didn't. As far as she could see there were animals, until they blended into the woods. All of them were facing her, watching her intently. Slowly she reached out, touching the nose of the tiger.

"Okay, okay, I get it," she spoke softly. "I'm not alone." Katie raised her head, from her knees. The kitchen was still in its messy state. Invigorated, she got up and started to clean.

The rest of the week flew by, as Katie adjusted to her new reality. She not only had all the extra credit homework due; she also had to keep up with her regular school work. She had lost all patience, in Miss Smith's English class. She figured out her grade. If she got 100% on everything, she barely passed with a D minus. Since she had never gotten a 100% on any English assignment, she decided to cut her losses.

She worked on her other homework during Miss Smith's fourth period. Miss Smith had other plans for her. She called on Katie regularly. She first tried to pay attention to what was going on in class, while doing her other homework. She finally had enough, and told Miss Smith she could care less what Chaucer said in his stupid poems. Miss Smith sent her to the office. Katie, having no intention of repeating the episode in Principal Davis' office, walked to the library to study.

The principal soon caught up with her in sixth hour. She stood quietly, as she was told she would have additional days in detention. Since detention was a great place to get homework done, she didn't mind in the least.

The next day, Katie showed up in English class. Before she could pull out her books, she was again sent to the principal's office. The librarian never said a word to her, as she came in and sat down at one of the tables. Principal Davis, didn't show up to reprimand her. She never bothered, going back to Miss Smith's class.

She brought a sack lunch that included food for her, and Mr. Kelly. During lunch, they both ate while he tutored her. She would stay long after detention was over, working on her homework. Arriving home she would eat dinner, and work on her homework until it was time to go to bed. A couple of times, Jackson came into her thoughts. She told him to leave her alone.

She was working on her homework at the kitchen table, when her mother walked in the front door. Startled, she glanced up from her work. She had avoided all phone calls, including her mother's all week. For a few minutes, she sat staring at her mother, wondering why she was there. She then deduced it was Saturday, the day her mother was supposed to come home. She still felt resentful over her mother's last words to her. Her mom made small talk, to which Katie merely grunted or ignored.

Finally, her mother sat down at the table. "Katie, we need to talk," her mother said in a determined voice.

Exasperated, Katie looked up from her books. “No, Mom, we don’t.”

“Yes, we do.” Her mom raised her voice. She then took a deep breath, and said quietly, “Look, I can tell, you’re still upset. But, I’m upset too. You told me I could count on you, and you decided to take that trust, and throw it back in my face, by skip-”

“I WAS SICK!” Katie interrupted. “Did I have friends over? Did I have a great big party?” Katie pushed herself, from the table. “I am so sick of your telling me what a disappointment I am to YOU!”

“I never said you were a-”

“Do you know what an unexcused absence means?” Katie interrupted. “It means you get a zero for that day, and you can’t make it up.” Katie looked at her mother’s shocked faced. “I got six days of zeroes. SIX DAYS!” she shouted.

“I am your mother, and I know you have never been sick that long in your life.”

Her mother still didn’t believe her. Katie walked over, and started shoving books into her bag. She was so angry, but she knew she had to shake that familiar heat in her belly. She walked into her room, grabbed some clothes, and shoved them in her book bag. She headed, for the front door.

“Where, do you think you’re going?” Her mother’s raised voice came from the kitchen.

“OUT,” Katie shouted back.

“Oh no, you don’t. We are going to talk this out.” Her mother’s voice sounded a little nearer.

“No, Mom, we’re not,” Katie opened the door, and ran to the woods. It felt good, to give into the heat. Her change was simultaneous to her entering into the woods. She paused only to reach down, and grab her bag with her mouth. She ran to the only refuge she knew.

Katie walked up the steps to Forrest's log house. The front door opened easily. It was surprising, how large and spacious it was on the inside. Even though the outside of the house looked as if nobody had been around in years, the inside didn't have much dust. Stairs led up to a loft, where a large bedroom could be seen. The kitchen area was surprisingly modern. She checked the lights. They didn't work.

There was a back door, leading out of the kitchen. Katie could see a note from Forrest, telling her the generator was out back. Not knowing how to work a generator, let alone start one, she decided to leave that for the next visit. She glanced above the cupboards, and saw about ten oil lamps placed in a row. The lamps were familiar to her. Her mother had several in case the electricity turned off in a thunderstorm.

Katie climbed up on the cabinet and got a couple of them down. She placed them, on the kitchen table. She pulled out her books and began again on her homework. She stayed at the cabin until Sunday afternoon. Every time she thought of her mother, a knot formed in her chest. She knew her mother was probably worried sick about her. She also knew her mother had no idea what was really happening in her life, so it was unfair how Katie had reacted to her. It still didn't lift the hurt she felt.

Katie reached the edge of woods. She paused when she saw Sam's car in the driveway. Turning back into human form, she reached into her bag pulling out her clothes. Mentally preparing for the ordeal ahead of her, Katie walked out of the woods towards the house. As soon as she reached the clearing, her mother burst out of the house at a dead run. She grabbed Katie in a huge bear hug and started crying.

"It's okay, Mom." She tried to comfort her mom. She had never seen her mother cry before, let alone so uncontrollably.

"Where were you?" her mom demanded. "I've called everyone, I could think of. I just...I just couldn't' find you." Her mom pulled out of the embrace, and started physically checking her out for any damage done to her.

Feeling like a two-year-old, Katie endured the torture a little longer, for her mother's sake. "I'm fine, Mom."

She looked behind her mother and saw Lizzy and Sam standing there, watching the scene. Sam had her arms folded with a disapproving look on her face. Katie grimaced at her and turned back to her mother.

"Come on; let's go in."

Her mom grabbed her face with both hands. "I'm sorry Katie. I'm so sorry, for not believing you. Sam told me you were really sick and couldn't go to school. I wish...."

Irritated, Katie pulled out of her mother's embrace. *She believed Sam, but not me, s*he thought. She wanted to start arguing the point, until she looked into her mother's tearful face. All anger drained from her.

"It's okay, Mom. I understand." She didn't, but she no longer wanted to fight about it either.

"We need to celebrate!" Her mother demanded. "Lizzy and Sam can come too. I have something I want to tell you."

Katie glanced back, at her two friends. Lizzy shrugged, in acceptance. Sam hesitated for a moment, and then slowly nodded her assent. Katie tried to walk into the house. Her mother kept grabbing her, to make sure she was still there. Grabbing a change of clothes, she showered and changed. When she reached her bedroom, Sam and Lizzy were sitting on her broken bed.

"Where were you?" Sam demanded in a hushed voice. "Your mom called half the county. She even had the forest rangers looking for you."

"I stayed in a cabin I found in the woods," Katie whispered back.

"You found a cabin in the woods?" Lizzy asked, looking behind her to make sure Katie's mom wasn't standing in the doorway.

"Yeah, someone by the name of Forrest," Katie could see Lizzy straighten up.

"There's an actual man named Forrest?" Lizzy demanded.

"Yeah, he owns a cabin about ten miles from here," Katie explained.

Lizzy's excitement showed on her face. "Do you guys remember that man at my grandma's funeral? He said I must be related to Forrest, because I look just like him."

"I thought that name sounded familiar. I just couldn't remember where I had heard it before," Katie said in a rushed whisper.

"Your mom has been going crazy," Sam interrupted.

Katie glanced towards Sam. The disapproving look was back. "I'm sorry, Sam. It was either stick around and change into a wolf in front of her, or leave. Which one do you prefer?"

Sam sighed, her frustration immediately leaving her. "Okay, I understand. There has to be a way, for us to communicate with you. So, if you decide to disappear again, we have a valid excuse for you."

"Girls, are you coming?" All three girls jumped, when Katie's mom called from the living room.

"Uh, be right there," Katie called back.

The smells of the restaurant made Katie's mouth water. She was so hungry, she could hardly control herself. Sitting down, she drummed her fingers on the table impatiently. When the waitress finally came, she was so ready to order.

"For an appetizer, I want a large order of buffalo chicken wings. I would like to have a 20-ounce steak, medium well... No, make that rare. I want two full orders of baby back ribs, French fries, instead of any vegetables, and for desert, I want a cheesecake, as well as the chocolate swirl delight."

Katie glanced up from the menu, to see three sets of eyes staring at her. Heat filled her cheeks, as she realized she had ordered more than all the rest of the table combined. She also didn't want to take anything back. She turned back to the menu, ignoring everyone's stares.

"Ah, I will also have a salad, with dressing on the side please." She casually gave the menu to the waitress. Before the waitress could leave, Katie could not resist. "Could you make sure, we don't run out of bread?"

Katie's mom sat back on her chair with a questioning look on her face. Katie knew she was trying to choose her words carefully, not to offend her. She patiently waited for her mother to start. It didn't take long.

"So, Katie, I sort of noticed there was no food in the house."

Surprise reflected on Katie's face. She did not expect that to be the conversation. "I've been getting hungry lately," she responded.

"Yeah, I guess you have. I even noticed you ate the fruit cake I was going to give away. Her mother gave her a wry smile. "I didn't think you liked fruit cake."

Katie remembered her early morning binge and started turning red. She didn't really know what to say.

"I ate the fruit cake, Mrs. Johnson," Sam jumped in. "I'm sorry if you had plans for it."

Her mother gave Sam a startled look. "That's okay. I'm sure I can find something else for Forrest."

Katie could see Lizzy's response to the name Forrest. She glanced at her friend and gave a small shake of her head. If her mother knew they were interested, she would clam up. She reached for a piece of bread, resisting the urge to shove the thing in her mouth whole.

"Forrest?" she asked casually "Who's that?"

Her mother gave a quick glance towards Lizzy. "Oh, just someone I know," she mumbled. It was obvious she was uncomfortable with the conversation.

Katie gave Sam a how-do-we-proceed? look.

Sam gave her a slight shrug before she turned to Katie's mom. "I heard you tell my mom, you had forest rangers looking for Katie." She said, as nonchalantly as possible. "Did you have the forest rangers, or is this Forrest person?"

Surprised Katie, looked quickly towards Sam. The idea had not even crossed her mind. She quickly looked back at her mother. Her mom glanced from one girl to the next. She seemed to realize, each girl was hanging on her every word. She shrugged, trying to ease the tension from the table.

"Katie didn't take her car," she said in explanation. "She must have taken off in the woods. Forrest can find anyone, so I called him. He told me he lost Katie's scent, the minute she walked into the woods."

“My scent?” Katie interrupted. She gave her two friends a quick startled look, before returning all attention back to her mother.

“I’m sure he meant your tracks,” her mother waved her hand as if to ward off an unwanted fly. "He doesn’t talk all that much, so when he does, he mixes his words up.”

Lizzy leaned in. “Who exactly is Forrest?” she asked, obviously tired of all the subterfuge Katie and Sam were playing.

Startled, Katie’s mom glanced at Lizzy, and immediately changed the subject. No matter how many times, each girl tried other ways to broach the subject of Forrest, her mother clammed up and changed the subject.

Katie could feel Lizzy’s disappointment. She reached over, clasping Lizzy’s hand. “Don’t worry," she whispered when her mother’s attention was somewhere else. “We’ll find out who he is.”

Lizzy smiled appreciatively.

Katie finished her first desert and grabbed her second. She was finally starting to feel full. She glanced at her friends and mother. They had been finished, with their dinners for quite some time. Shrugging, she started digging into the chocolate, savoring the taste.

“Katie, I wanted to tell you something,” her mom began.

Katie looked up from her chocolate, licking every inch of the spoon. All she could say was, “Mmmmhhhhm”.

Her mother looked disgusted. She didn’t know if it was because of the amount of food she just consumed, or her lack of response. She didn’t dare glance at her friends to see their reaction. She kept digging into her dessert, waiting for her mom.

"As you know, I went to Chicago. The trip was a complete success. While I was there, several of my pieces sold. I need to send them more of my stuff."

Her mother's excitement eventually registered against Katie's need for more calories. She stopped and noticed for the first time how her eyes sparkled with enthusiasm. She had a confidence that was always there, but seemed to have been magnified over the weeks she had been gone. Katie put the spoon down.

"Wow, Mom, I'm really happy for you." She was not sure what all this meant. She waited for her mother to continue.

"You have no idea, how long I have waited for this." Her mother was bursting with happiness. "If my pieces keep selling like this, it will mean a whole new way of life for us."

"That means Katie's birthday party, will be more spectacular than last year," Lizzy inserted with a laugh.

Katie tried to kick Lizzy under the table to stop her. She heard Sam's exclamation and realized she missed. Glancing at Sam apologetically, Katie turned to her mother. Her mom had a frozen look on her face.

"I forgot your birthday." It was a statement instead of a question. She could see her mother mentally counting back the days. "Last Monday," she said softly. "Oh, Katie, I'm so sorry. There was so much going on."

"It's okay, Mom, really," Katie interrupted. "I understand." Up until then, she hadn't. She just wanted her mother to feel better. Looking down at her desert, she no longer wanted it. "Let's get out of here." Pushing herself from the table, she walked to the car not waiting for the others to join her.

Chapter 10
December 21

Wednesday, December 21st arrived. Katie felt proud as she entered each class. She pulled out the finished homework, handing it to her teachers. She had met every deadline. There were only two more days left of the term. For the first time since she got into trouble, she sat through detention impatient to leave. *Compared to what she had gone through, the next two days of finals would be a breeze,* she thought to herself.

She drummed her fingers on her desk, as she watched the clock slowly tick away the minutes. The teacher finally gave the signal she could leave. She jumped up and walked through the empty hall. Hearing a distant pounding sound she recognized, she found herself walking towards the gym. Taking a quick look inside, she could see the boys' basketball team practicing. Not wanting to be seen, she quietly walked up to the corner bleachers and sat down. Watching the game she loved to play, gave her a twinge of regret. She wished things, could have been different. Right now, she could be practicing with her team.

She watched David Black steal the ball and make a spectacular basket from the three-point line. She resisted the urge to clap or make herself known. She always enjoyed watching him play. He was clearly, the best player on the team. As if sensing her thoughts, David turned and spotted her. He smiled and gave her a casual wave. Not knowing what else to do, she self-consciously smiled back and returned the gesture.

Katie couldn't keep her eyes off of David. Like every other girl around, she thought he was the cutest guy in school. He was tall and muscular. He had high cheek bones, emphasizing his Native American heritage. His dark eyes always sparkled with laughter. Like his sister, he seemed always to find something funny in every situation.

Katie knew everyone well in the Black family, but she felt closest to Sam and David. She'd had such a crush on David for so many years. She felt her face get hot, thinking about the day she'd realized everyone in the Black family knew about her crush. Since then, she had avoided David. Now, she realized she missed being around him.

"*AAUUGH!*"

Katie jumped out of her reverie. "*What is it? What's wrong?*" she thought.

"I was gone for a couple of days, to let you study," Jackson replied. He made "study" sound like a four-letter word. *"I decide to drop in and say hello. When all of a sudden... I have all these soft and squishy feelings about some DUDE!* ***EEEOOOOWWW!"***

Katie felt Jackson, mentally shake himself. "*I was <u>not</u> having soft and squishy feelings,"* she thought back indignantly.

"Who is this guy anyway?" Jackson interrupted.

"What guy?" Katie thought back, trying to delay.

"Turn your head, so I can get a good look!" Jackson ordered.

Katie purposely turned, and stared at the wall. "*No.*"

"Come on," Jackson tried a coaxing voice. *"Turn your head, just a little."*

Katie got up and walked down the bleachers, careful to keep her eyes on her feet. "*I need a little warning, before you just pop into my head. What happens if I'm in the shower or doing... other things?*"

"What makes you think, I haven't seen you in the shower, or..." Jackson paused *"doing other things?"*

"ARE YOU KIDDING?" Katie exploded.

"Yes," came the casual reply. His chuckle vibrated throughout her mind.

"KATIE! HEY WAIT UP!"

Katie turned, at the sound of her name. Seeing David running up behind her, Katie quickly looked down.

"Ha! Loverboy comes running!" Jackson smirked.

"Shut up!" Katie quickly thought back.

David stopped in front of her, obviously out of breath. "I was beginning to wonder if you were going to stop."

"Oh, sorry. I guess I was in another world." She kept her eyes downcast, making sure Jackson could not see David's face.

David placed his hands on his hips. "Were you able to turn in all the extra credit homework today?"

Katie's head swung up in surprise, her eyes meeting David's.

"BINGO!" Jackson's thoughts rang out.

Exasperated, she quickly looked down. "Uh, yeah, I was able to get everything done."

"Hey, that's great. Sam was pretty upset the way Davis treated you."

"Who the hell is Davis?" Jackson's thoughts shot back.

"Shut UP!" she thought, as loudly as she could. "Principal Davis," she said slowly, "was a real prick."

"Ooooh! Sorry," Jackson replied.

"Listen, I wanted to invite you to our Christmas party," David began. "Sam didn't think you were up to it, but I thought you might like a break."

"Oh." Katie had completely forgotten it was so close to Christmas.

"Time to tell lover boy to get lost," Jackson interjected.

Katie was getting tired of following two conversations. "I'm not sure."

David stepped closer. "You've always come," he said persuasively. "What's so different about this year?"

"Oh, I don't know, she turns into a great white wolf and can eat you alive," Jackson thought sarcastically.

"Will you please, SHUT UP!" Katie thought wildly, to Jackson.

She was conscious, of David's proximity. He was watching her a little too intently, for her peace of mind. She was beginning to wonder if he could see she was talking to someone else in her head. She liked the idea that David was asking her personally to attend the party, and not just Sam. It gave her hope that maybe, just maybe, he liked her too—or, at least enjoyed her company, she amended to herself.

"We have better things to do loverboy, than go to a stupid Christmas party with you," Jackson replied. His thoughts were aggressive and filled with dislike.

Katie's back immediately stiffened at Jackson's onslaught. She smiled warmly up at David. "I would love to come to your family's party."

David smiled back, a look of relief evident on his face. "Awesome. It's Saturday around six." He backed up and gave a quick wave. He turned, and ran back towards the school.

"I'd love to come to your family's party," mimicked Jackson in a high-pitched voice. Katie wondered, how he was able to change his pitch, with his thoughts. *"I think I'm going have to go somewhere and puke."*

"Look, we're going to have to set some boundaries," Katie interrupted. "*I have to function like a normal human being. Which means, having a conversation without your input."*

"I've got news for you," Jackson interjected, anger evident in every syllable. *"You are **not**, a normal human being."*

"I'm going to live my life, as normally as possible." Katie thought heatedly.

"Yeah? Good luck, with that."

Katie was so caught up in her conversation with Jackson, she didn't notice Lizzy standing by her car until she almost walked into her. Startled, she jumped back. "Lizzy, you scared me."

"Katie, I feel weird," Lizzy said softly.

"What's the matter?" Katie asked worriedly.

"I'm so hot, I think I'm going to burst into flames," Lizzy answered.

Shock vibrated through Katie's body. "AAHH, HELL!"

"It was bound to happen," Jackson's thoughts rang out. *"She's the granddaughter, of Old Elizabeth Hawk."*

"What has that got to do with anything?" Katie said out loud.

"What has what, got to do with anything?" Lizzy responded.

"You, need to watch what you say, Katherine. People will think you hear voices," Jackson replied.

"The legend..." Katie paused, trying to collect her thoughts. "The legend said, only <u>one</u> descendant of Running Deer would change."

"I can't change into anything!" Lizzy's voice sounded panicky. "I have a life. I have school, cheerleading practice. I can't go through what you did, Katie. I know I won't be able to handle it."

"AAAUUHHH! Cheerleading practice is soo important in the grand scheme of things," Jackson retorted.

"SHUT... UP!" Katie thought back. She closed her eyes for a moment. Upon opening them, she focused on her friend. "Lizzy, I handled it, because there was nothing else I could do. You just deal with what's handed to you." She reached over and touched Lizzy's arm. "Have you had any dreams about The Great White Tiger?"

Lizzy shook her head, "No."

"You will," Jackson's thoughts and Katie's voice said in unison. "This is the first day, you were feeling hot?" Katie asked.

"Yes."

"I think you have a couple of weeks, till you change," Katie said. "Let's hope it's during Christmas break, so you won't miss any school." Katie stood for a moment, watching her friend. "The problem we keep having is, we don't know enough of what we're dealing with. I haven't had any time at all to do any research. Finding out about the legends has to be our first priority."

Lizzy nodded her head in agreement.

"Come on. I'll take you home." Katie pulled out her keys, to open the car door.

"I agree we need to do some research," Jackson inserted. *"Saturday night's a good time to start."*

Katie's lips twitched into a smile. "*Nice try.*"

Chapter 11
Lizzy's Dream

Lying on her bed, Katie couldn't go to sleep. She kept thinking of Lizzy, knowing what emotions she must be going through. She wanted to help her friend, but she wasn't quite sure how to accomplish it. She thought back, to when she first started thinking something was wrong with her. The dream with the white tiger, was the first indication.

She reached out with her mind. "*Jackson, are you there?*" She waited for his response. She had never been able to contact him. It was always he, contacting her. *Why was that*? she wondered. There was so much she didn't know.

"I'm here," came a sleepy reply.

"This is the first time I've been able to contact you," Katie thought in surprise.

Another long pause, *"I think our minds, are getting more in sync with each other."* The thoughts came out, hesitantly.

"You sound like, it's not a good thing," Katie responded.

"I'm not sure, it is."

"Why?"

"Is this why you contacted me, or did you have another reason?"

Katie instinctively knew Jackson was changing the subject on purpose. Once again, she felt that old frustration when Jackson took evasive actions with her questions. Irritation grew when she heard Jackson chuckling through his thoughts. Since he could feel her emotions, he could feel her irritation. Tamping down her emotions, Katie concentrated on why she contacted him in the first place.

Changing the subject, was probably a good plan she reasoned. "*I'm worried about Lizzy.*"

Another long pause. "I'm listening," Jackson finally inserted.

"Maybe I can help her."

"How do you propose to do that?" Jackson replied dryly.

"You helped me," Katie pointed out.

"That took a lot of effort on my part, I'm not sure you're strong enough for that."

Katie bristled, offended of Jackson's judgment of her. "*If I'm strong enough to turn into a wolf without tearing the place up, I'm strong enough to help my friend.*"

"I'm not saying you're weak. It just takes a lot of brain energy, to accomplish it," Jackson reasoned.

"Lizzy is probably having the dream with The Great White Tiger as we speak," Katie tried explaining.

"So?"

She was beginning to think, Jackson was being deliberately obtuse. "*If I'm there, then maybe I can help her.*"

"There's something you need to understand." Jackson paused.

Katie bristled, her frustration and anger spilling out at his words. She realized he wasn't even going to continue until she got her emotions under control. Trying very hard, she took a couple of deep breaths, and as soon as her nerves steadied, Jackson resumed. *"Facing The Great White Tiger is sort of a test. Not all people look around for the nearest weapon, to defend the toddler. Some people actually run, leaving the baby defenseless."*

Astonished, Katie listened quietly to Jackson words.

"If you remember, I showed up after you had proven yourself. You must have done something special, because the tiger took a great liking to you. Hence the protectiveness she displayed."

Katie thought about, what Jackson had said. The white tiger showed her strong protectiveness, against Jackson. *"Since I will be in Lizzy's dream and not mine, will the tiger react to me as she did to you?"* Katie asked.

"No, the tiger will react to you as she always has."

"Why does she react negatively to you?" Katie asked.

A long pause followed. Katie wasn't surprised. Jackson always stepped around questions, or gave no answer at all, if he didn't like the question. She sighed, in response to the quiet.

"The Great White Tiger, didn't like a decision I made," came the quiet response.

Katie had ten questions, she wanted to fire back at him.

He seemed to realize this. Before she could start asking, he quickly said, *"You want to enter Lizzy's dream?"*

Knowing she was being sidetracked, she decided to let her questions go for another time. "*Yes, I would like to enter Lizzy's dream."*

"Don't you have school tomorrow?" Jackson asked.

"Yes. What does that have to do with anything?" Katie replied.

"There are side-effects; you need to be aware of."

"Look, I want to do this, so don't give me any crap about side-effects." Katie's frustration resurfaced with a vengeance.

"I'm not giving you any crap, I just thought you should be aware-"

"Jackson please," Katie interrupted, her frustration bubbling over.

A long sigh pervaded throughout Katie's mind.

"Concentrate really hard on Lizzy. Think about the essence of who she is, and then reach out with your mind the way you reached out to me."

It took several tries. Katie learned she had to let go of all emotions and somehow drift towards Lizzy. A couple of times, Jackson told her she had achieved her goal. This didn't make any sense to her, until Jackson explained. Lizzy must be having cold chills, instead of the hot flashes.

Katie was on the verge of giving up for the night when it just happened. She was transported into Lizzy's dream so quickly, she at first thought she must have fallen asleep herself. She was standing in the trees, looking towards the clear pool she remembered so well in her dreams. She saw Lizzy, stepping towards the toddler. Lizzy reached out for the little girl, when she glanced up, seeing the tiger advance towards the child.

Katie could see the terror in Lizzy's face. She wanted to step out and help her friend, but held back keeping in mind the things Jackson had told her. For a couple of seconds, Lizzy stood frozen. Katie wondered, what she was waiting for. Then with careful steps, Lizzy quickly picked the baby up and ran. The tiger didn't follow, but watched her leave the clearing. The tiger looked towards the trees, where Katie was standing. Knowing, it was probably safe for her to come out. Katie walked into the clearing, towards the tiger. She could hear Lizzy crashing through the woods, in her attempt to get as far as possible from the scene.

Not knowing what else to do, Katie started running after her friend.

"What are you doing?"

Katie stopped, looking around for Jackson. He hadn't materialized in this dream as she'd expected. He was obviously monitoring, everything through her.

"I'm chasing after my friend, she replied. *What does it look like*?"

"You're in a dream world. You don't have to run after anybody, just transport yourself in front of Lizzy."

Katie slowed down to a walk. "*I'm new at this, you know,"* she grumbled. "*How, am I supposed to know all the rules?* "She was still walking towards the crashing sounds Lizzy was making. "*How exactly, do I transport?"*

"There's nothing different from what you did in my room," Jackson explained. *"Just think about exactly what you want, and then it will happen for you."*

Katie closed her eyes, concentrating on the sounds Lizzy was making. She opened her eyes to see Lizzy trip over a log in front of her. Lizzy sprawled on the ground and started cussing up a storm. Katie couldn't help grinning. This was a new experience for Lizzy. She was always so graceful. She never thought in her life she would see Lizzy so out of her element.

As she stepped towards her friend, a rustling sound made her glance into the trees. She froze. A Cheetah was walking towards them. Katie couldn't help, but admire the graceful animal. Its long legs paused, before stepping over the log Lizzy had tripped over. Not knowing what to expect, Katie watched the animal lower its head. Rubbing her hands to get the dirt off, Lizzy was unaware the animal was just inches from her.

The animal daintily put its body in the same position Lizzy was in, and gracefully sidestepped into Lizzy.

Surprised Katie stood watching as Lizzy, struggled to her feet. Once again Lizzy plunged into her flight. In her haste to keep going, Lizzy almost ran over the top of Katie. She jumped and gave a startled gasp when she saw Katie standing there.

"KATIE!" She grabbed Katie's hand and tried to run. "Come on, we have to get out of here. There is a huge tiger behind me, reeeeally HUGE!" Her eyes were wild with fear, as she looked behind her before frantically tugging on Katie's hand. "WE have to go! NOW!"

It took several tries, for Katie to get Lizzy's attention. Eventually, she yanked her hand away from Lizzy's tight hold.

"LISTEN TO ME!" She yelled, as she gently shook Lizzy's shoulders. Lizzy gazed at her blankly, while her eyes kept darting towards the woods.

"This is a dream," Katie repeated, for what seemed like the tenth time. "This is only a dream. The tiger will not hurt you!" Katie could tell, Lizzy was finally getting a hold of her emotions as her struggles slowed down.

Lizzy stepped away from Katie, folding her arms in a defensive gesture. "No tiger?" she said in a quiet voice.

Katie reached over and hugged Lizzy tightly. "Remember me telling you, about the dream I had with The Great White Tiger?" She could tell Lizzy was listening, because her breathing became less ragged. Her terrified eyes stopped searching the wooded area.

Lizzy stepped back, tears were streaming down her dirty face. Katie watched Lizzy, slowly pull herself together. She daintily brushed off the dirt from her knees, and sat down on a fallen tree. She did it so gracefully, Katie was reminded of the cheetah. She had a suspicion, she knew what animal, Lizzy was going to turn into. She decided, to keep it to herself, until she knew she was right.

"Are you real?" The question sounded defiant and pleading all at the same time.

Katie smiled. She remembered, wanting to know the same thing about Jackson. She walked towards her friend and sat down, putting her arm around Lizzy's shoulders. "Yes, I'm real." Katie paused, not knowing how much more Lizzy could take in one night. "I was worried about you. I thought I might be able to help. I'm using a sort of telekinesis, to transport myself into your dream."

"How did you know you could do that?" Lizzy said, a trace of tears still evident in her voice.

Katie frowned. She didn't know how to answer. Something stopped her from telling her friend about Jackson.

"I don't know. I just did." Katie was relieved, when Lizzy seemed to take this at face value. "Come on; lets' go home. You're going to be very hot, when you wake up. Don't worry, it's all a part of the great plan."

"What plan is that?" came Lizzy's shaky reply.

"I have no idea," Katie stated truthfully.

Katie opened her eyes. She was lying on her bed, when a headache began forming in the back of her skull. She was so exhausted, she could hardly move. She closed her eyes and was fast asleep.

Chapter 12
Side Effects

The alarm went off, causing excruciating pain to slice through Katie's brain. Desperate to turn the sound off, she fumbled around, knocking the clock onto the floor. Stooping down to finally locate the blaring object, she succeeded in finding the button used to turn it off. The pounding in her head seemed to vibrate to the back of her eyes. Opening her eyes brought more pain.

Fumbling around in the dark, she located the small lamp next to her bed. The light sent shockwaves through her system. Her eyes felt as though they were going to fall out of their sockets. Desperate to turn the light off, she eventually smashed the lamp against her bedpost. Blessed darkness descended into the room.

If she lay quietly on the bed, the pounding in her head was less intense. If she tried to move or attempted to get up, the pounding would increase to intolerable measures. She would have loved to get up for some pain reliever. She didn't know how to get it, without causing more torture. She ended up just lying there, keeping her eyes closed. She didn't know how she accomplished it, but she eventually drifted off to sleep.

"What are you still doing, in bed?"

Katie didn't know if it was the sound of her mother's raised voice, or the overhead light being flicked on that caused her to double up. The pounding increased to such a level Katie just wanted to die and get it over with.

"What's the matter?"

Katie realized, her mother was still in the room. She tried to form words, but all that seemed to come out of her mouth were small moans.

She knew she was going to be sick. Katie rolled over and threw up in a potted plant. Keeping her eyes closed. "Turn off the light," she whispered.

Her mother quickly turned off the light. Once again, blessed darkness descended into the room. Katie opened her eyes, into slits. Daybreak was making the room lighter. Her mother returned, with two pain relievers. Grateful, Katie took the two tablets with the water being offered. Her mother smoothed out her hair, and asked her a few questions. Answering them, seemed to take all her strength. Her mother left for a couple of minutes. When she returned, she had a blanket in her hands. Katie watched, as her mother placed the blanket in front of the window, blocking all light coming into the room. Katie closed her eyes and gave into exhaustion.

She slept all day. Her mother periodically came in to give her more pain relievers. By nightfall, she felt well enough to leave her room. Her mother's worried face swung around from the living room. Giving her mother a half-hearted smile, she walked into the kitchen and got a glass of water. Sitting down on the couch next to her mother, Katie lay her head on the armrest.

"How are you feeling?" her mother asked quietly.

"Better."

"I called the school to tell them you were sick."

A huge weight crashed down on Katie, making the pounding in her head start up again.

"School!" She moaned the word. "I completely forgot." She was supposed to take, some of her finals today. If she couldn't make them up, all her work would be for nothing.

"Don't worry about it," her mother insisted. "I talked to Mr. Davis, and he said you could take all your finals tomorrow. That is, if you're feeling better by tomorrow."

"Tomorrow's end of term, I have to feel better," Katie replied. Her emotions were making her head pound again. Excusing herself, she went back to bed.

Katie, woke up startled. She automatically turned her head to look at her alarm clock. Remembering it was somewhere on the floor, she rolled over, peering over the side of the bed. An upside down red six thirty was blinking in the darkness. The blinking didn't hurt her eyes. Cautiously, Katie sat up in bed. The pounding was gone. Slowly, she walked into the bathroom. Flicking on the light, was something she knew she had to do. Her eyes, immediately snapped shut and squinted. No pain shot through her, with the unexpected light. Relieved, Katie got dressed for school.

She was eating a bowl of cereal, while she reviewed some of her notes.

"Good morning, Sunshine. How is your head?"

Katie was getting used to Jackson popping in and out. She continued eating her cereal, as if she didn't hear him. His words, eventually sunk into her conscious mind. She bolted upward, in her awareness.

"Are you telling me, you knew I was going to have... whatever it was, I just had?"

Katie could hear Jackson chuckling. *"I told you, there were side effects."*

"You said side effects, not a mind-numbing migraine. It gave the word "torture" a whole new meaning." Katie shot back. "*I cannot believe this. I missed finals and another day of school."*

"If you recall, I did ask you if you had school in the morning." Jackson pointed out. "I believe the exact quote was: Look, I want to do this, so don't give me any crap about side effects." His thoughts once again, went up an octave as he mimicked her.

Katie shook her head. *"All I'm saying is you could have been more forceful, with your warning."*

Jackson's chuckle turned into a wholehearted laugh. *"You seemed to have a personality, that wants to find out for herself, regardless of what she's told. 'Katie, that water is hot; do not touch it.' Then when you say, 'Ouch I burned my hand!' the only reply I can come up with is, Auuuhhh DUH!"*

"Go away," Katie muttered under her breath.

"Where do you want me to go?" her mother asked as she entered the kitchen.

"No, sorry, I wasn't talking to you," Katie said apologetically.

Her mother looked around the small kitchen, to make sure they were alone. She acted as though she wanted to continue the conversation, stopped, then shook her head in confusion. "How do you feel?"

Relieved that her mother didn't react to her talking to herself and annoyed that Jackson seemed to be having such a good time at her expense, she decided to ignore the laughing in her head and concentrate only on her mother. "I'm fine. I believe I will be able to keep up today. Thanks for yesterday, by the way."

Her mother seemed to want to pursue the conversation, but Sam's horn sounded outside. Relieved, Katie grabbed her things, and ran out to the car.

By the time lunch rolled around, Katie was dragging. The stress of the last two weeks, plus being sick the day before, was taking its toll. Katie only picked at her food, worried about some of the questions on her last final. Wondering how she did on it was driving her crazy.

"Katie? Did you... like…appear in my dream, the other night?

Katie glanced up at Lizzy, sitting across from her. For the first time, she took a really good look at her friend. Lizzy, whom always took great care with her appearance, looked horrible. Her hair was pulled back, into a quick ponytail. She had no makeup on, and there were definite bags under her eyes. Her shirt was rumpled as if she'd slept in it the night before.

"Yes, I was there," Katie answered. "Are you all right? You don't look so hot."

Lizzy looked around, to make sure no one was paying attention. "It was real?"

Katie pushed her tray of food out of the way, and leaned forward so she could talk in a lower voice. She was aware Sam leaned in, right beside her, to hear.

"I was there, Lizzy. I saw you. The Great White Tiger came into the clearing. It took you a while, to figure out what you were going to do. Then you stooped down, grabbed the baby, and started running as fast as you could through the woods."

"I was so frightened." Lizzy's eyes were brimming with tears. "It didn't feel like a dream. It felt so real. I…" She reached out and grabbed Katie's hand. "I almost left the baby, Katie." Her voice trembled, with each syllable she uttered. "I was on the verge of turning around, and running, leaving the baby behind."

Katie squeezed her friend's hand. "You didn't, Lizzy. It doesn't matter, what you felt like doing. What matters is, you did the right thing in the end."

"How, were you there, Katie?" Lizzy demanded. "How were you able to be there?" Her troubled eyes were searching Katie's.

"I don't know… I just closed my eyes and focused on you. Next thing I knew, I was in your dream." Katie knew, it had taken a lot more work than that. She didn't know how to explain it any better without bringing Jackson into the picture. The only reason she knew it could be done, was because Jackson had done it in her dreams. All the old questions she had lined up for Jackson, came flooding back. Shaking her head to clear her mind, Katie squeezed Lizzy's hand.

"Lizzy, the one thing you need to know is you're not alone. We can all get through this, together." The bell sounded, and all three girls looked up from their table. The lunch room was almost completely empty. Katie jumped up and dumped her tray. Her two friends followed suit.

"Whoooaaa! What are you doing?"

Katie gave a small start of surprise, before she realized Jackson was once again invading her life at the most inopportune moment. "*Leave me alone. I'm taking a test*," she replied as testily, as she could. hoping he would get the message.

"Stonewall Jackson did not die on the battlefield of Gettysburg."

Katie looked down, at the test she was taking. "*What?*"

"Come on, Katie, I only attended a small fraction of your study sessions. The answer is C, not B. Stonewall Jackson, was killed by friendly fire."

"I don't see the words friendly fire anywhere in C."

"It doesn't exactly say friendly fire, but he was killed by one of his own sentries," Jackson explained. "Here, I thought you were a true southern girl."

"I guess I did know that... I just... I keep reading the same sentence over and over, and I'm not understanding the question." Katie replied wearily.

"Turn the page to the front, and let me check your work," Jackson responded.

"I can't do that; it's cheating."

"Katie, I did this to you. Let me help. I know the answers, because I saw them through your eyes. Trust me, Katie. I can help you."

Katie slowly turned the test to page one. Jackson quickly told her what answers she needed to change. By the end of sixth hour, Katie's head was once again pounding. Jackson helped her through two more finals. She had taken pain relievers, but they didn't seem to work.

Mr. Kelly looked up from his desk, and asked her how she was feeling. Shaking her head, she sat down and pulled out her pencil to take her last final. After handing out the test, Mr. Kelly called her into the hallway. Not knowing what to expect, she quietly followed him out.

"Katie, you don't look very good." The teacher's concern was evident on his face.

Her head was starting to pound so much, she was starting to see stars. "I'm sorry Mr. Kelly, I have a really bad headache."

Kelly stood there for a moment, then told her to go to the office. He thought she needed to call her mom. He then told her he would be there 9:00 am sharp the next day, for her to take the final. Katie, couldn't believe it. Nodding her head in agreement, she went into the classroom and gathered up her things. Giving Kelly a smile of gratitude, Katie walked to the office and called her mother.

"That is the best teacher, I have ever seen." Jackson's thoughts quietly acknowledged.

"Yes, he is," Katie thought back.

Chapter 13
Christmas

Katie opened her eyes. Bright sunshine glistened off her bedroom furniture. Turning over, she could not help smiling. Christmas! Bouncing out of her bed, she walked into the living room. Her mother was sitting on the couch.

"Hello, sleepyhead. I was beginning to wonder if you were ever going to wake up." Her mom patted the couch by her.

Katie sat down, "Merry Christmas, Mom."

"Did you have a fun time, last night?" Her mother was grabbing small pieces of her hair, and was running them through her fingers.

"Yes, I did."

Her mother had attended the Christmas party at Sam's house with her, but Katie came home much later. Katie stifled a yawn, and then automatically glanced over at the Christmas tree. The sight confused her. The only present under the tree was hers to her mother.

When Katie was six, her mom stopped putting presents under the tree early. Katie would prod, shake them, and figure out what she was getting long before Christmas morning. She had continuously tried over the years, to find her mother's hiding place. Eventually, she had given up. This year with her secret wolf self, and exceptional sense of smell, she probably would have found it. Christmas, seemed to have just snuck up on her.

Her mother gracefully got up from the couch, and mumbled about having to make a phone call.

"What call do you have to make on Christmas?" Katie asked.

Watching her mother walk towards the kitchen, she got up and retrieved her mother's present. She gave another look, under the tree. Nope, nothing there. There wasn't even a small box she may have missed.

A little hurt, Katie sat back down on the couch. She was holding her mother's present when her mom walked back into the living area.

"Here, Mom. Merry Christmas." She handed the package over.

Her mother smiled, and slowly opened the gift. Her mother's smile brightened, when she saw what was there. Katie had painted a picture of the waterfall, and pool in her dreams. She knew she didn't get the colors quite right, or the light as is played off the water.

"Oh, Katie, it's lovely."

"I know it's not as good as your work," Katie said softly

"Don't you dare apologize," her mother scolded. "An artist never apologizes."

"You really like it?" Katie asked quietly. A shy smile, forming on her lips.

"Where is this place? It looks familiar to me."

Katie watched her mother, very closely. "You know this place? The exact location?"

"Don't you? You're the one who painted it."

"No, I've never seen it in real life," Katie pointed out.

The doorbell rang. Whoever was there, started pounding on the door yelling for her to open up. Bewildered, Katie got up from the couch and opened the door. There stood, David Black. His nose and cheeks were red from the cold. He took one look at her and started laughing. Katie self-consciously ran her fingers through her hair. She had no idea, what she looked like. She just got out of bed, for crying out loud.

"Merry Christmas!"

He picked her up, twirled her around, and gave her a big bear hug. When he let her go, her back faced the front door. David's laugh was infectious. Katie couldn't help giggling, as well. She had no idea, what she was laughing about.

Sam, came in next. "Merry Christmas, Katie."

"What is going on?! I just saw you guys last night." Katie pointed out.

Sam shrugged. "We just wanted to be here, when you got your present."

"My present?" This had to be something big, Katie thought.

"Yes, you dope. You didn't think your mom, was going to forget Christmas, too, did you?" Sam was shaking, with excitement.

"Hold on, I'm being left out!"

Katie turned to see Lizzy, running up the sidewalk. Her eyes caught, on a big red bow. The kind of bow, you put on something like a... CAR! Katie started screaming and jumping up and down. There in the driveway, was a sporty, baby blue, Camaro. She ran out, to get a better look. Her bare feet, making tracks in the snow. Opening the door, she could see the dark gray interior. She touched all the controls, making sure they were all there. Glancing up, she saw her mother standing in front of the car, smiling. Getting out of the car, she ran to her mother and threw her arms around her. "Thank you! Thank you!"

Before her mother could say anything, she ran back to the car. The cold, finally registered on her bare feet.

Getting in, she reached down and started the car. The purring of the engine sent thrills through her. Turning on the heat, Katie rolled down the window.

"Whoever wants a ride, better get in quick?"

She rolled the window back up. Three people started tussling, for the passenger seat. Katie laughed when she saw David win.

Backing out of the driveway, she made sure she didn't hit her old Honda. Katie paused and put the car into drive. "Let's see, what this baby can do."

Squealing tires and a few fish tales later, she was racing down the road. Eventually, she let all the passengers drive for a while. Finally, they all made it back to her house. Katie was a little hesitant about getting out of the car. She still, didn't have any shoes on. The only one way to get to the house and that was making a run for it.

The door jerked open, David reached down, picked her up, and carried her into the house. She snuggled into his arms, as the cold air hit her senses. Her face close to his, she could smell the light cologne, she associated with him. He turned his head, smiling down at her. Sam opened the front door. With a flourish, he set her on her feet. Katie thanked him hesitantly, before looking around for her mother. She was making breakfast for everyone.

Katie excused herself for a minute, and ran to her bedroom. Looking into the mirror, Katie was horrified to find her hair tasseled. It was almost useless, to get a brush through it. Fifteen minutes later, Katie emerged. Showered, changed, and with a little make-up on, she now felt she could face anyone in the kitchen.

Sitting down at the table, they had a good time laughing and talking. This is what she really needed, she thought, a chance to get away from all the worries and frustrations she felt, when she first turned into a wolf. This was the world as it should be. Turning her head, she could see Lizzy holding her head down. Sweat pouring off her face.

From experience, Katie knew exactly what Lizzy was going through. A small idea began forming. She decided to test it out.

"Lizzy, can you pass me the salt?"

Directing her thoughts towards her friend, Lizzy reached over grabbed the salt, and placed it within Katie's reach.

"Can you pass me the pepper?"

Lizzy looked around the table. "I don't see the pepper," she said out loud.

"Oh, I'm sorry. The pepper is above the stove," Katie's mom said, getting up to get the pepper. She placed the pepper in front of Lizzy.

Lizzy sat looking at the pepper for a minute, before the realization finally dawned. She glanced up into Katie's eyes. "*I was the only one, who heard you ask for the salt and pepper.*" Her thoughts came through very clearly.

"Yes," Katie thought back.

"We can communicate through our thoughts?" Lizzy questioned.

"Yes," Katie replied.

Instead of accepting this, Lizzy seemed to be freaking out over the idea. She started hyperventilating, the air coming in and out in short breaths. Her face turned white, indicating she wasn't getting enough oxygen. Sweat was running down her face. Katie jumped up from the table, and ran around to Lizzy.

Katie grabbed Lizzy and pulled her from the seat. Lizzy halfheartedly resisted. It looked as if she was going to start screaming at any second. Using more force than necessary, Katie pulled Lizzy out of the kitchen and into her bedroom. Lizzy's terrified eyes darted around the room. Katie whispered softly trying to calm Lizzy down, but it still looked as if she was going to start screaming. Katie, felt she had no choice. She hauled Lizzy into the bathroom, forced her into the shower, and turned the tap on cold. Water cascaded down, soaking them both. Katie could see, Lizzy was finally gaining control of her emotions.

Katie looked down at her damp shirt, and decided to change it before returning back to the kitchen. Walking back into the kitchen, three faces turned towards her.

"Uuuuhhh... Lizzy needed to take a shower. Soooo, I decided to help her." It was really lame. As soon as it was out of her mouth, she knew it wouldn't fly.

Sam raised her eyebrows in surprise. Katie refused to look in David's direction. Shrugging her shoulders, she started clearing off the dishes. Sam and David got up and started helping her.

"What was that all about?" Sam whispered. She had come up behind Katie, while David was convincing her mother the three of them could handle cleaning the dishes.

She glanced over at David and her mother, to make sure they couldn't hear. "Lizzy started freaking out," she whispered.

"She seemed just fine to me, maybe a little sweaty," Sam whispered.

"She started freaking out, when I spoke to her through my thoughts."

“WHAT?” Sam said loudly, David glanced in their direction giving them both a questioning look.

“SHHHHHHH” Katie whispered, giving David a smile that was supposed to say everything is fine over here.

Sam swiveled her head between Katie and David, finally coming up with a decision. “David, you need to go home,” she said with authority.

“What?” Katie and David said in unison.

Sam ignored Katie and spoke directly to David. “I’m sorry, David, but it’s time for you to go home. Katie will drive me home later.”

“You don’t have to leave.” Katie insisted.

David gave Katie a smile as he shrugged into his coat. “I was wanting to meet up with Robbie and Steven anyway.”

Steven Bends was Robbie’s age and was best friends with David and Robbie forever.

“I cannot believe, how rude you were to him,” Katie said, as she watched David drive away.

“He’s my brother. He has done a lot ruder things to me.” Sam said dismissively. “Now we need to go into the bedroom, and sort a few things out.”

Katie shrugged her shoulders and walked back into her bedroom. She lay down, on her broken bed. Apparently, Lizzy was still in the shower.

“She had to have used all the hot water by now,” Sam muttered.

“I don’t think she’s using hot water at all.” Katie retorted, still peeved over David's leaving.

“Do you think, we should check on her?” Sam asked, ignoring Katie’s tone.

"Lizzy, Sam is worried about you. Do we need to come in, and check on you?" Katie reached out with her mind.

"NO, I'M FINE… DON'T COME IN," Lizzy, hollered from the bathroom.

Sam swiveled around to stare at Katie. "How did she-" Her face cleared. "Wow! That's some trick," her voice whispered in awe.

"Yes, it is," Katie agreed.

"How far does it go?" Sam asked, "I mean how far can you two be a part, and still communicate?"

"I don't know; do you want to experiment?" Katie asked, the idea growing along with Sam.

"Tell Lizzy she needs to come out," Sam ordered.

Shrugging. "*Lizzy, Sam's going to come get you, if you don't come out right now,"* Katie relayed.

The water immediately turned off in the bathroom. A few minutes later, Lizzy came out, wrapped in a large towel. Her eyes were bloodshot and puffy. Katie and Sam looked knowingly, at each other.

Between the three of them, Lizzy was the drama queen. Katie got up from the bed and rummaged through her drawers. She threw Lizzy a pair of jeans, a T-shirt, and some clean underwear. Lizzy caught the clothes and turned back into the bathroom to change.

When Lizzy returned, Sam softly cleared her throat. "Katie and I were wondering. How far can you two be apart, and still communicate with your minds? Would you mind, if we conduct a few experiments?"

Lizzy sat on the bed. "Fine," she said in a fatalistic voice.

Katie had to stop herself from rolling her eyes. She glanced towards Sam, who was doing just that. Trying to hold back a grin, she decided to continue the conversation. "We can probably go farther than the distance between Lizzy's house and mine," Katie explained.

"What makes you- Oh! Yeah, the dream. You entered into her dream," Sam quickly surmised. "Why don't we try this? Why don't Lizzy and I get in Lizzy's car and head east, while you drive west. We'll bring our cell phones when the contact is broken, so we can gauge how far the connection is."

Katie told her mother they were going out, then headed for her car. Getting into her new car again gave her a huge thrill. She couldn't believe, her mother had been able to afford such a vehicle. Of course, the car wasn't brand new, but probably still under factory warranty, Katie figured. That was a lot newer than anything they ever had before. It didn't take her long, before she was eating up the miles. She checked periodically with Lizzy, still able to hear loud and clear. After the girls drove over a hundred miles away from each other, they decided to turn around and head for home.

Driving back towards her house, Katie reached out her mind towards Jackson. *"Jackson, are you there?"*

A long silence prevailed. Not knowing if she was too far away, or if he couldn't hear her. Katie sighed. *"Merry Christmas, Jackson."*

Turning into her drive, she a heard his soft reply. *"Merry Christmas to you too, Katie."*

So, he had heard her, but for some reason, he didn't want to communicate. She could respect his wishes. After all, it was Christmas.

Chapter 14
Trail of Tears

"Did you know, Appalachia used to be attached to the African continent?"

Katie looked up, from the book she was reading. Sam had been throwing out trivia information, all morning. All three girls were in the county library. They were trying to look up *anything,* that would give them information on Native American folklore and legends. So far, they had found out the Appalachians were the oldest mountains in the world. They somehow had a "sister" forest, somewhere in China. Large mammals like the mammoth and saber tooth tiger roamed freely, but there were absolutely no legends on animal spirits turning people into animals.

Frustrated, Katie threw the book she was reading, onto the table. "We're wasting our time," she muttered.

Sam flopped down on a chair, next to Katie. "Do you know, what I don't understand?" She didn't wait, for the others to comment. "The tiger turned this Running Deer into a tiger, when the first white man appeared. How come it didn't show up, when the white man came again?"

Katie leaned away from Sam, to get a better look at her. "What do you mean?"

"How come The Great White Tiger didn't show up, when the *Trail of Tears* was happening? I mean, as far as a 'great evil.'—Sam put her two fingers together, doing the quote sign—"That would have been, at the top of my list."

"Maybe the Tiger did, we just don't know about it." Katie glanced around the room, spotted Lizzy, and motioned for her to come over.

"To tell you the truth, I really don't know all that much about the *Trail of Tears*." Katie swung her head back and forth, between the two shocked faces of her friends.

"Okay, I know the white man stole the land, and forced the tribes to move a thousand miles to Oklahoma," Katie shrugged. "The details are kind of sketchy," her voice trailed off.

Lizzy leaned back against a low bookshelf resting her elbows behind her. "My grandma Elizabeth used to talk about it, all the time."

Katie turned to Lizzy, interested, "What did she say?"

"President Andrew Jackson worked hard to pass the '*Indian Removal Act*' that forced all natives off their lands. She said most of the country was actually against the law, but the government in Washington decided they knew better than the people they represented.

"The Creek and Choctaw Tribes were the first to leave. The Cherokee decided to fight the law in court. It took a couple of tries, but the Supreme Court ruled in favor of the Cherokee, saying the Cherokee Nation, was actually a sovereign nation. The removal act didn't affect them."

Katie frowned. "In that case," she interrupted, "how were they forced to leave?"

Lizzy pushed up from the bookshelf and sat down next to Katie. "The Cherokee had a representative government, a lot like the U.S.

government at the time. They were ranchers and farmers and they built roads and schools. They even dressed, like their white counterparts. The principal chief of the Cherokee was a guy named Ross."

Lizzy paused for a moment. "I think his first name, was John." She shrugged. "Yeah, John Ross sounds right. Anyway, he fought really hard against the white encroachment on Indian lands, and he did it really smart. Like I said before, he took the case through the U.S. court system.

"Rumors started raging throughout the United States, that gold was found in the mountains owned by the Cherokee Nation. The white people were really desperate to take the land. A small majority of about 500 Cherokee thought it would be best to leave the land to the white man. One man by the name of Ridge was a representative in the Cherokee government. He took the idea to the tribal council, and it was swiftly voted down."

Lizzy locked her hands together on the table, as she leaned towards Katie and Sam. "Ridge actually ignored the tribal council, and negotiated a treaty. He sold all the Cherokee land, for 20 million dollars. Which was about 5% of what the land was actually worth at the time. He then took himself, his friends and family, and moved to Oklahoma in style."

"NO WAY!" Katie exploded.

"Hush!" came a strong whisper from the librarian.

Katie gave the librarian an apologetic smile. "Sorry," she whispered.

Lizzy waited patiently. When Katie turn back towards her, she continued in a softer voice. "It would be like a senator from Arizona, selling the whole state of Arizona to Mexico, without the approval of anyone else in the government. Ridge didn't have the authority to broker a treaty, let alone sign it. Just like that," Lizzy said, snapping her fingers, "all the land the Cherokee owned no longer belonged to them."

"Weren't there people who could see it wasn't right?" Sam asked.

"There were a lot of people who were totally against it, and knew the treaty was bogus," Lizzy explained. "People like Henry Clay and Davy Crockett fought like crazy in the Senate. The treaty was ratified, by a majority of only one vote."

Katie pushed up from the table, anger and frustration welling up inside of her. "So in reality, the Cherokee people were betrayed by one of their own."

Lizzy nodded. "That is what always made Grandma Elizabeth so angry."

"Weren't there about 4,000 Cherokee who died in the march?" Sam asked quietly.

Lizzy nodded in agreement. "The first ones who were forced to leave were gathered up and taken to rat infested holding pens. The worst ones were in Chattanooga. There wasn't much thought given to how they were going to be fed, either. They were dying like crazy. Chief Ross, negotiated a deal with the U.S. general. He started moving the people in smaller groups, where they could forage for food as they went. He was credited with saving a lot of lives."

"If my family had to go through that, I would have hunted Ridge down," Katie said in a quiet, angry voice, forgetting once again she was in a library. The resulting hush whisper had her again apologizing to the librarian.

"I believe that was exactly what happened." Lizzy agreed, her voice remaining soft. "Chief Ross took care of the traitor real quick, right after his arrival in Oklahoma."

"Maybe The Great White Tiger is only there to help the Sugaree," Sam said, referring to the original topic.

"No." Katie shook her head. "The Sugaree died out when the first white man came. Running Deer then joined, and was numbered among the Cherokee. If you think about it, we only have a small fraction of the Sugaree left in us. We're more Cherokee than Sugaree."

"I always thought it was strange, that Grandma Elizabeth always stressed about the Sugaree lineage, when the Cherokee is most dominant," Lizzy said.

"My mom is into genealogy," Sam said quietly. "What I have learned from her is... Genealogy is usually messy." She paused noticing the questioning look on her friend's faces, so she explained. "What I mean is… It's not all cut and dried. People meet, maybe they marry, maybe they don't. Babies were born, out of wedlock all the time. Who the daddy was, sometimes only the mother knew."

"I thought people in the "*olden days,*" didn't do that sort of thing," Katie muttered.

"Sex has been around longer than us," Sam said dryly.

"I know that," Katie said, her cheeks starting to burn. "It's just adults keep saying how things are much worse now than when they were young."

"That doesn't mean, it was nonexistent. Look at King David, for example." Sam said.

"I don't remember a King David," Lizzy inserted.

"I'm pretty sure we didn't have a King David," Katie added.

Sam gave each girl an exasperated look. “King David, from the bible?”

Lizzy and Katie gave Sam a blank stare.

“You know David, who killed the giant Goliath?” Sam tried explaining.

“AHHH! Wasn’t he just a poor shepherd?” Lizzy asked.

“Oh for crying out loud!” Sam exclaimed. Now it was Sam's turn, to apologize to the irate librarian. Turning back to her two friends, she whispered. “David later became King David. He had over 600 wives. Instead of being happy with his wives, he still wanted his neighbor's wife.”

“Sounds like a perv,” Lizzy asserted.

“Yep,” Katie agreed, “Definitely a pervert”.

Sam shook her head in frustration. She obviously decided to change the subject. “It looks to me like, Old Elizabeth Hawk was a huge source of information. Yet, she lived with us our whole lives.”

“We didn’t know we needed her, until she was gone,” Katie agreed. “I started having the dreams, and getting hot flashes as soon as Old Elizabeth had the stroke.

“Do you think it’s all connected?” Lizzy asked.

“I think we shouldn’t rule it out until we know for sure,” Katie said.

Sam got up and started pacing the small area around the table. “I think we need to talk to our mothers again, and try and get more information about the ceremony we missed.”

Katie and Lizzy gave each other a knowing look. It was no use, saying no to Sam or, "We already tried." Sam was going to keep insisting, until they did exactly what she said.

Sam stopped in front of Katie. "If that doesn't work, I don't see any other option than to tell your mom you turn into a wolf."

"What?" the thought, was mortifying to Katie.

Sam ignored her, "I know she'll come up with all kinds of information then."

Chapter 15
The Black Panther

"Mom, can I talk to you for a moment?"

Butterflies in her stomach, Katie was pacing the small living room. She had come to the same conclusion as Sam. Her mother should be told. Her mom would have already known, if she had not gone to Chicago for two weeks. Still, it was much easier telling her two friends, than her mom.

"What is it, Katie?" Her mother walked into the room, from the kitchen. Her hands were all muddy, from the clay she had been rinsing.

Katie paused. "Do you want to clean up first?" She knew she was stalling, but couldn't seem to help herself.

Her mother walked back to the kitchen. Katie followed, at a leisurely pace. She leaned up against the dividing wall, between the kitchen and living room. When she saw her mother was almost finished, she turned around and headed back towards the living room. She still had no idea, how she was going to proceed. Her mother came in and sat back down on the couch. The moment had finally arrived.

Katie looked down at her hands. "Uh, Mom, I have something I need to tell you." She paused and cleared her throat. "Do you remember, when all of us were at the campfire, and Old Elizabeth Hawk was telling that story about The Great White Tiger?"

"Katie, we've been through this. We only attended the ceremony, because of our respect for Elizabeth Hawk," Her mother said, impatiently.

"Mom, please listen." Katie pleaded. She looked down at her hands, "The thing is... The story Elizabeth Hawk told..."

The ringing of the telephone interrupted Katie. She wanted to grab the offensive object, and throw it against the wall.

Her mother reached for the cell phone, immediately checking the caller ID. "I'm sorry Katie, I've been waiting for this call. Can I get back with you?" Without waiting for a reply, her mom jumped up and headed back into the kitchen.

Frustration and anger began warring in her chest, the heat filling her body. She had come so close to finally telling her. She started pacing the living room like a caged animal. Periodically, she would glance towards her mother.

"Mom..." She could hear the anger in her own voice. "I turn into a great big white wolf." She watched her mother. Her mom was still talking animatedly on the phone.

"MOM," she said in a louder voice. "I turn into a GREAT BIG WHITE WOLF." The anger was building into a crescendo in her belly. She knew it would only take just a second to let it go, and she would change right there in the living room.

"MOM!" she yelled, **"I TURN INTO A GREAT BIG WHITE WOLF!!!"** she screamed at the top of her lungs.

"Katie, would you keep it down. I'm on the phone."

Katie let the heat flow into her limbs, making the change instantaneously. She stood in the living room, facing her mom.

Look up, Mom, she thought. *Just look, for one second.* With the eyes of a wolf, Katie watched her mother laugh, her eyes sparkling. She was so happy. In that moment, all of Katie's anger and frustration left. All of her mother's dreams were coming true. Who was she to mar it? Turning back into human form, Katie bent over to retrieve her ruined clothes.

"KATIE!"

She jumped.

"What are you doing without any clothes on?!"

"So, there I was, naked as a jaybird, saying... 'Um, Mom, I have this mole on my hip. Do you think it's cancerous?" Katie stood up from the chair she was sitting in and acted out the last part of her story.

"NO WAY!" Lizzy said.

Sam covered her mouth with her hand as her laughter rang out through the room.

All three girls were sitting in the local diner. "I'm telling you, it was a total disaster." Katie couldn't help chuckling through her embarrassment, as Sam went into another fit of giggles. "We have to come up with another plan, because I can't go through that again."

Shaking her head, Katie sipped on her soda. The air around her ears popped and sizzled. Lowering her drink, she felt a tingling sensation run up her spine. Katie reached out and touched Lizzy's hand. *"Do you feel that?"*

Alarmed, Lizzy swiveled her head from Katie, then towards Sam who was staring out the large window.

"What is she doing?" Sam asked.

Following Sam's gaze, Katie turned to look out the window. There in the snow, Candace Franklin was stripping off all her clothes. Underneath the baggy clothes were shorts and a t-shirt. She was stuffing a coat and warm clothes into an oversized duffel bag. She reached up, pulled her long hair into a ponytail, and fanning her face like it was 100 degrees outside.

Lizzy pointed her finger towards Candace. "Isn't that the girl from Central High who keeps beating you?"

Ignoring Lizzy's remark, Katie stared, as Candace pulled her hair around into a tight bun. "I don't believe it," she whispered.

She recognized the signs Candace was portraying all too well. Shaking her head in wonderment, Katie reached out with her mind. "*How are you feeling, Candace?*"

Candace's head snapped up and looked directly towards them. She had a questioning look on her face. Katie was close enough to the window by then, to actually see Candace's pupils start to elongate and turn more cat-like.

Sam grabbed Katie's arm. "She's turning right there, in front of everybody."

Lizzy immediately started freaking out.

"Run!" Katie told Candace. "*RUN! I'll catch up.*" Pulling away from her friends, Katie grabbed her keys and threw them towards Sam. Running for the door, Katie could see Candace was already across the street. She was heading towards the woods on the other side. Katie stopped at the edge of the woods, flipped off her shoes, and undressed. Changing into wolf form, she grabbed her clothes with her mouth and followed Candace's tracks. She was amazed at how far Candace ran in such a short time.

She soon came across a scent she didn't recognize. The hairs on the back of her neck began to rise. Placing her clothes on the ground, she crept cautiously forward. Candace was on the ground, rolling around in the wet snow. She seemed to be crying and screaming for help at the same time. Her voice seemed to fade in and out, from human to cat then back to human again.

A black panther was slowly circling her, as if it was waiting for something. Katie could smell the evil emanating from it. She didn't know what the panther planned, but she instinctively knew it wasn't good. Not wanting to wait till the panther attacked, Katie struck first when the panther's back was turned.

A few things became clear. Katie was larger and heavier, which in her mind meant she could beat the black cat. She fought, acting on pure instinct. The panther was faster, and knew much more about fighting. She was completely outclassed. Several times the panther could have killed her. Instead, it backed away as if giving her an out. It never occurred to her to run. She just got her bearings and plunged back into the fight.

The fighting and snarling grew more intense. Still, she stayed, getting tired with every passing minute. Finally, she could see she was backed up against a rock with no way out. The panther went in for the kill.

"This is it," she thought. *"I'm going to die!"*

The panther came within inches of her face, then suddenly stopped. He stared into her eyes intently, then slowly lowered his head, placing his forehead on hers.

"I'm sorry Katie."

The words echoed through her mind, until recognition shot through her. "*Jackson?*"

The panther closed his eyes, nodded in ascent, turned, and ran into the woods.

Stunned, Katie watched Jackson until he disappeared. Slowly getting up, Katie shook off the dirt and snow caked in her fur. Exhausted and completely confused, she slowly walked over to Candace. Her eyes kept scanning the trees where Jackson disappeared. Her cuts from the fight were starting to sting. She clenched her teeth together, resisting the urge to lick her wounds. *That was just way too gross,* she thought.

"What is happening to me?" Candace's thoughts screamed.

Katie turned her attention towards the snow leopard in front of her. *Why is everyone turning into some kind of cat, while I'm a wolf?* She thought in disgust. Shaking, she once again looked towards the trees, where Jackson had disappeared, her confused thoughts returning to the black panther and Jackson. She desperately tried to reconcile the person she knew, who had helped her so much to the panther's evil scent.

She could still smell the scent as it clung all around her. Its pungent odor kept her tense, as every cell in her body screamed the word evil to her brain.

The leopard was rolling around on the ground crying, as if in a lot of pain.

"Calm down; you're going to be all right," Katie communicated to Candace.

"Calm down? There's a great big wolf standing over me going to eat me!"

Katie rolled her eyes. "*I have no intention of eating you,"* she thought in annoyance.

"I'm talking to the wolf?"

Katie couldn't believe it, but the cries from the leopard actually went up another octave. "*Will you please calm down!*" The cries were really getting on her nerves. "*I need to get you indoors before you turn back into a human.*"

"I'm not human?" The leopard looked down at her feet, let out a screech, then toppled over into blessed silence.

Katie contemplated what she should do. Eventually, she contacted Lizzy, who told her, both Sam and she were in her car, waiting for her to give them orders. She told them where she thought she was in relation to her house. She was going to try and get Candace there. She grabbed Candace by the scruff of her neck and slowly started dragging her home.

It was hard work. A few times the leopard shuddered as if she was going to turn human. She had left her own clothes in the forest, and Candace's were shredded. She was at a loss as to what she could do, if that scenario happened. Thankfully, the back of her house came into view.

She reached out with her mind, and was told *yes*, Lizzy and Sam were waiting for her. She continued to drag the leopard to the back porch. Sam opened the door, while Lizzy stood back in the kitchen. Both girls had a look of shock and awe on their features. Katie backed into the house, dragging the leopard behind her. When she pulled enough for Sam to close the door, she dropped Candace.

Turning, she went into her room, changing into human form as she went. Digging through her clothes, she was mortified. She realized her clothes were dwindling to almost nonexistent. She was going to have to buy some clothes before school started again. Returning back into the kitchen, she was surprised both girls hadn't moved.

"What's wrong with her?" Sam asked, as soon as she saw Katie.

Katie shrugged. "I think she just passed out." She stepped around the leopard and started rummaging through the fridge. She was always starving after she exerted herself in wolf form. Digging out some meat loaf, she popped it in the microwave. She had to restrain the urge, to wolf it down cold. Finishing the meat loaf, Katie started rummaging for more food.

"Am I going to eat like that, when I.... you know.... change"? Lizzy asked.

"Who knows?" Katie shrugged. "Maybe you'll turn into a dainty cheetah, and hardly eat a thing."

"I didn't mean it to sound rude," Lizzy mumbled.

Katie looked up, from the three huge sandwiches she had just made for herself. "I'm sorry, Lizzy. I know you're having a hard time, but at least you were warned. Candace, apparently, didn't have a clue. She freaked out so badly, she passed out in the snow. Come to think of it, I think I passed out when I first saw my wolf face in the mirror."

Sam shuddered. "Who wouldn't?"

Finishing up her sandwiches, Katie got up and nudged the leopard with her foot. "Candace... It's time to wake up!"

The leopard rolled over, its feet straight in the air.

Katie nudged a little harder. "Candace, you need to wake up," she said a little louder.

The leopard still didn't move. Katie walked over to the kitchen sink and filled up a picture of cold water. Sam and Lizzy, seeing what Katie was about to do, ran into the living room. Walking back to the cat, she dumped the cold water on its head. Two seconds later, a screaming Candace in human form appeared.

Chapter 16
Candace Franklin

The screaming reached an all new level. It pierced Katie's sensitive ears. She tried to tell Sam, to go get a robe from her bathroom. Sam stood there, with a horrified look on her face. Her head kept swiveling, from Katie to Candace and back again. Finally, Katie reached out with her mind, for Lizzy to get the screaming idiot a towel and robe. Lizzy turned, to do her bidding.

Coming back with the items, Lizzy threw them towards Katie. She draped the towel around Candace's shoulders, dropping the robe in her lap. She thought she was being rather patient, but the screaming didn't stop. She tried to talk over the screaming, or in the intervals when Candace had to take a breath. Seeing that didn't work, she reached out with her mind.

"Candace, we don't have a lot of time on our hands. Can you please calm down, so we can discuss what is happening to you, in a civilized manner?"

The screaming continued, unabated. Katie glanced up. Sam and Lizzy, had their hands over their ears. *How can anyone, keep screaming like that?* she thought. It was really, starting to drive her crazy.

"Look, if you don't stop screaming by the time I count to ten, I'm throwing your ass out in the snow." She slowly started counting to ten.

Sam shook her head and tried to say something to her, but Katie was unable to hear. She continued counting *"8...9...10..."* The screaming stopped. The silence was deafening.

Surprised, Katie looked down. Candace was taking the towel, and drying herself off. She stood up, put the robe on, and walked into the living room. Speechless, Sam, and Lizzy backed away from her. Candace made a sweeping glance, around the living room. Her eyes, resting on Katie's painting. Slowly, she walked towards it. She studied it for a while. She sat down with much dignity, as if she were the Queen of England.

Ears still ringing, Katie walked into the living room. Now that there was quiet, she was a little lost on where to start. All three girls stood together, as they watched Candace pull her long blonde hair out of her eyes and sweep it into a bun. Composed, Candace eyed them back, wearily.

'I'm ready to talk in a civilized manner."

Katie had to squash a smile. *She didn't like the way I talked to her,* she thought.

"You did say we didn't have a lot of time," Candace said, in a perfectly cultured, controlled voice.

Katie turned. "Sam, can you do the explaining to Little Miss Cry Baby about what has happened to her?" She smiled broadly, when she saw Candace's lips tighten around her mouth. She sat down on the floor, while Sam took over.

Katie had to hand it to her. Candace didn't interrupt. She quietly listened, to the old legend. A couple of times she looked up at Katie's painting, studying it in detail. When Sam was finished, she sat there as if she was waiting for more.

"Is that all?"

Lizzy shrugged. "That's pretty much all we know."

"Let me get this straight." Candace got up from the couch and started pacing the small room. "This *old Indian legend* says, that when evil threatens the Sugaree people, then someone turns into animal form, and takes care of this evil."

"That is what the legend says," Sam answered. "But it seems to be wrong, on several points."

Candace turned to watch Sam, intently. "What exactly, has the legend been *wrong* about?"

Katie was looking up so much, her neck started hurting. Feeling the bruises from the fight with Jackson, she slowly got up. "First of all, only one person was supposed to turn into a great white tiger. Obviously, that's not right. I turn into a white wolf. You turned into a snow leopard, and Lizzy is on the verge of turning into... something." She gave a dismissive gesture, with her hand.

"Second," Sam followed, "The last time we know of someone turning into a tiger, the evil was white men entering the mountains."

"I don't want to sound pessimistic, but the tiger was unable to stop white men from entering the mountains," Candace interrupted.

"Yeah, well maybe that's why The Great White Tiger decided to bring reinforcements," Katie muttered.

"What I'm trying to say," Sam said over Katie's muttering, "is we just assumed the change would only happen to people like... us."

Candace stood there, not commenting at all. She was either unable to contemplate their meaning, or she just decided to ignore it.

"What we would like to know..." Katie decided to spell it out. "Do you happen to have any Native American blood in your DNA?"

Candace swung around, “I understood what Sam was saying.” She gave Katie a haughty, disdainful glare. “The answer to your questions is no. I’m quite positive, I have no Indian blood in me.” Her clear cultured voice, still resembled a queen addressing her peasant subjects.

"Are you sure?" Katie decided to push. “From what I understand, genealogy can get pretty… messy… Who knows? A great grandmother could have had a thing for the gardener. She decided, no one would know...” Her voice trailed off, suggestively.

“That may, or may not be the case,” Candace interrupted. “Since her family didn’t know then, how would I know now?”

Sam gave Katie a watch yourself look and turned toward Candace. “How long, has your family lived here?”

Candace shrugged. “We’ve lived here forever.”

Katie couldn’t help it. “Not forever, blondie.”

The cool facade disintegrated in an instant. “WHAT IS YOUR PROBLEM?” Candace exploded.

Katie could see the anger, vibrate through Candace’s body. Katie yelled at Lizzy and Sam to get out of the way. She slammed against the wall, trying to get out of the way. She was glad to see her friends had made it to safety, as they both hightailed it into the kitchen. Katie watched in fascination, as Candace tried to control herself. She almost made it, until she glanced towards Katie. The loss of control was instantaneous. One second Candace was there holding onto the couch for support, the next instant a huge snow leopard was in her place.

Katie watched in horror, as the leopard sunk its sharp claws into her mother’s new couch, making huge slash marks.

"STOP!   WHAT ARE YOU DOING?" Desperate to stop her, she reached over to grab the leopard. The leopard twisted around and attacked. Acting on instinct, Katie changed. She was much larger in mass than the leopard, and was able to quell her onslaught easily.

"GET OUT OF MY MOTHERS HOUSE! "she shouted with her thoughts. Grabbing the leopard by the scruff of the neck, she pulled it towards the door. "*Lizzy! Open the door!*"

Waiting for Lizzy to do her bidding, she threw the cat out. It bounded down the small steps, turned, and attacked again. Katie had enough. She grabbed the leopard by the scruff of the neck and forced her to the ground. She lay down on top of the large cat, crushing her to the ground.

Snarling and growling, Candace tried repeatedly to bite or claw her. Panting for breath, the cat eventually slowed down to a stop. " *Will you get your fat butt, off me?*"

Katie heard the words in her mind and decided to ignore them just a little longer.

"What do I have to do, to get you off me?" Candace snarled.

Katie couldn't help gloating. *"Say please."*

Candace, let out a string of curses.

Katie couldn't help laughing. The "Queen of England," facade was completely gone. *"Now... Now, do you let your mother, hear you say that?"* she tittered.

Sam came out of the house. "Katie!! Lizzy tells me you are being mean to Candace, and won't get off of her until she says, please. Is this correct?"

Katie glanced up, from her position. She recognized the look Sam was giving her. Since she didn't want to deal with an angry Sam, she casually got up, took a few steps, and sat down. Candace jumped up, took a swipe at Katie with her claws, turned, and ran into the woods. Yelping at the sudden pain on her nose, Katie started running after the leopard.

"Just let her go!!!" Sam yelled.

Katie kept running, fear clutching her throat. Because of her, Candace was trying to get as far away from her as possible. Jackson, was somewhere in the forest. She had no idea what he would do, if he found her alone and defenseless. How could she live with herself, if anyone including Candace was hurt because of her? She wanted to shy away from the thought of Jackson being evil. He had helped her, in so many ways. Yet, she knew very little about him. There was no denying, he had purposely kept her in the dark on a number of things.

Jackson could have killed her, if he wanted to. Katie remembered how quickly, she was able to defeat Candace. If Candace had to fight Jackson, she didn't have a chance. The thought spurred her faster. She reached out. "*Candace, can you stop? I need to talk to you.*"

All she got for her trouble, was a string of curses. Katie shook with frustration and fear, making her run faster. Reaching out with her mind, she tried again. "*Candace, you can't be alone, it's dangerous out here.*"

No response. *Maybe that's good,* she thought. Candace could run all she wanted, but she would never run so far that Katie couldn't communicate with her. "*Look, I'm sorry. You have every right to be mad. I guess I went a little over the top.*"

"You guess?" Candace's thoughts broke through.

"Hey, I said I was sorry. Can you slow down, so I can catch up?" Katie asked.

"I don't get it," Candace snapped back, *" What have I done to you, to make you hate me so much?"*

Katie was at a loss for words.

"You beat her in every sport you play against her", Lizzy chimed in.

"Stay out of this, Lizzy," Katie interrupted.

"Whoa! Are you kidding me?" Candace chortled.

Candace started snickering. Katie clenched her jaw in frustration, but continued to follow Candace's tracks. It didn't take her long till she found her. Candace was relaxing under a tree, gently preening her paws. Obviously, what Lizzy had said had pacified her. Seeing her there alive and well, most of her frustration left.

She sat down across from the leopard. *"Now, what do we do?"* Katie thought.

"We could go back to your house," Candace suggested.

"No, my mom will be coming home soon. She doesn't know about all of this yet." She sighed. "Although, it's going to be hard to explain the couch."

"I'm sorry about that, I didn't really mean..."

"I know you didn't," Katie interrupted, *"Come on; let's go."*

"Where to?"

Katie got up, *"I know of a cabin. We can stay there for a couple of days."*

"Katie, Sam says she doesn't trust you, to be nice to the new girl. She wants us, to come to the cabin also." Lizzy relayed.

"Fine!" Katie thought irritably.

"UHH... How are we going to get there?" Lizzy asked.

"Candace and I are going to scout around," Katie answered.

"Okay, let us know," Lizzy answered.

Katie glanced around, got her bearings, and started running for the cabin.

"How do you know which way to go?" Candace asked.

Katie paused. "*I don't know... It's automatic... My house is south, Town is southwest. The cabin is northeast from here.*"

Candace stopped, "*Where is southwest?*" she asked, her thoughts obviously confused.

Katie tried to quell her frustration. "*Since we are headed to the cabin, then town is behind us.*"

"Are you saying, when I was running away from you, I was heading deeper into the woods?" Candace asked.

Katie began running, "*Yeah, that's exactly what I'm saying.*"

Candace started running, to keep up. "*That just bites.*"

Katie couldn't help smiling. So, Candace had a terrible sense of direction. Finally, she was able to see a chink in an all too perfect, Candace Franklin. Things were starting to look up.

They ran in silence, till they reached the cabin. Candace read the sign on the door. *"Who exactly is Forrest?"*

"Your guess is as good as mine. I came upon this place, a couple of weeks ago." Katie answered. "Come on, let's see if there's a road or something."

Not waiting for Candace, she ran around to the back. In satisfaction, she saw an old road. It was covered in snow, but looked serviceable. Candace came running up behind her. *"I need to follow this road, to see where it leads. I think it is best, if you stay with me. The last thing I need is for you to accidentally turn human."*

"I think I can handle it," Candace answered.

Katie could tell, she had irritated Candace. A small idea started forming. *"Are you sure?"* Katie replied. *"Maybe you need to go back, and stay in the cabin?"*

Candace didn't bother answering. She took off running, down the road. Grinning, Katie followed. She could tell, her idea worked. If she kept Candace angry, then she would stay in leopard form. Twenty minutes later, the trees began thinning. Katie recognized, the old plantation house immediately. This was one of her mother's, favorite places. The old mansion was built before the civil war. The large pillars and porch were covered in dead vines.

Candace stopped. *"Wow!"*

Katie knew the feeling well. She always experienced a sense of regret and sadness about the place. Several times, she had investigated inside the old home, while her mother painted. "*Lizzy, are you there?"*

"Yes, we're here." Lizzy responded immediately.

"There's *an old road, by the Martineau Plantation. It leads to the* cabin."

"Sam thought, we probably needed a four-wheel drive, so we switched your car for David's Jeep. Is that okay? "Lizzy asked.

Katie didn't know what to think about that, but realized there wasn't anything she could do about it. *"Soooo David's driving my car?"*

"Yeah! He's pretty ecstatic over it. Lizzy responded. *We have clothes and food. We also came up with a solution, about our parents. Your mom and Sam's parents, think you two are staying with me. My mom thinks I'm staying with Sam. We're bringing our cell phones, so Candace can call her mom and make arrangements."*

Once again, it looked like Sam has covered all the bases. Katie shuddered to think how her mom was going to react when she walked into her house. Since she couldn't change or fix it, she had to just not think about it.

Chapter 17
Lizzy Hawk

Sam and Lizzy followed Katie and Candice into the cabin. Sam made a quick assessment. "This is exactly, what we need."

Lizzy's eyes kept darting to every drawer and closet she could see. Katie knew she was eager to not only explore, but to figure out everything she could about the cabin's owner. Candice flopped onto the floor still in leopard form, and was fast asleep within minutes.

Katie followed Sam, into the kitchen. She watched as Sam spotted the note on the back door then slipped outside. Within minutes, Katie heard the generator start up. She couldn't help smiling as the lights flickered just a little, and came on. Leave it to Sam, to know how to start a generator.

Sam came in, stamping her feet. "Do you want to help me with the groceries?"

Katie nodded, happy to be doing something.

Walking back into the living room, Katie could hear drawers being opened upstairs. Sam cocked her head towards the sound. "Lizzy's already snooping," she said in a hushed tone.

Katie tried not to feel guilty. "If I didn't want answers so badly, I'd tell her to stop, that it's rude."

"I know exactly, what you mean." Sam agreed.

It didn't take long before all three girls were rummaging through everything. There were plenty of things you would find, in a hunting cabin. Sam came across an extensive collection of arrowheads, but absolutely no written documents of any kind.

"I was so sure, we would find something," Lizzy said, dispirited.

All three girls were sitting at the kitchen table. "There's not even a single book. How can you not own a book?" Sam lamented.

Exhausted and disheartened, Katie sat back on her chair. "I'm too tired to think anymore, let's go to bed."

Sam swung her eyes around automatically, resting on the snoring leopard. "What should we do about Candace?"

"Don't try and wake her," Katie cautioned. "She may attack."

Sam got up and put her hands on her hips. "We can't just leave her on the floor."

Katie shrugged. "Throw a blanket over her if you want." She glanced out the window. "I'm going to go outside, and check the surroundings."

Sam gave Katie a questioning look.

Katie felt obligated to explain "I don't think we're in danger, I just want to make sure. Okay?"

Not waiting for a response, she took off her clothes, turned into wolf, and walked out the door. Circling the cabin, there weren't any new tracks. Her senses on alert, she couldn't find anything amiss.

Not wanting to go back in, she sat in the same spot where she first found the cabin. She tried to remember the conversation she had with Jackson. He was trying, to tell her something that night. She tried hard to remember. She thought he was angry with her. He told her he couldn't contact her, because of the full moon. What did that mean?

The idea of what she was about to do had been forming all day. She patiently waited, until she was sure Lizzy was sound asleep. She then reached out with her mind.

"Jackson, are you there?"

No response. Did that mean he couldn't hear her, or he didn't want to talk? For a moment, she sat in the snow wondering how to proceed.

"Jackson, I'm so confused. What were you going to do with Candace?"

She waited. The silent night did not give her any answers. She glanced around. There was very little wind. The only thing she could detect, was the soft clouds that exuded from her own breathing. She decided, to try one more time.

"Jackson, I consider you my friend. I'm willing to..."

She stopped. What was she willing to do? Since she didn't know what he wanted, how could she bargain anything with him?

"Jackson, what is going on? This is driving me crazy." She wanted to say so much. She needed so many answers from him. The silence was deafening. Shrugging her massive shoulders, she got up and headed back into the cabin. She wanted him to know she still called him her friend. *"I miss you,"* came her last plea, before she changed back into human form.

The sleeping leopard had a blanket draped over her, with a pillow lying next to her head. Pajamas were folded neatly in a pile, next to the pillow. The hide-a-bed was pulled out, bed made. Once again, Sam was making sure everyone was taken care of. Katie lay down, resting her head on the pillow. Within minutes, she was fast asleep.

Katie opened her eyes, as early morning light was coming through the window. She realized, she had a warm body snuggled next to her. A little confused, she extricated herself from the bed. Sometime through the night, Candace had turned human and crawled into bed with her. Realizing she probably would have done the same thing, if she woke up on a cold hard floor, Katie dressed.

Katie started fixing breakfast for everyone. She looked up, saw Candace enter the room.

"Good morning. Breakfast is almost ready."

Candace didn't pause as she headed straight for the pan of bacon. She reached her hand into the hot pan and tried to snag several pieces.

"Hey, what are you doing? You're going to seriously burn yourself." Pushing her out of the way, Katie actually heard a growl, coming from the girl. "If you're that hungry, there's a plate of bacon, on the table."

Candace turned, and headed for the table. Katie watched in fascination. She not only ate all the bacon, but everything else on the table. There was nothing left. Getting up from the table, she headed for the loaf of bread. There was no way to describe it. She tore the bag open, and scarfed down the whole loaf.

"How's that bacon coming along?"

Katie was so busy watching Candace, she forgot all about the bacon. "Um, just a minute." She quickly scooped out the sizzling pieces of bacon, and set them on a plate. Before she could do anything else, Candace grabbed all of the bacon and wolfed it down. Katie raised her eyebrows, when she realized bacon was still sizzling in Candace's mouth. Obviously, Candace was oblivious to the burns, because she turned to the refrigerator and started rummaging through it. She found a bag of sliced ham. Sitting down, she consumed the whole bag. Katie was relieved, when that seemed to stop the girl's appetite.

Hearing Lizzy and Sam moving around upstairs, Katie started rummaging through the refrigerator to see if she could make something else. She started frying the last four eggs. By the time her friends entered the kitchen, she was standing guard over the eggs she'd cooked.

Sam came in with a big smile. "Wow, it smells really good. I just love bacon in the morning." She stopped dead, when she noticed the table. She first looked at Candace and then Katie with a questioning look.

Katie cocked her head, trying to point it towards Candace. "We no longer have bacon."

The two girls looked confused.

Katie moved behind Candace and started pointing with both fingers at Candace's head. "We don't have toast either, or ham for sandwiches."

Understanding dawned slowly on Sam's face. She slowly walked, towards the table. "Oh, that's okay; we weren't very hungry anyway."

"What do you mean, we're not hungry? I'm starving!" Lizzy walked over to the stove. "There's got to be something left."

Katie handed her one of the plates, she had been guarding. She walked over and placed the other plate in front of Sam.

Sam glanced up and smiled, "Oh, this is plenty. Thanks, Katie."

Katie looked towards Candace. Her head was bowed so low, she couldn't see her expression. Bending down a little, she saw tears running along her chin. Not knowing how to react, Katie sat down across from her. Katie looked up at her two friends. Each girl shrugged in response.

Katie took a deep breath. "When I first exerted myself in wolf form, I woke up so hungry I actually ate everything in the kitchen, including a frozen fruit cake." She shook her head at the memory. "I hate fruitcake."

Sam came over, sat down beside Candace, and lay her arm on her shoulders. "We went to a restaurant, and Katie ordered not only a large steak, but two large orders of baby back ribs. She consumed four baskets of bread, a salad, and two desserts. It had to be the most disgusting thing I have ever seen in my life."

"It wasn't that bad," Katie muttered under her breath. She thought Sam was going overboard with her explanations.

Lizzy laughed. "Oh yes it was, it was awful".

Candace gazed at each girl intently.

Sam jerked a thumb towards Katie. "Her mom kept staring at her like she was an alien or something."

Shaking her head, Katie raised her arms trying to block the insults. "Okay, you guys have had your fun. It was not as bad as all that."

"You ought to see the amount of food her mom buys, to make sure she has enough," Sam continued.

Lizzy started picking up the dishes. "It's definitely enough to feed an army, instead of a girl in high school."

Katie got up to help. "You just wait!" she said, pointing the pile of plates in Lizzy's direction. "You are going to be eating just like that before long."

She looked up just in time to duck, as dishes were slung towards her head. Holding the dishes firmly between her fingers, she stared at the mess on the floor before returning a wide-eyed gaze back at Lizzy.

"I can't believe you're so mean to me!" Lizzy screamed, and ran from the room crying.

Katie watched her friend flee from the room and run upstairs. Surprised, she looked back towards Sam. "What the heck was that?" She said each word slowly, her astonishment clear.

Sam waved her hand, "Oh come on, you don't recognize the signs?"

Katie was completely stumped. "No."

"That's how you acted, just before you changed," Sam said.

"Excuse me," Katie said a little offended. "I did not throw anything at my friends, and scream about how mean they were to me."

"No, you just tried to wipe out the whole Central High basketball team, and then cried when I called you on it," Sam inserted.

"OH! I definitely remember that," Candace piped up. She gave Katie a knowing look, "What kind of drugs were you on anyway?"

Katie could feel the heat, rising to her cheeks. "I wasn't that bad."

"Yes! You were," Candace and Sam said in unison. They both looked at each other and cracked up laughing. The crying upstairs, intensified. The two girls clamped their hands over their mouths, as they tried to control themselves.

Candace leaned over and whispered, "So you changed into a wolf, close to the time we played against each other?"

"I changed that very night," Katie whispered back.

"That's funny." Candace shrugged her shoulders. "That's the night, I first dreamed about The Great White Tiger."

Katie paused, before she started cleaning up the mess on the floor. "Don't you think, the timeline is a little short?"

"What do you mean?" Candace asked.

"I went through those horrible cold and hot flashes, for several weeks," Katie said, as she dumped the dirty dishes in the sink. "It looks to me like you had the dream, and then changed within a three-week period."

Sam started filling water in the sink. "Lizzy had her dream the night before finals. She acts like she's on the verge of changing."

The droning sound of the generator Katie had gotten used to took a couple of sputters and died. All three girls glanced up, just in time for the lights to flicker and die. Silence echoed in the house. Katie could hear Lizzy, running down the steps. Her head appeared in the doorway. Her startled, bloodshot, puffy eyes, were questioning.

"Oops." Sam grinned. "I forgot to check it this morning." She walked over and started pulling on her coat and boots.

Katie watched her for a couple of seconds. "I think I'll join you."

Katie watched Sam carefully, trying to remember all the steps it took to fill the generator with gas, prime the engine, and pull the cord until the engine roared back into life. It seemed easy enough.

"We need to refill these gas cans, we've been using," Sam said, as she straightened up. "If we are going to stay here any longer, we're going to have to get more food."

"I don't think it's a good idea, for Candace or Lizzy to be seen in public," Katie said, as she followed Sam back towards the cabin. "Nor is it a good idea for me to leave them."

Sam turned and stopped, her steady gaze never left Katie's eyes. "Why are you so sure, they're in danger?"

Katie looked into Sam's dark, frank eyes. She almost told her friend right then about Jackson. To Sam, everything was black or white. This was right, that was wrong. Jackson could not be good and evil at the same time. If she told Sam her fears, she would make an immediate judgment. Odds were, Sam would decide he was evil. That would definitely make things more complicated, Katie thought. She had to find some way to learn more about Jackson before she could tell her friend.

Katie started kicking snow off her shoes. "It's just a feeling I have," she mumbled.

Sam shrugged. "You're the expert." Sam turned back towards the cabin.

Katie wanted to debate the point. If she was the expert, they were all in trouble. She knew absolutely nothing.

It was soon decided Sam would go for more supplies. The other three girls stayed behind. Since there didn't seem to be any cell phone service at the cabin, Sam was going to touch base with their moms, so they wouldn't worry. Katie had learned through past experience, moms trusted Sam.

It only took three hours for Sam to return. It felt like three days. Lizzy continued to blow up, or start crying at everything and anyone. Every time Lizzy started blubbering about how mean everyone was to her, Katie wanted to throw her outside in the snow.

Candace was turning into a snow leopard and back into human so often she started wearing a towel so she wouldn't ruin any more clothes. Once Katie explained what the cold and hot flashes meant, Candace could feel a change coming on and get ready for it. She not only accepted her new condition, but was learning quickly how to adapt. Watching her excel irritated Katie even more than Lizzy's crying.

Katie heard Sam's vehicle long before she saw it driving slowly down the rutted road. She stepped out on the porch in anticipation. She needed to vent some of her frustration, or she was going to explode.

Pacing back and forth, she waited impatiently for Sam to stop the vehicle. Before it came to a complete stop, she grabbed the door.

"I thought you were never going to get here."

"Why? What's wrong? Has something happened?" Sam asked worriedly.

"No! Nothing's wrong." Katie had a hard time, explaining her feelings. "I'm just really glad you're here." She reached in and grabbed a gas can, and started walking towards the back shed. Just having Sam there calmed her. "I was about to tell you we have two really crazy girls in the cabin, but I'm afraid the count is three." She smiled towards Sam. "I'm afraid you're the only sane one here."

"Hey, I know this is rough." Sam stomped her feet as she entered the shed, "I can't tell you I know what you're going through. I can only be there to support you."

Sam and Katie entered the cabin, their arms full of groceries. The air slapped Katie in the face, as it snapped and popped with electricity. "Do you feel that?"

Sam shook her head and glanced around the room apprehensively, her confusion evident.

"It must have been going on before I left the cabin, but I didn't feel it until we walked back in," Katie said softly. Putting down the groceries, she followed the electrical current she could feel. Walking up the stairs, she saw Candace now wearing a sheet, toga style, leaning up against the wall watching Lizzy.

Lizzy was thrashing around on the bed, covered in sweat. "I can't stand this, I'm so hot!" she moaned softly.

"How long has this been going on?" Katie whispered.

"Not long," Candace whispered back. "Watching her is giving me some serious flashbacks."

"It was only yesterday."

Candace grimaced "It seems a lot longer than that."

"What can I do to help?" Sam said, as she walked over to the bed.

Katie and Candace shrugged, in unison.

"Don't stand too close," Katie cautioned. "We don't know how she's going to react, once she turns."

"I feel so helpless," Sam said as she stepped back.

The room plunged into semi-darkness, as the generator's consistent hum died. All three girls looked up at the dead light fixtures.

"It's not out of gas," Sam whispered. "It ran all night last night."

The hairs on the back of Katie's neck started to rise. "Stay here and watch Lizzy," Katie whispered to Sam.

Candace immediately changed. A soft growling echoing low in her throat.

Katie crept down the stairs, a large snow leopard on her heals. She first peered out a window, careful not to show herself. She didn't see anything unusual. It looked like, they had less than an hour till nightfall. Walking as softly as she could, she locked the front door.

"Do you smell anything unusual?" She directed her thoughts towards Candace.

"I'm not sure," Candace thought back.

"Is there anything, or anyone in the house?"

"No."

Katie slowly crept towards the kitchen, trying hard not to make a sound on the hardwood floor. Peering outside, she could see her and Sam's footprints leading in and out of the shed. She could also see a set of prints coming from the woods into the shed, then leading out heading around the front of the cabin. Katie reached over and locked the back door.

"There is someone out there," she relayed to Candace.

The low growling intensified.

Katie touched her pointer finger, to her lips.

The growling lowered, a couple octaves.

Katie took off her clothes and changed into wolf form. She reached her nose into the air, sniffing cautiously. What she smelled, made her heart drop. She thought she could smell Jackson. No. There was a similarity to the smell of Jackson, but it was not he. The only way to describe it was Jackson had a cleaner smell. The pungent evil smell was much stronger on this individual. She crept back to the small living quarters, to the front of the house.

She looked up and saw Sam with a look of pure terror, sitting on top of the stairs. Sam pointed to a window, in the front of the house. There was an ugly face peering in. Katie ran to the front door changed to human form for a split second, to open the door. She changed back into a wolf and dashed out.

"Lock the door behind me," she directed Candace.

The man was no longer there. Katie could see exactly where he had changed to animal form. He was just ahead of her. Katie stretched her long legs, to give chase. The tracks were easy to follow, and the scent was strong. She felt she was gaining, and sprinted even harder. She could tell the scent was getting fresher. She had to be closing in.

"KATIE STOP! IT'S A TRAP!"

The thoughts busted through her resolve. "*Jackson?*"

"TURN AROUND!"

Katie stopped. "*Jackson, what the hell is going on?*" she thought back.

"I don't have time to explain. There are several Seekers, ready to jump you over the next ridge."

"I need you to expl"

"THEY ARE AFTER LIZZY! GO BACK! HURRY!" Jackson interrupted. *"The snow leopard is too young, to fight them all."*

Katie immediately turned around and started running. Her heart in her throat, she raced towards the cabin. "*Candace, are you guys okay?*"

"Where have you been? I've been, trying to contact you for several minutes," Candace shot back.

"I'm trying to get back, as fast as I can."

"Sam needs to know, if you are in the front right corner of the house," Candace relayed.

"No!" Katie stepped up the pace even faster. *"I'm approaching the back of the cabin."*

A gunshot rang out, followed by another. She heard an animal yelp in pain. Fear taking over, Katie could see the back of the cabin. *"I'm coming up to the back door. Let me in."*

Candace was there in human form, to open the door. Katie threw herself towards the door. Candace slammed the door and locked it. "What do you think you were doing, running off like that!"

"I'm sorry I wasn't thinking."

"That's pretty obvious," Candace said fuming.

"Where's Lizzy?"

"Upstairs!"

Katie ran towards the stairs, intent on seeing Lizzy. Reaching the top, she stopped in surprise. The electrical current in the air, was almost tangible. Lizzy was exactly where Katie had last seen her, lying on the bed moaning. Sam was across the room, with the window opened just a crack. She was holding a shotgun, with shells scattered on the floor around her. She was busy reloading the gun.

She grinned. "I know I got one. Did you hear the yelp?"

Flabbergasted, Katie nodded.

"I didn't kill it, just filled its snout with buckshot," Sam said, as she slipped the gun through the crack.

It looked as if Sam, was taking care of Lizzy just fine. Turning, Katie ran back down the steps. Candace was pacing the living area in leopard form, keeping watch over all windows and doors. Katie decided to join her.

Her heart slowing down to normal, Katie had time to think about what just happened. The electrical current was now coming in waves. She hadn't felt it this strong, when Candace was changing. Why was this so different than when she or Candace changed? Jackson used the term *Seekers*. Why were they so determined to go after Lizzy?

Katie turned, went back upstairs and crouched down next to Sam. She could see just as well in the dark as in daylight, but Sam couldn't. She didn't see any movement out there. Glancing towards the bed, Katie was just in time to see Lizzy turn into a Cheetah. She gasped. The noise must have caught Sam's attention, because she turned too.

"Oh, isn't she beautiful?" Sam said in a soft whisper.

The electrical current flowing through the air came to a complete stop. Candace must have felt it leave, because she ran up the stairs. She stopped in awe. The Cheetah tried to sit up too close to the edge, and fell on the floor with a bang.

Katie tried, to stifle a giggle. She glanced around, and saw Candace doing the same thing. They looked at each other and started giggling louder. Sam quickly punched Katie in the hind flank to quiet her. Katie roared with laughter.

"What's so funny?" Lizzy's thoughts reached out.

"Nothing… Nothing at all," Katie responded, "*I'm just so glad, you made it."*

Katie and Candace, both decided they would take turns keeping watch through the night. Katie's turn to keep watch had her wandering the cabin. The questions about Jackson kept coming back. Tired of the merry go round in her head, she reached out with her mind.

"Jackson, are you there?"

No response. Did she actually think he would answer?

Looking out the window in the quiet night, it was hard to believe a few short hours ago Lizzy had been in great danger. What exactly, was a Seeker? She remembered her dream, when Old Elizabeth Hawk told her she was in danger from Seekers. She tried to remember, what else she was told. It seemed to be something like… they will try and convert you. What did that mean? Were they part of a religion or cult?

"Stop trying to contact me."

"Jackson?""Surprise and relief welled up inside of her.

"You're bringing attention not only to yourself and friends, but to me as well."

"I'm sorry. I-"

"Look, I know you have a lot of questions, but now is not the time. I'm having a hard time keeping our conversation private, if you know what I mean."

"You can keep our conversations private?" Katie asked in surprise. *"What do you mean, I should know what you mean?"* Her annoyance rushed to the surface.

Jackson sighed. *"You probably haven't noticed, but it's a full moon. I lose a lot of my mental powers during the full moon. That is why I'm having a hard time keeping things private. When you reach out to me, it's as if you have a radio signal, broadcasting to the whole world. Not only is it your location, but everything you say."*

"I'm sorry. I didn't know. Katie's frustration increased. *The problem is, I don't know about a lot of things. I've been thrown into this stupid little game where everyone knows the rules except for me, and my friends."*

"It's not a game, Katie. I'm sorry, I'm losing control... talk later, okay?"

"Are you a Seeker?"

Katie rushed the words, afraid to know the answer. She waited patiently for an answer, but none came. Katie got up, frustrated, and started pacing the floor again. Talking to Jackson only increased the number of questions. She felt a lot better about him. He had warned her about the trap she was running into, and about the Seekers who were trying to get to Lizzy. Her gut feelings still told her not to completely trust him. When it came to push and shove, she always did exactly what he instructed.

If that wasn't trust? What was?

"Yes."

Katie stopped her pacing. "*What?"*

"The answer to your question is yes, I am a Seeker," Jackson's thoughts said softly.

Katie lowered herself onto the floor, closing her eyes in defeat.

Chapter 18
Back to School

Katie walked down the hallway, a frown on her face. She had assumed the start of a new semester meant exactly that, a fresh start. Glancing at her schedule, her frown deepened. She was not going to have English class with Miss Smith for a teacher.

NO WAY!

Walking towards the counselor's office, she saw a long line that stretched around the corner. The line didn't bother her at all. She didn't care how long she had to wait, she was changing her schedule. Reaching the end of the line, she leaned up against the line of lockers, intending on standing there all day, if she had to.

The sound of the bell had several students leaving the line running to their respective classes. Katie watched them leave, with satisfaction. Principal Davis came out of his office and glanced towards the line of students. Walking towards them, a few of the younger students vanished making the line shorter. Taking several steps forward, she leaned up against the lockers watching Davis under hooded lashes.

Davis began waving his arms like he was herding sheep. "Come on people, let's get to class. If you have a problem with your schedule, I suggest you come back later."

The line completely vanished. Ignoring the principal, Katie walked up to the counselor's door. This shouldn't take long at all, she mused.

"Miss Johnson, I suggest you go to class." Principal Davis said in a stern voice.

Katie bit her lip. She debated how she should react. She couldn't afford to anger the principal; nor could she leave without changing her schedule. She decided to try and explain.

"Principal Davis," she said in the most respectful voice she could muster. "I need to change my schedule. It won't take long to-"

"You need to get to class immediately," Davis interrupted, his features set, in a determined line.

"If you would just listen," she said meekly, "I need-"

"Go to class now, or deal with the consequences." The principal pointed down the hall.

Heat coiled in her chest and rose into her cheeks. Katie took a couple of deep breaths. She knew she couldn't afford to lose it here. She stared intently into Principal Davis' stern features, turned and walked to class.

Five minutes before first hour was over, Katie walked to Mr. Thompson's desk. "Can I go to the bathroom?"

The teacher glanced at the clock, "You only have about five minutes-"

"Yeah, I know, but I really need to go now." Katie felt her face turning red. "You know, monthly-"

Thompson immediately waved his hand in a gesture that clearly said, *I don't want to hear any more.*

Katie grabbed her things and left class. She always made fun of girls who continuously used the "monthly" excuse to get out of class, but she only had another hour before she had to be in Miss Smith's class. She had to change her schedule immediately.

Walking towards the counselor's office, she tried to come up with an excuse as to why she wanted out of the class besides the obvious. She knew, "*because I hate Miss Smith,*" would not get the desired result. She came up with, "I need more time to study for my other classes, so, I need a study hall. The counselor, wouldn't have to completely rearrange her schedule. She would be able to get her homework done during school, and she could have more time for other things. She would have to make up her English credits, her senior year. A small price to pay, for not having to deal with Miss Smith.

Knocking on the door, Katie poked her head into the counselor's office. A haggard looking, Mr. Chandler, looked up from his desk. She gave him a bright and friendly smile. "I was wondering, if I could have a word with you, about my schedule."

Mr. Chandler nodded, and gestured towards the two hard seats in front of his desk. "Hello, Katie, come on in, and have a seat."

Katie sat down quietly and waited for the counselor to pull up her record. She saw her name, appear at the top of the computer screen. She leaned towards the counselor, across the desk. "I was wondering, if I could change third hour into a study hall."

Mr. Chandler frowned, keeping his eyes on the screen. Deciding it wasn't a good sign, Katie felt she needed to explain a little more. "I have never taken a study hall, so actually I have more credits under my belt than others. I really would like to have the extra time, to keep the rest of my grades up."

“I don’t see a problem in your doing that...” Mr. Chandler stopped in mid-sentence, his frown deepening. “Let me get back with you.”

“If you don’t see a problem, then...” Katie paused. The counselor was no longer staring at the computer. He was intently looking at his desk avoiding her eyes.

She decided to try again. “I don’t understand…” she paused for a moment, studying the man’s features intently. “You are the one who changes schedules?” Her voice trailed off into a question that hung in the air.

“Just come back in an hour.” Mr. Chandler's gesture was dismissive. “I’m sure I’ll have it all changed by then.”

Realizing the interview was over, a confused Katie got up, and went to her next class. Before the end of second hour, Katie was called into the principal’s office. A feeling of dread filled her chest, as she went slowly to the office. Seeing her, the secretary waved her forward, indicating she was expected. Knocking tentatively, she entered.

Principal Davis was leaning back in his chair, his fingers steepled together. He indicated a chair, and Katie sat down, waiting for him to start. “I understand you want to change your schedule, to include a study hall instead of English.”

Once again, Katie didn’t know how to react to the principal's words. She was afraid if she showed how important it was to her, he might make her take the class. On the other hand, if she acted as if she didn’t care, there would be no reason to change.

“Mr. Davis.” Katie cleared her throat, trying to give herself a couple of seconds to form her words. “I just thought, that if I took a study hall during third hour, I could keep my grades up in my other classes.”

"You seem to forget, Miss Johnson, that I know your dislike for Miss Smith." Mr. Davis pushed himself forward, his elbows resting on the desk. "Your records indicate, you received a failing grade in English last semester."

"I know, but I have my senior year to..."

"I believe it unwise, to put off anything for another time, Miss Johnson. You have no idea what the next year will hold,"

"I have never taken a study hall. I will have plenty of credits to graduate," she argued.

"Miss Johnson, it is this school's duty, to not only give you a basic education, but teach its students how to become responsible members of society. This means teaching you how to get along with," Davis paused, "your superiors."

Katie frowned. She knew she had lost. She had inadvertently tipped her hand that morning, when she refused to go to class. It was obvious he wanted a reaction from her. Keeping her emotions in check, she carefully made her expression blank. Satisfied, she watched disappointment flicker across the principal's features.

"Your schedule will not change," Davis informed her needlessly.

Holding herself perfectly still, she waited patiently, for the dismissal.

Davis watched her carefully, his eye's narrowing. "If there's nothing more you would like to say, you may go."

Furious, Katie watched Davis dismiss her, as if she were a five-year-old child. At that moment, she wanted to rant and rave the way she used to. She knew it would be disastrous if she lost control. It would mean her secret would be out, for the whole world to see. A part of her wanted to change and see the fear in his eyes. She wanted to see him cower and cringe as the magnitude of her wolf form filled the room. Forcing herself to calm down, she took deep gulps of air, and slowly released them.

She searched her mind, trying to find something to grasp, something she could cling to. She remembered how Candace had acted in her living room. Holding onto that memory, she fashioned her features emulating Candace. She slowly stood up, straightened her shoulders, and walked out of the office with as much dignity as the "Queen of England".

At lunch time, Katie walked into the cafeteria, stopping in surprise. She couldn't help smiling through the sea of hot pink t-shirts. She had forgotten that Sam was planning on stepping up her campaign of getting the dance team to wear more *appropriate* outfits. Almost every girl in the cafeteria, was sporting a hot pink t-shirt with the inscription "Modest is Hottest!"

Katie headed towards their standard table, sitting down across from a beaming Sam. "It looks like the t-shirt idea, was a big hit."

"I completely ran out of shirts. I wish I had more money. I could order more."

Katie shook her milk. "Maybe you should charge the next time around. You know, to cover your expenses."

"That's a good idea." Sam frowned. "I still need to come up with the money for the order."

Katie picked up her fork, wondering if she really wanted to eat what was in front of her. "You should take orders from the girls and get the money up front. Then you will have the money for the shirts."

"Wow, that's awesome." Sam pulled out a notebook and pencil. "I'll start working on it right away."

The seat next to Katie remained vacant. Afraid she would *turn,* Lizzy had refused to come to school. There had been no further incidences in their stay at the cabin. It had only taken Candace two days, to control *her* changing. It had taken Lizzy, three times as long. Afraid their parents would start getting suspicious if they stayed any longer, the girls started taking turns with Lizzy until she could control herself.

Both Katie and Candace kept insisting Lizzy could go to school. Lizzy still refused. Sam eventually halted the argument, by acknowledging that Lizzy would know when she was ready, just as long as Lizzy understood she was getting behind in school.

"Did you change your schedule?" Sam asked.

"Nope."

Sam gave her a small frown, before leaning forward, "Why? What happened?"

Finally able to vent, Katie allowed her frustration to spill, explaining in detail what happened earlier.

"How did Miss Smith react, when you walked into class?"

"She completely ignored me," Katie answered. "I can handle that."

Sam sat there, deep in thought. "Maybe we're going about this all wrong."

"What do you mean?" Katie asked nervously. She was afraid Sam was going to come up with one of her "big" ideas.

"I don't know; let me think about it." Sam reached into her bag. "By the way, here are your shirts." She handed Katie three hot pink t-shirts.

Good naturedly, Katie took the shirts, promising to put one on as soon as possible.

“Sam, I love you. You know that, right?” Katie was trying, to keep her frustration in check. “I don’t think I can do what you’re asking.” Katie was driving home from school, when Sam decided to voice her “big idea” about Miss Smith.

“Hear me all the way before you judge it can’t work.” Sam had completely turned in her seat. Facing Katie, she was using her most persuasive voice, her hand gestures emphasizing her excitement.

“No one knows anything about Miss Smith. I think we could soften her heart if we do something really nice for her.”

Katie gave Sam a quick glance before returning her eyes to the road. “You can’t soften what’s not there.”

“Everyone has a heart. Besides, the Grinch’s heart grew ten times bigger than it once was,” Sam responded.

“A fictional character <u>and</u> not human,” Katie bellowed.

“Mr. Scrooge then…”

“Another fictional character,” Katie quickly pointed out.

“This will work!” Sam raised her voice to the same level as Katie's. “I know if we do a service project for her, she would soften towards you.”

This had to be the worst idea Sam had ever come up with. Katie knew it was not going to work. She shook her head, as she eyed her friend. “You do realize, it will look like we are trying to bribe a teacher.”

“I don’t care what it looks like,” Sam responded, “We are doing a good deed, by making someone feel special.”

Katie shook her head. She did not want to have anything to do with Sam and her “big idea”.

“Can you at least think about it?” Sam said persuasively.

Katie stopped looking in Sam's direction, "Yeah, sure, I'll think about it." She was willing to say anything, to get off the subject.

The next morning Katie wasn't surprised, when Sam got into the car with a plate of cookies in her lap. It had a big red bow on top. She reached over, to read the attached note. "Here's something sweet, because I think you're neat." Little pink flowers, were formed around all the vowels in the note.

Katie wanted to gag. "I am not handing her that," she said in determination.

"You don't have to hand it to her. Just set it on her desk before school," Sam explained with a laugh.

Katie rolled her eyes and glanced in the rear-view mirror. She could see Lizzy covering her mouth, trying not to laugh. Walking into the school, Katie took off her coat and covered the plate. There was no way she was going to be seen by anybody with the evidence. Sam stood watch outside of the classroom, while Katie quickly placed the cookies on the desk, and ran back into the hall.

"She's going to wonder all day who the nice person was who gave her cookies," Sam gushed, grinning from ear to ear.

Katie didn't think so. Walking into third hour, confirmed her suspicions. The red bow could be seen, hanging out of the trash can.

Sam didn't sound disappointed when Katie told her the fate of the cookies. "I'm going to have to come up with something else."

Watching her friend, Katie decided Sam was in a class all her own—A force of nature, no one could survive against.

Chapter 19
Day Dreams

"PLEEEASE! STOP!" Katie's thoughts rang out. *"I'M DYING HERE!"*

The vision, or whatever it was she was being subjected to vanished.

"What's wrong?" Lizzy's thoughts asked.

"Was that you? Did you just do that?" Katie asked in shock.

"Do what?" Lizzy's thoughts were cautious.

Katie had been sitting in the back row watching Miss Smith, when she found herself in the middle of a mountain meadow. The grass was tall, and filled with wildflowers blooming in every imaginable color. The air was thick with the scent of flowers. A whippoorwill was calling, above the singing of the other birds in the trees.

Katie looked down, she could not see her hands. She could feel the desk beneath her fingers. She waved her hands, in front of her face. She looked down around her, but she could not see any part of herself. It was as if she was completely invisible, in this beautiful meadow. She looked up to see Lizzy, walking through the tall grass. Her hair was longer than normal. She tossed her hair as if she was in a shampoo commercial. Her dark tresses glistened in the sun, as it fell back into place.

Lizzy was smiling at something, to her right. Katie turned and saw Tyler Sanders, standing with a rose in his hand. Lizzy ran to him, and Tyler dropped the rose. Picking her up, he twirled her in a small circle. Lizzy laughed out loud, resting her forehead against his. Placing her on the ground, he reached over with both hands. He cupped her face, bent down, and kissed her passionately.

"What's wrong? Is everything all right?" Candace's thoughts interrupted.

"Nothing happened," Lizzy immediately responded.

"Nothing happened?" Katie mimicked her to tone, disbelieving. *"I was somehow, transported to a meadow where Lizzy was kissing Tyler Sanders."*

Her shock was giving way to amusement. She kept staring at the back of Lizzy's head. She desperately wanted to see Lizzy's face, but her friend kept her body turned towards the front of the class.

"I was under the impression, nobody could read my thoughts," Lizzy replied, her thoughts angry.

Katie tried to think about what just happened. *"I can't read your thoughts. The daydream was so strong, I was able to see. No. That's not right. I felt like I was actually there. I even smelled the flowers, and heard the birds singing for crying out loud."*

"How is that possible?" Candace asked

Katie shook her head, *"I don't know."* She tried to form in her thoughts what she had seen. *"I couldn't see myself. Yet there I was, in Lizzy's daydream."*

"I wouldn't call it a daydream," Lizzy said defensively.

"Oh, yeah? I was afraid it was going to turn "R" rated," Katie responded. *"I didn't think, you liked Tyler Sanders."*

"I don't."

"Yeah? OH! Okay!" Katie said disbelievingly.

"I don't!"

"I saw you, Lizzy. You want me to describe in detail, what I saw?"

"You know? This sucks!"

Katie was so surprised by Candace's outburst, she didn't say anything. Not being able to stand it, she finally had to ask *"What sucks?"*

"You guys all together, while I'm in a completely different school."

"Oh. Well, at least you don't have to deal with, an eternally angry English teacher." Katie eyed the old woman, who was still giving a lecture in front of the class.

It was Candace's turn to sound surprised, *"Why angry?"*

"I can only guess, but I believe she's mad because a house fell on her sister," Katie answered.

"I don't get... OOOOH!"

"I'm going to get you my little pretty, and your great big wolf too?" Katie mimicked.

Lizzy and Tyler Sanders laughed out loud. Stunned, Katie could only watch, as Tyler turned and faced Lizzy. His eyebrows cocked, in a devil may care attitude and winked.

"Do you two have something, you would like to share with the rest of the class?" Miss Smith was looking over her bifocals, using her most pinched expression.

Still smiling, Tyler turned his attention to the teacher and shook his head no.

Katie couldn't see Lizzy's face. Seeing her friend squish down in her chair was indication enough how embarrassed she was.

"Maybe you would like to explain to Principal Davis, what you find so amusing in my class." Miss Smith said disapprovingly. "Katherine Johnson, you may join them."

"What?" Katie was a little distracted, watching her friend gather her things.

"You can join them," Miss Smith repeated.

"I didn't do…"

"You were distracting the class with all the arm waving, you were doing earlier." Miss Smith explained, as if to a five-year-old child.

"Arm waving?" She was first at a loss, before it dawned on her. She must have actually raised her arms and waved them while she was in Lizzy's daydream.

"Get out of my class, Katherine."

"Fine by me!" Katie started grabbing her things, slinging them as fast as she could into her book bag.

"Oh, Miss Johnson, I have your assignment."

Katie glanced up from her books, immediately mortified. Miss Smith was holding her first assignment up, so the whole class could see. A large D- in red was emblazoned on the front. Katie slowed down, putting her things into her bag. She let Miss Smith stand there a little while longer, as she wrestled with her emotions. Completely in control, she blanked her face before turning towards the teacher. Straightening her shoulders, holding her head up high, she walked towards her. "Thank you," she said with as much dignity, as she could muster.

She could see disappointment and rage in the old woman's eyes. Realizing the teacher wanted a stronger reaction from her, she carefully kept her face completely void of emotion. Head held high, Katie turned and walked through the door. Reaching the hall and out of sight, she took off running after her friend.

She found Lizzy up against a locker, while Tyler was slowly leaning in. Not knowing if she should interrupt or turn around, she eventually cleared her throat. Without looking in her direction, Lizzy ducked under Tyler's arm and started walking towards the office. It looked as if he was going to grab her, and pull her back.

"Hold it there, lover boy."

Tyler didn't move as he continued watching Lizzy walk away. He turned facing her. Katie could see, why Lizzy found him attractive. He had a certain devil may care style, that emulated every bad boy movie character she had ever seen. His black hair and dark eyes, were in complete contrast to his white skin. His clothes were obviously hand me downs. He always had a sort of scruffy look about him, which somehow made him look more appealing. His bangs were too long and covered one eye. He was eyeing her warily, waiting for her to continue.

Katie didn't know how to start. "How much did you see and hear?"

He shrugged.

Katie stared at the good-looking guy. *"You heard Candace speak, from Central High?"* She directed her thoughts towards him.

Watching her intently, he nodded.

Katie saw a bead of sweat, forming on Tyler's upper lip. "Have you been having hot and cold flashes?"

All she got in return, was a nod.

"Have you had any dreams, about a big white tiger?"

Surprise flittered across his face, then a slow nod.

"We need to talk."

Tyler raised his eyebrows.

"I mean in private, away from here." Katie waved her hand, indicating their surroundings.

"What's going on, what happened?" Candace's thoughts interrupted.

Tyler looked up, his eyes darted around, his expression thoughtful.

It was obvious he heard her. *"It looks like we have a new member, to our team,"* Katie answered.

A weighted pause. *"What's her name?* Candace asked.

Staring into his eye's, she gauged his reaction. *"His name is Tyler Sanders."*

"Another example, where the old legend is completely wrong on key facts." Candace's thoughts rang through.

Katie nodded in agreement, to Candace's assessment. Thinking about Jackson this time, she wasn't in the least surprised.

"Miss Johnson and Mr. Sanders, I believe you're supposed to come see me." An impatient Principal Davis, was motioning them towards him.

Katie, Lizzy, and Tyler were required to attend after school detention. Since they couldn't really talk with other people around, they had to wait until everyone congregated at Katie's house later that night.

Tyler entered the small living room. His eyes immediately drawn to Katie's painting. Studying it the same way Candace had, he waited till Lizzy sat down. He boldly walked over and sat next to her grabbing her hand. Lizzy halfheartedly tried to pull her hand free. He didn't let her go. He changed his right hand with his left, and draped his arm over her shoulders. He pulled her back against the blanket Katie's mother had draped over the couch to cover the slash marks. Lizzy's cheeks a bright red, she leaned against his arm, a small smile forming on her lips.

Katie watched the display, a little apprehensively. She knew Tyler complicated things. Lizzy and Tyler as a couple could quickly turn problematic. Looking up, she caught Sam with a worried expression on her face. The same thought must have occurred to her too. Shaking her head, she glanced at the clock. Her mother was due home in an hour, this meeting had to be over by then.

"We need to get started." She really hated this part. "Candace, can you do the honors, and tell Tyler what's going on?"

Surprise chased across Candace's face, "I'm not sure I'm qualified."

"I'm sure you'll do fine," Katie waived her off.

"If you need any help, I'll jump in." Sam offered.

Candace got up, and started telling the legend. Katie watched Tyler carefully. He communicated quite well with his eyes, and expressions. Candace would explain in greater detail, just by the guy raising his eyebrows. Disbelief and humor, became the dominant feature. Katie could tell, he didn't believe a word of it.

"Stop."

Candace's voice trailed off in mid-sentence, as she glanced towards Katie. Getting, up, she indicated for her to sit down.

Frustration and anger started warring in her chest. "You don't believe us," Katie stated.

Tyler cocked his head to one side and shrugged. *"Give him time, Katie,"* Lizzy pleaded with her thoughts.

"We don't have time," Katie said out loud.

"Katie, I'm not so sure this is a good idea," Sam cautioned.

Katie started pacing, in the little space she was standing in. "He doesn't believe a word of it," she said, pointing in his direction.

Tyler let go of Lizzy and folded his arms. He looked relaxed, but an air of tension emanated from him. Beads of sweat formed on his forehead.

"Heat is coursing through your body right now." Katie continued her pacing. "You wake up in the middle of the night so cold, you think you'll never get warm. The next minute you're so hot, you think the heat will consume you. You can communicate with your thoughts. Yet, you still don't believe. What's going to make you believe, Tyler?"

He shrugged.

Katie had to admit he was more irritating then Candace ever was. Did the guy know how to talk? "You want to see? You won't believe, unless you see with your own eyes is that it?"

Again no sound, just a quick nod.

Katie knew, it was going to eventually come to this. The heat rose through her belly, and into her chest, immediately changing. She watched in satisfaction, as Tyler's eyes grew large. He jumped up, his feet landing on the seat of the couch. He toppled out of sight, as he fell over the back. A string of curses could be heard from behind the couch.

"Well, well girls. The boy can speak."

Chapter 20
Close Call

"I don't think you're allowed to smoke in here." Sam's disapproving voice could be heard from Katie's bedroom. Deciding she needed to hurry, she put clothes on in record time.

A clearly shook up Tyler, was trying to light a cigarette. Small sparks kept flying out of his shaky hands, as he repeatedly used the lighter. When it finally was lit, the cigarette was wobbling around so much the flicker went out.

Deciding she had seen enough, Katie walked over and grabbed the cigarette out of his mouth. "No smoking in my mother's house," she stated firmly.

Seeing her, Tyler jumped back quickly. His eyes wide with fear kept darting around the room. Katie noticed they kept resting on the windows and doors. He was looking for exits. She stepped back, giving him space. "Meetings over, everyone go home."

"We still have things, we need to discuss."

"I know, Sam." Katie grabbed his coat, walked over, and opened the door. "Tyler has had enough for one night. Let's just go home for now." As she expected, Tyler jumped up and ran for the door. She shoved his coat in his arms on his way out.

Lizzy ran after him. "You want a ride home?"

Katie wasn't surprised when he kept walking. She had no idea, where he lived. She hoped it wasn't far.

"I was wondering, if I could talk to you a little more," Candace said quietly.

Immediately taking the hint, Sam grabbed their coats and Lizzy headed for the door. Giving her a quick smile, they waved and they were gone.

Katie closed the door wondering if she really wanted to hear this. Slowly walking to the couch, she sat down, patiently waiting for Candace to continue.

"During Trig, I started getting that tingling sensation. You know... The same thing we felt when Lizzy changed."

Katie raised her eyebrows. *Oh great, she's taking trig her junior year, which means, she's extremely smart. This is ridiculous, Doesn't the girl have any faults?*

"I followed the feeling, till I realized where it was coming from." Candace got up and started pacing the small room. "The girl's name is Jackie Oaklin."

"So it's happening two at a time again," Katie interrupted. "Did you go talk to her? How come, you didn't bring her with you?" Katie's thoughts already jumped into gear, of another person changing into a were-animal.

"I can't stand her!"

"What?" Katie looked up in surprise.

"I really cannot stand her at all!" Candace emphasized. Her hands outstretched, as if warding off a foe.

Not missing the irony of the situation, Katie sat in silence for a moment, collecting her thoughts. "Candace, this isn't a club where we get to pick and choose who gets to join."

"I know.. I know…I just couldn't…" Candace made a pleading gesture with her hands, and sat down. "In eighth grade, this girl used to be the biggest bully."

Katie decided not to judge Jackie too harshly. "Not only does she need to be told what is going on," Katie stressed, "but she's actually in very real danger."

Candace rubbed her forehead, in distraction. "I was wondering if you could talk to her."

Katie studied her options. "No, Candace, and I'm not saying that just to be snotty or mean." She rushed in, when she saw Candace was getting ready to object. "She has to be told immediately. I cannot get to Central High, and back to my school in time, not without getting myself into trouble again."

Studying Candace's downcast expression, she felt a little sorry for her. "Look, just tell her you would like to talk to her after school. I'll drive over there, and meet you. Okay?"

Candace nodded, a relieved look on her face.

"I'll bring Sam," Katie said. "She always, makes people feel comfortable."

Candace nodded, grabbing her coat. "I have some things for you, in my car," she said, obviously changing the subject.

Katie followed Candace to the door and waited patiently while she reached in her car for a big garbage bag. She struggled, pulling it out of her back seat. Seeing it looked heavy, Katie went out to help her. Lights swung around blinding them, as Katie's mother pulled into the drive. Reaching the porch, the girls hauled the bag up the steps to the front door.

"Katie, get in the house, and shut the door now!" her mother yelled, from the car.

Surprised and a little apprehensive, Katie did what she was told. She glanced over at Candace, who stood a little nervous, fingering the large bag.

Her mother came in and bolted the door. Turning around she faced the girls, a strained smile evident on her face. "Who is this?" she asked politely.

"Ah, this is a new friend of mine, Mom. Her name is Candace," Katie mumbled, still trying to gauge her mother's mood.

"Hello Candace, it's nice to meet you."

"She was just about to leave," Katie said still watching her mother closely.

Her mother actually backed up, blocking Candace from leaving. Surprise, had both girls glancing at each other.

"We need to talk," Her mother said. "I believe all your friends need to hear this, so Candace might as well stay for a couple more minutes." She gestured towards the couch, indicating the girls to sit.

Katie sat down next to Candace, watching her mother closely.

"A week ago I came home, and found the house in a complete wreck. Both the back and front doors were ajar, and my couch was ruined. There were huge animal footprints, all over the place."

Katie exchanged a quick glance with Candace, who was looking guilty.

"I was so thankful, you were not here. I jumped at the chance, for you to stay at Lizzy's. I called Forrest. He came down immediately. He told me, there have been sightings of larger than normal animals roaming the woods. People have started turning up missing." Her mom started pacing the small room. "Tonight I received a call from Forrest. He said they found a body, where animals had been feeding on it. Large animal tracks were found, everywhere in the snow."

"A body was found?" Katie asked in a stunned voice.

"Something ate it?" Candace stammered.

"The forest rangers are afraid of it's getting out of control, and ruining the tourism in this area." Her mother continued. "I could care less, if we have tourists. I'm really worried about the residents." Her mother rubbed her eyes, looking exhausted. "I was so afraid, I couldn't get home fast enough."

"OH NO!" Katie jumped up from the couch. "Tyler is out there, walking." She grabbed her coat and started looking around for her keys.

"Where do you think you're going?"

"Mom, I have to go. A friend was here. He got upset. He's now walking home by himself. I have to go get him."

"Katie, you're not going anywhere," her mother said firmly.

"Mom, you don't understand. He's walking home all by himself. I don't even know, if he knows any shortcuts, but if he does he'll be walking through the woods." Katie couldn't finish the sentence. "I have to go to him." Katie turned to Candace, silently asking for her help.

Candace hadn't moved her hand, over her mouth. Her shocked eyes not registering.

Realizing she wasn't going to get help in that direction, she automatically started reaching out to Lizzy. Jackson's words the last time they spoke, stopped her. Reaching into her pocket, she found her cell phone. Impatiently, she waited for Sam to pick up her phone.

"Sam! My mom has just been telling me, that a body has been found where large animals had been feeding on it."

Sam paused for a couple of moments. "Your mom is standing right there with you?"

"Yes."

"You can't say what you want to say," Sam finished.

"Yes."

"You're worried about Tyler?"

"Yes."

"Why don't you reach out with your mind?"

"I'm afraid." Katie glanced up, to see her mother watching her intently. Not knowing what else to do, she turned and walked into her bedroom. Candace jumped up, following close behind.

"I'm afraid what we say to each other, is not private." She said quietly in the phone.

"So if others are listening, and Tyler tells you where his location is…"

"They may get to him before we do," Katie finished the sentence.

"Lizzy, do you know where Tyler lives?"

Katie waited impatiently for Lizzy's muffled replies.

"Lizzy thinks he lives, near the old Smokey Mountain Campgrounds."

"What?" That's over ten miles from here." Katie was completely mortified. "He'll freeze to death, before anything else."

"Maybe he called someone for a ride," Sam suggested.

Katie thought about it. "No way, Tyler is a loner. He won't call anyone for help." Katie pictured Tyler in her head, with the hand me down clothes he was wearing. The chance of him owning a cell phone, were slim to none. "I have to go after him."

"I'm going with you," Candace announced.

Katie turned and gave her a grateful look. Her coat still on, she came back into the living room. Her mother was sitting quietly, watching the news. The look she gave Katie, almost stopped her in her tracks. Strengthening her resolve, she continued to the door.

Her mother stood up to block her. "You can't go, Katie."

"Mom, what if it was me out there. Wouldn't you want someone, to go after me?" she tried to explain.

"Katie, I'm sure he called his parents or whatever."

"No, <u>I'm</u> sure he didn't," Katie replied.

"Katie, you are not going!" Her mother shook Katie's keys, in her hands. "I have your keys, and I have disabled your car. You are not leaving this house."

Katie looked down, trying to control her emotions. Looking up into her mother's eyes, she had a quiet intensity in her voice. "I am going to make sure Tyler is okay. If I have to crawl out my bedroom window and follow his footprints in the snow, then that's what I'm going to do."

Tears welled up in her mother's eyes. "You're all I have."

"I know, Mom. I'll come back. I promise."

Her mother quietly stepped aside. Katie gave her a quick hug and ran out the door.

"Do you have an idea how to find him?" Candace asked as she ran behind Katie.

"I think I'm going to have to follow his scent," Katie answered. "Let's take your car. I don't want to leave any tracks, around the house."

"Good idea."

Katie started taking off her clothes, the minute she got into the cold car. It was freezing. Candace turned up the heat, which didn't help. "Soon as I find him, I'll contact you to come pick us up."

Her house disappeared behind them. The car stopped, letting her out. Stepping into the cold snow was not fun at all. She changed before she shut the car door. Tracing her steps back, she caught onto the scent. Running full out, she followed. It wasn't long before she heard footfalls behind her. Glancing over her shoulder, she was surprised to see a snow leopard following close behind. "*I thought I told you, to stay with the car.*"

"Anyone can drive a car. I want to help," Candace replied.

Not wanting to waste time arguing, Katie kept running. The scent was getting stronger. Candace was much smaller than she and had to take two steps to her everyone. Katie had to hand it to her, she kept up without complaining.

Katie could tell, she was getting close. Reaching out with her mind, "*Tyler are you there? We really need to talk.*" No response, Of course not, the guy didn't know how to speak.

"Tyler, we're coming up behind you."

"Hurry!" Came the quick reply.

"Are you in trouble?"

"I'm gonna be."

"What is that supposed to mean?" Candace vented. "*Can you give us a heads up, of what to expect?"*

"Something, or someone coming up hard and fast, in front of me."

"Are you sure it's not us?"

"Yeah, I'm sure."

Katie stretched her legs out, increasing her speed. Finally able to see Tyler in the distance, he was climbing a tree as fast as he could.

Smart boy, she thought. He was about fifteen feet in the air, when an object hurled itself towards the branch he just occupied. The branch snapped, under the weight. The tree swayed, losing most of the snow on its branches. She was surprised Tyler was able to stay up there.

"Hang on we're coming!" Katie threw out needlessly.

The large cat, was beginning to climb the tree after Tyler.

"Oh no, you don't," Katie thought.

The cat was so intent on reaching Tyler, it didn't look around when Katie hurled herself up in the air. She grabbed its hind quarters with her mouth, and brought him down to the ground. Before she could loosen her hold, Candace went for its throat. In a matter of seconds, it was over.

Both girls backed away from the cat, as it slowly started turning back into human form. Fascinated, they didn't notice Tyler climbing down, and standing next to them.

"What kind of cat was it, do you know?" Candace asked.

"I think it was a mountain lion." Tyler said out loud, "The biggest mountain lion I have ever seen."

"I just killed someone!" Candace's thoughts rang out. A note of hysteria in her voice.

Katie stood their silent, as the implications of what Candace had said sunk in. They had both killed a person.

"Thank you," Tyler said quietly.

Both girls turned. Tyler, shivering in the cold, was trying very hard to express himself. "I don't know what else to say." He shrugged his shoulders, nodded his head towards the young corpse. "That could have been me. I'm not ready to… You know…" He nodded again, his voice failing him.

Katie decided, to have pity on the guy. "*You're welcome.*"

Chapter 21
Score a Point for the Other Guys

"She's not here!"

Katie was walking towards her most favorite class in the whole world, when she was distracted by Candace's thoughts. *"Who's not there?"*

"Jackie Oaklin. I thought, I just wasn't seeing her. I have her in third hour. She is not coming into class. She's really not here."

Katie stopped just outside English class, not wanting to go in just yet. *"Maybe she's late."*

"No, the bell rang, she's not coming in."

Katie looked up, as her school's bell rang, announcing she was late for class. Why does something always happen, during third hour? She peeked into the classroom. Both Tyler and Lizzy were watching her. She quickly moved out of sight, so Miss Smith couldn't see her.

"Katie, are you there?" Candace reached out impatiently.

"Yeah, I'm here."

"I've been having the tingling feeling, all day. It's getting stronger. I'm afraid she's out there, all by herself."

Katie, recognizing the panic in Candace's thoughts, and gave a sigh. *"I'm on my way."* Thrusting her book bag on her shoulders, Katie started walking down the hall.

"Katie, wait up."

She turned, to see Tyler running up behind her.

"I want to come too," he blurted out.

"I appreciate your offer, but I don't think it's a good idea."

He raised his eyebrows.

"I don't want to hurt your feelings, but you're only going to slow me down."

Tyler nodded, looking down at his feet.

She reached out and patted and his arm. "I'm sure, it won't be long."

"Mr. Sanders, Miss Johnson, aren't you supposed to be in class?"

Katie closed her eyes, this could not be happening. Turning, she faced the principal. "I need to leave, Mr. Davis."

"I don't think so, Miss Johnson. You turn around and go to class, or face the consequences."

Katie stood there, weighing her options. Every time she tried to be respectful to this man, he ran over her. Frankly, she was sick and tired of the threat of consequences. Slowly turning back down the hall, she started walking away.

"Miss Johnson, you will come with me."

"No, Mr. Davis, I need to leave."

Walking into the office she signed herself out, the reason for leaving she left blank. Her heart thumping, she turned back around and walked out.

Mr. Davis was standing in the same spot, she had left him. "You need to learn, the proper respect."

“Respect goes both ways, Mr. Davis.” She walked out of the building. Reaching her car, she flew out of the parking lot, her back tires squealing behind her. Consequences be damned, she thought in disgust.

It took thirty minutes, to reach Central High. She pulled into the pull around. Candace ran out and jumped into the passenger seat. “Do you have any idea, where we should start looking?”

“I think so. Do you feel that tingling sensation? It’s coming from that direction.” Candace pointed to her right.

Katie had been so pent up about her run-in with the principal, she hadn’t felt anything. Leaning back and relaxing, she felt the stirrings.

“Yeah, I feel it.”

Putting her car in drive, she started driving slowly. Taking a few turns, she ended up on the edge of some kind of park. Getting out of the car, the two girls started walking towards the wooded area. They went just beyond a swing set, when they heard a cat like scream. Both girls started running, towards the woods. Taking off their clothes as fast as they could, they changed and took off. The tingling waves built up to a crescendo, then stopped. Running as fast as they could, eventually, they entered a small clearing.

This is where Jackie, had changed. Human footprints entered the clearing. Dirty snow and mud showed the place, where she had rolled around in the snow. Large tracks of another cat came from the east, circled, and even resting a few times. Two sets of tracks left the clearing together.

Katie smelled the other animal's scent. Relief washed through her, when the evil, pungent smell was a little stronger than Jackson. Score one more for the other guys, she thought to herself. She didn’t see any reason, to follow the tracks. Turning, she headed back. The two girls dressed, in silence. Going back to the car, Candace turned the heater up high. She started sobbing.

Katie didn't know how to comfort her. "We are not going to be able to save everyone."

"My fault!" Candace said between sobs.

"No, it's not your fault." Katie objected. "Look, we don't know what just happened. She didn't die. We didn't see a body. They walked off together, just like you and I did when I came and got you.

Candace looked up, a small frown forming. "I don't remember walking off with you."

"That's because you passed out. I had to drag your sorry butt, all the way to my house."

Candace laughed softly "I didn't handle changing well, did I?"

"Nobody handles changing well."

Candace looked out into the trees. "Do you know what the hardest thing about all of this is?"

"Yes."

Candace quickly glanced towards Katie. "Being naked all the time?"

"Yep." Katie sat back in the seat. "It's only going to get worse."

"How's that?"

Katie chuckled, "Tyler, is going to be naked all the time."

"OH! Crap! I didn't think of that."

Katie couldn't help grinning over the comical frown on Candace's face. "Yeah, well, I'm sure Lizzy has."

Katie got back to school when lunch was getting over. She felt pretty good about only missing one class. Sitting in seventh hour, the tingling sensation began running up and down her spine. Just to make sure she followed the sensation, she quietly stood outside the boy's restroom until Tyler walked out. His face was wet. She didn't know if he was sweating, or if he threw water in his face. It didn't matter. He was on the verge, of changing. It was a good thing it was Friday. If they were lucky, they could be completely done by Monday morning.

"If I see that boy naked one more time, I'm going to scream," Sam said in a hushed voice. "I know it's not his fault. It just seems he is having a little harder time controlling himself, than the rest of you."

Katie glanced out at the falling snow. "Maybe we are not handling this very well," she said softly. "If it were me, I'd be mortified, if I kept flashing my naked body in a room full of guys."

"We're here to..."

"I know why we're here," Katie interrupted Sam. "But it's obvious, Tyler is a loner. When Candace and I were running through the woods, it almost killed him to ask for help."

Candace leaned in. "The only thing he said was, hurry!"

"Now we're all here trying to help and support him, when maybe all he needs is to be alone." Katie looked back out at the falling snow. "I believe the dangerous time, when the Seekers would have come for him, has passed. Let's go home, and give the guy some space."

Hearing footsteps, Katie looked up to see Tyler walking into the room. A sheet was draped around his shoulders, toga style. He stopped dead, when he saw all the girls huddled together whispering. He nonchalantly leaned up against the wall, his eye's hooded. He acted, as if he didn't have a care in the world. Katie believed it was all an act. He did care that they were talking about him. Smiling towards him, she motioned him forward. Slowly standing straight, Tyler swaggered towards them. Sitting down, he cocked his head to one side.

"Tyler, we've been thinking." Katie reached over and touched his shoulder. "Maybe you wouldn't mind being alone, until you conquer changing."

Tyler raised his eyebrows.

"We have never had any problem with Seekers, after the original change." Katie found herself explaining. "That's when the tingling sensation goes away. So I believe, you will be relatively safe here."

"Do you think you will like that?" Sam interjected, "or would you like us to stay."

Relief washed over Tyler's face. His features relaxing into the first smile Katie had seen in the last twenty-four hours.

"You would like us to go?" Katie wanted to clarify.

A definite nod.

Sam got up and started putting on her coat. "Okay, that settles it. We need to leave, before the storm gets any worse."

Katie reached over and started grabbing her homework. "We will check on you every day."

"We'll take turns, to make sure you have enough fuel and supplies." Candace started grabbing her things and throwing them in a bag as fast as she could.

Lizzy was the only one, still not moving. She was staring longingly towards Tyler. Katie could tell, she wanted Tyler to ask her to stay. Not wanting to embarrass her friend, she decided to start packing

Lizzy's things too. When everything was packed, she grabbed Lizzy's coat, placed it on her shoulders, and pushed her out the door.

A final wave and they were all headed down the rutted road. A smiling Tyler, standing in the doorway. Katie gave a sigh of relief, she was glad she was going home.

Chapter 22
A Good Deed

"Katie? Katie? Wake up! Someone is here, to see you."

Katie raised her head out of the pillow, trying to see who was waking her up. Blinking a couple of times, she finally focused on her mother standing in the doorway. "What?" she said groggily.

"David Black is here. He wants to see you," her mother said.

Katie laid her head on the pillow, her thoughts still unclear.

"Katie, did you hear what I said?"

"Yeah, David Black is... Whoa, DAVID is here!" Jumping up, Katie stumbled around, tripping over the huge black garbage bag, Candace had given her. She crashed into the dresser, causing several nick knacks to fall on the floor.

"Are you all right?" her mother asked quietly.

Katie glanced quickly at her mother, then frowned, when it became obvious her mother was trying not to laugh.

She tried to muster whatever dignity she had left. "Um, tell David I'll be right there." Watching her mother leave, she turned to the large garbage bag. She lifted it up, and heaved it onto her bed. The bag rolled over and spilled some of its contents on the other side.

Digging through her bare dresser, she came up with only one clean shirt. Reaching over, and grabbing the jeans she wore the day before, she dressed. Dragging a brush quickly through her hair, she finally felt presentable enough to face David.

He was standing in the living room, with a big smile on his good-looking face. "Good morning sleepy head."

Her lips twitched, "Hello. What are you doing here?"

Ignoring her question, David rubbed his hands together giving her a mock evil smile. "I've got plans for you."

"What?" Katie asked suspiciously. After all, David was Sam's brother. The possibilities were endless.

"I'm not telling, until I have more control over you." He raised his eyebrows, still trying to look like an evil villain. "Make sure you're dressed warm. I don't want you to get frostbite."

Going back to her bedroom, Katie dressed as warm as she could with her limited wardrobe. Coming back into the living room, she heard her mother ask David how long they would be gone.

"Several hours," he replied.

Hearing her mother's parting, "Have fun," she was off. Katie waded through the new fallen snow, crawling into David's old jeep.

David patted the steering wheel. "This old jeep doesn't drive as well as your car. Which by the way, I'm very happy to drive. It's nice, when you and Sam go off on your secret rendezvous. My jeep is the only thing that will make it to where we're going."

"Where are we going?" Katie asked innocently.

Laughing, David put the gear shift into reverse. "I have to get you away from your safe warm house, before I tell you anything."

Katie waited patiently, not wanting to distract him while he negotiated the hazardous roads. When they finally started driving on cleared roads, she felt it was safe enough to ask again where they were going.

"Almost there," was his only reply.

Pulling over to the side of the road, Katie sat up in her seat to look around. They were in a quiet neighborhood. The older homes were small, with small yards. Some cars were barely visible, as the snow plows had almost completely buried them.

Suspicious Katie folded her arms and turned her body to face David. "What are we doing here?"

David had the grace to look a little uneasy. "Sam told me about your problem with Miss Smith."

"WHAT?" she said before he could say anything else. Katie was shaking her head, "NO WAY!"

"Sam said you would act like this. That's why she told me not to tell you, till we got here."

Katie still shaking her head, glanced out the window wondering where the old lady lived. Then she decided, she didn't care. "You need to take me home, right now!"

David tapped his hands, on the steering wheel. "Just listen to the plan okay?" he said, sounding remarkably like Sam.

Katie sat there, her posture defiant. "Okay, let's hear the plan," she said sarcastically.

David eyed her wearily. He must have decided, this was his only chance to explain. "I did my Eagle Scout Project in this neighborhood, so I know most of the residents here." He pointed his finger, towards a little blue house. "Miss Smith lives there."

Katie took a greater interest in her surroundings. "What was your project?"

David smiled, "Most of the people who live here are older. Some of them want to live in their homes, as long as possible. Some residents have been ripped off by contractors, promising to do work around the homes. They take their money, then leave without doing the work."

Indignation welled up in her chest. "That's just horrible."

"Understandably, they are cautious," David continued. "They also are getting too old, to do the work themselves. Some members of my church and family did quite a lot of work for most of the homes here."

Katie wondered where she was when all this was going on. She wouldn't have minded helping.

David pointed to the cars now buried. "Every time it snows, cars get buried. It's hard for the residents, to get out. I still come out here, shovel snow, clear the driveways, dig out the cars. Things like that."

Katie looked out, over the snow-covered homes. "That's very kind of you."

David paused. "I'm not telling you all this because…" he stopped shaking his head. "The reason I'm telling you this is to give you some background."

He started drumming his hands, on the steering wheel. "My plan to help you with Miss Smith, is for you to help me shovel snow. First of all," he said, holding up his a finger. "We won't be singling her out. We are doing something, for the whole street. Second..." He held up another finger. "She will see you out here, and have to see you're the good person we know you to be. Third..." He held up another finger. "She will soften her heart towards you, and give you a break."

Katie sat there for a moment. "I think, you're doing a really good thing here. I have absolutely no problem, shoveling snow." She paused a moment, gathering her thoughts. "I think you're wrong, about Miss

Smith. Her anger runs deep." She shook her head. "Far deeper, than what the normal situations call for."

"We'll see," David said confidently, opening the jeep door.

Katie got out, followed him to the back of the jeep. He started pulling out shovels. Handing her a smaller shovel, they both got to work. After only half an hour, Katie wanted to quit. It was freezing. Not wanting David to see what a wimp she was, she continued. Katie glanced around her. They had only uncovered one car and partially cleared one driveway. Looking down the street, Katie counted a total of seven homes. Removing snow was going to take all day. She was going to freeze to death, before they finished the first house.

It would be much nicer she thought, *if I could do this in wolf form.* She would be unable to use the shovel, but at least be toasty warm. Just the thought of it caused heat to fill her chest, which in turn warmed her. She let the heat course through her body as she was going to change, but stopped it from actually happening. Heat and energy surged through her body. *This feels more like it,* she thought.

They finished the first house. David led her back to the jeep, where he pulled out a thermos of hot chocolate. Turning on the vehicle, he started up the heat. Katie adjusted her own body heat, accordingly. She didn't have to concentrate very hard. This was a really cool trick, she could hardly wait to share it with the others.

"I think you're doing awesome," David said interrupting her thoughts.

"What?"

"Sam, usually makes me take two breaks per house," David explained. "We're going to get done, in record time."

"Where's Sam today?" Katie couldn't help asking.

"Sam had some responsibilities at church today," David answered. "Besides," he grinned, "she thought you'd get suspicious, if she showed up too."

"Yea, she's probably right." Katie took a sip of hot chocolate, not really needing it. "You're not supposed to do work on Sunday, are you?"

"This is different."

"How?"

David put the lid on the thermos. "This is a service project. We're helping people. That is a really good thing, to do on Sunday."

Turning the key off, David got out of the jeep. Taking his cue, Katie followed. Crossing the street, they started working on the next house. Miss Smith's home, was the fourth house they approached. Eyeing the home wearily, Katie followed David's lead immediately started digging out the car. Keeping an eye on the home, she saw the curtain move a couple of times.

David seemed to notice too. Smiling towards Katie, "I believe she's seen us. It's going to work."

Getting a little nervous, Katie kept working. Walking up the drive, David started working on the small sidewalk, while Katie stayed on the driveway. A red light caught Katie's attention. Looking up she stopped, when a sheriff's car pulled up.

David started walking towards the car, a puzzled look on his face.

A middle-aged man got out of the car, zipping up his jacket. "Hello, David".

"Hello Sheriff Tate," David said, in a friendly voice.

Katie walked slowly down the driveway, dragging the shovel behind her. Instinctively, she knew why the sheriff was here.

"We have had a complaint of trespassing, and vandalism," the sheriff informed David.

David shrugged his shoulders, looking around. "We've been here a couple of hours' sheriff, and I haven't seen anyone out here, but us."

Katie thought David a little slow, on the uptake.

The Sheriff looked down at his feet, nodding his head. "The complaint is about you, and your friend."

Katie glanced behind her. She saw the curtains twitch, as a shadow backed quickly away from the window.

"What?" David's shocked face looked around the snow-covered neighborhood.

"The person who called wants to press charges," the sheriff continued. "They want me to arrest both of you, and bring you down to the station."

Stunned, David stood there not quite comprehending. "I have been coming here helping these people…" his voice trailed off. He shook his head.

Katie stepped up and grabbed his arm. "I'm sure all the people on this street, appreciate you, David. There's only one person who called, isn't that right officer?"

The sheriff nodded his head. "I know the good things, you've been doing here." The sheriff looked towards the little blue house. "Frankly, I don't understand, why today is any different."

Katie could feel David's gaze on her, before he turned back towards the sheriff. "What happens now?"

"I'm not going to arrest you." The sheriff kicked the ice, forming behind the tire well. "I just thought I would come out, and tell you about the complaint."

"Thanks, sheriff, I appreciate it." David shook his head. "We'll be leaving."

Katie gripped David's arm, "We have to finish."

The sheriff looked over, his eyes narrowing.

"We won't work on the house of the complainer," she tried to explain. "The others shouldn't be penalized, because of the one."

"That's up to you." The sheriff turned, and opened his car door. "I'm sure the other residents, would agree."

David and Katie, watched the cruiser pull away in silence. His movements jerky, David started walking towards the jeep.

"Where are you going?"

"Home!"

Katie followed trying to catch up. "We need to finish."

"No, we don't."

She grabbed his arm, "We need to talk about this."

"Do you know how much work, I've done for these people?" David waved his arm towards the homes. "Do you have any idea, the hours I have spent shoveling snow, mowing lawns, and fixing things?" Raising his voice, it was shaking with emotion. "I have actually grown, to care about these people. For what? What do I get in return?"

"Only one person called the cops," Katie tried to point out. "You cannot tell me, Miss Smith has ever acted grateful for the things you did for her."

David paused in his tirade, a stunned look on his face.

"She hasn't, has she?" Katie brought home her point. "Never once did she let you know she was grateful for the things you did for her." She could tell he was listening. "I bet you and Sam worked harder on her house than any of the others." She pointed her finger, against his chest. "I can just see you and Sam, trying to kill her with kindness, while the crotchety old lady gave you two nothing but grief."

David looked down, his shoulders slumped.

"That woman has a hatred and anger, that runs deeper than... than the Grand Canyon." Katie pointed at the other homes. "You cannot penalize these other good people, because of her."

She lifted her shovel on her shoulder. "I'm going to finish this. You can either help me or go home. I don't care."

Katie started walking towards one of the unfinished homes and started shoveling. A couple of minutes later, she heard the sound of another shovel scraping the concrete.

The sun was lowering in the sky, when David pulled into Katie's driveway. For the rest of the day, David hardly said two words to her. She hoped this episode hadn't killed their friendship. Katie opened the jeep door, when David reached out and grabbed her arm.

"I just wanted to thank you."

"I didn't..."

"Yes, you did," David interrupted. "You were right. The other residents had repeatedly warned me about her." He paused, "I didn't want to listen."

"Did you notice, she waited until after we uncovered her car, before she called the cops?"

David shook his head, a wry smile forming. "No, I didn't."

"She probably thinks, you're going to forget all about it, by the time the next snow falls."

"I'm not going to forget this, for a long time." David let go of her arm. "I'll see you tomorrow."

Getting out of the jeep, Katie waved goodbye and headed towards her house. Her mother was sitting on the couch. She gave her mother a quick rundown of their activity for the day. Heading to the bedroom, she saw the large garbage bag on her bed. She walked around her bed, to the side where the contents were spilled over. She paused, grinning from ear to ear. She grabbed her cell phone and called Sam.

"Get over here, Now! Bring Lizzy!"

By the time Sam came back over in David's Jeep, Katie had everything organized. Sam and Lizzy squealed in delight, seeing the piles of clothes. Most of the outfits still had price tags on them. All the items, were top of the line designer quality. It was Christmas, all over again.

Chapter 23
Samantha Black

"I'm not sure this is a good idea." Katie's thoughts were cautious, as she watched Mrs. Hawk in the kitchen.

"We have tried everyone else," Lizzy demanded. "*I am sick and tired, of not knowing."*

"Yeah well, maybe it's none of our business."

Katie tried to get more support, from anyone else. The whole team was assembled around Lizzy's kitchen table. Tyler sitting close to Lizzy would vote for whatever she wanted. Candace kept exchanging weary glances, between her and Lizzy. Shrugging apologetically to Katie, Candace told her what she was voting for. Only Sam, sat with her arms folded. A frown on her face, showing her disapproval. This was why Katie was questioning whether they should proceed.

"I have a right to know," Lizzy communicated.

Katie leaned back in her chair, defeated. "*It's your life. Go ahead.*" She turned to watch Mrs. Hawk stoop down, to pull a casserole out of the oven.

"Mom, who is Forrest?" Lizzy said, in a loud clear voice.

Katie could only watch, with a shocked expression. The casserole slipped out of Mary Hawks hands and slammed onto the floor scattering food and glass everywhere. Sam jumped up, and ran over, to see if she could help. Katie followed, not knowing what she could do.

"Guilty!" Candace and Lizzy's thoughts said in unison.

Katie quickly glanced over, seeing Tyler nod his head in agreement. Reaching the sink, she turned the cold water on. "Here Mrs. Hawk put your hand in here."

"I'm all right, I must have just slipped," Mary Hawk said, her face turning a bright red.

Sam was grabbing paper towels, trying to pick up the glass and scattered food.

Mary glanced towards them, then did a double take studying the others.

Katie followed her glance. All three teenagers, had their arms folded. All had the same look, of condemnation on their features.

"Lizzy, it's time for your friends to go home," Mary said firmly.

"Mom they just got here," Lizzy protested.

Sam made a trip, to the trash can. "Let me help you clean this up first, Mrs. Hawk."

Mary gave Sam a grateful smile. "Thank you, Sam, but I think it's time for everyone to go."

"Why do they have to go? That's not fair," Lizzy said in agitation. Her voice rose, into a whine.

Katie looked down feeling embarrassed and started gathering her things. "I'll see you later, Lizzy," she said, giving an apologetic smile to Mrs. Hawk. She walked out the door, the others following close behind.

"That didn't go well," Katie mumbled, fiddling with her keys.

"I think it let us know who Forrest is," Candace answered.

"NO! It did not!" Sam whispered furiously. "The only thing it showed was, Mrs. Hawk is sensitive about the subject."

"Can you believe it?" Lizzy thoughts rang out. "*The adulteress sent me to my room!"*

Sam, looked like she was going to explode. "*You do not know, if she's an adulterer Lizzy. I will not have you, calling your mom names around me."*

Everyone stood staring at Sam, shocked expressions on their faces.

"What?" Sam said out loud.

Katie's lips twitched. "You answered Lizzy with your mind, Sam."

"I what?" Sam's head swiveled from face to face, for confirmation.

"You answered Lizzy with your mind," Katie said through her thoughts.

"I did?... I did! "Sam communicated. "Oh my gosh." She clamped her hand, over her mouth. "I was beginning to believe I wasn't worthy to become a were-animal."

"What?" Katie shook her head. "That has got to be the most ridiculous thing I have ever heard." Grinning, Katie opened her car door. "It's been over a week, since Tyler changed. I was beginning to wonder, if we were going to slow down."

"Wow!" Sam exclaimed happily, "It's finally going to happen to me."

Candace shook her head in wonder. "You're the first person I know who is excited about turning into an animal."

"I've had a long time to get used to the idea," Sam replied. "You guys don't realize it, but there have been whole conversations I've missed because I couldn't hear."

Katie frowned in reflection. "I'm sorry, Sam, I had no idea."

"I'm not telling you to complain," Sam rushed out. "I know you didn't *mean* to exclude me." She shrugged. "I knew it was the situation."

Katie had a good time watching Sam experience becoming a were-animal. The first time she got hot, she started squealing. She had to show everyone her sweat. She was just as dramatic with the cold flashes. Bundling up, she complained with a large smile on her face. The tingling sensations started early Wednesday morning. Katie decided they all needed to be at the cabin Thursday after school, just to be safe. Telling Sam her plans, she was surprised when a frown crossed her face.

"What?" Katie wanted to know. "I thought you were excited."

"Oh, I am," Sam responded. She looked down, a little embarrassed. "I don't know how to explain without sounding judgmental."

"I'm not sure…" Katie's voice trailed off, hoping Sam would explain herself.

"Katie, you were able to go through the change by yourself," Sam said in a rush. "I've watched the others go through the change, and well…" Sam shrugged her shoulders. "it's not pretty."

Katie rolled her eyes. "Sam, we don't care-"

"I would like to be able to do this with my dignity intact," Sam interrupted.

"I am not going to leave you alone, not with Seekers out there," Katie objected.

"I'm not saying for you to leave me completely alone..." Sam's voice trailed off. "I just don't want people to see me at my worst."

Katie sighed. "What's your suggestion?"

Sam smiled in relief. "When it looks like I'm getting close, I just want you and Lizzy to step out."

"What about Candace and Tyler?"

With a guilty look, Sam shrugged her shoulders.

Katie started to understand. "You don't want Candace or Tyler there?"

"It's not that I don't like them," Sam tried to explain. "Tyler is a guy, so I really don't want him around, when I lose control. The thought of him seeing me naked as many times as I saw him is just way too embarrassing."

"And Candace?"

"I really like Candace a lot." Sam shrugged. "I would just like to have my oldest friends, there only."

"What happens, if the Seekers appear worse than when Lizzy was changing?"

Sam smiled, knowing she was going to get her way. "I know you can handle it."

Katie shook her head. Sam always knew how to talk her into anything. "OK, I'll make the arrangements."

Actually, changing the arrangements wasn't hard at all. Tyler, clearly relieved, couldn't stop grinning. He must have been stressing about it all week. Candace understood Sam's request, and told her she would just hang out with Tyler. She would be closer to the cabin if she was needed.

Katie sat down on the front porch steps of the log cabin. She was conscious of Sam inside. The electricity emanating from the cabin was coming in much stronger waves than she had ever felt before. Watchful of every sound coming from the nearby trees, she was jumping up regularly, ready to change into wolf form if needed. Lizzy was watching the back door. The change was going to happen any minute. This was the time, she expected the Seekers to come. Getting up, she walked to the end of the porch. All was calm.

"Lizzy, is everything all right with you?"

"I don't see, or hear anything," she replied.

Katie leaned up against the post. Maybe she was wrong. Maybe the Seekers wouldn't come for Sam the way they did Lizzy. Another shock wave came from the cabin. If she could feel that, she was sure the Seekers could.

"Beautiful night, isn't it?"

Katie felt a wave of pleasure, when she recognized Jackson's thoughts. *"Where have you been? I haven't heard from you in several weeks."*

"Missed me?"

Katie glanced around the woods. It was still quiet. *"Yes, I missed you,"* she admitted.

"Have you seen the moon?"

Katie glanced up, the moon was behind the cabin. *"No."*

"You have to see it."

Katie walked down the porch steps, and walked a little away from the cabin. Keeping a careful eye on the woods, and the cabin behind her. She looked up.

"Can you see it?"

"Yes, It' full and bright," Katie answered.

Katie heard Jackson chuckle in her thoughts. *"It's completely full tomorrow."*

"How do you know?"

"I just do," Jackson replied.

"Where have you been, Jackson?" Katie changed the subject. She waited patiently, for a response. Just as usual, he wouldn't answer if given a direct question. Jackson?

A scream came from the cabin.

"SAM!"

Katie ran to the steps. Before she reached them, two objects hurled themselves out the window onto the porch. Katie jumped onto the stairs, to see two large cats fighting. She saw them go up, and over the rail. The snarling came to an abrupt stop, when they both hit the ground. One of them ran off. Katie recognized Jackson's Black Panther form, as it paused for a moment before he took off into the woods.

Lizzy's scream split the night. Katie took the last two steps onto the porch, and burst through the front door. She first saw Lizzy, her hands over her mouth screaming. Her shocked eyes, looking down. The strong odor of blood assaulted Katie's senses. Fear clutching her throat, Katie rounded the couch. A gouge was ripped from Sam's neck. She was bleeding, profusely a large pool of blood, already forming on the floor.

"NO! NO!" Reaching Sam, Katie tried to stop the blood with her hands. "Lizzy get a towel. NOW! OH PLEASE! Not this! Please, NO!" Reaching up, she grabbed the towel Lizzy threw her. "It's going to be all right," she promised.

"Sam! Hang in there. OK?" The towel, became immediately soaked. Katie looked around, trying to find something else. Not seeing anything that could help, she pressed the soaked towel to Sam's throat. She tried desperately, to stop the flow of blood.

"Candace call 911," she screamed with her thoughts. ***"WE NEED HELP! HURRY!"***

"PLEASE NO!" Katie begged, cradling Sam. "I need you. You can't leave me!" Throwing her thoughts out again, ***"CANDACE HURRY! DID YOU CALL 911? WHERE ARE THEY?"***

She began rocking back and forth, pressing the bloody towel against the large wound in Sam's neck.

"Tyler called, they are on their way." Candace was finally able to penetrate through Katie's incoherent thoughts. *"What happened?"*

Katie shook her head, unable to describe the horror she was facing. Holding the useless towel against Sam's neck, she watched life bleed out of her best friend. "Sam... Please...Please don't leave me."

Unable to speak, Sam's eyes held no fear. She gazed, into Katie's eyes. Her face turning white, as blood pumped out of her body unabated.

"Please Sam," Katie begged. "Please don't leave... Please."

Katie watched in horror, as the spirit of The Great White Tiger, lifted itself from her friend. "No! No! Come back! She needs you," she begged the spirit. "Come back. You can fix her... Please... I'll do anything. Anything! Please help! I know you can."

The spirit stepped away, and looked back first towards Sam, and then at Katie. Turning towards the wall, it disappeared.

Hearing a rattle, Katie looked down, and watched her best friend breath her last. She stared, into her best friend's dead eyes. She gently shook Sam's body, hoping her friend would blink, and come back to her. Shaking her head in shock, the resounding question pushed out of her lips.

"WHY!" Katie didn't realize, she was screaming. *"WHY!"*

She threw her thoughts out. ***WHY? JACKSON! WHY?***

There was a pause, as her screams vibrated through her thoughts.

"I told you, you would hate me." Jackson's thoughts, slapped down whatever control she had left. She screamed and screamed, until she literally had nothing left inside her.

It took almost two hours, for the authorities to arrive. Holding her friend, she was vaguely conscious of a snow leopard and African lion presence. Their heads bowed, viewing the scene. She heard jumbled comments. The ambulance cannot make it down the road. Rangers have been called. She held onto Sam, until she realized Sheriff Tate, was trying to pull her away from the body. Not understanding the words he was saying, she eventually let him pull her away.

She stood with her friends, as Sam was loaded onto a stretcher. The sheriff began asking questions.

What were they doing there?

How did they know, about the cabin?

How long, have they been coming here?

Katie stood frozen, not making a sound. Her friends taking her cue, followed suit. Sheriff Tate tried to scare them by telling them they were trespassing. Charges could be brought against them. His voice became rough and demanding. His questions more pointed.

Not saying a word, Tyler turned to the front door. He grabbed the sign off the door and handed it to the sheriff. The sheriff read the note, scrunched it in his hands, before jamming it into his pocket. Realizing he was not going to get any answers, the sheriff eventually left, muttering under his breath about teenage kids.

Katie overheard a couple of forest rangers, talking about animal attacks, and how they were becoming a problem. She shut them out when they started expressing their own opinion, stating how teenagers had no business being this deep in the woods.

One of the Forrest Rangers drove them home. They were told David's jeep would be delivered to the Black family. Arriving home, Katie walked into the arms of her mother. She looked at the moisture, streaming down her mother's face, and realized her mom was crying. She vaguely wondered, how come she couldn't cry. She hazily understood her mother, commenting on her clothes. She glanced down, noticing she was completely covered in blood.

She fingered her shirt. Seeing Sam's blood, she started reliving Sam's death, seeing Sam's dead, vacant eyes, knowing they would never sparkle with laughter again.

"Sam's dead," she whispered to her mother, horror vibrating in her voice.

Her mother gently took her hand, and led her to the bathroom. She slowly undressed Katie, and push her into the shower. Hot water cascaded onto her hair and down her body. With dead eyes, Katie watched Sam's blood slowly run down the drain. She stood in the shower, not understanding what she was supposed to do. Finally, her mother opened the shower curtain, and started washing her hair, as if she was a little girl. Katie stood motionless. Her eyes never left the drain as the last of Sam's blood vanished.

Her mother gently dressed her. Sitting down on the bed, her mother gave her a sleeping pill. Without hesitating, she dutifully took the pill swallowing the glass of water offered her. Lying down, her mother tucked the covers close around her. Katie closed her eyes, silently, pleading to the God Sam so diligently prayed to.

Please! Please! Please! Change this night, into a horrible dream, a nightmare I can wake up from and in the morning realize was just a bad dream. Sam will be alive. Her eyes sparkling with life, joy, and laughter.

Feeling the effects of the sleeping pills, Katie closed her eyes, welcoming the drug-induced oblivion.

Chapter 24
Life without Sam

Katie opened her eyes, automatically squinting as bright sunshine shown through her bedroom window. For a minute, she lay there, no memories of the previous night invading her consciousness. She was vaguely aware of a foreboding feeling she instinctively didn't want to pursue. Without any warning, memories of the previous night came crashing down around her. Grief welled up inside her so strong, it consumed her.

Sam's dead.

The statement rammed itself, into Katie's consciousness with the force of a bayonet. The picture of her friend's lifeless body raced across her mind, the sight of Sam's unseeing eyes haunting her, eye's, that no longer held her best friend's soul.

Sam's gone. She is actually gone.

Katie kept saying the words in her mind, trying to come to terms with reality. Shaking her head, she tried to get the image out of her head. It remained to haunt her. Nothing she could do was going to make it go away.

"I can't stand this."

Reaching inside, she clamped down hard on the emotions she was feeling. It became a hard knot, in the middle of her chest, which physically hurt for several minutes. After she took several calming breaths, the knot remained but was less painful.

Rolling over onto her back, she looked up at the ceiling. *What happened? She thought she was being so careful.* She remembered standing out on the porch, watching and listening for every sound. Ready to turn into wolf form, the second there was trouble. Jackson had reached out to her, and started talking about what a beautiful night it was. She'd stepped off the porch, and walked away from the cabin.

Realization struck her. She had walked far enough away from the cabin, to not be able to hear what was going on inside. That was when Jackson and the other "Seeker" were able to get in. She remembered, she tried to talk to Jackson, but he didn't respond. He was probably distracted. He was not listening to her, so he could do what he wanted to Sam.

Betrayal rippled through her body. Jackson was her friend. He had helped, in so many ways. Katie ran through her mind, all the times she had talked and laughed with him. She thought of the time she had first changed into wolf form. He had been her lifeline. Why didn't he kill then? She was vulnerable and weak. She remembered, when she saw him with Candace. She instinctively knew he was evil. She could actually smell, the evil on him. When she attacked, he could have easily killed her. And yet... he didn't.

Why?

When Lizzy was changing, he had warned her about the other Seekers. None of it made any sense. His very actions contradicted themselves. Why would he help Katie, but be so intent on going after Candace.

She remembered fighting him. Jackson's Black Panther was a much better fighter than she was. He could have easily killed her, and then did whatever he wanted to Candace. Yet, he stopped. She remembered how he placed his forehead, against hers.

"Sorry Katie," he had said with his thoughts to her.

That is when she realized, who he was. She would never have known, who the Black Panther was. He gave himself away.

She closed her eyes, as she remembered seeing the Black Panther, fighting the other cat. They had both simultaneously gone through the window. As the fight continued, they went up and over the front porch railing, landing on the ground. That was when the other cat ran into the woods, but the Black Panther paused for just a moment, his indecision clear, and then he ran after the other cat.

Katie shook her head. If Jackson's intent was anything else but to kill, then it would have taken longer. She was desperate to find a reason for Jackson to be there, other than the obvious. Her mind returned to Jackson's telling her it was a beautiful moon, and she had to see it. He was the one who purposely distracted her. She would never have left the porch for anyone else but him. He was the one she trusted.

She closed her eyes remembering the shock, as it vibrated through her soul. She remembered, how she screamed. "Why? Jackson Why?"

His response clanged like a death toll, as it bounced around her shocked consciousness.

"I told you, you would hate me!"

The knot in her chest moved up into her throat. She clamped down. She shoved it back into her chest, where it throbbed. Jackson's words vibrated in her mind, until she thought she would go mad.

Trying desperately to get her thoughts away from Jackson, she remembered seeing what animal spirit left Sam. The Great White Tiger, was going to be Sam. It made perfect sense, once she thought about it. Sam, was a natural leader. She had a strong sense, of right and wrong. The tiger would have picked her for herself.

The spirit tiger made sure it was protected, while changing. There would have been four others guarding her, but she never had four there. Candace and Tyler were miles away. Katie and Lizzy were outside, watching the doors, not the windows. Leaving plenty of room for Seekers to destroy the body the tiger planned to possess.

Katie got up and looked out the window, not seeing anything. If she'd been in wolf form, she would have smelled Jackson. She could have heard him, easily. Lizzy had followed her example and didn't change either. She had been lulled into a false sense of security of her own making. Jackson may be responsible for the actual kill, but she allowed him to do it. In the end, Sam was dead because of her.

It was her fault. The knot rose again, threatening to choke her. Clamping down hard, she forced it back into her chest.

"Katie."

She turned, noticing her mother for the first time. She wondered, how long she had been standing there.

"David Black is here to see you."

A sickening cold enveloped her body. The knot slammed into her throat, choking off whatever words were starting to form. Shaking her head, she began gasping for breath.

"No." She finally was able to whisper, through tight vocal cords. "I can't..."

Her mother nodded, turned, and left the room.

Katie turned back to the window. She was thankful, her window faced the back of the house. She did not want, to have to see David leave.

The next couple of days followed a pattern. She barely left her bedroom. She refused to eat, until her mother threatened to hand feed her. She only picked at her food. She would stare for hours out the window, going over and over the things she should have done. Grief, betrayal, and guilt were at war with each other, each emotion, intent on destroying her.

Sometimes she would feel a pushing sensation against her mind. Through her pain, she realized the other were-animals were trying to speak to her. A couple of times, she almost opened her mind and allowed them access. She had no idea what she would say. In the end, she closed her mind to all.

Her mother insisted she go to Sam's funeral. Not having the energy, to argue, Katie eventually agreed to go. But, she was determined to drive herself. Seeing her mother leave, she waited until she knew she was late. Entering the chapel, she sat in the back pew.

Wearing sunglasses to hide her eyes, she closely watched the front pews. Four large pews, were corded off for family members. She recognized, almost everyone in the family. She wasn't surprised, when she saw Tyler, Candace, and Lizzy all sitting together in the family section. She saw Robbie had come home from college. Her eyes drifting down the row to Steven Bends. Robbie and David's best friend was sitting between Robbie and David. He must have come home from college for the funeral. That was nice of him to do that Katie mused quietly to herself.

Her eyes eventually rested on David. He looked handsome, in his suit and tie. He kept glancing around, as if he was looking for someone. She vaguely wondered who he was looking for.

Feeling a little uneasy, Katie slowly moved over, until her view of David was blocked. She had to admit it, Sam's funeral was nice. Instead of focusing on the tragedy of her death, her life was celebrated. Katie briefly forgot her grief, when she was forced to laugh over some crazy things Sam had done. Most of the stories she had witnessed herself.

After one of the speakers, Katie glanced towards the family pew. David had not only moved, but his body was turned sideways. He was staring straight at her. Quickly looking down, very slowly, nonchalantly, she moved down the pew to block his view. When the closing prayer was over, David jumped up heading in her direction. Panic seized her, until she realized he was stopped by several people, offering their condolences.

She quickly left the church and got in her car. She drove a little down the street and parked. She waited patiently, for the motor brigade carrying Sam's casket, to drive buy. She could then follow. She stayed in her car, as the family did one last prayer over the grave site. She didn't understand her feelings. She desperately wanted to be a part of Sam's last farewell. She wanted to stand next to the family, and be counted as one of them. She knew the people standing over the grave would welcome her with open arms.

Guilt stopped her. It was her fault.

"My fault," she whispered.

Grief flamed up, consuming her once more. Unable to endure the heartbreak, she looked down trying to get her emotions under control. Finally suppressing her feelings, she glanced up. Surprised and shock rebounded, through her consciousness. David was walking towards her, with a purposeful gate.

Sitting up in her seat, she leaned over and started her car. Seeing him break into a run, Katie slammed the car into gear. She punched the gas. The Camaro's tires jumped and squealed. She almost lost control before she let up on the gas. Looking in her rear-view mirror, she saw David's hands on his hips watch her drive away.

She knew it was only a matter of time. He was going to find a way to talk to her. After all, he was Sam's brother. Defeat was not a part of their vocabulary. As long as it wasn't today or in the near future Katie could live with it.

The next morning, her mother informed her she needed to go back to school. She listened to her mother with empty eyes. Shrugging her shoulders in acceptance, she turned to get ready. Opening her dresser drawer, a hot pink t-shirt lay on top. Pulling it out, she fingered the fabric, the words "Modest is Hottest" emblazoned on the front. Without even thinking about it, she put the t-shirt on. Katie couldn't explain it, but it made her feel better.

Katie's number one goal was to stay out of David's sight. She soon developed a sixth sense. It was almost as if she could smell his presence. She never went to lunch and avoided all common rooms where he might see her. When school was out, she left for home immediately. Lizzy and Tyler tried repeatedly to talk to her. Unable to completely avoid them, she would mumble yes or no answers, and then find an excuse to leave.

She wore Sam's pink t-shirt every day. Since she only had two, she was continuously washing one to be ready for the next day. They soon started to fade and look worn out. When she couldn't find the shirts, she found out her mother had thrown them out. Screaming at the top of her lungs, she dug the faded shirts out of the trash and continued to wear them.

A month later, her mother refused to give her any more sleeping pills. Katie was so afraid she might dream, she lay awake for hours. Eventually, she drifted off into an exhausted sleep. She found herself on the edge of the small pool. The waterfall was cascading down, shutting all sound. Looking around, she expected to see The Great White Tiger. Instead, Jackson stood close to the edge of the trees. He took a couple of steps towards her, his arms stretched out in a pleading manner.

Shaking her head, she took a step back. He said something to her. She couldn't hear him. "NO!" She took a couple of steps back, shaking her head. **"I TRUSTED YOU!"** she screamed. **"WHY! WHY!"**

She felt the familiar tug on her mind. She realized he was trying to reach her. Backing away, she started screaming. Her arms were outstretched, trying to ward him off.

"Katie wake up! WAKE UP!"

She opened her eyes. Her mother was shaking her. Dripping in sweat she glanced around, afraid she may have given something away. Her mother, watching her intently, got up and left the room. She soon returned with a sleeping pill. Grateful, Katie welcomed the oblivion she craved.

"Hello, Katie."

Katie inwardly cringed, recognizing the voice. She didn't want to look up, making her worst nightmare a reality. Unlocking her car door, she opened it, intent on ignoring the voice as long as possible. She wasn't surprised when her car door slammed shut. She felt David's warm body close to her. She slowly raised her eyes from his pants, to his shirt, his neck, his unsmiling lips until they rested on his eyes. His eyes were so much like Sam's. She quickly looked down, unable to hold his gaze.

The moment had arrived. David was going to insist on answers. She had no idea how to act, or what to say. She stood quietly, ready to take flight with whatever means necessary. David watched her intently, not saying a word. Finally sighing, he looked out over the parking lot.

"I have something for you." He handed her, two of Sam's hot pink t-shirts. They looked brand new, compared to the faded one, she was now wearing.

Surprised, Katie mechanically took them. Unable to stop the small smile, she lifted them to her face. The soft cotton texture comforted her. She closed her eyes, unable to stop the hard knot in her chest as it rose up threatening to choke her. Clamping down on it, she forced it back down into her chest. Dropping her book bag, she whipped off her old faded pink t-shirt, and pulled one of the new shirts on.

"UHH..."

Katie looked over, at David's red face. He was looking everywhere, but at her. She realized she had just taken off her shirt, in front of him. "I'm sorry. I didn't think."

"UHH, it's okay," he said. His eyes darted towards her, and then quickly looked away. His face turned into a deep shade of purple.

Katie could feel the heat, rising into her cheeks. She was such an idiot. Becoming a were-animal, the first thing you stopped thinking about was personal modesty. She couldn't help see the irony, when she quickly donned the hot pink shirt declaring, *modest is hottest.* She wouldn't have stripped naked in front of David, but a bra was almost the same as the top of a swimsuit. Except to a Black family member. They would always see the distinction.

"I'm really sorry. I..."

David shook his head, his cheeks returning to a more normal color. "Hey, at least I get to tell my friends, I've seen you in your bra." He gave her a tight smile. "For some reason, they think I'm square."

Katie shook her head. "David, you are square," she retorted.

"OH Yeah?" David leaned towards her, his warm body invading her personal space. His smile, suddenly turning genuine. "A square, who got to see the prettiest girl in school, without a shirt on."

A warm glow developed in the pit of her stomach. She couldn't help the smile, creeping into her lips.

David brushed a hair, away from her face. "Don't be a stranger," straightening he walked away.

Katie watched him go. She had expected questions, accusations, demand for answers. What she got, was the complete opposite. She shook her head. He was very much like Sam. Still smiling to herself, she drove home.

Chapter 25
Forrest

"You look like your mother."

Katie looked up from her homework. The older gentleman standing in front of her looked out of place in the high school library. Cocking her head to get a better look at him, she saw he was tall and thin, his hair pulled back into a long gray ponytail. His eyes were a striking gray color. She had only seen that color eyes on one other person, her friend Lizzy. Suspicious, she watched the man, sit down across from her.

Neither one spoke, as they eyed each other wearily. Katie waited patiently, for the man to speak.

The man looked around the room and leaned towards her. "You are not much of a talker, are you?"

Katie shrugged.

"My name's Forrest." The old man said unnecessarily.

Katie nodded.

"You seem to have made yourself at home, in my cabin."

Not knowing how to respond, Katie shrugged.

"Can you tell me, what you kids were doing there?"

Katie sat in silence. Her features showed no emotion.

"Could you at least, tell me what happened?"

Katie didn't move, afraid to give anything away.

"If I didn't know any better, I'd say you were…." Forrest paused shaking his head.

Katie felt a tug on her mind. Someone was desperately, trying to speak with her. She ignored it, concentrating on the man in front of her.

The old man stared at her for a couple of minutes, not saying anything. "My mistake." Shaking his head, he rose from the seat.

Katie watched Forrest start to walk away, when several ideas occurred to her at once. She was afraid, he would disappear? "Seekers," she whispered.

The man stopped dead, and turned back to face her. Now she had committed herself. She was having a hard time following through. "Two seekers killed Sam," she forced the whisper through dry lips.

Again, she felt the tug on her mind. She looked up, "I can't hear you. Since Sam, I shut my mind off. I'm not sure I know how to turn it back on."

Forrest sat back down, studying her intently, "Are you alone, or have others…"

"There are four others," Katie said softly. "Sam would have been five."

"Five." Forrest shook his head. "I have never heard of that many, at one time."

Katie eyed him closely. "Maybe you and I are not really talking about the same thing. So you tell me what you're talking about, and I'll tell you if you're right." Again, Katie felt a familiar tug on her mind. "I told you, I cannot hear you. Quit trying to speak, through my mind."

Forrest looked around, making sure they were not overheard. "What form of animal, do you change into?" he asked quietly.

Katie's heart jumped, "I turn into, a great big white wolf."

Clearly startled, Forrest sat back into his chair. "A wolf?"

The bell rang, indicating she needed to leave and go to class. "I've been hoping, to meet someone with answers." Katie stood up, and started quickly packing her books. "We need to talk, maybe after school…?" She looked up, in time to see a guarded expression on the old man's features. "What?"

"I'm not sure I have any answers…" His voice trailed off.

Anger immediately raised, causing heat to course through her body. "You don't think you have answers?" She mimicked him. "You don't even know what questions I'm going to ask," she stated. "If you haven't noticed, pal, we've been trying to figure out what the hell is going on for months." Throwing her book bag over her shoulder, she rounded the table. "My best friend died. Her throat was ripped out." She stepped closer, her voice rising with suppressed emotion. "I held her, as she bled out. I tried to stop the bleeding, but there was absolutely nothing I could do."

She realized, she had been holding her emotions in for too long. It was hard to stay in control.

"Why?"

She held out her hands. "Why? Because we didn't understand what we were up against."

She jabbed him in the chest, and took satisfaction when he took a step back. "We've been '*Forrest Gumping*' our way through for months." Stepping closer, she allowed her eyes to change, for a split second before returning human. "Now, I know you have answers. I'm going to hunt you down."

Forrest took a couple of steps back. "I believe I'll be able to answer a few of your questions."

"Thank you," she said sarcastically. "Where do you want to meet?"

The man paused for a moment. "How about the old trading post?"

"The what?" Katie had lived in the area her whole life, and has never known anything called the Trading Post.

"You know they tore it down, and called it *Paul's Diner* for a while."

"The only diner I know close to here, is called *Mountain Meadow Diner*."

"Yea, that's the place."

"Fine, I'll meet you there after school." Katie stepped closer, letting a threatening tone enter her voice, "3:30 pm. I expect you there."

Turning around, she stopped dead in her tracks. David, was standing in the doorway. His shocked expression and white complexion showed he'd been standing there for a while. Not knowing how to respond, she pushed past him and headed for class.

For the first time in weeks, Katie had a spring in her step, as she walked through the halls. She couldn't wait, to find Lizzy and Tyler. Walking into class, she tried to catch Lizzy's eye, but she was unable to do so. She walked up to her. "You are not going to believe, who I talked to this morning."

Lizzy seemed to be looking everywhere else, but her.

Katie paused a moment, studying her friend. "You're not going to believe, who I talked to this morning," she repeated.

"Oh, are you talking to me?" Lizzy said, in a dramatic way. "I wasn't sure, since you decided you no longer wanted to be my friend."

"What?" surprised Katie just gaped at her friend, "What are you talking about?"

She felt a tug on her mind. Looking around, she saw Tyler watching her closely. Turning back around, she saw Lizzy smile a triumphant smile. Not really understanding what was going on, she decided to ignore the drama and get to the point.

"Look, if you are trying to talk to me with your mind," she said in a hushed whisper. "I can't hear you. I somehow turned it off, and I don't know how to turn it back on."

She felt Tyler's presence behind her, as he listened intently to what she was saying. Another tug on her mind distracted her.

"I realize you're saying something, but I can't hear." Geez... how many times, did she have to repeat herself? "Look, I don't have time for..." She waved her arm "whatever game you're playing. So, if you don't want to know I talked to *Forrest,* I'll just sit down."

"What?" Lizzy's face froze. All pretense dropped. "When, Where?"

"He came into the library before school," Katie tried to explain.

"Katherine Johnson, leave my class."

Katie looked up and saw Miss Smith.

"I'm sorry, I'll just..."

"You will leave my class, and go to the principal's office now!"

Katie glanced around the classroom. Everyone was closely watching her. Giving Tyler and Lizzy a significant look, she shrugged her shoulders and walked out. Sitting in the principal's office, she waited patiently for Davis to appear.

"Miss Johnson, I was hoping to have a word with you."

Katie sat back in her chair. She remembered through previous experiences, how she'd trembled with anxiety. Now, she could care less what this man said or did.

"Miss Johnson, I've been talking to your teachers. They are concerned your grades have been continuously slipping since ..." He paused, searching for the right word "the incident with Samantha Black".

Katie raised her eyebrows. She thought she was doing pretty well, under the circumstances. Homework was actually a relief. It kept her mind off other things.

"Now, I hear you're disruptive in class," Davis continued.

"Disruptive?" Katie couldn't help repeating. "Where did that come from?

"Apparently, you had an incident, with a long-standing member of the board this morning." Davis reminded her. "Just now, you refused to sit in your chair."

"Refused to sit?" Katie repeated stupidly.

"I know, you have been having a rough time. We do have a counselor, willing to sit and listen to you. They can help you sort things out."

Katie almost laughed out loud. *Oh yeah, like that's really going to work with me,* she thought derisively.

"Believe it or not, Katie, I have your best interest at heart."

She choked, coughed, and sputtered looking around for relief. Not seeing anything to help her, she finally got herself under control. Shaking her head, she stared at the principal in disbelief.

"I take it, you don't believe me," Davis said dryly.

"No, I don't."

"Miss Johnson, I have four hundred students in my care. Most of those students go through high school with very little help from me. Others, I have to punish, to keep them in line. I only have to do it a couple of times, until they straighten up. Then there are the few who seem to think, I'm out to get them. The teachers are just horribly mean, only to them. They expect, special treatment. If they don't get it, they have a chip on their shoulders. It's always everyone else's fault."

Anger rushed through her system to a boiling point, Katie took a couple of breaths to try and calm down. Her chest heaved. "You're worried about my grades?" She said softly, her voice barely under control. "You weren't worried, when you gave me six days of zero's last semester." Gaining momentum, her voice became stronger. "You forced me to take Miss Smith's class." Digging into her bag, she pulled out her English folder. She grabbed one of her graded papers, and she stood up. "Do you see my grade?"

She held it up, replicating the English teacher's voice. "Katherine, I have your homework." She held up the paper, as if she was in front of the class, making sure everyone could see.

"Every week, Miss Smith tries to humiliate me in front of the class. Do you see any other markings, on this paper besides the D minus?" She threw the folder, onto the desk. "Look for yourself. Why don't you grade my homework, and see if I really deserve the grades I received."

She started pacing the office, her voice rising a little higher. "For the record, I did not refuse to sit down. The bell had just rung, and I was not seated."

She paused, in front of the desk. "I tried to apologize, and sit. Was she willing, to just let me sit?" She shook her head, "No way!"

Stopping in her tirade her chest heaving, she expected Davis to defend the teacher. Instead, he was watching her closely. Reaching over, he gathered her English papers into a pile, opened his drawer and placed them out of sight.

She wanted to say a lot more, but all the energy drained out of her body. She sat down, her shoulders slumped. "I'm doing the best that I can, Mr. Davis." She shrugged "I don't know what else to say."

Davis sat there for a couple of minutes, not saying a word. Finally, he got up from his desk. "Katie, I want you to go to the library for the rest of this hour, and then continue with your schedule for the rest of the day."

Relieved, Katie got up, and left before he could change his mind.

Katie pulled into the parking lot, of the old diner. Parking her car, she got out and looked around for Forrest. Walking into the restaurant, she made sure he wasn't there before walking back out leaning up against her car. She looked at her watch. 3:30 pm. She was on time. Where was he?

Watching every car that went by, she wasn't surprised when she saw David's jeep pull into the drive. She watched the occupant, as he sat behind the wheel. Finally, opening the door he got out and slammed it shut. Walking towards her, he leaned up against her car.

"Beautiful day isn't it?"

Katie shook her head. Once again, he surprised her. She never knew what he was going to say. "Yeah, it's really starting to get warm."

David squinted in the sunlight. "If it keeps up, all snow will be melted in a couple of days."

Katie nodded. Glancing at her watch, a cold suspicion entered her thoughts; 3:40 pm still no Forrest.

"You're afraid he won't show?"

Only able to nod, Katie narrowed her eyes.

"Who is he?" David asked quietly.

Surprise flitted across her face, before she masked her emotions. "His name is Forrest. I don't know, if it's his first or last name."

"How is he connected?"

"He owns the cabin. You know, the cabin in the woods."

David nodded. "This morning it sounded as if…" his voice trailed off. He shook his head and tried again. "It sounded as if... What happened to Sam, was not a random animal attack."

The knot in Katie's chest that had been dormant, rose up into her throat choking her. Trying to fight the grief, and guilt she struggled inwardly. Pushing off the car, her only thought was to flee, when a car pulled up beside her. Turning, she saw Lizzy and Tyler jump out.

Lizzy came running around the car. "Is he here? Did you see him?"

Her throat still tight, she could only shake her head.

"Why? Isn't he here?" Lizzy demanded.

Another car pulled into the parking lot. Candace jumped out and came running over. "I got here, as quickly as I could. Where is he?"

Katie only shook her head.

"He didn't show up?" Lizzy rounded on Katie. "Why did you let him get away?"

"What?" Katie croaked, still fighting to calm her emotions.

"You did this on purpose," Lizzy yelled at Katie. "So I, wouldn't find out who my real father is."

Katie glared at Lizzy, her voice deadly quiet. "This may surprise you, Lizzy, but the world doesn't revolve around you and your little daddy quest."

Lizzy fell back, as if she was slapped.

"Sam's dead, or don't you remember that small detail."

"I remember," Lizzy defended herself, "I didn't just lose one best friend that night, I lost two."

"I'm still here, Lizzy. I haven't left."

"You haven't been here. Where were you during Sam's funeral? No one saw you there, except for that ridiculous display at the gravesite, where you zoomed away tires squealing." Lizzy stepped closer, her voice louder. "Do you know how many comments, the Black family made about you?" She pointed her finger, into Katie's chest. "They were all so worried about poor little Katie, while you didn't even give the courtesy of a single condolence."

"IT'S MY FAULT, SHE'S DEAD!" Katie screamed back. All the guilt she was experiencing, rang out in every syllable. **"SAM'S DEAD, BECAUSE OF ME!"** Heat enveloped her. She knew, she was on the verge of losing complete control. **"YOU DON'T HATE ME, AS MUCH AS I HATE MYSELF!"**

Turning, she blindly reached for the car door handle. Jumping in, she started the vehicle. She pulled out so fast, she saw all her friends jump out of the way.

Pulling out of the parking lot, she fishtailed through the stop sign. Not wanting to go home, she raced down the highway. Going through the canyon, she tried to concentrate on the road instead of her thoughts. Pushing the gas pedal, she desperately tried chasing away emotions as they consumed her. Reaching other vehicles on the road, she went around them as if they were stopped. Still, she raced through the narrow road, going faster and faster.

Turning one of the hairpin corners, she saw snow completely blocking the road. The warm weather had caused the snow to melt, creating a small avalanche. Slamming on her brakes, she hit the slushy snow going way to fast. The car went air born. The wheels caught the railing, in its first roll. Katie lost count, how many times the car turned over, and each turn jarring her body.

Her car, resting at the bottom of the ravine, she raised her throbbing head. Automatically, reaching for the handle, she tried to open the door of the crushed car. Looking around, all the windows were gone. The roof smashed down, level with the doors. The only way out, was through the back. She fumbled, trying to unbuckle her seat belt. Crawling slowly, through the small space she pushed herself out landing with a thump on the ground.

Dumbly, she patted her pockets looking for her cell phone. It wasn't there. Night was falling. No one knew where she was. Lying in the slushy snow, she knew it would refreeze during the night. She was in trouble. She tried to reach inside herself for the familiar heat, to keep her warm. Nothing happened. The effort made her light headed. Trying to reach out with her mind, she echoed the words she used when Sam died.

"Candace call 911... We need help.... Hurry." Then darkness enveloped her.

Chapter 26
Refuge

"OH NO! NO! NO! Please NO!"

Katie opened her eyes.

"Katie?"

"Thank God!"

"I'm going to get you out of this. Hold on! Okay? Please just hold on."

The voice sounded familiar.

Raising her hand to her eyes, she felt a sticky residue on her face. The sun had lowered, causing the temperature to drop. Shivering, her teeth chattered.

"Cold," she mumbled.

"I've got you. Just give me a minute, I'll get you warm."

Darkness enveloped her once again.

Opening her eyes, the first thing she felt was warm. She was on a small bed, next to an old-fashioned fireplace. The fire hurt her eyes, as the flames danced and popped. Turning her head, she saw a figure crouch down beside her. Recognizing him, she reached out and touched his hair. "Jackson?"

His head jerked up. He reached out and grabbed her hand. "Katie, I thought I'd lost you."

Her head in a fog, it was hard to speak. "I've missed you," she said softly.

Shaking his head, he raised her hand to his lips.

"What are you doing here?"

Again, he shook his head.

"Here we go again. You are avoiding my questions." There was something in the back of her mind, warning her about something. She wrinkled her brow, trying to remember.

"Go to sleep Katie... We'll talk later..."

Reverting to old habits, she closed her eyes. Trusting Jackson, was as natural as breathing.

Katie opened her eyes. The small amount of light was streaming through a dirty window. Looking around, it looked like she was in some kind of one-room log cabin. The room was so small, the bed was touching one of the old wooden chairs pulled up to an old rough table. It had a dirt floor. The fireplace dominated the room. There was a small walkway between the bed and the kitchen table. To the side of the bed, was an old fashion wardrobe with a hinge missing.

Sitting up in the small bed, her eyes unfocused, her body gave a small sway. A deep throbbing in her head caused her to raise her hand. She felt material wrapped around her head, in a makeshift bandage. Looking down her wrist was wrapped, as well as her leg. She could see dark brown spots, where blood had soaked through the bandages.

She heard steps, on some kind of wooden porch outside, before the door was opened. Sunlight made her eyes squint, as a dark figure walked into the cabin. When the door shut, the cabin was plunged into semi-darkness again. The figure walked in and placed wood by the fireplace.

Turning, he sat down on the floor facing her with his back up against the wall.

"Hello Jackson," Katie said quietly.

Nodding, Jackson's features stiffened, his eyes guarded. "How are you feeling?"

"I'm a little sore, my head still hurts." Looking around the room, "What is this place?"

He sat for a moment not responding, before giving a small shrug. "I found this place several months ago."

Absently, rubbing the bandage on her wrist, "What happened?"

His eyes narrowed. "You don't remember?"

Katie frowned. When she tried to remember, her mind shied away. "No, I don't."

Glancing up, she caught relief dance across his features, before it settled back into a mask. "Do you realize, this is the first time I've seen you in person?"

A slow smile spread across his face. "Hello, Katie Johnson. It's nice to meet you." He said in a soft mocking voice.

Katie's stomach rumbled, causing heat to rush to her face. "Sorry, I'm a little hungry."

Jackson jumped up. "No problem, I was hoping you'd be hungry." Heading for the door, he grabbed the handle. Turning back around he paused, "are you needing to relieve yourself?"

A quick nod, had him walking back over to her. Helping her up, he walked her to the door. Looking at her bare feet he picked her up, and carried her out to an outhouse. "Sorry about the accommodations, this is the best I could do."

"I'm pretty sure I can walk," she grumbled.

“I’ll tell you what, I’ll get your shoes, and put them just outside the door. This way you can walk back.”

Nodding, she shut the door.

When she re-entered the small cabin, she saw Jackson had the small table full of several different kinds of meats. Sitting down, not wanting to embarrass herself, she resisted the urge to shovel the food in her mouth.

Jackson watched her closely. “What are you waiting for?”

“Nothing.”

“I know you’re hungry, so dig in.”

The food was making her mouth water.

Picking up a large turkey leg, Jackson held it under her nose. “I know you want it.”

Not able to stand it anymore, she grabbed the leg and started wolfing it down. It didn’t take her long before everything on the table was gone.

Jackson smiled, “finished?” He got up and started cleaning off the table.

Now her body wasn’t demanding food. She was embarrassed not only over the amount, but the speed she'd consumed it. “I’m sorry.”

Jackson paused. “What are you sorry for?”

“I don’t know… for being such a pig?”

“Katie, you just went through a traumatic accident. If you were completely human, you’d be dead. The wolf spirit inside, was the only thing that kept you alive.” He sat down beside her. “Don’t apologize, for the animal characteristics you display. That’s a small price to pay, for everything it has done for you.”

Listening, Katie’s eyes began to droop. She tried not to yawn.

Jackson got up. "It looks like it's time for you to go back to bed, sleepy head."

Trying to protest, she lay down and was sound asleep within minutes.

When she opened her eyes, it was dark again. Her head no longer throbbed.

"How do you feel?"

Katie followed the voice, and saw Jackson in his usual spot sitting on the floor. His eyes had the guarded look again.

"Better."

"Are you hungry, or thirsty?"

"No, I don't think so."

"Good." Jackson nodded his head. "Do you remember anything?" he asked softly.

"About what?"

Jackson got up, frustration marring his features. "About what happened before… before you got hurt."

Katie wrinkled her brow. She had a sense of foreboding, when she tried to remember. She shook her head. "Is it important I remember?"

"Yes." Jackson ran his fingers through his hair, his frustration evident. "Look, let's do something different."

"Jackson, I have a lot of questions, I would like you to answer." Katie began. "It's been driving me crazy, not knowing things about you."

The guarded look was back in his eyes again. "Katie, I promise I'll answer all your questions, but you're going to have to wait."

"I've been waiting, for quite a while, Jackson." She got up to face him. "I believe, I've been pretty patient up till now."

"Believe me, Katie, I want to tell you, but you're still going to have to wait."

She raised her arms, "What are we waiting for?"

"You."

"You're waiting for me," she said disbelievingly.

"Yes, I'm waiting for you." He smiled, walked over, and put a strand of hair behind her ear. "Hurry up, so we can get it over with. The wait is driving me crazy."

Katie swallowed. He was such an incredibly nice looking guy. He was standing so close to her, she could feel his warmth radiating from his body. She immediately became aware of how alone they were. His stormy eyes held hers for a minute, before he slowly stepped away.

"How about we play chess?"

Katie groaned, letting the tension she was feeling drain away from her body. "What is it with you and chess?"

"Hey, all the great ones play chess," Jackson countered. "Besides, what else are we going to do in this place?"

Katie looked around the small room. "What was I thinking?" she said sarcastically.

"You have got to be the worst chess player, I've ever seen."

Katie glanced up. "What?"

"You have to let someone die, Katie."

"No, I don't."

"If you keep moving trying to protect everyone, you'll lose the game," Jackson tried to explain. "The smaller players, are expendable.

"No one is expendable," Katie defended.

"You can't move around very well, if you're determined to keep all your men alive."

Katie grinned, "Haven't we had this conversation before?"

"Obviously, you haven't taken my advice," Jackson shot back. "Where did you get this philosophy anyway?"

Katie looked down and picked up a pawn. "Sam," she shook her head smiling. "It used to drive David crazy, when she did nothing but move the players around so they wouldn't get hurt." A small tear appeared in her eye. "She was the most caring, loving person I have ever known." Katie stopped, realizing she was describing Sam past tense. Staring at the chess board, her brows knitted together, she slowly raised her head and looked into Jackson's guarded eyes. A deluge of memories flooded into her. "You killed her," she said softly.

"Katie listen to me," Jackson said desperately.

Following the sound of his voice, her eyes rested on him. "YOU!" She jumped up ignoring the chair, as it crashed to the floor. **"YOU KILLED HER!"**

"Katie it's not what you think."

"NO!" she screamed **I TRUSTED YOU!** She brought up her arms, trying to block his words with her hands. "Even after Candace, I STILL TRUSTED YOU!!"

Jackson reached out, and grabbed Katie by the shoulders "Let me explain…"

Struggling, her only thought was to flee. "Let me go!"

Strong bands came out of nowhere and wrapped themselves around her arms and legs. Unaware of them at first, she was only fighting Jackson's grip. When he let her go, she was dragged over to the bed, where the bands tightened down on the bed posts.

The more she fought the tighter the bands became, till they were biting into her flesh. Looking up, she saw Jackson, leaning up against the wall watching her closely.

"If I have to gag you, I will," he said softly. "You will hear, my side of the story."

Chapter 27
Answers

Feeling heat course through her body instinctively, she tried to change into wolf form. Surprise and anger flashed in her eyes, when she realized she couldn't. Struggling, the binding tightened again. Her fingers began feeling numb. "What is this?" She tried to lift a hand, indicating the bindings. "What are you doing to me?"

"I just want you to listen," Jackson said in a controlled voice.

"These ties are cutting into my hands." As soon as the words came out, the bindings loosened enough for her fingers to stop tingling.

"How did you do that?" Katie asked, unable to resist the question.

Jackson folded his arms and shrugged. "I wouldn't try changing, if I were you. I wasn't expecting company, so I don't have any extra clothes lying around." He cocked his head, to one side. "Of course, it's all up to you, if want to be naked. It will make things, more interesting."

"Shut-up!" Kate spat out. "You know I can't change. I already tried. You've done something to me."

Jackson raised his eyebrows.

Looking around the small room, Katie could see no way out. Starting to panic, she started struggling with the restraints.

Jackson watched her struggle. "Don't be afraid, Katie. If I wanted to hurt you, I would have already done it."

"I'm not afraid," Katie lied.

Jackson gave a derisive smile. "I can feel your emotions," he said slowly.

Katie centered all her anger and hatred towards him. "You feel that?"

"Yeah, I feel it. Hatred makes you ugly."

Stung, Katie pulled back and sat on the bed, quietly eyeing him.

Jackson's eyes narrowed. "You can't hate me *and* get your feelings hurt when I say something to you... It doesn't work that way."

Katie numbly stared at Jackson's handsome face. "You want me to listen?" She shrugged. "I'm listening."

Jackson stood there for a couple minutes, eyeing her warily.

"What are you waiting for?" Katie eventually asked. "I'm your captive audience," she said, indicating her restraints. "Let's hear your explanation, for killing my best friend."

His face colored. Pushing himself off the wall, he agitatedly ran his fingers through his hair. Shaking his head, he stood in front of her. "I used to be a senior, at Central High School," he began slowly. "I was an average teenage guy who enjoyed sports and chased girls. I have a mom, a dad, and a little sister."

He leaned back against the wall. "I thought I was coming down with something when I got the hot and cold flashes. I didn't have a clue as to what was going on."

He paused, shaking his head. "I've learned, when a person is on the verge of changing, he instinctively runs into the woods."

He shook his head. "I was no different. I found myself in the woods, rolling around, wondering what was happening."

"A large bobcat stood above me, talking to me in my head. He gave me a choice. I join him, become a Seeker, or die." Jackson pushed himself off the wall. "That was my choice, Katie." He looked imploringly at her. "I was seventeen. I wanted to live. I didn't even know, what a Seeker was. The only thought I had was, If I can live, I'll do and be anything you want.

"Steven, the name of the bobcat, had me bow down and say an oath. I had to repeat it, word for word in my head. The second the words were said, I felt something rip out of me. The pain was so intense, I screamed."

Katie nodded, remembering when she and Candace tried to get to Jackie Oaklin. They had heard a scream and started running into the woods.

"I was told, I could never go home again, or my family would be killed. My life was now theirs. They have complete control over every portion of my life. They give off this superior air, as if they are all-knowing. If I tried anything, they would know. I went to a training camp of sorts, where I was taught how to fight. When my training was over, I was assigned to this area of Appalachia. I have learned this part of the mountains is considered dangerous to Seekers. The survival rate is non-existent."

"Why?" Katie couldn't help asking.

"Elizabeth Hawk," Jackson replied. "She has a formidable reputation, among the leaders. They both fear, and respect her."

Katie frowned, "I don't understand".

"Old Elizabeth Hawk used to be The Great White Tiger," Jackson explained.

Katie sat, dumbfounded.

"She has protected this area, for over 170 years."

"How is that possible?"

"I haven't figured it all out." Jackson shrugged. "My guess is, the animal spirit elongated her life."

"That means, she was alive when..." Katie was trying to subtract in her head.

"When the Cherokee Nation, was forced to march the trail of tears," Jackson answered.

Trying to absorb all the information, Katie looked down. Her hands were no longer tied. Lifting her hands, she rubbed her wrists.

"I never wanted to hold you down, Katie."

She nodded, understanding, and motioned him to continue.

"Since this area was considered so dangerous, I was basically left alone." Jackson folded his arms. "I felt the first electrical currents, pretty quickly. Instead of staying away, like I was told, I found out who you were. I followed you, I even watched you play ball... I was thinking about you one night."

He shook his head. "I don't even know how I was able to do it, but I found myself in your dream. I watched you fight off the tiger. I followed you. You know what happened then," he finished.

"I felt so intrigued. I wanted more contact with you. Despite the consequences of a severe headache, I tried again. This time, I tried to control the situation, so the tiger wasn't the one in control. The tiger found a way anyway.

"I couldn't stay away, Katie. You were so trusting, happy, and good. You were this bright light, in my darkened world. When you asked questions, I didn't know what I could or couldn't say. When I found out you knew Elizabeth Hawk personally, I thought it was only a matter of time. I was going to be dead anyway. So why not break the rules. When you told me Elizabeth Hawk had been dead for months, I wondered how come the *all-knowing* leaders were not aware of it?"

"You were different than all the other were-animals in several ways. It took you months to finally turn, when it took others only a week or two."

Jackson started pacing the small room. "When you finally changed, the instinct to flee into the woods didn't happen. The electrical current, informing all seekers you were changing was minimal. You changed into a wolf, when everyone else I knew, changed into a member of the cat family."

Jackson sat down, on the bed next to Katie. "Since I got to know you, I didn't have the heart to turn you into a Seeker."

"I was afraid to draw attention to you, so I physically stayed away. I only spoke through my mind. When Sam and Lizzy came over, I watched them closely. I wanted to know which of the girls was related to Elizabeth Hawk, because I figured she would be the next Great White Tiger."

Jackson got up, agitated again. "I was lying on my bed, watching everything through your eyes, when I was roughly pulled off my bed by other Seekers."

Jackson turned his back to her, his shirt melted away into thin air. Katie gave a gasp, when she saw his back. Massive scars crisscrossed his back. Some scars looked older, while others still looked red and tender.

"What happened to you?" she whispered.

“I was punished for not turning you into a Seeker.” Anger vibrated through his voice. “I was tied down while the other Seekers clawed me, until there was no flesh left.”

Jackson turned, a shirt materialized on his body again. “The leaders, or whoever they are, decided they would make an example of me. I’m surprised I survived.”

His lips tightened. “I was locked up in a dark little room. There was very little food and water. My contact with you was the only thing that kept me sane. I would go to school with you, and participate in everything you did. They had no idea I was communicating with you.”

He shook his head. “More proof they are not all-knowing, like they would like us to believe.” “Then everyone felt the stirrings, of another were-animal about to turn.” Jackson got up and started pacing the room again. “You should have seen them.” Jackson gave a dry laugh. “They were still afraid of Old Elizabeth Hawk even in death, or maybe they were afraid of you?”

Jackson looked at her. “The decision was made to send me out, to give me another chance. I recognized Candace Franklin, from school. I was pretty desperate, to change her…” His voice trailed off.

Katie remembered, finding Candace rolling around in the snow. A black panther circling her, intent on something she didn’t know. She had fought Jackson, but he hadn’t actually hurt her.

“I think I know, why The Great White Tiger likes you so much.” Jackson interrupted her thoughts.

Katie blinked, “Why?”

“You have no thought of self-preservation. I repeatedly showed you, I could kill you. You never ran away. You just kept trying. It was only until I realized, you had no intention of quitting. I decided to concede."

Katie was afraid to ask. "What happened to you?"

"I really don't know, how I survived," Jackson said softly. "I wanted to die." The shirt he was wearing disappeared, and he slowly turned. The claw marks and welts were crisscrossed all over his torso. His chest, up around his neck, and down below his waistline. The shirt materialized back onto his frame.

Katie wanted to ask how his shirt kept disappearing and reappearing, but was afraid to get off the subject. "You stopped talking to me. I thought it was because you didn't want to."

Jackson shook his head. "I was unable to do anything."

"What happened when Lizzy changed?"

"Young Elizabeth Hawk. Everyone thought she would be the next Great White Tiger. She had to be stopped at all cost. Of course, our fearless leaders are still too afraid to come here personally," Jackson said sarcastically. "They sent six Seekers with the orders to kill everyone, especially Lizzy Hawk. Of course, I was one of the six. Another chance to prove myself."

Jackson sat down on the bed again. "The plan was to draw you out, and ambush you. Then we would go in, and kill everyone in the cabin. Personally, I thought you were too smart to fall for it. I couldn't believe it when I saw you running up the hill."

"I just acted on instinct." Katie tried to explain herself.

Jackson smiled. "During the full moon, the others, I don't even know what to call them. They have a strong control, over our minds. I don't know how I was able to break loose from them, to warn you. I used the techniques learned in the prison to cover my thoughts. The other

Seekers didn't know how you stopped and turned back to the cabin. They were too afraid, to attack you."

Jackson reached over and grabbed her hand. "Of course, they haven't actually seen you fight. If they had, they would have seen how terrible you are."

"It's not my fault. I don't know how to fight." Katie defended herself.

"To everyone's surprise, someone started shooting a gun." Jackson started chuckling. "Here we are, animals trying to attack a fortress. Someone pulls out a gun, and starts shooting."

"Sam," Katie answered with a sad smile. "She always knew what to do."

Jackson watched her closely before he decided to continue. "Everyone was afraid to go back, because they saw how I had been punished. While they were debating on what to do, you reached out with your mind so everyone could hear.

"Jackson, are you there? What's going on?" He mimicked in a high voice.

Jackson started chuckling again. "That threw everyone into a tizzy. You should have seen them; they were freaking out…Who's Jackson? Is there another were-animal, we don't know about?" He laughed. "Everyone decided to get out of there, fast."

Katie frowned. "How come they didn't recognize your name?"

"Jackson isn't my real name," he quietly explained.

Katie raised her eyebrows.

"When I first contacted you, I was breaking the rules. I didn't want to get caught. It was a good thing too, or..." He looked at her and smiled. "You reaching out, would have been my undoing."

"Were you punished again?" Katie asked softly.

"Not too bad. Since there were six of us who were incompetent, there weren't enough Seekers around to hurt us." Jackson shrugged. "Besides, I figured my way around punishments."

"What do you mean?" Katie asked.

He smiled. "I promise I will explain everything, but you have to be patient. I don't want to get side tracked."

"What is your real name?" she questioned.

Jackson shook his head. "The person I used to be, is dead, Katie. I'm Jackson."

"But..."

"Katie, do you want to hear what happened when Tyler was almost attacked?" He interrupted.

She nodded, indicating to continue.

Jackson sighed. "The leaders over us decided for us to go and grab Tyler before he actually changed. This would ensure, we had control over him."

Jackson put three fingers in the air. "They sent three of their best fighters to do the job."

"There was only one cat out there in the woods." Katie interrupted.

"No, there was only one after I killed a huge saber-toothed tiger," he answered. "Believe me, he was tough. I almost lost." He grabbed her hand. "The only thing that kept me fighting was picturing you trying to fight the beast."

"You were there," she said needlessly.

Jackson nodded. "I was pretty impressed with the debutante. She didn't hesitate, when she went in for the kill."

Katie's eyebrows knitted together. "What do you mean by debutante?"

Jackson gave a startled look. "You don't know?"

"Know what?"

"Candace is related to Tom Franklin, the senator." Jackson retorted. "You know Franklin Industries? They are one the richest families in three states."

"Are you sure?" Katie said disbelievingly.

"Yes, I'm sure. I went to school with her since the eighth grade." Jackson replied. "The BMW she drives must have given you some indication."

"I've seen her car several times," Katie interrupted. "She drives an old Toyota."

Jackson raised his eyebrows, shaking his head.

"Why does she drive an old car around us?" Katie asked

Jackson shrugged, "She probably doesn't want you to know she has money."

"That's ridiculous," Kate stated.

Jackson grinned.

Katie sat for a few minutes, digesting everything Jackson had told her. Her heart pounding in her chest, she finally asked the most important question she wanted answered. "What happened when Sam died?" she asked quietly.

Jackson stood up, his movements jerky. "I didn't want to be a Seeker," he said quietly. "I did not want to be any part of those people." He turned, to face her. "How can a decision I made under stress, control who I am?" Agitated, he ran his fingers through his hair. "I wish, I could relive that day again. I would have attacked Steven, or died fighting.

Instead, I just accepted my fate." He started pacing the small room. "I was desperate to join you and your friends. I was already helping.

"I thought about it in my head so much, it was driving me insane. I wanted to get back to where I was, before I became a Seeker. I knew, no way out." He stopped in front of her. "I was afraid you wouldn't accept me." His words came out softly. "Since I felt your emotions, I knew how much you loved Sam. I came up with this crazy plan... In hindsight, it was incredibly stupid." Jackson walked over leaning against the wall. "I thought, if I turned Sam into a Seeker, then you would accept me."

"What?" Katie asked incredulously.

"I thought, I could change Sam into a Seeker," he repeated. "She would then want to be with you. Since you loved her so much, you would accept her into your group as a Seeker. This would ensure your accepting me." Jackson tried to explain his reasoning.

"I was already accepting you," Katie almost shouted. "I knew you were a Seeker, after Candace. Didn't I still try, and talk to you, follow your directions?" She couldn't believe what she was hearing. "I knew you were helping me. I trusted you completely, Seeker, or not."

"I had to be sure!" He shot back. "I was so desperate, to get out of the situation I was in. I knew it was selfish," Jackson replied.

"What happened?"

"Steven saw me on his turf," Jackson answered. "I listened regularly, to your conversations. I knew you and Candace, were going to try and get to Jackie Oaklin before she turned. I also knew, you were going to be too late. I was afraid of you running into Steven."

Jackson pushed off from the wall and started pacing the small area again. "I was afraid, he might try and take you down. I got too close, and he saw me. Unbeknownst to me, he was suspicious and started following me.

"Usually, the change takes place, on a full or new moon. This time around, the leaders were unprepared. Sam was changing on the day before the full moon. I knew of the change, because I was listening to your conversations."

Jackson sighed, and looked down. "My plan was to get into the cabin, turn Sam into a Seeker then get out." Jackson looked up, his eyes haunted. "Everything was working well. Lizzy was outside, on the back porch. You were away from the cabin. I was crawling in the window..." He paused for a moment. "Steven appears out of nowhere. He knows what I'm about to do. I couldn't come up with a reason he couldn't *tag along*. I didn't have time, and I rushed the process. I gave the ultimatum to Sam before she turned." Jackson stopped, unable to go on.

Katie covered her mouth with her hand. "What happened?" she whispered, afraid she already knew the answer.

Jackson looked up, unable to find the words to explain.

"She chose to die," Katie voiced her fear.

Jackson slowly nodded his head in ascent. "I have never heard of anyone choosing to die. It never crossed my mind she would make that choice." Jackson said in a defeated voice.

Katie nodded, picturing the scene in her head. She wasn't surprised, given Sam's personality, rooted in her strong religious faith. She was never afraid to stand alone. She faced whatever adversity came her way, if her standards were questioned. Katie had always admired Sam for living what she believed. She could see Sam making the decision quickly, unselfishly, knowing her decision would bring about her death.

“I didn’t kill her, Katie. I swear I didn’t kill her.” Jackson's rushed words broke through Katie’s thoughts.

Katie nodded, accepting the truth. “Steven.”

“It was all over, before I could do anything about it…I was so sure, she would accept…I was wondering, what do I do now?... I didn’t expect him to... He moved so fast.” Jackson stopped, unable to go on.

“I saw you fighting,” Katie said softly. “You both broke through the window.”

Jackson turned, his back to her. “He wanted to feed,” he said so softly. Katie was unsure, if she heard correctly.

“What?”

“He wanted to feed,” Jackson said a little louder. “He thought were-animal, would be a tasty treat.”

Unable to say anything, Katie stared at Jackson’s stiff back. Her mind, couldn’t quite comprehend his words.

Jackson eventually turned around. “When I changed, he was an ordinary Seeker like me.” He shook his head. “Now he’s so dark and evil, the leaders welcome him with open arms.” He shook his head, “He has changed his name to Surgious. He will fight with anyone who calls him anything but Surgious. How stupid is that?”

He sat down, next to Katie. “The leaders don’t trust Seekers, but now they completely trust Surgious. He has graduated to another level.”

Katie sat motionless, taking in the information. “The Rangers, have found a body eaten by large animals…” Her voice trailed off.

Jackson nodded. “I can’t be like that, Katie. I don’t want to change.” His voice was pleading. “I’ll do anything. I’m so sorry for Sam. If I could change it, I would...You have no idea, how much I wish I could change things." He knelt down beside her. He grabbed her hands and held them between his own.

"Please, let me join you."

Chapter 28
Letting Go

Katie looked down, fumbling with her fingers. She thought about the night she turned into a wolf. She was so scared and helpless. If a were-animal appeared and gave her an ultimatum like that, what would she have done? She shook her head. She hated to admit it, but she would have said yes to life. She would have become a Seeker like Jackson and joined him.

She thought about Sam, so strong in her beliefs. Everything was always black or white. That was the main reason she never told Sam about Jackson in the first place. She instinctively knew Jackson was a gray area Sam would never accept. She closed her eyes, her friend's face appearing in her mind. Even now, she could picture Sam in a disapproving stance. She would tell her to stay away from evil, even the appearance of evil.

Sam was dead.

The ache in her chest intensified. She would never get the chance to try and persuade her of Jackson's plight.

It was just her, Katie, making the decision. She knew what her answer would be. Jackson in her life seemed right. When she thought, he had betrayed her, she was lost. He had helped her through so much. Glancing up, she realized he had gotten up and was once again leaning up against the wall. He was trying not to show any emotion, but it was vibrating throughout his body.

She took a deep breath. "Jackson, you have my vote."

Making a loud whooping sound, he gathered her up and twirled her around. Both of them laughed as he placed her on the floor. "You won't regret this, I promise."

"It's going to be hard to convince the others," she said cautiously.

"You're their leader," Jackson answered cheerfully. "I know you can convince them."

"I'm not the leader," Katie stressed. "Sam was the leader."

"No way!" Jackson laughed confidently. "I listen to all your conversations regularly."

"You didn't listen very closely..." Katie tried to stress again. "Sam was always the natural leader. I always looked to her and enforced what she said."

Jackson stopped and looked intently at her. "What are you trying to tell me?" he asked quietly.

"I saw the spirit of The Great White Tiger leave her, when she died," Katie explained. "She was supposed to be our leader."

Deflated, Jackson sat down on the bed. "Sam, was The Great White Tiger?" he asked, not really wanting an answer. "Are you thinking, The Great White Tiger may not accept me?"

Katie sat watching Jackson as different emotions flitted across his face.

Jackson shook his head in confusion. "Do you know how I found you?"

Katie shrugged. "I just assumed…" her voice trailed off. "How did you find me?"

"I heard a noise outside. I came out to investigate. The Great White Tiger, was standing about fifty yards off. As soon as it saw me, it turned and ran. I followed, and then I found you."

Jackson got up and started pacing. "The tiger could have gone to anyone on your team, but she came to me to save you. There must be a reason, Katie." He grabbed her arms. "The tiger wanted me, to save you. Can you see that?"

Katie nodded quietly.

"This is important. I can feel it," Jackson said excitedly. "I just have to figure it out."

Katie looked around feeling exhausted. "How long ago was the accident?"

Jackson glanced over. "Four days ago," he said distractedly.

"WHAT?" Horrified, Katie covered her mouth with her hand.

"Oh No! My Mom!" She glanced around the small room. "I have to get out of here! My mom is going to be so upset."

"Are you sure, you want to leave?"

Katie turned frantic to get out of the small cabin. "My mom will be so upset." Realizing what he asked, she turned to face him. "Jackson, I have to go."

"I know," he shrugged. "It was just nice, having someone else around."

"Things are going to be different, Jackson. You're not going to be alone for very much longer," Katie assured him. She looked around the small room. "Do I have any of my stuff here?"

"No," Jackson answered. "I could only carry you."

Realizing how he must have struggled to save her. Katie reached out and hugged him "Thank you, Jackson. I owe you my life."

Jackson felt stiff in her arms for a moment, before wrapping his arms around her, and holding her tight. "You don't have to thank me, Katie. I would do anything for you."

When he released her, she stepped back. "How do I get home?"

"The easiest way, is for you to change."

"I can't change, I've tried," Katie wailed. "I don't know what's wrong with me."

Jackson studied her for a moment. "I have a pretty good guess."

Katie stopped eyeing him closely, she folded her arms waiting patiently for him to continue.

Jackson leaned back against the wall, in his usual spot. "The emotions, you've been carrying around with you. The spirit animal does not know how to handle them. In fact, I believe they are slowly destroying the spirit inside of you."

"I don't understand."

"Betrayal, guilt, grief, anger, and self-hatred," Jackson ticked them off with his fingers. "What does a spirit animal know about any of them, Katie. When grief envelopes your soul, it incapacitates me. I'm miles away from you. How can the wolf inside of you, handle it?"

Katie sat back down on the bed. "I don't understand. How does it incapacitate you?"

"There have been times, when I was in panther form. Without any warning at all, I felt a grief so intense, I could not hold my animal form. I turned human." He shook his head. "It was pretty uncomfortable, until I could figure out how to keep warm despite your emotions."

"I cannot control how I feel," Katie rushed out angrily.

"Yes you can, Katie," Jackson said quietly. "You can't stamp feelings into submission as you've been doing, because they will come out unexpectedly and swamp you."

"I don't know how to do anything else," she said quietly.

Jackson pushed off the wall and came closer. "I don't think you have cried." He was looking into her eyes. "I would have felt the release, Katie. The emotions build up to a point, and then you crush them into submission. You need to let go." He touched her cheek. "When the emotions come on, let them wash over you, so you can release them. The wolf inside of you will then be able to recover and protect you better."

Katie could feel the knot in her chest, rising to her throat. Looking into Jackson's eye's, she almost let it happen. A reflex, she didn't know she possessed grabbed the knot, and jammed it back into her chest where it burned.

Jackson turned, but not before she saw the disappointment in his eyes. "I'm trying, Jackson," she pleaded.

Nodding, he kept his eyes averted. Grabbing his coat, he gave it to her. "We've got a long slow walk, ahead of us. I suggest we get going."

Jackson wasn't kidding, about the long walk. It took three hours, before they came upon a small rutted road. Most of the way, she stumbled and slid, on the muddy terrain. She would have fallen several times, if Jackson hadn't been there to grab her. She was exhausted by the time they came to the road. It took a while, for her to notice a camouflaged Hummer. It was parked, blocking everything in its path. Relieved, she didn't have to walk anymore, Jackson helped her into the large vehicle. Katie closed her eyes and was fast asleep within minutes.

Jackson gently shook her awake. Opening her eyes, she realized she was in her driveway. Slowly rising, she looked around. She stumbled out of the vehicle, but Jackson was there to help her up the drive. She was so tired, she stood there for a few moments, not really knowing what she should do, Jackson reached over and knocked on the front door.

Her mother opened the door, and let out a scream. She vaguely registered her mother was crying and laughing, at the same time. She dumbly watched, as Jackson was enveloped in a bear hug. It wasn't long before her mother had her back in a car racing to the hospital. She tried to tell her mother she was fine, but she was just too tired to care. Closing her eyes, she let sleep claim her once more.

The next several hours were a blur. She got so tired of questions being thrown at her, she stopped talking altogether. Ignoring everyone, she closed her eyes and tried to sleep. Eventually, she was placed in a hospital room for observation. She wanted to bite a nurse's head off, when she was woken up to take a sleeping pill.

Katie opened her eyes. Looking around, she realized she was still in a hospital room. Her mother was asleep in a chair, next to her bed. Reaching out, she touched her mother's hand. She watched her mother, slowly open her eyes.

"I am so sorry! The car, I think it's totaled. I was driving too fast. I lost control."

Her mother's smile trembled with emotion. "I thought I lost you..." Her mother covered her hand. "I don't care about the car. I wish I never bought it."

"You know about the wreck?"

Her mother nodded, her frame shaking. "I was frantic, when you didn't come home. I started calling all your friends. David told me what transpired in front of the Diner. He said you drove out of the parking lot and almost lost control then. He told the sheriff what road you took."

Her voice trembled. "It didn't take long, for the sheriff to find your car."

Her mother stopped, to compose herself. "He said, there was no way you could have survived the crash. They had search teams looking all over, trying to find your body."

Her mother paused, tears spilling onto her cheeks. "I didn't know why the Rangers, were called on the scene. I called Forrest. He told me several different large animal tracks, were found around your car. One had drag marks, where they think you were carried away. They started hunting, trying to find what was left."

Katie sat horrified as she realized what her mother went through. "I'm so sorry, Mom. I'm so sorry!"

She got off the bed and embraced her mother. She felt her mom give in to her emotions. Sitting back, she watched the tears roll down her mother's cheeks. When was the last time she cried? She reached up and touched her dry eyes. Why couldn't she cry?

Katie looked up when she heard the door open. Sheriff Tate came walking into the room. Letting go of her mother, she faced the sheriff. *How long is this going to take*, she wondered to herself. Defiantly, she folded her arms and eyed the sheriff wearily. Every question he asked was met with complete silence. Her mother tried to get her to answer. She turned to her mom, softly patting her hand, but would not say a single word.

Katie watched the sheriff get up, frustration and anger in his features. She watched him pull out a small book, and started filling it out. She couldn't believe it when he handed her a citation. She wondered vaguely, how much it was going to cost her. She thanked him sarcastically. Her mother, giving her a warning look, followed him out.

She got up and started looking around, for her clothes. Finding them, she was completely disgusted by how much blood and mud was caked all over them. She promptly threw them in the trash. She looked around, for something else to wear. She was delighted, when Jackson walked in holding a shopping bag.

"I thought you might want some clothes," he said casually.

Smiling, she grabbed the bag. "Thanks".

"I would have been here sooner, but I saw you had company."

Smiling, she headed for the bathroom, "Yeah."

"What did you say to him?" Jackson asked casually, referring to the sheriff.

"Nothing."

"What kind of nothing?" Jackson asked.

"I mean, I didn't say anything at all to him."

Jackson cocked his head and smiled. "So you took the fifth amendment to a whole new level."

Chuckling, she shut the door in Jackson's face. She then showered and changed. Coming out of the bathroom, she paused when she saw her mother eyeing Jackson warily.

"How did you say you found Katie?" her mother was asking, in a too-sweet of a voice.

Jackson folded his arms and leaned up against the wall. Katie could tell he was trying to figure out what to say. He didn't want to offend her mother, but he also did not want to answer any questions. She wished she could communicate to him with her thoughts.

Walking into the room, she distracted her mother enough, to watch Jackson slip out of the room. "I'm ready," she announced.

"Ready for what?" her mother asked cautiously.

"To go home."

She could see her mother, start shaking her head. Before her mom started talking about doctor's orders, she decided she needed to take control of the situation.

"Mom, I'm fine. All the tests came back fine, didn't they?" She didn't want to play her ace, but her mom kept insisting she stay in the hospital. Finally, getting tired of the argument she played it. "I'll just get Jackson to take me home. I'm sure he's just outside the door."

Her mother frowned, argued a little longer, but fifteen minutes later, Katie was in the car on her way home. Pulling into the drive, her mother had to go around the large Hummer. Katie casually looked around for Jackson. He didn't seem to be around. Walking up the drive, she saw a note on the door.

Keep the Hummer as long as you want. I hope it keeps you safe.

Jackson

Her mother read the note, her frown deepening. Katie wasn't surprised, when her mother turned to face her. "Who is this Jackson? How long have you known him?"

"Mom, I know you're worried, but Jackson is my friend," she tried to explain.

"Who gives someone an expensive car like that?" her mother demanded.

"He didn't give it to me. He's just letting me use it. I'm sure he'll ask for it back in a couple of days," Katie replied.

Her mother sighed, and rubbed her eyes. Katie could see she was exhausted. Walking over to her, she gave her another hug. "Mom you're exhausted. Go to bed. I'm sure things will not look so bad once you have some rest."

Katie could tell how tired her mother really was when she nodded and walked back to her room. She sat down and waited patiently for her to fall into a sound sleep. An idea had been forming ever since her mother's emotional release in the hospital. Glancing up at the clock, she saw it was past 10:00 am.

Katie quietly left the house and got into the Hummer, starting the vehicle. The engine purred softly. She drove the familiar route, she had taken hundreds of times. Pulling into the driveway of the Black home, she wasn't surprised, when it appeared empty.

Sunday morning meant every member of the Black family was at church. Getting out of the vehicle she paused. She could imagine Sam opening the front door, bouncing down the steps to greet her. The memory created an ache in her chest.

Getting out of the vehicle, she stood for a moment. She relived hundreds of little moments. She loved this house and the people who made it such a loving home. She slowly walked up the steps and opened the screen door. Reaching down, she felt the knob, as always unlocked. The old familiar scents of her favorite hangout drifted out. Stepping into the living room, she saw the walls covered with pictures of the Black family in various ages. She stepped into the kitchen. The table was littered with empty bowls of cereal, the gallon of milk, sitting on the table. She could imagine Mrs. Black scolding the kids for leaving the milk out again. Walking over she grabbed the gallon, opened the fridge, and placed it on the rack.

She turned back around. There were the stairs, leading to Sam's room right in front of her. Walking up the steps, she paused before slowly pushing the door open. She didn't know what she expected, but it came as a shock, for the room to be exactly the way Sam had left it. The bed was unmade, as if Sam had just gotten up that morning. A sweater was tossed on the floor. A book bag was dumped in the corner, with books and folders strung out as if she was in a hurry.

Katie slowly drifted into the room. Reaching down, she picked up the sweater. Rubbing it with her fingers, she sat down on the bed. Lifting it up to her face, she could still smell Sam's essence. The hard knot in her chest lifted to her throat.

Trying not to fight the feeling, she slowly glanced up. He was standing in the doorway, watching her intently, dressed in a white shirt and tie. She always thought David handsome in his Sunday clothes. She looked down at the sweater, the knot still lodged in her throat. Unable to stop herself, she lifted the sweater again to her face. The moment she smelled Sam, tears welled up in her eyes. "I miss her," she forced through her tight throat. "I miss her so much, it hurts."

Tears glistened in her eyes. She looked up, her eyes so blurry, she barely could make out David's face. He reached out to touch her. The moment his fingers touched her cheek, the damn broke inside of her. Tears came in a torrent.

David took a couple of steps closer. He reached his arms around her, holding her tight. Unable to stop the raw emotion engulfing her, she cried for her best friend, who would never grow old, the missed opportunity of a courageous spirit, the complete waste of a beautiful person.

"I need her in my life." She cried in anguish. "She was my anchor. I don't know how, to go on without her."

David quietly held her, until her emotions were finally spent. Getting up he left the room, coming back he handed her a box of tissues. Her eyes felt gritty, as she quickly blew her nose. Sitting back down on the bed, he leaned up against the headboard. He pulled her down, to lie next to him.

He softly stroked her hair. "It's not your fault. Nobody blames you, Katie."

She shook her head, automatically denying his words. "I could have-"

"It's not your fault." He interrupted her. "She wouldn't have wanted you to take the blame this way, Katie."

Katie thought of her friend. Her thoughts tried to shy away from the hurt, as a picture of her friend appeared in her mind. She imagined Sam telling her off like she did after the disastrous basketball game.

"I no longer have her around, to tell me what's right." The tears close to the surface started spilling over again. "I wish it were me."

David's arms tightened around her. "We just went through almost losing you, Katie. I thought I had lost you too. I.." He stopped talking and held her tightly. "I can't lose you too, Katie. There's only so much..." He stopped took a couple of swallows. "Promise me, you won't do anything like that again."

"I'm sorry. I wasn't thinking," Katie tried to explain.

David touched his finger to her lips. "No more apologies, Katie. I need promises and smarter actions."

He reminded her so much of Sam. Tears again slid down her cheeks. "I promise," she said hoarsely.

David snuggled down and got a little more comfortable. "Do you know what I regretted most, when I thought you were... no longer going to be around?"

"No."

"I never asked you out."

"What?" She pulled away from him.

He pulled her back down beside him. "I knew you liked me," he stated in an honest, direct way she always associated with the Black family.

Katie buried her heated face into his chest.

"When you stopped coming around, I missed you. I discussed it with Sam, what I could do to make you more relaxed around me." He shrugged. "She told me to just stay away from you until you felt more comfortable. It seemed to take an incredible amount of time. So, I have decided to take matters into my own hands."

He twined her hands with his. "Now, I have a second chance. Would you go to Prom with me?"

"Prom?" Surprised Katie lifted her head, and stared at him, dumbfounded.

"Yes," he said with a smile. "I know it's a little early, but I have to ask before someone jumps in before me."

A warm glow enveloped her. Nodding her acceptance, she laid her head on his chest. For the first time in months, Katie was finally at peace. Katie closed her eyes and felt content.

David continued to stroke her hair. "How did Sam die, Katie?"

Shock jolted through her body. Jumping up, she eyed David suspiciously. "Were you just really nice to me, because you wanted to... to know how she died?" She stumbled over the words.

Frustration and annoyance danced crossed David's face. "I have a right to know how my sister died, Katie." He jumped off the bed, facing her. "I was not just being nice to get information from you."

Still suspicious, Katie folded her arms defensively.

Frustrated, David rubbed his fingers through his hair, reminding her of Jackson. "I have always cared about you. Even when you were a snot-nosed five-year-old, running around here like you owned the place, I was nice to you."

"That's because your mom said you had to, or you would be grounded." Katie shot back. "I overheard the conversation."

David raised his eyebrows. "You heard that, huh." He sat back down on the bed. His shoulders hunched over in defeat.

"Nobody comes in here," he said softly. "Everything's different. My mom cries all the time. My dad, never speaks at all."

Katie lowered her head and stared at the floor.

"Sheriff Tate thinks you all were at the cabin having a big party."

Shocked, Katie quickly looked up, with denial on her lips.

"My parents, are all thinking the worst. Since nobody is willing to say what they were actually doing there, that is confirmation."

"You know Sam, David." Katie interrupted. "She wouldn't have put up with any of that."

"Yeah, I know, but I see no plausible reason for you to be there either."

Feeling cornered, Katie felt the urge to flee. "I got to go." Turning quickly, she reached for the door handle.

David moved so fast. She didn't realize, he was directly behind her, until his arms wrapped around her tightly. "Don't leave, unless you promise to come back."

She leaned back her head against his chest, reveling in his touch. She didn't want to deny him anything.

"I promise," she whispered.

"I'm sorry if I pushed too hard, Katie. There is going to have to be a time when we are told what exactly happened. You do see that don't you?"

Katie bowed her head, not really wanting to leave, but not wanting to tell him anything either.

With a sigh, David let her go. "I'll walk you outside."

David opened the front door, allowed Katie to walk out first. Smiling at his gentlemanly behavior, she hadn't noticed the dark figure leaning up against the Hummer. David and Katie saw Jackson, at the same time. She stopped in surprise, while David stepped forward. His hand outstretched.

"Jared isn't it?"

Jackson sauntered closer, ignoring the outstretched hand. His eyes had a devil may care attitude, that rubbed Katie the wrong way. Fearing what he may do in front of David, she stepped in between the two. "Jackson, I'd like you to meet Sam's older brother, David."

Jackson's attitude immediately changed. A haunted look entered into his eyes, as he looked back at the Black home. Katie knew David was too intelligent, not to notice the change.

"You knew my sister?"

Agitated, Jackson rubbed his fingers through his hair. "Yes." Turning, he started walking back towards the Hummer.

David followed close behind. "Were you there, when she was killed?"

Jackson opened the door of the Hummer. "Yes," he said quietly.

"Was it a random animal attack?" David asked relentlessly.

Jackson walked back, grabbed Katie by the hand, and pulled her mercilessly towards the vehicle. When she tried to climb in, her aching muscles protested. He picked her up unceremoniously and threw her into the passenger seat.

"No."

Katie struggled to right herself, as her legs dangled outside precariously.

"Was it an accident?"

"No."

Jackson quickly walked to the driver's side and opened the door.

"Was she murdered?"

"Yes!"

Climbing up, Jackson slammed the door. He jammed it into gear and backed away. Katie turned to see David's white, stormy face disappear as they drove out of sight.

Chapter 29
A New Member

Jackson drove, in controlled silence. Katie kept glancing towards his face, trying to gauge his emotions. When they were a mile from her home, Jackson pulled over and shut off the engine. He sat there for a couple of moments, not saying anything. She waited patiently, quietly watching him.

He reached out for her hand, and intertwined his fingers with hers. "That was some release," he said quietly. "I know you feel better. I can feel it."

Her emotions were so close to the surface, tears immediately filled her eyes and started spilling down her cheeks. "I'm sorry. I'm turning into such a cry baby."

Jackson shook his head. "You had too much emotion bottled up, Katie. You needed to let go. I just wish…"

He stopped talking and looked out the windshield. "I'm just glad you were able to get it out." He said finally. Looking towards her, he smiled reassuringly at her. She was watching him so closely. She noticed his eyes darken, his features turning into a concentrated frown.

"What is it? What's wrong?"

"Everyone is all coming to your house. I have been listening to their conversations, all morning. I was afraid, if you took too much longer in the… in there." He stumbled over the words. "I was going to have to come in, and get you." He shook his head. "Of course, I didn't know it was Sam's house…" his voice trailed off.

"Why is everyone coming to my house?" She said, trying to stay on track.

Jackson frowned. "They want to hear what happened to you, and…." He stopped again, his face in concentration.

"What is it?" she asked softly.

Jackson looked at her apprehensively, "Lizzy seems to think….." he paused for a moment. "Not only is she the leader, but she can kick you out."

"What? No way!" Katie shook her head, laughing a little nervously. She looked back at Jackson, hoping he was joking. "Lizzy's my friend. She wouldn't do that to me."

"She's tasted power, Katie. She wants more," Jackson said. "The other two have not really commented one way or the other. That makes me believe, they are still loyal to you. Or, they both want to wait and see how you react, before they decide. I'm not sure." Jackson tapped his fingers, on the steering wheel. "You may have to fight her, to show who's the Alfa in the pack."

"What?" Katie shook her head in surprise. "I'm not physically fighting my friend, to show who's going to be the dominant leader."

"That's how it works, Katie."

"Yea well, I think we have evolved a little." Katie couldn't believe where this conversation was heading. "We may be animals and have an animal spirit inside us, but I believe we can talk things out."

"Is that how we're going to fight the evil that is threatening us, by talking?" Jackson shot back sarcastically.

"No. I just mean, I believe I can talk reasonably with Lizzy."

Jackson looked out the windshield. "Maybe it's not such a good idea to let them know I'm a Seeker."

Katie thought about it for a while. She shook her head. "No, I think we need to be up front, with everyone. Not telling them, and they've find out another way looks like we are intentionally being deceitful."

"We can tell them," Jackson said persuasively. "Just not today, when the situation is a little dicey."

"No, Jackson," Katie said. "We have to tell them everything. Lay all the cards on the table, then they can decide what they want to do."

"What if they won't accept me?"

"Then we will be a pack of two," Katie stated.

A slow smile spread on Jackson's face. "You won't abandon me, huh."

Katie smiled back, "No, I won't abandon you."

Jackson started the vehicle. "Let's go face the music. They should be at your house by now."

Spotting her house, she straightened up. Sure enough, Lizzy and Candace's cars were parked in the driveway.

Jackson pulled in front of the house. "How are you going to tell them?" he asked nervously.

"I'm not sure. I'll just see how it goes."

Katie got out of the car and walked towards her house.

Jackson followed, cautiously behind. "They know you're here," Jackson said quietly. "They're not sure who I am, and trying to gauge if you know anything."

Katie turned and started walking around the back of the house. "Tell them, I'll meet them out back in the woods."

Jackson let out a chuckle. "Now they're completely freaked out."

"Jackson, I want you to promise me you won't hurt them."

"What do you plan to do?" Jackson asked wearily.

"I'm not sure yet," she said quietly. "I just don't want anyone to get hurt."

"I don't see you, extracting a promise out of them."

"I know you can take care of yourself," Katie answered heatedly. "You could seriously hurt one of them, and I don't want that happening."

Jackson sighed. "Whatever, Katie. You have my promise."

Katie entered the woods. She walked until she reached a small clearing. Sitting down on a fallen tree, she waited. Jackson sat down beside her. "Are they coming?"

"I'm not sure. They stopped speaking, thru their thoughts."

Katie heard a branch snap. Looking in that direction, she could see three figures walking slowly towards them. She quickly looked towards Jackson, his features had turned into stone. Tyler was walking ahead of Lizzy. Candace was quite a distance back, following slowly behind. Entering the clearing, Tyler gave Katie a quick smile. His features became unreadable, as Lizzy entered the small area.

Katie waited until Candace was in the clearing. Casually she got up, and smiled at all three of them.

"I'm glad you could all make it," she said warmly, pretending she was the one who called the meeting. "First off, I would like to apologize for the theatrics in front of the diner. I shouldn't have spouted off like that. Lizzy, I am truly sorry."

Lizzy folded her arms, her mouth twisted into a pout.

Katie could feel a pressure in her mind. "I believe I have already told you this, but if you're trying to speak to me with your mind, I cannot hear you. I somehow turned it off when Sam died. I don't know how to turn it back on."

Lizzy looked triumphantly at Katie, her smile deepening maliciously. Katie quickly glanced over at, Jackson.

"She's pointing out why you should no longer be the leader, because you can't speak through your thoughts," Jackson said under his breath.

Lizzy looked at Jackson.

Katie felt that familiar pressure in her mind. Her eyes kept darting from Lizzy, to Tyler, to Candace, and then back to Jackson.

Jackson shrugged. "If you want to talk to me, you're going to have to speak out loud, so Katie can hear."

Again, she felt the strong pressure in her mind. She glanced back at Jackson. He was looking directly at Lizzy, not making a single sound.

"FINE!" Lizzy burst out "We'll have it your way. Who are you?"

Jackson smiled. He turned towards Katie, gesturing for her to continue.

"This is my friend, Jackson," Katie said formally. "We've been friends, for several months now. He has helped me and all of you a great deal." She paused, not knowing how to continue. She glanced back at Jackson, his head shook imperceptibly. Ignoring his gesture, she turned back to her friends.

"Jackson is a Seeker," she rushed out. "He was there when Sam died."

Katie quickly glanced back at Jackson. He shot her an *Are you kidding me?* look. Giving him a shrug, she glanced back towards her friends. It took about 30-seconds, for the information to sink into their consciousness. The change from human to cats was instantaneous. Katie jumped out of the way, as three snarling large cats attacked Jackson at once.

Slamming to the ground, Katie turned over just in time to see Jackson pull the coolest move she had ever seen. He jumped about fifteen feet in the air, did a black flip during the rotation, and turned into panther form. Coming down, he landed ten feet from the others. She watched, unable to take her eyes off him. He maneuvered around her three friends, everyone intent on killing him. He merely pushed, scratched, and eluded them. Finally deciding he had enough, bands came out of nowhere. They wrapped around the cat's legs, hog-tying them together.

Katie got up and brushed off dirt and leaves from her pants. Her friends, unable to do anything else, were snarling and spitting towards her and Jackson. Walking towards the panther, she folded her arms waiting for the loud snarling to dissipate. She felt pressure, against her mind again. Shaking her head, she glanced back towards the panther.

"What are they saying?"

Jackson turned into a human.

Katie watched in fascination as hair receded, clothes appeared covering his body. "You have got to teach me, how you do that."

Jackson gave her a cocky smile "They are calling you a traitor," he said, referring back to the snarling cats.

Katie looked down. Candace and Tyler were lying quietly watching the exchange, between her and Jackson. Lizzy was still snarling, fighting against the binding.

Jackson shook his head. "The more you struggle, the tighter the ropes will become."

The snarling became louder.

Jackson gave a tut-tut sound, through his teeth. "Does your momma, know you use those words?"

Lizzy kept spitting and snarling.

Katie waited patiently, until Lizzy finally calmed down. "Are they in pain?" she asked Jackson. She remembered, how the binding had cut into her wrists.

"Lizzy is uncomfortable," Jackson answered.

"Loosen them, will you?"

Jackson nodded.

Looking back towards her friends she leaned back and started telling them everything. She left nothing out, as she explained her friendship with Jackson. How he had helped them survive attacks, and eventually how Sam died. She told them about the accident, how Jackson had come to her rescue. When she was finished, she looked towards her friends. Tyler and Candace were no longer in bindings. They were in a relaxed position, watching her intently. Lizzy was still bound, her eyes refusing to meet Katie's.

She glanced towards Jackson, giving him a questioning look. He shrugged. "I can't tell how she feels about anything." He said softly. "She's still tied up, just to be safe."

"Go ahead, and let her go."

Jackson shook his head, "I'm not sure that's a good idea."

"Jackson, let her go."

Jackson eyed her wearily, then shrugged his body tense. Katie looked towards Lizzy, expectantly. As soon as the binds disappeared the cheetah jumped up, and lunged for Katie. A black blur jumped in front of her, blocking the cheetah. Katie jumped up in time, to see the panther on top of Lizzy.

"Jackson no. Stop!" she pleaded.

Glancing towards the other two cats, she could see they were again tied up.

She could tell Jackson was speaking to Lizzy. Frustration warred inside of her. She wanted desperately to know what he was saying to her. Slowly the panther got off the cheetah, and walked back to her side. Turning into human form, he eyed the other two large cats their bindings now gone.

Katie leaned towards him, "What did you say to her?"

Jackson shook his head, eyeing the cheetah.

She could tell she wasn't going to get anything else from him. Turning back towards her friends, she sighed.

"We need Jackson on our team, guys. He has just demonstrated, quite effectively I might add, how he can beat us in a fight. I know you don't know him and are afraid to trust him. I'm asking for you to trust me until you do get to know him. I'm not going to force this issue. If you will not accept Jackson, then that's fine. We'll just go off, and be a pack without you. I just want to stress, there is a great evil out there that we are going to have to fight against. It's better for us to be together than apart."

Katie got down on her haunches, so she could look directly into the eyes of her friends. She noticed, Lizzy still refused to look her in the eye. "I want you to vote. If you're willing for Jackson to be on our team, cross over, and stand next to us. If not, stay where you are."

"Tyler," she said, facing the African lion. "You don't get to vote for whatever Lizzy wants. You need to step up to the plate, and make the decision on your own."

Standing up, she stepped back next to Jackson. For a moment, nobody moved. Katie felt her heart sink, when the seconds ticked by. Then the snow leopard stood up gracefully and stepped next to Katie. Turning, she watched the other two cats. The African lion started swinging its head between the cheetah, and Katie. Eventually, it stood up and sat next to the snow leopard.

Katie watched the proud cheetah, as she struggled. She desperately wanted to put her arms around her friend and tell her, how much she cared for her. She almost took a step towards her. Jackson anticipating her move, quickly grabbed her hand. She glanced towards him. He shook his head, in a small discernible move. She turned her head quietly, watching Lizzy.

Eventually, the cheetah got up, took a couple of steps forward, then sat back down.

"Was that a yes or a no?" Katie blurted out, unable to stand it anymore.

Jackson arched his eyebrows, "Yes."

Katie whooped for joy, jumped over, and hugged the cheetah. She could tell Lizzy was stiff in her arms, but she knew it wouldn't take them long to be good friends again. Running over, she gave the other two cats a warm hug. Laughing and crying she jumped up and embraced Jackson. He picked her up and turned her around smiling at her antics.

Jackson looked down at the cats and smiled. "Candace wants to know if you could go to her car, and get her backpack. She wants to change into human form."

"Oh yeah, no problem, I'll be back in a minute." Hurrying away, Katie ran to get the items.

Katie stood next to Jackson, while the rest of the team was changing into their clothes.

Candace emerged from the bushes first. “I want to know how you can change into human form with clothes on,” she demanded.

Jackson smiled. “Hello to you too, Candace.”

“Hello,” she mimicked in a too sweet voice. “Jackson isn’t it,” she said sarcastically.

“Yes, that’s right,” he shot back.

Candace placed her hands, on her hips. “Are you going to tell us or not. After all, you are now a member of the team. Are you not? Share and share alike, Jackson.” Every time she said the name Jackson, she would emphasize the word, in a disbelieving voice.

Katie raised her eyebrows, questioningly.

Jackson glanced towards her, chuckling.

“She knows my real name,” he said indicating Candace.

“Ah,” Katie nodded in understanding. “David called you Jared.”

Jackson frowned. “My name is Jackson.” He said it loud enough for only Katie and Candace to hear. “My family would be in grave danger if my real name was ever connected to me.”

Candace frowned, nodding in agreement. “I’m sorry Jar… I mean Jackson. I didn’t know.”

Jackson watched Candace closely and stuck out his hand to her. “Thanks, Candace I-”

“Well great leader,” Lizzy said sarcastically. “Where do we go from here?”

Candace's head shot up, giving Katie a warning look. Katie didn't understand, what Candace was trying to say. Instead, she smiled at Lizzy, including her and Tyler into their group.

"I've been thinking about several things. If you guys are willing to listen, and I can get your ideas and input I'd appreciate it."

Lizzy snorted and folded her arms defensively.

Katie glanced around, the rest of the team was listening attentively. She decided to ignore Lizzy, and continue. "There are a number of things, Jackson needs to teach us. First, how we can fight effectively."

She started ticking them off, with her fingers. "Second, how the heck does he change into human form, and still wear clothes? Third, how is he able to tie us up?" Everyone nodded in agreement. Katie could see, that Lizzy was even interested. "Fourth, we need to set up a time and place to meet."

Katie looked around the group, "Does anyone have any ideas?"

"What's wrong with the cabin?" Lizzy asked.

Katie shook her head. "Too many bad memories. I'm not sure, I'll ever be able to go back there."

Everyone nodded in agreement.

Katie glanced at Candace, who was looking down at her feet. She saw the small shake of her head, before she noticed Jackson's eyebrows rise questioningly.

What was that all about? she wondered.

She decided to move on. "I would like to work after school and weekends. I know everyone has sports, and other activities." She tried to forestall any complaints. "We don't have to meet all at once. In fact, Jackson may be able to teach better, if it's one on one."

Katie looked around the group, satisfied with their response. She turned towards Jackson. “Could you tell us how you are able to wear clothes?”

Jackson cocked his head to one side and smiled. “I’m not wearing any clothes.”

“Yes, you are.” She reached out and touched his sleeve. She rubbed the fabric between her forefinger and thumb.

“I’m projecting an image.”

“This isn’t an image. I can feel the fabric in my hand,” Katie demanded.

“It’s an image all the same,” Jackson repeated.

Candace reached over and rubbed the shirt with her fingers. “How is that possible?”

Jackson shrugged. “If the mind believes it’s real, who am I to tell you otherwise?”

“What about those ropes you tied us up with?” Lizzy snarled.

“What about them?” Jackson said cautiously.

“Are you going to tell us they were not real either?”

“Yes, that’s exactly what I’m saying.” Jackson shrugged. “Your mind thought you were tied up. Therefore, you were.”

“The bindings actually hurt,” Katie blurted out. “That was in my mind too?”

“Wait a minute,” Candace interrupted. “When were you tied up?” she demanded.

“You don’t think I quietly listened to him, after I saw him jump out the window when Sam died do you?” Katie retorted.

Candace nodded, giving her an understanding look.

“Is this like the daydream, Lizzy had in class?”

Everyone looked towards Tyler, surprised he said anything.

"What daydream?" Jackson asked.

Much to Lizzy's annoyance, Katie described Lizzy's daydream during English class. Jackson listened carefully, nodding in understanding. "I believe it goes along the same idea. Except, to be able to portray it in such detail, in such a large area, is truly a unique gift." He turned to Lizzy. "You need to work on it, so you can create any circumstances you want on demand."

"I don't know how I did it, in the first place," Lizzy said awkwardly.

"Don't you think that's how I figured out how to do what I can do?" Jackson replied. "It happened by accident. I figured out what I did to make it happen, so I could do it again."

Everyone sat there deep in thought for a couple of minutes.

"I must warn you. There are people out there who don't have the gene or whatever it is, to be able to see." Jackson said cautiously. "I found that out the hard way. I walked into a convenient store, to pay for gas. The attendant asked me, why the hell wasn't I wearing any clothes? It was 10 degrees outside."

Katie started laughing, at the picture in her mind. Looking at Jackson's dubious expression, made her laugh even harder. Soon, Candace and Tyler joined in. She looked towards Lizzy, who had an odd smile on her face. It felt good to laugh.

"Come on let's go home," Katie said, still chuckling.

"Can I talk to you in private?" Candace asked quietly.

"Sure." Giving Jackson, and the others a small wave. She waited until they were completely alone, before she turned to Candace.

"I just wanted you to know I did not go along with Lizzy's plans," Candace burst out. "I didn't agree with it from the start. I wanted to warn you, I just didn't know how..."

"Hey, it's all right," Katie said reassuringly.

Candace looked down. "I wanted to thank you," she said quietly. "For fighting for me...."

Katie didn't understand what she was talking about.

"I seem to remember two large animals fighting around me, when I was changing. I blocked it out I guess. If I was faced with the same decision as Jar... Jackson, I probably would have chosen the same thing," Candace said softly.

"Me too," Katie agreed.

"Did he happen to tell you anything about me?"

Katie carefully studied Candace, she was still looking down, her expression hidden. "He told me you are from a powerful family, with lots of money."

Candace looked up, her eyes filled with tears. "I was hoping he-" She stopped in mid-sentence and shook her head.

"I don't understand," Katie said surprised.

"My family's money does not define who I am." Candace interrupted vehemently.

Katie waited patiently, for Candace to continue.

"I wanted you to like me, for me." Candace sat down on the log, her shoulders slumped. "Now I don't get the chance to really know."

Bewildered, Katie sat down next to Candace. "I had a good idea you had more money than we had when you gave us all those clothes," Katie explained. "For your information, that normally doesn't happen around here."

"I couldn't help it." Candace gave a shaky smile. "You guys kept wearing the same thing over, and over again. Each time you *changed,* your wardrobe was getting smaller and smaller. I was beginning to think, you only had two pairs of pants left."

Katie reached around and put her arm around Candace. "I do consider you my friend... Despite the annoying fact that you have beautiful blond hair, eye's the color of the sky, you're incredibly smart, you can beat me at sports, and now you're rich. What's not to like? Have I missed anything?"

"I'm loyal," Candace said softly.

Katie nodded. "Loyalty is good."

"Since you know I have money, there's no reason to not tell you, we have a hunting lodge with extensive grounds about 20 miles from here," Candace said casually.

"You have a hunting lodge, with extensive grounds?" Katie repeated dumbly.

Candace waited patiently, watching the words sink into Katie's consciousness.

"You have a hunting lodge, with extensive grounds," Katie repeated again, a slow smile forming on her face. "Why didn't you say anything?" she demanded.

"Jar...Jackson was trying to get me to say something about it, but I didn't want to tell anyone I had money unless I had to."

"How does Jackson, know about the hunting lodge?"

"He's been there several times, with my family," Candace explained. "His dad is a business associate, and friend of my dad."

"Oh really!" Katie said, with meaning. "Funny, how he didn't explain that fact."

"Jackson is in the same situation as I am. In fact, I copied him."

Katie frowned. "What do you mean?"

"He wanted to live a normal life, and go to a regular high school. I saw him, when he started attending a public school. So, I insisted on going to Central High too," Candace explained. "He was always able to play the part, better than me," she said quietly. "He seemed to fit right in. While I struggled, just making friends. You and Sam were the closest thing I had to real friends. Now she's gone, and I don't want to lose you too."

"We're in this together, Candy," Katie told her quietly. "Through thick and thin, we're in this together."

Candace's head shot up. "You called me Candy."

"I'm sorry. It just came out. I didn't mean to." Katie immediately started apologizing.

"No, it's not that." Candace tried to explain. "Nobody has ever called me by a nickname before. I like it."

"You want to be called Candy?" Katie asked surprised.

"Yes," she said formally in her soft cultured voice. "I would love for you to call me Candy."

"Candy it is." Getting up, she reached out for her friend's hand to pull her up.

"Do you think it's possible to let Jar…Jackson's parents know he's alive? His family was devastated, when he disappeared." Candy asked as they headed back.

Katie shook her head. "Jackson could be right, about the immediate danger. He would know more about it than us."

Chapter 30
David Knows

Katie walked confidently through the hall of school, ignoring the stares and whispers. She smiled wickedly, when a girl saw her and dropped her books. She had been getting that same reaction, all morning. Her apparent death may not have caused a whole lot of gossip, but her resurrection was causing a huge response. Walking into the office, with a note from her mother excusing her from four days of school, was a true classic. The office secretary took one look at her and broke into tears.

Principal Davis came out of his office, and just at that moment turned white. When he saw her, he reached over and gave her the biggest bear hug of her life. She kept repeating over and over, she was fine. They each gave her a dressing down, on driving too fast on slick roads.

Entering third hour, she could tell, Miss Smith hadn't heard the great news of her resurrection. The shocked look, followed by a stack of papers crashing to the floor, was a picture Katie was going to treasure for a long time. Stepping over the papers, she couldn't resist a cheerful "Hello Miss Smith" before sliding into her chair in the back row.

"Nice to see you... Alive." Miss Smith said, through clenched teeth.

"'Yeah, well rumors of my demise, have been greatly exaggerated,'" Katie quoted in the most hillbilly accent, she could come up with. She had always loved Mark Twain. Looking towards Tyler and Lizzy, she gave them a wink. Tyler chuckled, while Lizzy stared stonily at her. Katie frowned a little, at her friend's reaction. She decided, to ignore Lizzy's stony presence. She was pretty confident, her friend was going to eventually thaw out.

"Katherine,. I would like to see you, after class."

Katie looked up, just as the bell rang. Tyler gave her a thumbs up, while Lizzy looked nervously from her to Miss Smith.

"I'll meet you guy's later," she said quickly, as she watched them head for the door. Waiting patiently for the last person to leave, turning, she faced Miss Smith not knowing what to expect.

"You think you're pretty clever, don't you?" Miss Smith said, in a very soft but angry voice.

Katie tried to think, of what she could have done. "I'm not sure-"

"You set me up," the teacher said thru clenched teeth.

"I... What?" Katie had no idea, what she was talking about.

"Are you telling me, you have no idea, how Mr. Davis got all your graded papers from my class?"

She had completely forgotten the episode in Mr. Davis's office, a week before. She now remembered, she had thrown her folder on the principal's desk. Wow! Davis must have looked over her homework. Her assessment of the man went up several notches.

"I see through your stupid expression, you know exactly what I'm talking about," Miss Smith said. "I'm not going to let a spoiled little girl, get the best of me. If you want to take me on, let's see how far you really want to take this." The teacher stepped closer. "Then rumors of your demise will be right on target."

The animal spirit inside jumped, as the threat lingered in the air. Katie took slow small breaths, trying to control the heat building inside her. "Are you threatening me?" she asked in a soft voice.

"I've stomped on bigger things, than a smart ass little girl like you," the teacher shot back.

Katie couldn't believe what she was hearing. "I really don't know what your problem is, lady, but you need to get over-"

"What do you know about problems," Smith interrupted. "What do you know about anything?"

Katie felt she was on a tightrope with no safety net. She kept watching the older lady, get more heated by the minute.

"What do you know?" Miss Smith demanded, her voice rising.

Katie tried sustaining her own heat, as the animal spirit recognizing an unknown danger, was awakening. It was coming to life, in her chest. Keeping silent, Katie took steady breaths.

"All you kids, are just like Elizabeth. You think you always know better, than anyone else. You sit there judging people, spreading her filthy lies." The old women mumbled, under her breath.

Katie caught the name, and stepped a little closer, despite her better judgment. "You knew Elizabeth Hawk?"

"Of course, I knew Elizabeth. I knew her, long before she called herself Elizabeth." The old woman said bitterly. "What is she saying about me? Lies all lies," she yelled. "Her and Forrest," the old lady spat the names out. "They are laughing at me. All these years they're laughing at me, telling everyone about me. How I couldn't keep my man. Everyone thinks, she's so loving and kind. Well, I know different. She stabbed me in the back, and took my man from me."

Shock vibrated through Katie's body. She tried not to show any emotion. She was trying to get as much information as possible, before the old woman came to her senses and stopped speaking.

"She thinks she's so smart, warning me. Telling me, I can't retaliate against you kids. She thinks she can keep me in line. I am no longer under her command. I can do whatever I want."

Miss Smith zeroed in on Katie. "I'm no longer under her orders and you-" She pointed a bent finger towards her. "You're my first target."

Katie felt the threat wash over her, ignoring the heat for a moment longer. "How long exactly, have you known Elizabeth Hawk?"

The old head snapped up, her unclear eyes sharpened. "What do you know?" the old women demanded. "How much do you know?"

Katie felt the heat reaching out, starting to consume her. Turning blindly, she ran for the door. Opening the door, she bolted with the old lady screaming behind her. Rounding the corner, she ran headlong into David.

"Whoa, where are you going? I need to talk to you," David said, trying to hold on to her.

"I'm losing control!" She yelled struggling, she jerked her arms free and ran to the door.

She had a large parking lot to cross, before the outline of trees meant safety. Running as fast as she could, she felt the heat building inside of her, wanting to explode. Running full out, she thought she was going to make it, when someone grabbed her from behind. Whirling around, she frantically fought the arms, that held her tight.

"Why are you so afraid of me?" David demanded. "Why does a total stranger give me more information about my sister's death, than her best friend?" He held her tight, his voice raising, and his face contorted in anger.

"I can't," frantically she fought to get out of his grip.

They both heard a growl, coming from the woods. David's hold loosened, his eyes growing wide. He placed himself between her, and the large Black Panther that stepped out of the trees. The large cat snarled louder, stepping closer to the couple, and looking like he was about to attack.

Katie took the opportunity, to pull out of David's arms.

"No! Jackson go back, he's not hurting me."

Knowing she had only seconds, she took three steps away from David and changed. Two more steps, she was in the safety of the woods. A weight lifted off her shoulders, she felt free and alive.

"I'm back!" Her thoughts rang out.

"You just couldn't have waited another ten feet before you changed?" Jackson said dryly.

"Hey, I'm lucky I didn't change, in the classroom in front of Miss Smith," she retorted. She started rolling around in the grass.

"What are you doing?" Jackson asked.

"I have no idea, but it feels really good. You should try it," said Katie reveling in the feel of the grass on her neck and back.

"Aren't you forgetting something?" Jackson said in a low patient voice.

Katie rolled over on her stomach. "*Oh, crap.*"

"I wouldn't exactly say that, but yeah. Oh, crap!" Jackson lay down beside her. *"Do you want to take bets, on him following you into the woods?"*

Katie didn't have to think very hard. The Black family had no idea, how to quit on anything. She lay there quietly for a minute, wondering when David was going to show up. It didn't take long.

"Katie, are you in here?" the words came out softly hesitantly.

"I have to give him credit," Jackson said. *"He's got a set."*

Katie laid her head down, not really wanting to face David. "*I wonder, if he still wants to go to prom with me.*"

Jackson gave out a choking sound.

"Can you ask him?"

"NO! Not uh chance!" Jackson was shaking his head. *"It is not gonna happen, Katie."*

"Katie, are you all right?"

She laid her head on the ground, reaching out with her mind. "*Lizzy, can you bring me some clothes*?" She quickly explained, where she was. She heard Candy and Tyler, immediately start asking questions. Jackson shook his head over the noise and confusion that now bombarded their minds.

Looking up, she saw David step into view. His face was anxious, but not afraid. If she stood up, she would be face to face with him. She knew how big she was, she didn't want to advertise it. Lowering her head, she tried to appear as small as possible.

"Oh, for crying out loud," Jackson mumbled in her mind.

Turning into human form, Jackson stood in front of David. He folded his arms, in defiance. "Katie wants to know, if you still want to go to prom with her."

David's eyes never left Katie. "Why can't she ask me herself?"

"Because, if she changes back into human. She'll be naked." Jackson explained like he was talking to a five-year-old.

"So, my guess is, you have no problem being naked," David shot back.

Jackson's face registered surprise, then he turned to face Katie a cocky smile forming on his face. "You can't see me wearing clothes?" He stressed, staring at Katie.

"You're not wearing clothes," David pointed out.

"Says you," Jackson retorted.

Katie swiveled her head, between David and Jackson *What does that mean?* she questioned.

"It means, he doesn't possess the gene to turn into a were-cat," Jackson answered with his thoughts, the smile growing larger on his face. He started rocking back on his heels, trying to hold in his glee.

"Where are you guys?" came a loud voice behind David.

David turned around.

Katie could see Tyler, crashing through the underbrush. He stopped dead, when he saw David. "Uh, what are you doing here?"

"How did you know where we were?" David immediately questioned Tyler.

Tyler looked between Jackson, and Katie before he smiled.

"David's here, and he knows." Tyler announced to Candace and Lizzy. Questions and exclamations immediately bombarded their minds. Katie winced the same time as Tyler and Jackson.

David sat there, his head swiveling between the three of them. "You can communicate without speaking?" he guessed.

Tyler grinned; slapping David on the back. "Oh man, I've been dying to talk to you. I know, you must be freaked out. First time I saw Katie turn, I thought I must be in an old episode of the Twilight Zone. Katie was the first one to turn. No, sorry, I'm wrong... Jackson was the first one to turn. He turns into a Black Panther. As you can see, Katie turns into a huge white wolf. Lizzy turns into a Cheetah, and Candace turns into a snow leopard. I turn into a cool African lion."

Katie sat, watching Tyler speak. Before this moment, she was sure he had never said more than one sentence a day.

"We talk with our minds. Candace is now lamenting, over the fact that once again she's far away and missing out. Lizzy has gone, to get clothes for Katie."

"Candace is the girl Katie tried to take out, during a basketball game?" David asked. "Now she seems to be her best friend."

Katie had no idea, how observant David had been in her life.

"Yeah," Tyler agreed. "Katie saved her from..."

Jackson immediately turned back into a black panther and snarled loudly. Tyler jumped back, looking apologetically towards the black cat. "Sorry, dude."

"Just because he knows we are were-animals, doesn't mean we tell him our whole life story." Jackson retorted through his thoughts.

Tyler shifted, uneasily on his feet. "Sorry."

He turned to David, pointing to the panther. "He's the baddest fighter, I've ever seen. He can pretty much wipe the floor with me, and I'll be happy if he doesn't kill me." Tyler shifted again on his feet. "By the way, Candace is ecstatic you know what's going on. She thinks we all, need a little *Black* common sense."

David's eye's narrowed. "Sam, was a part of this?" Katie felt the hairs, on her back rise. Jackson sat down beside her. A low growl, emulating from him.

David looked swiftly towards the panther, then at Katie. "No offense Katie, I just would like to know what my sister was into."

Jackson growled, a little louder.

Tyler laughed, shaking his head. "None of us wanted this to happen. Well, Sam seemed to be a little too excited, when she showed the symptoms. The spirit of The Great White Tiger, chose us to protect this place. The people here," Tyler reiterated.

"The Great White Tiger?" David repeated.

Tyler frowned. "Yea, I thought all of you knew, the Old Sugaree legend."

Katie made a quick explanation with her thoughts towards Tyler. He cocked his head, listening to her.

"Oh, I didn't know," Tyler said out loud. "Katie says every year the women would sit around the fire, and Old Elizabeth Hawk would tell the women about the legend of The Great White Tiger. She says, you should go home, and ask your mom."

Elizabeth Hawk's name reminded Katie of her conversation with Miss Smith. *Lizzy,* Katie reached out with her mind. *I think Forrest, is your grandfather.* She quickly explained to everyone her conversation with the old woman.

Questions and speculations were swiftly flying around so fast, Katie had a hard time keeping up. Looking up, she saw David's eyes boring into her.

"Are you guys all communicating, without me being able to hear?" David eventually said.

"Sorry dude. It's easy to forget you can't hear also," Tyler apologized. "Katie just mentioned an argument she had with Miss Smith. She thinks the old bitty is connected to Forrest and Old Elizabeth Hawk. Katie thinks Forrest, is *our* Lizzy's grandfather.

Lizzy came crashing through the brush, a backpack dangling from her arm. "Sorry it took so long, I was parked on the other side of the building."

She threw the bag down. Katie looked at the three guys, expectantly. Jackson got up and turned into human form. He grabbed David by the arm, and slowly turned him away from Katie. All three guys faced the other way. David kept glancing over at Jackson.

Katie got up, expecting to change back into human form. She concentrated, still nothing happened. She hadn't felt this frustrated since her first week. Jackson and Tyler started chuckling, when Lizzy explained the situation to them.

"What?" David asked turning towards Jackson.

"Katie, can't turn back into human form. It's like, she's a puppy all over again." Tyler answered.

Katie laid her head, on the ground defeated.

"She hasn't been able to communicate, or change into animal form since Sam died," Tyler explained. "She almost lost complete control and turned into a wolf in the school building. Now, she doesn't know how to turn back into human."

The sound of the bell, had all the students lifting their head in unison.

"I'm going to get behind again," Katie lamented.

"One more day is not going to make that much difference," Jackson said out loud.

“Don’t worry, I’ll sign you out,” David said reassuringly.

Tyler and Lizzy started heading back to the school. David got down on his haunches. “I can understand why you had a hard time telling me, Katie. I’m glad I was here, to finally be able to understand.”

David stood up, eyeing Jackson wearily. “How did you get all those scars, Jared?”

“DO NOT CALL ME BY THAT NAME! “Jackson said, a threat evident in his voice. “You will get me and my family killed.”

David folded his arms, not backing down from Jackson’s threat. He gave a quick stiff nod, showing he understood. Jackson gave him another long stare and changed back into a panther. Flicking his tail in the air, he disappeared into the brush.

David watched him go, then turned to Katie. “We’ll talk later.” His smile was tight. “Just so you know, I still want to go to prom with you,” he said quietly.

Katie nodded. Getting up she turned and followed Jackson out of site.

Jackson was running at full speed, knowing Katie would follow. She stretched her legs, to catch up. It felt good to run again. She laughed jumping over fallen trees and dodging boulders. It didn’t take long till she was running beside him. Looking his way, she could tell he was going as fast as he could.

Making her legs stretch further, she passed him. laughing in exhilaration. Leaving him behind, she eventually slowed down to wait for him. Pausing by a large tree, she waited. Lifting her head up to smell the air, she was just in time to jump out of the way. He came crashing down, from up above her.

Rolling around, they played and fought for a while. She could tell, he was again limiting his fight to match her.

Stopping to rest, Jackson leaned over. *"You really are, a terrible fighter."*

"Well, I hope to remedy that. Katie pouted acting offended."

Jackson chuckled. *"When I think of all those Seekers scared to death of you."*

"Well, that's what happens, when I get credit for something I didn't do." Katie frowned, looking over the trees.

"What is it?"

Katie turned towards Jackson. He was so attuned to her every emotion. "*I was just thinking about, some of the things Miss Smith said."*

Jackson got up and moved closer. *"What exactly, did she say?"*

Katie went into greater detail on everything Miss Smith said to her. Jackson listened attentively, not interrupting. When she was finished, he lay down and rested his head on his paws. *"It sounds like, she maybe a were-animal."*

"No way." Katie shook her head. "*She is the most hateful person I have ever met.*" She went into detail about the time she and David shoveled snow and she called the cops on them.

"Did you hear, the terms she used?" Jackson pointed out. *"She has known Elizabeth, before she called herself Elizabeth. 'I am no longer under her command,'"* Jackson quoted.

"Tyler, Lizzy, and myself are all in her English class. We not only talk to each other, but that is where Lizzy, had her little day dream. She never responded, or even showed she could hear us."

"The Seekers talk to each other, you can't hear them," Jackson said. "Maybe it's a different frequency or something."

"Can you hear the Seekers, talk to each other?" Katie asked.

Jackson nodded. *"It's just as easy for me to hear the Seekers, as it is for you to hear Candy. I used to have to concentrate really-hard, to even talk to you. The headaches were incredible."*

Katie nodded, remembering how bad her headache was, just trying it that one time.

"Now I can hear both sides, with no problem at all."

"That night when Lizzy was changing, I reached out to you. You told me everyone could hear me. How was that possible, if they couldn't hear me before or after?"

Jackson stopped to consider. *"I was new to my abilities then. I wasn't sure what was going on. You must have accidentally, gotten into the frequency of the Seekers. You were trying to reach me, a Seeker."*

Katie thought about it for a moment. "*When you warned me to turn back, it was a trap. I reached out to Candy. She asked me, where I was. She couldn't get through to me, for several minutes.*"

Jackson nodded. *"It makes sense. For those moments you were only tuned into the Seeker frequency."*

Katie remembered, talking to Forrest in the library. She told him how she thought Forrest, was trying to talk to her. She felt the pressure in her mind, but couldn't hear him. "*Is it possible for Forrest, Miss Smith, and Old Elizabeth Hawk to be were-animals?"*

Jackson shook his head. *"I don't know... When I first became a Seeker, I was told not to go around that particular cabin; unless I wanted to die an early and painful death."* He turned his head to face her. *"Remember when I asked you where you were, when you first found the cabin? You told me you didn't know, some cabin in woods owned by a guy named Forrest. I was once again, reminded I was walking on fire."*

Katie felt the wind shift. Her nose twitched, when an unfamiliar smell filled her senses. She felt Jackson tense. "*You smell that*?"

Jackson got up and faced the wind. He started trotting, towards the smell. Katie watched him leave and then decided to follow. They were deep in the forest, following the scent. It became stronger. The closer they got, the more unpleasant it became. Katie was surprised, when they came upon fresh four-wheeler tracks.

Following them, they came upon a camp. One of the poles was broken in the circular tent, causing it to cave on one end. Clothes and camping equipment were scattered around haphazardly. Katie felt uneasy, as she surveyed the destroyed camp. Jackson had disappeared, from around the tent. Deciding to follow she stopped short, when she saw two bodies. It appeared to be a man and his pre-teen son.

Katie immediately stepped back, feeling sick. She couldn't believe it, when Jackson stepped closer. His nose to the ground. *"Katie, come here."*

"What? No way!"

"Katie, you need to come here."

Not really understanding, Katie slowly stepped forward averting her face, from the bodies.

"Smell this," Jackson commanded.

"No." Katie was breathing through her mouth, trying not to smell at all.

"Katie, you want me to teach you. School starts now," Jackson stated. *"Come over, and smell this."*

Katie took another step. Her stomach twisted, when she saw the frozen scared expression on the boy's face. She slowly lowered her head, and gave a small inhale. She had smelled this scent before, she realized.

Breathing in deeper, the memory flashed into her mind. She smelled this when she and Candace were trying to save Jackie Oaklin, from Central High.

"*Surgious?*"

"Yes." Jackson stepped around the body sniffing, *"Smell here."*

Katie hesitated a moment, then came over and sniffed. The scent was unfamiliar.

"James Schmidt," Jackson informed her. *"He became a Seeker, after I became one."* He shook his head. "*I felt sorry for him and tried to protect him. Now, look at him. Look, at what he's become."* His head close to the ground, he went around the camp. He made sure, Katie followed close behind, as he showed where the attack originated, and how the two humans tried to fight and lost their battle. He showed her where the two Seekers left.

Katie was ready to leave long before Jackson. She finally breathed a sigh of relief, when he headed back towards her home. They traveled for several miles, before either one said anything more.

Unable to stand the silence. *"What makes them change, Jackson?"*

"I don't know, Katie. The only thing we are asked to do is, turn were-animals into Seekers. We are not trusted with any other information, or duties other than that."

"If that's the case, how come you have never felt the urge to eat human flesh?"

Jackson didn't say anything for a while. *"Maybe, it's because I never actually changed anyone into a Seeker."*

"You think that's it?"

"I don't know Katie, I honestly don't know. There's another thing, that's really bothering me." Jackson waited a couple of moments to formulate his words. *"This is my territory."*

"I don't understand." Katie was afraid, to hear Jackson's reply.

"They are moving, into my territory, which means they no longer consider this area dangerous."

Chapter 31

Forrest's Judgment

Katie woke up from a nightmare. The young boy's scared face, echoing in her mind. She knew it was going to be hard to go back to sleep. Getting up, she walked into the kitchen, looking for the bottle of sleeping pills her mother used to give her. Finding the bottle, she shook out a pill, debating whether to take one or two. Opening the refrigerator, she glanced at all the little notes, her mother placed reminding her of appointments, or things to buy. She stopped, staring at a hot pink post-it note, a phone number with the name Forrest right next to it. The sleeping pill now forgotten, she studied the neat handwriting of her mother.

She couldn't believe it. She remembered the many times her mother told her she had called Forrest. When the house was broken into by large animals, she had called Forrest. When she couldn't find Katie, she had called Forrest. When Katie had wrecked her Camaro, she had called Forrest. She grabbed the note and walked back into her bedroom. Looking at the clock, she realized it was after midnight. She could care less, if she woke him. Finding her cell phone, she dialed Forrest's number. She waited impatiently, as it rang several times. She wasn't surprised, when an answering machine picked up.

"This is Forrest. If you need me, leave a message."

"Forrest, this is Katie Johnson, I have several things I need to discuss with you. For one thing, a friend and I found a man and his son in the woods, half eaten. Second, Miss Smith, my English teacher is threatening me, telling me, I'm just like Elizabeth Hawk. Third, I believe you promised me some answers. So, if you're too afraid to have a conversation with me, then go run and hide. If you're not, I would appreciate your getting your ass down here, and giving me some answers."

She hung up, smiling to herself. She thought she laid it out pretty well, till she remembered she hadn't left her phone number. She studied her cell phone, debating whether to call back, finally deciding it would lose the effect she was trying to make. He knew where she was. She lay back down on the bed.

"You may look like your mother, but you don't have her sweet disposition."

Katie looked up from her books. She had been expecting Forrest to show up sometime today. She came early to school, just to help him contact her. Glancing at the clock, she still had thirty minutes before the first bell rang. She leaned back in her chair and gestured toward the seat in front of her.

He sat down, eyeing her warily. "I believe you said you found a couple of bodies?"

Katie narrowed her eyes. "I want an assurance that you won't take off, leaving me hanging, as soon as you get information from me."

Forrest look affronted. "I'm a man of my word."

Katie wanted to debate the point, but decided it was in her best interest not to point out the obvious. Hoping her silence spoke volumes, she waited for him to continue.

Forrest pulled out an old worn map. His fingers shook a little as he spread it out on the table. Katie could tell it was the Appalachia Mountains in their immediate area. "Can you point out the approximate area where you found the bodies?"

Katie studied the map to get her bearings. "You will find them right here," she pointed to the spot.

Forrest frowned. "Are you sure?"

Katie gave the map a closer look. She could see a red marker line that encircled natural barriers, rivers, and mountain lines. She could see the place she pointed was inside the marked line.

"Yes, I'm sure. They had a four-wheeler, so there has to be a way in there by trail." Katie pointed to the red line. "What is this for?"

Forrest stared at her for a while. "This is a protective line, Elizabeth Hawk drew a long time ago," he eventually answered.

"They are no longer afraid to come into the boundaries," Katie said, hoping he would explain more.

The old man nodded, studying her a little harder. "I've been watching you, Katie Johnson. I've been watching you real close. What I see, I don't like."

Katie lifted her eyebrows, in surprise.

"You've been courting around with that Seeker. Including him in your team, making the others accept him. He was there when your friend died, did you know that?"

Katie sat up straighter. "You don't know him," she said defensively.

Forrest shook his head, a cynical smile playing on his lips. "Do you know how many times I have heard that, little girl? I've been on this mountain for 140 years. Do you know how many lives I have seen come and go? It's always the same—different people, different names, living the same life, over and over.

"He's different than the rest," Forrest said in high pitch voice. "Now you listen to me, and you listen good. When a were-animal goes on his knees and makes the oath to become a Seeker, the heart or soul of the animal leaves. It cannot live in a corrupt vessel. What is left, is just an essence of what the spirit once was. Without the animal soul, the human becomes corrupt. There is no going back. They all become Malus." He leaned forward and grabbed Katie's hands. "They all become corrupt," he repeated. "No exceptions!"

"What's a Malus?" Katie couldn't help asking

"It's the monster your little boyfriend is going to turn into," Forrest replied.

She pulled his hands away, from his tight grip. "Maybe this time is different." She said grasping.

"Elizabeth thought that same thing."

Katie looked up, into the old man's face, not wanting to hear any more.

"Elizabeth fell in love with a Seeker." Forrest shook his head, his eyes becoming watery. "She gave her whole heart, to that boy. She tried real hard, to save him too. In the end, she knew he had to be killed. She couldn't do it herself, so she asked us, to do it."

Katie felt sick to her stomach. She didn't want to hear any more. Gathering her books, she started jamming them in her backpack as fast as she could.

"I'm not finished."

Katie wanted to walk away, and never see the old man again. She reminded herself, that she'd asked for this meeting. Sitting down, she folded her arms and slumped in her chair.

"The wolf is second in command. That's how it's always been." The old man tapped, his pointed finger on the table. "Second, not first."

Katie was at a loss, what the old man was trying to say. "What's your point?"

"What I'm saying is, when The Great White Tiger makes its appearance, you have to step down," Forrest stressed. "You're only in charge, until it arrives. You can save a lot of heartache and contention just stepping down and being supportive, instead of fighting for control."

Stung from the accusation, Katie was not sure how to respond. "This is here and now, old man. I'm not repeating an old play, where Romeo and Juliet continuously die."

"Romeo and Juliet? I'm talking more along the lines of Judas or Brutus."

Katie had no idea, who he was talking about. "Anything else Obi-Wan?" Katie said sarcastically.

Forrest watched her closely. "I see, I've given you a lot to think about."

Katie watched the old man get up and walk out of the library. She waited until he was completely gone before grabbing her bag, and running for the door. She needed to find somebody smarter than she was. Walking down the hallway, she spotted David. He was talking to three of his buddies. Her immediate impulse was to turn around and avoid him. Giving herself courage, she walked up to him and tapped him on the shoulder.

"Can I talk to you for just a moment?"

David gave her a tight smile and walked with her. She looked around making sure, they were by themselves. "Who is Judas?"

"What?" David smiled his first genuine smile. "I was expecting you to talk to me about something else."

"Yeah, well, I plan on talking about that later. Right now, I would like to know who a Judas and a Brutus was... or... is... or... whatever." She waved her hand in agitation.

"Are you talking about Judas Iscariot?"

"I don't know. Just Judas. How many people have that name anyway?" Katie said, frustration etched on her features.

"Judas Iscariot was an apostle of Christ. He betrayed him, by giving him a kiss on the cheek, telling the soldiers who he was. That's where the term, the Judas kiss comes from."

Katie nodded. "Who is this Brutus guy."

"Caesar, acting as emperor of Rome, was assassinated by Brutus, and other members of the senate."

Katie was starting to understand, what Forrest was implying. "Were Judas and Brutus, good friends with the people they betrayed?"

David smiled. "Oh yes, very good friends."

Anger and resentment flushed her features. She wanted to find the old man, and knock his head off. How dare he judge her? Nodding her head, she gave David a distracted smile.

"Thanks." She turned to walk away.

"Whoa, wait a minute there. We need to talk." Grabbing her hand, he pulled her back towards him.

Katie eyed him apprehensively. "What?"

"Oh, I don't know. What did you and your naked friend do together?"

Katie laughed. "He wasn't naked," she said, coming to Jackson's defense.

"I was there. He was naked as a jay-bird," David replied.

"I saw clothes," Katie answered.

David cocked his head to the side. "How?"

She wasn't sure how to answer. "Our minds are connected some way. He projects an image from his mind to ours." She shrugged. "I can actually feel the fabric."

"So, when he made a point to you, about me not being able to see his clothes..." David's voice trailed off.

"He was really making the point that you don't have the right gene or mind, to become a were-animal."

"Wow, that just breaks my heart." David patted his chest, giving her a sad mocking look.

Katie laughed. "Did you talk to your mom, about the Sugaree Legend?"

He nodded, giving her a speculative look. "I always wondered, what you women did on those camp fires."

"Hey, I only attended one, and it was cut short." Katie laughed. "Jackson told me Old Elizabeth Hawk, has been protecting these mountains for over 170 years."

David's eyebrows raised, in surprise.

"Do you want to hear something else?" she asked quietly.

David leaned in closer.

"Forrest just told me, he has been around for 140 years." Katie looked around, making sure no one was within hearing distance. "I wonder how old Miss Smith is?"

"How do you know Miss Smith is a.... were-animal," David stumbled over the word.

"I don't." She shook her head. "Jackson thinks she is, because of the way she acted, and the terms she used yelling at me yesterday."

"How does... Jackson, know so much?"

"I don't know," Katie said quietly. "If he hadn't been around helping me and the others, we wouldn't have made it." She didn't know who she was trying to convince, David or herself.

"Do you know, what I don't understand?" David said quietly. "The legend says the descendants of this Running Deer, turn into were-animals. None of us are related to each other. My family is Navajo, and we are the first generation to live in these mountains. How can we possibly be related to anyone, in the Cherokee nation?"

He shrugged his shoulders. "How come Sam was chosen?"

Kate nodded. "I know!" she said in frustration. "The only thing that is right so far about the legend is, that someone becomes a were-animal. Sam used to say, it was because the legend was never written down. Each generation that passed the story on, would add or take away from the original."

David acted like he wanted to pursue this line of questioning, when the bell rang signaling they needed to go to class. Katie gave David a quick wave and walked to her first class. She tried to chase away her feelings, but an unfamiliar dread settled in her stomach. Sitting down, she went over her conversation with Forrest again. Doubt clawed its way into her consciousness. How could she trust Jackson now? Giving in to her doubts and fears, she hated Forrest.

Chapter 32
Indecision

Katie was now, officially freaked out. Walking out of English class, she looked back towards Miss Smith. Who made it a point, to give her a small wave. An ugly grimace stretched over her tight teeth. If it didn't look so frightening, Katie would have laughed at the teacher trying to smile.

Turning back around, she voiced her concerns. "What did we just witness?"

Chuckling softly, Tyler shook his head.

"Maybe, she decided you're not the daughter of Satan," Lizzy said, in speculation.

"Overnight? I don't think so." Katie gave a nervous laugh. "I don't believe I'm going to say this, but I think I prefer her mean. At least I know, where I stand."

Looking over, she saw Tyler still laughing quietly.

"I'm glad you're enjoying yourself at my expense," Katie grumbled.

Tyler glanced her way, giving her a wink.

Smiling back into his handsome face, she felt better. "Are we still on for tonight?" she asked him.

Lizzy put her arm, around Tyler's waist. "Are you sure it's okay, if I come later?"

Katie nodded. "We already discussed coming at different times, then we could have more individual lessons with Jackson."

"I can't wait to learn how to wear clothes," Lizzy said.

After school, Katie found Tyler, through the throng of people spilling out of the building. Giving him a wave, she headed towards the Hummer. Tyler gave the large SUV a loving pat, before climbing in. His smile contagious. Katie laughed, as he stroked the dashboard.

"You want to drive?"

Needing no encouragement, he jumped out and ran around to the driver's seat. Katie scooted over, to the passenger seat. Watching him, she noticed he was looking particularly nice. He was wearing a nice pair of jeans, and a shirt that set off his eyes.

Remembering him always, in ragged hand-me-down clothes, "You're looking nice today," she commented.

Tyler gave a quick laugh, as he turned the engine over. "Candace."

Nodding in understanding, Katie grinned. "She gave us clothes too. Pretty sweet, Huh!"

"My foster mom, thinks I'm selling drugs," Tyler said, as he pulled onto the road.

Surprised, Katie looked over. He was always so quiet. She had no idea, about his home life.

"Drugs?"

"Yeah, she told me when I get arrested, she's not going to bail me out. She's going to call child services to move my butt out of her house."

Katie nodded, trying not to show her feelings. "I guess, we don't have to worry about that?"

"I imagine what her face would look like if I ever changed in her presence. It usually gives me a laugh, just thinking about it."

Katie noticed Tyler was once again uncharacteristically verbal. He seemed more confident than he used to be.

"Do you know where I should turn?"

Katie looked down at the GPS, on her phone. Giving him directions, they headed up through the canyon. Katie remembered going through this area, with her Camaro. Going around the corner where she lost control, she couldn't help looking down the ravine. Tyler slowed down, so she could get a better look. Shaking her head in wonder, she realized how lucky she was to be alive.

"I turn here?"

Katie, glancing back down, gave him the rest of the directions. Coming to a gate, a small electronic box was placed by the driver's side window. Katie gave Tyler, the numbered code to get in. The gate swung open.

He drove carefully, down the lane. "Do you get the feeling, Candace has more money than she lets on?" Tyler asked casually.

Katie smiled. "Yeah, she finally fessed up when she told me about this place."

Not really knowing what to expect, Katie gave a quick gasp when the lodge came into view. Tyler gave a low whistle. Large could hardly describe the place. It was huge. It was made out of the biggest logs, Katie had ever seen. It had a large sweeping porch, that had at least fifty chairs, posed in various groupings. The door was hewn from a single piece of wood.

Getting out of the vehicle, they both tentatively stepped onto the porch. Looking around, she looked over at Tyler, who gave her an uncertain smile. Walking towards the massive door, she turned the large knob. It opened gracefully, with very little noise. Entering the premises, she could see a massive fireplace on the far wall. Everything was clean and polished to a fine sheen. Furniture lined the walls, leaving a large open space. Looking up, she saw a loft upstairs, which left the middle of the room open to vaulted ceilings.

Turning in a small circle, she could see railing surrounding the whole upstairs. In the corner, she spotted movement. Concentrating, she could see a dark figure in the shadows. She watched the shadow carefully.

Jackson? she reached with her thoughts.

The dark figure stepped out, swung over the railing, and dropped the twenty feet to land lightly on his feet. Jackson walked gracefully towards them, with a cocky smile on his lips.

Immediately upon seeing him, the doubts and fears she felt all day, ran to the forefront of her mind. Frowning slightly, she watched him as sadness enveloped her soul. Jackson immediately stopped, watching her carefully. She realized, he was feeling her emotions.

"Well teacher here we are," she said brightly.

Jackson kept watching her carefully. Turning to Tyler, he directed him where he could change out of his clothes. Turning back, he waited until Tyler was safely gone. "What's wrong Katie?"

She shook her head, unable to talk about it.

Stepping closer, he reached out softly touching her cheek. "Do I have to remind you again? I can feel your emotions."

"Not now Jackson. I have to learn how to fight." She tried to brush him off.

Nodding, Jackson directed her, where she could go to change. Changing quickly, Katie returned in wolf form. She watched Jackson, teach Tyler a few moves. He then turned to her. This time around, he didn't hold anything back. When she did something wrong, he quickly moved in, usually causing some kind of pain.

She liked the way he taught, giving the instructions first. They tried them out on each other, before trying the moves out on Jackson. She appreciated the fact that he gave her no preferential treatment. It didn't seem very long at all when Lizzy and Candy showed up. Realizing how fatigued she was, she went in and dressed. Going up the stairs, she leaned on the rail watching Jackson work with the girls.

Tyler came up and stood next to her. "He's really good."

Katie nodded quietly, the sadness entering her heart again.

"We're lucky, you found him."

"I didn't find him, Tyler, he found me." She noticed Jackson, looking towards her. She couldn't help chuckling, when Lizzy took advantage of his distraction. She took him down, for the first time that day.

"Tyler come down here, I want to show you something." Jackson reached out with his mind.

"Doesn't he get tired?" Tyler mumbled, before leaving.

Candy soon came upstairs, leaning on the rail next to her.

"This is some place."

Candy smiled. "I almost told you about it that first day, when you were trying to figure out what to do with me."

Katie smiled at the memory. “I’ve never seen logs, this large before.”

“The trees came from around here.” Candy explained. “The lodge was built, just after the civil war. It was around the same time loggers came and cut all the trees.”

Katie turned around to see the large logs. “The trees were that big?”

“It seems a real shame, doesn’t it?”

Katie agreed. Looking down she watched the fighting.

“Is there something wrong?”

Katie quickly glanced, towards Candy. She needed to talk to someone, and get another perspective. Her first choice, was no longer available. Confiding in Lizzy, didn’t feel right. Making a decision, she started telling her about the bodies she and Jackson found, and then her conversation with Forrest.

Candy frowned, looking down at the play fighting continuing below. “What are you going to do?”

“I don’t know.” Katie mumbled softly, “What do you think, I should do?”

Candy didn’t say anything, for a while. “You can’t judge him for something he hasn’t done, or on something he may do in the future.”

Katie nodded.

“Look, my outlook on this may be a little twisted in Jackson’s favor,” Candy stressed. “But if there was anyone out there, who has the will and courage to beat this, it would be him.”

Katie desperately wanted to believe her. “Should I tell him, about Forrest?”

Candy nodded. “I would.”

"What if it becomes, a self-fulfilling prophesy?" Katie pointed out. "If it's going to happen anyway, why fight it."

"No, you're looking at this wrong, Katie. Better to be forewarned. He knows what he's fighting against."

Everything Candy said, made sense. Hope was finding its way, into her heart. Looking down, she noticed Jackson looking up at her.

"We need him, Katie," Candy stressed. "He needs us. I don't think we can do anything, without him."

Katie listened intently, feeling better. "Thanks," she said quietly.

Jackson soon called a halt for the night. Sending everyone home, he grabbed Katie's arm, stopping her from leaving. "I'll drive you home."

Katie watched the others leave. Knowing a conversation was inevitable, she sat down on one of the large chairs.

"What's going on?" Jackson didn't waste any time.

Katie gave a deep breath, then proceeded to tell him everything Forrest had told her.

Jackson listened, his eye's drifting away. "I'm not going to change Katie," Jackson said emphatically. "I don't care what that old man said." He got up and started pacing the small area in front of her. "What were you and Candace talking about?"

"I told her what was worrying me."

Jackson gave her a twisted smile. "What did the debutante have to say?"

Katie sat up straighter, resenting his judgment. "The debutante told me to give you the benefit of the doubt. Not to judge you, on something you didn't do. And," she stressed, "to tell you immediately."

Jackson had the decency, to look ashamed.

"You keep calling her the debutante, like having money is something truly terrible. She tells me, your family has as much money as hers."

"My family's money doesn't define who I am," Jackson shot back.

"Wow! That's truly amazing." Katie dramatized her words. "I believe Candy, said exactly the same thing."

"She was always a copy-cat."

"I believe this time around, you're copying her."

Jackson gave her an assessing look. "She really said all those things?"

"Her exact words were, 'Look, my outlook on this may be a little twisted in Jackson's favor, but if there was anyone out there who has the will and courage to beat this, it would be him.'"

Jackson stared at her in disbelief. "I always thought..." he stopped staring off into space. Looking down, he grinned. "I always thought she was like her mother."

Katie raised her eyebrows.

"Her mother. Augh!" Jackson shook his whole body, in mock agitation.

"She can't be that bad."

Jackson nodded. "You have no idea."

Chapter 33
Full Moon

The proceeding weeks took on a pattern. Every chance they got, they were at the lodge learning how to fight. It was decided they would work on their mental capabilities on Friday night and Saturday. This way they could recuperate from the horrible migraines on Sunday.

Jackson was relentless in his teaching. He would have them do the same move over and over again until they had it perfected. Being athletic, Katie was naturally competitive. The others followed suit, trying to beat each other in their play fights. Each time the team would perfect a new move, Jackson would have a counter move, which would make the original move obsolete. Katie wondered if he did nothing but work up new fighting techniques while they were at school.

Lizzy was the first to figure out how to project clothes. The next week Candy had the technique mastered. Unable to stand it anymore, Katie worked on it during the week. She was able to figure out how to do it the following week. Tyler soon followed suit.

Jackson worked with Lizzy on her ability to project a "*daydream*". He had the others step out around the yard, to see how far she could project. They soon figured out, she could project 25 feet radius from herself. Jackson worked with her until she was able to quadruple the area. He had her change the scenes from winter to summer. He then worked on her to change the scene from outside to inside. She eventually could create a scene from anywhere she wanted to.

Through the week, she would look up pictures on the internet and recreate them. It kind of freaked everyone out when she got pictures from the Space Hubble. They all knew they were still standing on the floor, but each felt as if they were floating in space.

When they all reached a point where the migraines weren't so bad, Jackson would introduce another mind exercise. Eventually, he had them split into partners and see through each other's eyes, the way he did with Katie the first night she changed. It took several tries for Katie to finally allow Candy in. Reaching into Candy's mind, Katie was able to do it the first time. Looking over at Tyler and Lizzy, Katie could see they had it mastered quickly.

Jackson set up an obstacle course. They, in turns, would be blindfolded. Partners would have to go through the course, using the eyes of their partner, who was sitting down watching the course from a distance. Trying to gauge the correct perspective, took a lot of work. When Katie was trying to go through the obstacle, Candy swung her head around to stare at Jackson, who was obviously laughing at her antics. Turning in his direction, she told him to come out and try it for himself. Katie watched through Candy's eyes as he immediately frowned, his eyes turning a light gray, and abruptly walked away. Katie began to wonder what she said, when Candy reminded her he had been in a bad mood for a couple of days.

Later that night, Katie happened to glance at her mother's calendar. The full moon was two days away. Wondering if that had any effect on Jackson's mood, she decided to watch the situation carefully. His mood became increasingly worse. A couple of times she snapped at him for being so rude. She could tell, he was fighting the urge not to change and fight. She watched him as he controlled his impulse, and again walked away.

The doubts and fears of Jackson being a Seeker, were once again in the forefront of her mind. She silently watched him, as he had the three other were-animals attack him at once. He again formed a spectacular move that had two of the three at a disadvantage. She knew they had all reached a level of fighting that could beat anything that was out there. Yet, every time they succeeded, Jackson exceeded to a whole new level she had previously thought was impossible.

What if he turns into a Malus? How are we ever going to fight him? She wondered. The thought of actually fighting him made her stomach clench uncontrollably. It would be like losing Sam, all over again. Yet, the picture of those two campers she and Jackson had come across haunted her. What if he was killing innocent people? He would no longer be the person she cared about, but someone she would need to stop.

How? How could she stop him?

He was so much better, than all four of them combined?

Katie looked back, towards Jackson. He had stopped and was watching her closely. Giving him a smile, which trembled slightly, she turned and walked away.

The day of the full moon, Katie's nerves were shot. Getting out of the SUV, she glanced around, noticing no one else had arrived. She waited patiently, for Jackson to appear. Giving the clock a watchful glance every few minutes, she realized he wasn't going to show.

She remembered all the times he tried to explain the hold, the leaders had over him. When Lizzy was turning, he was able to break through only a couple of minutes to warn her.

She pictured Jackson, in her head. He was so strong in mind, spirit, and body. How could someone or something have so much control over him? She laid her arms on the table, resting her head. She silently communicated to the others not to bother coming. She squeezed her eyes shut, remembering Forrest's words.

"When a were-animal gets on his knees, and makes the oath to become a Seeker, the heart or soul of the animal leaves. It cannot live in a corrupt vessel. What is left, is just an essence of what the spirit once was. Without the animal soul, the human becomes corrupt. There is no going back. They all become Malus." *There's no going back*, kept repeating itself in her mind. How she hated that old man.

She thought about Old Elizabeth Hawk, falling in love with a Seeker. She made the decision to kill him. She imagined making the decision, then asking her friends to do the deed for her. Katie raised her head. Would she be able to make that decision? Her mind immediately shied away from the idea. She didn't even have the means to kill Jackson, but if she did... could she?

Shaking her head, the answer was a resounding, NO. The thought of losing him was something she couldn't handle. He hadn't done anything yet. She knew "yet" was the operative word. She would just keep watching him, and the situation. She would learn, as much as she could from him. If he turned into a Malus, she would just have to deal with it.

That night she dreamed she was running through the woods. She smelled the distinct odor of death. Following the scent, she came across a campsite. The tent was made out of cloth. Odd looking ropes, were swinging in the breeze. An old fashioned cooking pan, was sitting next to the fire. Walking around the makeshift tent, she saw a Black Panther, head lowered over a body, blood dripping from its mouth.

Katie turned human. "NO!" she screamed "NO! How could you?

The Black Panther turned, and walked towards her.

"You said, you wouldn't change. You promised me!" She was crying so hard, she could hardly see, as the cat stopped in front of her.

The panther turned human. Instead of Jackson, it was a young warrior, his naked body glinted off the sun. "I didn't kill them!"

"I saw you," she said. "The blood of the innocent killed drips from your lips."

"It was not me. Look around, see the evidence. The one who killed these people, lies over there dead." He pointed towards a low embankment.

"I knew it. I always knew, you would change. There's no going back. Once a Seeker makes the covenant, the human becomes corrupt." She changed into animal form and ran. Her tears streaming down her face, her thoughts rang out.

"*He's changed.*"

"*What's wrong*?" a voice Katie didn't recognize, rang in her thoughts.

"*Hawk has changed, he is a Malus.*"

"*Are you sure*?"

"*Yes, I've seen him with my own eyes.*" She choked, as another round of tears engulfed her.

"*Don't worry, we'll take care of him.*"

She knew the choice was hers. She could tell them to stop. Her mind shied away from the decision. She wanted to beg, her pack to cease. She wanted them to continue. Knowing her silence, condemned the man she loved. She ran away as hard, and as fast as she could. She ran until she couldn't run anymore.

Katie woke up, sweat pouring down her face. Getting up, she took a cold shower. Lying back down on her bed, she went over the events in her dream. Her eyes felt gritty, as if she had been crying. She still felt the heartbreak in her chest. She no longer had to wonder how Old Elizabeth Hawk felt in making the decision to kill her Seeker. She knew in vivid detail every heart-wrenching moment.

Katie went over the events in her head. There was so little evidence the panther had killed the people in the campsite. Elizabeth had expected him to change. As soon as she had the slightest evidence, she condemned him. She didn't even look around or listen to him.

The name of the warrior was Hawk. The name seemed significant, knowing Elizabeth's chosen last name. Katie wondered, if Elizabeth went over the events in her head, and questioned her decision.

How could she not?

Katie closed her eyes, trying to ease the heartache she felt for Elizabeth. Once a decision is made, there is no going back. It has to be right. It has to, or the heartache will not only last one lifetime, but forever.

Using the technique Jackson had taught her, she reached out to him, keeping her thoughts private from everyone else. "*Jackson, are you all right?*"

It took a while, for his answer to come back. *"I'm here, Katie."*

"*Are you....*" She didn't know how to frame her question. "*Are you with the other Seekers?*"

"Yes."

She closed her eyes, her heartache increasing.

"Don't give up on me..."

Wiping a small tear from her eye, she shook her head. She realized, he couldn't see her. "*I'm not.*", The last part of her sentence left unsaid, not... yet.

Chapter 34
Practicing

Katie was practicing the mind technique Jackson wanted them to accomplish. She was seeing and hearing everything Candy was doing in Central High. She was aware of her own surroundings and functioning normally. She was determined to be the first to accomplish it. She didn't care about being the first, she amended, she just needed to learn it before Candy. She was beginning to think, she was getting the hang of it.

"Oh yeah, I can do this. No problem."

BAM!

She found herself sprawled on the floor, her head felt like it just exploded as pain lanced through her brain. As she slowly sat up, she thought she could actually see stars.

"Hey, are you all right?"

Recognizing the voice she didn't want to register, she realized David had just seen her hit a wall. Reaching up, she felt a warm sticky substance, she could only assume as blood, on her forehead.

"I believe, I need to take you to the nurse."

Katie shook her head, trying to reach around and find her bag.

"What are you reaching for?"

"My bag, where's my bag," she said softly, still clutching her head.

"Hold on, you've got stuff everywhere."

Katie lifted her hand away from her face, to see almost everything in her overloaded book bag had been dumped on the floor, including, an extra pair of clothes, a bra, and underwear. Mortified, Katie started grabbing things, making a pile next to her. *Why did something like this always happen to her, when David was around?*

"Hold on, I'm getting it. You just sit there until I take you to the nurse."

Katie watched as David in swift movements put everything back in her bag for her. Coming over, he examined her head. "You're going to need stitches."

"I'm alright, I just need..."

"What were you doing anyway?" He stood up and reached down to help her up. "I was watching you. You had to have seen it."

Katie shook her head, softly.

"I may be wrong, but I believe that wall has not moved since the school's been built."

"Ha! Ha!" Katie said sarcastically.

David chuckled softly. "Come on, I'll take you to the nurse."

"No, I just need to go to the restroom," Katie objected. "Thanks."

Turning, she headed for the nearest ladies room. Finding a paper towel, she wiped the blood from her face. Reaching into her bag, she pulled out a clean shirt. Changing quickly, she combed her hair. Taking one last look at herself, she walked out into the hall. She should have known, David was waiting patiently outside.

"Hold it there." David grabbed her arm. "I still need to take you to the nurse."

"No, I don't..."

He leaned over and moved her hair. Starring at her forehead, he looked down into her eyes. "It looks like a minor scratch."

Katie shrugged, "I heal quickly".

David narrowed his eyes, not letting her go.

"You didn't think I survived that car crash, by divine intervention, did you?" she said flippantly. "One of the perks," she shrugged, "you know."

"You were gone for four days," David said quietly.

"I was hurt pretty bad. Jackson found me."

David's spine stiffened, at Jackson's name. He shook his head a little. "What were you trying to do just now?"

"Jackson has us working on mind exercises. I was trying to look through Candy's eyes, while still functioning in my environment."

David paused a moment. "Let me see, if I got this right. You are trying to see through Candy's eyes, Candy who is attending Central High?"

"I didn't say that," Katie countered. "I can already see through Candy's eyes. I am attempting to see through her eyes, listening to what she hears, while still functioning in my environment. It's a lot harder than it sounds."

David nodded his head, a frown forming on his face, "How is learning this important?"

"I don't know. Jackson says we should learn it," she shrugged.

"Do you do everything Jackson says?"

"Absolutely," she nodded. "I'm going to learn it first this time." She said determinedly.

David sighed, "Your mom, has been talking to my mom."

Katie closed her eyes. She didn't know, if she wanted to hear what he was about to say. Opening her eyes, she braced herself for him to continue.

"She thinks Jackson, is a bad influence on you."

Katie grinned, that wasn't very bad.

"She doesn't like the idea that you drive his very expensive SUV. You're gone all the time. You seem to be incapacitated every weekend."

She nodded in agreement. "That's exactly, what's been happening."

"Care to explain?"

"Jackson's teaching us, how to fight. We meet in a lodge, owned by Candy's family. We go there every day after school. On the weekends, we work on our mind exercises. This, in turn, causes everyone to have massive migraines on Sunday." She shook her head. "It's not pretty."

"Who are you planning on fighting?" David asked quietly.

Katie shook her head. She almost turned, and walked swiftly away. Looking into David's face, she could tell he expected her to do just that. "Do you remember hearing about those campers, who were attacked by animals?"

David nodded, staring intently into her eyes.

"We have to stop them. They are no longer afraid of Elizabeth Hawk, and encroaching on her territory."

"What exactly are we talking about?" David asked quietly.

"Forrest calls them *Malus*." She shook her head. "I'm not even sure they are the worst things out there."

"How do you become, a *Malus*?"

Realizing she spoke too much. She hefted her bag on her shoulders, backing away. "I'm sorry, I have to go." Tears came to her when she saw the frustration and hurt on his face.

David stepped closer, blocking her way. He backed her into a locker, the lock digging into her back. "We have to know Katie. My family, your mom, everyone that's close to this thing has to know what's going on around us. Not knowing is killing us. Can you understand that? We've got to know…" He let her go and backed away from her. "Just think about it. Please?"

Shaken, Katie walked away.

"That was quite a conversation". Candy said through her thoughts.

Katie jumped. "*How much did you hear?"*

"Probably all of it. Your emotions were jumping all over the place, so I decided to investigate."

Katie grimaced. "*Jackson always complains, my emotions swing in every direction.*"

"Are you okay?"

She felt Candy's concern, through her emotions. "*Yeah."*

"He's probably right you know," Candy pointed out.

"You think we should tell our parents, and the Blacks?" Katie asked in surprise.

"No. I think we need to tell your parents and the Blacks. We need to leave my parents, completely out of this."

"Hey, if one parent is told all parents are told."

"Okay, forget I brought it up, Candy answered."

Chapter 35

The Black Family

"Katie this is ridiculous; we've been to every store in the mall."

Katie glanced up from the rack of dresses. "I don't see what I'm looking for."

"How do you know? You never even tried a single dress on," her mother shot back, frustration and fatigue etched in her features.

Since David had asked her, Katie had been casually looking for a prom dress for months. She had exhausted all the local stores in the surrounding towns. Since she had not found what she was looking for, her mother finally suggested they drive to Knoxville. Through the long hour and a half drive, Katie had enjoyed her mother's company. Now she was just tired. Everything she saw she knew wasn't going to work.

"I thought shopping was supposed to be fun," she mumbled.

"If you could tell me what you're looking for, I could probably help you find it," the helpful sales lady suggested.

That was the problem, Katie decided. She didn't know, what she wanted. She just knew everything she saw was not it.

"This bright red would look very pretty next to your dark skin. Not very many people would be able to wear this color, but I think it would be just beautiful on you."

Katie looked at the strapless dress, and shook her head, no. It didn't take her long to flip through the rest of the dresses. Looking up, she indicated to her mother she was ready to go.

"What exactly, are you looking for?" Her mother sighed, as they left the store.

"I don't know, Mom." She didn't know how to describe what she was looking for in her mind. "Let's just go home." Defeated, she walked back to the car.

"Did you find the right dress?" Candace asked through her mind.

"No."

"Do you need help?"

Katie realized she did need help, but not from Candace or her mother. She wished she could talk to Sam. Since that was no longer an option, Katie bit her thumbnail, going over her options. An idea forming in her mind.

Arriving home, she looked at her watch. "Mom, I'm going to take off for a while. Okay?"

She saw her mother's lips, compress into a frown. She wanted to tell her she wasn't going to see Jackson, but decided it might set a dangerous precedent. Climbing into the Hummer, she pulled out of the drive and headed towards the Black home. Pulling into the drive, she sat outside for a couple of minutes.

Finally, getting the courage she needed, she slowly got out of the vehicle and walked up the drive. Knocking on the door, she waited patiently. Butterflies were doing flip flops in her stomach. Mrs. Black answered the door. For a second, she gave Katie a bright smile. The smile faltered, followed by a deep sadness in her eyes.

Katie wondered if she should be here. "Hello, Mrs. Black."

"Hello Katie, David's not here."

Katie felt a little relieved. "I came here to see you actually."

Seeing the door opened wider, Katie carefully stepped into the living room. Looking around, she was assaulted by the sights and smells of Sam's home. Trying to fight the urge to flee, she waited for Mrs. Black to shut the door. Now that she had her full attention, she didn't really know where to start.

"Uh... I'm going to prom with David," she blurted out.

"Yes, I know." Mrs. Black pasted a smile that didn't quite reach her sad eyes.

Katie stood there, fiddling with her hands. "I can't find the right dress."

Mrs. Black raised her eyebrows.

This wasn't going very well, she decided. "I don't want to wear a sack, but I would like it to look nice or... I don't know, elegant." Shrugging, Katie didn't know how to describe what she wanted.

Mrs. Black waited patiently, for her to continue.

"Sam," she stumbled over the name. "Sam always said, modest was hottest." Tears came to her eyes. "I want to find a dress, Sam would be happy to wear. I would like David to feel comfortable, with what I'm wearing." She shrugged her shoulders, her arms outstretched. "I don't know where to look. Will you help me?"

Sarah Black stood frozen in place. Katie wondered if she was going to say no. The Blacks had always been so warm and kind. It never occurred to her, she might be turned down.

After what looked like a great effort, Mrs. Black stepped towards Katie and gave her a warm hug. "Of course, I'll help you."

"Oh great!" Katie was so relieved, she felt like doing a little dance.

"Wow, I didn't know if that was going to turn out all right," Candy interjected, with her thoughts.

Katie jumped. "*You need to give me a little heads-up if you're listening.*"

"Oops, sorry. Your emotions were all over the place again."

Katie followed Mrs. Black, into a cluttered room. Every wall was covered in shelves, that went up to the ceiling. Every flat surface, was covered with something. Katie took a closer look.

"That's all my scrapbooking stuff."

"All of it?"

"Yes, I used to work in here for hours. Now, I just don't feel like doing it anymore."

Katie leaned over, her eyes drawn to a large book marked "David." Pulling it out, she flipped through some of the pages. Smiling at some of the baby pictures, she shut the book and placed it on the shelf. Drawn to the name Samantha, she pulled out the large book. She slowly turned each page. Some of the pictures showed her there, smiling next to Sam. A knot formed in her throat as she carefully placed the book back in its place.

Turning, she saw Mrs. Black watching her carefully.

"I miss her," she said softly.

Sam's mother, fighting her own tears, nodded and turned away. "We first need to take some measurements."

Katie was a little confused. Maybe Mrs. Black thought, she had to sew a dress. She didn't want to sound ungrateful, but she didn't want a homemade dress either.

"I don't think you noticed, she turned her computer on." Candy piped into her thoughts.

Katie closed her eyes. "*What?*"

"*I think she's going to order a dress on the computer,*" Candy reiterated.

"*How did you know I was worried?*"

"*Your emotions are so strong, it's easy to tell what you're thinking.*"

Mrs. Black turned around and started taking measurements. After writing them down, she sat down at the computer. Giving a sigh of relief, Katie sat on a sewing stool close by. Going through a list of websites, Katie made comments and speculations, that had Sam's mom smiling and giving suggestions. They were soon arguing, and laughing over some of the dresses they found, eventually, coming up with a perfect selection, Katie pulled out her mom's credit card and made the purchase.

Getting up from the chair, they both turned to find David leaning against the door, watching them closely. Katie felt dumb and wanted to make a quick escape. His mother insisted she stay for dinner. She tried to make up an excuse. Her mother might be wondering, where she was. Mrs. Black made the call herself, informing her mother where she was, and that she'd be home later.

Katie helped make dinner. She told several funny stories of her encounters with Miss Smith, embellishing on the good twin who now has taken over her job. David started telling stories of his own. They were soon laughing, and having a good time. Nora and Ben sat on chairs and piped up with comments and a few stories of their own. Mr. Black came home, quietly staring at the scene. He eventually joined in. The family sat down at the table. Katie, having eaten there many times, automatically folded her arms and bowed her head to say grace.

Looking up, she saw the whole family staring at her. "What?"

Shaking his head, Mr. Black reached out for his wife's hand. The family eventually joined hands in a small circle. Bowing their heads, Sam's father said the prayer. Looking up, Katie was a little confused when she saw tears in Mr. and Mrs. Black's eyes. Not knowing what just happened, she looked towards David who squeezed her hand before letting go.

Having had a pleasant evening, Katie eventually stood up to leave. David followed her out the door. He was quiet, as he walked her out to the Hummer. Staring at the large vehicle, he opened the door. "Thank you," he said quietly.

"I didn't do anything."

"Yes, you did. My mother," he shook his head. "I forgot how my mother used to act before…" his voice trailed off.

"What happened at dinner?"

He kicked a tire. "We haven't prayed as a family since Sam died."

Shocked, Katie stood there. She had always known the Blacks to pray about everything under the sun. She remembered when she was little, complaining to her mother that Sam's family made up things to pray about.

"I'm sorry, David. I didn't know."

"Don't be." David stopped for a minute, looking at her. "We needed you to come over, and remind us what's important again."

Katie climbed into the SUV, and David shut the door. She rolled down the window and reached over to turn the engine over.

David patted the vehicle, with his hand. "I used to love Hummers; I don't care for them anymore."

"You don't like the car?"

"Nope, can't stand the sight of it," David said with a grimace.

Katie backed out of the drive and gave David a small wave.

"That was so sweet", Candy piped in.

Katie wasn't surprised this time around. "*Were you present the whole time*?"

"I couldn't' turn away. It was totally awesome. What a wonderful family."

"Yes, they are."

Chapter 36
Prom

Katie opened her eyes, turned over, and looked at the clock 10:00 am. She had slept in. Excitement coursed through her veins. She was going to prom with David. This was going to be the first Saturday in several months, where she didn't spend the whole day, working out with everyone on the team. Jackson had grimaced, and made a few snide remarks, when Lizzy and Katie reminded him they were not showing up for practice. Grinning, she had taken it in stride.

Enjoying her lazy morning, Katie was lying on the couch flipping through channels, when she heard a honk outside. Getting up, she peered out the window. Seeing Candy in her sporty BMW, she walked outside.

"What are you doing?" she said with a laugh.

Candy rolled down her window half way. "Come on, we're going to be late."

"Late for what?" she couldn't help asking.

"I'm not telling," Candy laughed, "Hurry!"

Katie climbed in, squeezing herself next to Lizzy. She shot her a questioning look. Lizzy only shrugged in return.

"Where are you taking us?"

Candy only smiled. "You'll see."

Katie leaned back and didn't pay attention to where they were going. Laughing and talking to Candy and Lizzy, she felt happy and content. Noticing Candy had slowed down, she peered out the window with interest. Candy had pulled into a parking lot of a very impressive looking building. The grounds had small waterfalls and botanical gardens. Katie had no idea such a place existed so close to her home. Feeling a little apprehensive, she slowly got out of the car.

"What is this place?" she said in wonder.

Candy only giggled, and told them to follow her. Entering one of the doors, Katie could only gape at the elegant surroundings. Feeling underdressed, she wished she had worn her best clothes. Then she decided maybe her best clothes still were not good enough for this place. Candy walked confidently through the lobby giving a wave to the girl behind the counter.

Apprehensively, Katie followed.

"You don't have to worry. It's going to be fun." Candy's thoughts entered her mind.

"I'm not worried," Katie lied.

Candy giggled, *"I can feel your emotions, remember."*

Katie decided to ignore her.

Coming to another desk, Candy stopped and laid her purse down. "Hello, Michelle. These are the two girls, I was telling you about." She gestured towards Katie and Lizzy.

The woman behind the counter immediately stood up and smiled. "Very good, Miss Franklin." The woman motioned to them. "If you will follow me?"

Katie gave Candy a grimace, and then followed the woman. Four hours later, Katie and Lizzy left the building feeling as if they have never actually lived before. A full spa treatment was something to be worshiped. They had been soaked, caressed, manicured, pedicured, shampooed, cut, and styled. Every inch of her body glowed. Climbing back into Candy's car, she turned to her friend. "So, this is how the other side lives."

Candy sat grinning, from ear to ear. "Feels pretty good, doesn't it?"

Leaning back in the seat, Katie closed her eyes. "I just want to know one thing."

"What?"

"How come I wasn't your friend, a long time ago?"

Candy laughed contagiously. "I knew you would love it."

Katie stood in front of the mirror, not recognizing the elegant figure staring back at her. Turning around to see the back of her dress, she smiled. Her hair was twisted and braided, except for soft curls that lightly touched her neck. Hearing a sound behind her, she looked in the mirror. Jackson was sitting on her window seal. His eyes hooded. Slowly turning around, she faced him.

"Well, what do you think?"

"You're beautiful, Katie." He said it so softly, she could barely hear him.

She felt the blood, rush to her cheeks at the compliment. "Did you just crawl, through my window?"

Jackson smiled derisively. "I get the strongest impression, your mom doesn't like me very much."

"She doesn't know you like I do."

Jackson shrugged, getting slowly to his feet. Walking over to her I-Pod, he flicked through her music. Finding a song, he set it down on her I-home. A soft love song drifted softly from the speakers. He walked over to her.

"Could I have this dance?"

Without waiting for her to reply he stepped in and gathered her in his arms. He slowly rotated, in her small room. He lifted his arm gently, spinning her in a small circle.

"I don't know how to ballroom dance," she said softly her voice unsure.

He chuckled, "I can teach you."

They gently swayed to the music. She cautiously looked up into his eyes. They had turned into a dark turquoise. He placed his forehead against hers and pulled her closer to him. She could feel, the strong beat of his heart against hers. His body felt warm next to hers, causing heat to course through her system. She liked the feel of his arms, around her. She wanted him to… to what? She closed her eyes, her confused emotions vibrating through her body.

They both heard the loud knock, on the front door. Jackson stopped dancing, staring into her eyes. Letting her go, he dropped his arms, and backed away. Not saying a word, he crawled out of her window.

Katie watched him go. She could hear her mother, greeting David in the living room. She turned and stared at her reflection in the mirror. Her brows were knitted into a confused frown. Her face flushed, her eyes bright, she could feel her heartbeat fluttering in her chest. She stayed where she was, until her mother opened her bedroom door.

She tried to smile as her mother gushed over her dress and the way she looked. Slowly following her mother down the small hallway, she caught the handsome face of David Black. He looked incredible in his tux, the cumber bun and tie matching her dress.

His face first registered shock, then a slow smile spread across his features. She couldn't help smiling back. Going through the motions of taking pictures, she good-naturedly did everything her mother asked. When her mother obviously ran out of poses, David grabbed her hand and led her outside.

Katie didn't realize David had stopped until she stumbled into him. Looking up, she saw Jackson leaning up against the Hummer. He slowly tossed the keys in the air.

Pushing himself off the vehicle, he strode towards them. "Candy seemed to think, you were going to take Katie in your old jeep. I thought she was absolutely nuts, but I guess I was wrong."

David stiffened.

Jackson's cocky smile widened. "I told her, you could take the Hummer. She told me you hated the car, and would not ride in it."

Jackson continued, with his one-sided conversation. "She told me I could not allow you to take Katie in your old jeep, and you were to take her BMW." He gestured to the road.

Katie turned her head, she could see Candy's car sitting on the side of the curb.

"I have my own car, thanks," David said stiffly.

Jackson frowned and half turned to face David's Jeep. Sitting next to the Hummer, it looked old and decrepit. "Look, don't turn down the wheels, because it's me offering it," he said quietly. "The car is Candy's, not mine."

David stood stiffly, his hand clutching Katie's tightly.

"I'll tell you what. I'll just give you the keys." He tossed the keys to David, who automatically caught them. "I'll take off, then I won't know what vehicle you actually took. Sound fair?" Jackson turned, and climbed into the Hummer. "I'll see you later." He said casually, shutting the door. He backed out of the driveway.

David watched him go, with narrowed eyes. Giving his jeep a hard look he sighed, and turned to her. "You have some choice friends, Katie."

Katie didn't know what to say. "Candy is a generous person," she said softly. "I can see her, wanting this night to be special."

David sighed, and touched her cheek. "I want this night to be special too," he said softly.

"We don't have to take the BMW. We can take your jeep. I don't care," Katie insisted. "I love your jeep." She added for good measure.

David grinned, flicking the keys in his hand. "I've always wanted to drive a BMW."

Katie grinned, "Here's your chance," she said wickedly.

"It's Candy's car?"

She nodded.

David gently pulled her, to the sporty vehicle. He softly caressed the hood. Opening the car door for Katie, he helped her in. Running around to the driver's side, he slid behind the wheel. Turning the engine over, he revved the engine a few times. Smiling wickedly, he put it into gear and whipped the car around. Speeding down the road, he let out a whoop that had Katie laughing along with him.

David took the familiar route, to his place. Telling her to stay in the car, he ran around and opened the car door for her. She felt a little stupid but liked the gentleman-like behavior. She went into the Black home, so his mother could see them. They good-naturedly took more pictures, before giving them a final goodbye.

David took the longest route he possibly could take to get to the school. Pulling into the parking lot, she could tell he still wanted to drive.

"Dance's usually take a while to get going," she suggested. "We could probably be late."

Turning a grin towards her, he whipped the car around and headed for the canyon. He drove easily, through the narrow road. "I didn't think anything, could top your Camaro."

Katie grimaced. "I miss my car."

"You have a fancy Hummer to drive."

Katie looked over unable to read his face, "I still miss my car."

"I don't get it, Katie, don't his parents wonder where his vehicle is or something?"

Katie looked out over the narrow road. "His parent's think he's dead, or maybe a runaway."

She could feel David's glance, before it returned to the road. "Why would they think that?"

"Because he disappeared," she said quietly.

"He went to Central High. His parents live close by."

"If he goes near his family, they might be in danger." She was beginning to feel uneasy, where the conversation was headed.

"Is your mom in danger?"

"No."

"Then why?

Katie felt the familiar panic in her chest when David started asking too many questions. She looked out the window, not answering his question.

Letting out a sigh, David pulled over into a lookout area. Turning off the vehicle he turned. "I'm sorry Katie, I don't want to pressure you tonight. I want to have a good time."

Katie looked back at his handsome face. The last rays of sunlight putting his features into shadow. "I want to have a good time too."

"Let's not discuss Jared, Jackson, or whoever he is tonight, deal?" David held out his hand.

Katie reached out, and shook his hand. "Deal."

Returning to school, they walked into the gym. Katie looked surprised, at how much the old gym had been transformed. Seeing Lizzy and Tyler dancing, she gave them a quick wave. Walking over, they sat down, next to a bunch of David's friends. He held her hand, making sure she was close to him at all times. He included her in the conversations. He kept turning towards her, as if he couldn't keep his eyes off her.

Eventually, he got up, and he led her onto the dance floor, holding her close. Katie loved the feeling of his arms around her. She softly swayed to the music, thinking everything was perfect. She laid her head onto David's chest, breathing in his masculine scent. *This is perfect*, she thought to herself. *This is how she'd always envisioned dating David would be.*

Panic and fear jolted her. Katie immediately raised her head. Looking around, couples were entwined in each other arms swaying to the love song. Laying her head back onto David's chest, fear rippled through her body.

Where were these emotions coming from? Panic raced through her body, making her heart jump. Concern jammed through her consciousness, when she realized these were not her emotions but Candy's. Candy was gripped in fear and in trouble, automatically reaching out with her mind.

"Candy what's wrong?"

Candy gave a gasp in her thoughts, "*I'm sorry… I know you're at prom."*

Katie shook her head "*What's going on?"*

"It's Jackson he's gone..."

Katie could hear she was on the verge of tears.

Fear rippled through Katie's body, causing her heart to beat frantically. Realizing she was gently being shook, she opened her eyes into David's looming face.

"You haven't heard a word I said," he said softly.

"Something's wrong." Pulling out of his arms, she walked off the dance floor. "*Tyler, Lizzy, I need you now."*

Lizzy immediately began protesting. Katie gave a backward look, towards the other couple. *Tyler?*

"We're coming," Tyler immediately responded.

Walking out of the gym, she surveyed the group of parents acting as chaperones. Taking a quick left turn, she headed for the parking lot. "*What happened?"*

"We were planning on watching a movie, and eating pizza together. When I got here the place is tore up, and Jackson's not here."

Katie reached Candy's car and leaned up against the vehicle. Closing her eyes, she saw the broken windows first. Directing Candy to change into animal form, she had her walk around the lodge. Several of the chairs were turned over, stuffing was strung out over the floor. She could tell, Jackson had put up an incredible fight. She asked Candy to smell the ground. The clear scent of Surgious, plus four other Seekers was present.

Opening her eyes, she wasn't surprised seeing David standing within inches of her. He was watching her closely. Deciding to ignore him for the moment, she turned to Tyler and Lizzy.

"Five Seekers, have taken Jackson."

She felt Candy's presence, in her mind.

"Well it's about time, is all I have to say."

Shock rippled through her body, when she turned to stare at Lizzy, "What?"

Lizzy folded her arms defensively, "He's not one of us, Katie. We're better off if he's with his own kind."

"I didn't see you complaining, when he was teaching you how to fight, or stretch your mind." Katie shot back sarcastically.

"He was willing to teach me, and I was willing to learn."

Katie shouldn't have been surprised, by what she was hearing. Hadn't she had those same thoughts, herself about Jackson? Hearing it from Lizzy, sounded awful. She felt ashamed and inflamed at the same time.

"They are going to kill him, Lizzy. Does that mean anything to you?"

"Don't you dare judge me." Lizzy pointed her finger at Katie, her face growing ugly. "I haven't forgotten who's responsible for Sam's death. I haven't decided to conveniently forget."

She hadn't forgotten. Doubt clouded her judgment, making her vulnerable to Lizzy's onslaught. Keeping her face as blank as possible, she was racked with indecision.

"He didn't kill Sam." Candy pointed out privately in her mind. She could feel Katie's emotions, as they warred with each other.

"What if he becomes a Malus?" Katie asked Candace with her thoughts. Katie hated herself, as she gave voice to her most inner fears. "*He is far better, then all of us combined. What if this is our only chance, to stop him?*"

"Katie, we have already had this conversation. You cannot judge him for something he has not done."

"He may not have killed her, but if it were not for him, Sam would be alive."

"Are you telling me, you have not forgiven him for that? This whole time you have pretended to be his friend, only to harbor feelings of ill will?" Candy pointed out mercilessly.

"No". Katie sighed. She knew David, Tyler, and Lizzy were wondering what was going on in her head. "*I just need to throw out my doubts and fears, to ears that won't condemn me for them."* She felt Candy's understanding, and empathy.

"Katie, Jackson's going to die if we don't save him. We need to go and save the man of today. Not the one who made a bad decision of yesterday, or the man who may choose wrong in the future. But, the Jackson we know and love today."

Katie pictured Jackson's beautiful face, those clear blue eyes sparkling over something stupid she had said. In reality, she wanted to believe him. The choice was hers. Does she believe a Seeker can change? Or, does she end up being a fool.

Katie folded her arms defensively. She was highly aware David was listening closely to everything Lizzy implied. She knew he was burning with questions and accusations. She came to the only decision she wanted to make.

"We're wasting time. Jackson's in trouble. I'm not going to force anyone to go and help. As for me, I'm going to do everything in my power, to save him. Tyler, are you in or out?" She could feel Candy's relief.

Lizzy grabbed Tyler's arm. "This could be a trap. How do we know anything he has ever said is true? He can have us see anything, with our eyes. How do we know those scars on his body, are real?"

David cleared his throat. "I can see the scars, but I can't see him wearing clothes."

Katie gave him an appreciative glance. "He has never lied to me," she said realizing it was true. "Even in the beginning, he warned me I needed to stay away from him." She gave Tyler, a questioning look.

Tyler gently pulled out of Lizzy's grasp and stood silently next to Katie.

Katie turned, to get into the car. "*Hold tight Candy, we're on our way.*"

"HE KILLED HER!" Lizzy screamed "He killed Sam. How can you go, and risk your lives for him?" She spat out the last words, in hatred.

Katie felt David stiffen next to her, bowing her head she closed her eyes for a moment. "You saw him kill her?" she said softly. "You saw him make the killing blow?"

"He could have done it just as easily. You don't know if he did or not."

"Yes, I do Lizzy, because he has saved my life, yours, Tyler's, and Candace's on multiple occasions. We are a team; that means family." Katie stepped closer to Lizzy. "You voted to include him after you knew he was a Seeker. You accepted him. I did not force you."

Tears streaming down her face, Lizzy shook her head.

"There has to be a time in everyone's life, where you regret a decision or action. You wish with every fiber of your being to change the clock back, and make a different choice. But you can't. No one can. So, when the time comes, you go to the people you hurt. You ask for their forgiveness. You hope they will try, and forget what you can't." Katie sighed. "I don't want to be the person who refuses to forgive. I want to be someone like Old Elizabeth Hawk. She was loved and cherished, because she was kind and gentle. She was also ferocious, and fought evil threatening her people." She stepped closer to Lizzy. "Jackson is a part of us. He needs us to save him, with or without you. We are going."

"We're outnumbered," Lizzy mumbled.

"Yes, we are."

"We could die," she said softly.

"Yes, we could."

Lizzy stood uncertainly.

"Our courage has already been tested, Lizzy. The Great White Tiger tested us, before the animal spirit entered our bodies. We all passed. That is why we are here."

Lizzy nodded slowly, still not making a decision.

Katie was beginning to run out of patience. "We need to get there, before he dies, Lizzy. That's what saving him means," she said sarcastically.

Lizzy wiped her tears and nodded silently. "I'll get my car."

Tyler gave Katie a quick smile and lopped after her.

"I guess I'll just ride with them," she said turning towards David. "I'm sorry we ruined this night for you."

"Katie," David stepped closer to her, "I don't want you to go."

She shook her head, "I have too."

"It's supposed to be me running off. Saving the damsel in distress, not sitting back letting my damsel do all the fighting."

Katie smiled in the darkness. "I don't need saving, David. I can take care of myself."

"I don't want any regrets," David said quietly stepping closer to her.

He reached out and touched her chin gently, easing it upward. Taking his time, he let her know what he intended. His lips were soft and warm. Giving into the kiss, Katie's heart sang as the kiss deepened. She wrapped her arms around his neck, letting her body and her emotions take control.

She had dreamed about this moment, a moment when David Black kissed her, and it was exactly how she thought it would be. Her body felt warm and compliant, as she felt his arms wrap tightly around her. She didn't want this moment to end. A small honk, had them pulling apart. Her breathing labored, she could tell David was just as affected as she was.

David turned his head, to see Lizzy's car close by. "He hasn't you know."

Her mind foggy, Katie didn't understand what David was talking about. "What?"

"Jackson hasn't gone to everyone, and told them what happened, asking for their forgiveness."

Katie stiffened in his arms.

David tightened his arms around Katie, not letting go. "Sam's family has a right to know everything that happened to her." He gave her a little shake, his emotions spilling out. "We have to know Katie. Not knowing, is destroying us." He slowly loosened his arms, to let her go. "You're a big part of my life, Katie." He tucked a strand, behind her ear. "I need you in my life. Do you understand? I need you here, beside me."

Katie wanted to stay in his arms, and listen to the words she'd always wanted to hear from him. Instead, she gently pulled away from him, and walked towards Lizzy's car. She looked back at the handsome young man she had been in love with since she was eleven. She heard the words, softly in the night.

"Come back Katie. Please, come back."

Climbing into the car, she watched him standing alone in the dark. She watched, until he was no longer in sight.

Chapter 37
Saving Jackson

They drove in silence, each one mentally preparing for the fight ahead. Eventually, the dark lodge came into view. Katie could see a snow leopard, waiting impatiently on the porch. Getting out of the vehicle, Katie took a couple of minutes to get undressed, hoping Lizzy's car blocked most of her body from Tyler's view. Changing into animal form quickly, she ran towards Candy.

"I've already figured out where they came and left," Candy explained. *"I don't know how they were able to take him, without his being incapacitated in some way."*

Katie could feel the fear and concern for Jackson rippling through Candy's body. *"We'll find him, Candy."* Now she had committed herself, she was determined to follow through.

Not waiting for Lizzy or Tyler, she followed Candy till she caught on to the scent herself. She took the lead, stretching her legs running full out. *"How long ago, do you think they came, and got him?"*

"Over an hour, maybe a little more," Candy answered. *"I wasted time getting here."*

"Don't beat yourself up," Katie shot back. *"What would have happened, if we noticed him gone in the morning?"*

The trail was getting stronger. She could tell they were gaining. "*If they were picking him up, and dragging him it would take them a lot longer to get to their destination.*"

"How do you know, they have a destination?"

"Because, if they just wanted to kill him, they would have done it back at the Lodge," Katie answered. She could feel Candy's horror, at the thought of finding Jackson's body.

"W*e are going to save him,"* she said more confidently, then she felt.

Coming to the top of the hill, Katie quickly stopped breathing heavily. She gazed at the scene below. She counted twenty-three large animals, grouped sporadically in the valley below. They were all facing in one direction. A woman was standing in front, obviously speaking to the group. Katie strained her ears, but couldn't hear anything.

Candy hunched down next to Katie, viewing the scene below. "*They must be talking through their minds. Why didn't Jackson, teach us how to hear them*? "Frustration was evident in her thoughts.

"Obviously an oversight," Katie answered.

"There behind the woman," Candy pointed out, "*He's tied to that tree.*"

Katie moved a couple of feet over. She could see Jackson's back. His arms were stretched tight, over a couple of branches. His back was bare. Fresh scratches, streaked across his back. " *We have to come up with a plan and fast,*" she said cautiously.

Hearing Tyler and Lizzy coming up the hill, she cautioned them to keep quiet. She quickly gave them the information they'd learned and turned back towards the scene. "*Have any ideas?*"

"Actually I do, Candy inserted. *I don't think we have to fight them all, only the Seekers who have turned into a Malus, or are about to,* she pointed out. *I bet all of those other Seekers want out, just as badly as Jackson did."*

"How can we differentiate the two groups?"

"The hierarchy of the animal kingdom," Candy pointed out.

"What?" Katie was hoping Candy was going to make a point.

Candy gave a deep breath. *"I don't have time to explain the alpha and omega of the animal kingdom. I think the lower class of animals will be in the back, while the alphas of the pack will place themselves in front."*

Katie couldn't believe this, but it actually made sense. Who knew, she would actually use the stuff she learned in science class.

"So, how are we going to get past the ones who don't want to fight?"

Candy turned to Lizzy. *"Lizzy can virtually make us see anything she wants. I think if she projects an image of the scene below, we could basically walk past the Seekers in the lower pack. We could get to the alphas. If one of us can get to Jackson and untie him, Lizzy can project Jackson's image that he's still there."*

Katie was beginning to see the plan. Turning to the other two, she could see Tyler was on board. Lizzy was once again shaking her head.

"Do you see a hole?"

"There are over twenty were-animals. What if Candy's wrong, and they all fight us at once?"

Katie was losing patience. *"Then we'll fight like hell, and probably die."*

"We're going to die for a Seeker?"

Katie was tired of having the same argument again. "*NO, we're going to die, trying to save a member of our team.*" She looked back over the scene.

She could see a small ridge to the right. She pointed the ridge out to the others. "*Lizzy if you could sneak up there, you will have a commanding view and be able to project. Tyler, you go to the left of the group. Candy, you go to the right. I'll go up the middle, and try to reach Jackson.*"

She let the plan form in her mind. "*If you get close to an alpha, and he's not standing close to anyone else, go ahead and take him out. Lizzy can cover up the sound, and smell of the fight.*"

"How are we supposed to know an alpha, from one of the omegas?" Tyler asked.

"My guess is they will have a strong evil smell. Once you have smelled it, your instinct will step into overdrive. You will want to fight, Katie answered. *Everyone knows what to do?"* She waited till she saw a distinct nod from everyone. *"Okay, let's sneak up close while Lizzy finds her way to that ridge."*

Katie slowly and quietly, moved until she was just behind the last were-animal in the pack. Waiting patiently, she heard Lizzy's go ahead. It was unnerving to walk past the large animals without their being aware of her position. She could tell Candy's hypothesis that alphas were closer to the front was correct. The particular pungent smell grew stronger the closer she came to the front. Pausing for just a moment she identified Surgious's position.

Staring at the large cat, she fought the urge to attack. She needed to get Jackson down first, she told herself. Memorizing his position, she promised herself he was going to be the first one she attacked. She walked so close to the woman, she felt the soft breeze as she waved her hand in the air making an obvious point.

Getting a firsthand view of Jackson's back made her gasp. What looked like scratches from a distance were claw marks cut deep into his sinew. Walking around the tree, she turned human clothes automatically forming on her body.

"Jackson, we're here to save you, hold on let me untie your hands."

She wrestled with the ropes. She kept looking up over her shoulder expecting to be attacked. Getting one hand free, he swayed hanging from the other hand. In his place, a projected Jackson stood still in the same position. Working as fast as she could, she eventually had him completely untied.

"Jackson, we have to go."

His eyes were unfocused, she wondered if he'd been drugged. Shaking him, she got no response. She changed back into wolf, wondering what she could do now. If he was a panther she could carry him. In this form, she was afraid of causing more damage to his tender flesh.

"Jackson, please, I need you to snap out of it, and help me."

Jackson opened his eyes and focused on her for a moment. "Help me," he pleaded.

"What's wrong?" Candy asked uncertainly.

"He's not responding." Katie closed her eyes fighting tears of frustration. "*I can't drag him, because he's not wearing enough clothes. I can't pick him up, because he's human."*

"Something must be stopping him from changing. Candy's thoughts rang out. *Get into his mind Katie, and see what's going on."*

Getting down on her haunches, she closed her eyes trying to relax. She concentrated on the young man she had grown to care about. "*Trust me, Jackson, I need you to trust me.*" Emotions rippled through her body. She knew the moment she broke through. Despair filled her soul. Self-hatred clawed in her stomach. Not able to take the raw emotions, she collapsed turning human. Lifting her head up, she saw Candace fall on the ground in human form.

"What have we here?" The woman said in wonder. "Two more morsels, to fill your appetites bring them closer," she commanded.

Katie felt hands grab her, as she was dragged to the forefront kneeling. She watched Candy being dragged and placed heavily by her side.

"Bring the traitor also."

Katie turned her head, as Jackson was unceremoniously dumped next to her. *Jackson*? she pleaded with her mind.

He opened his eyes, finally focusing on her, "I'm sorry."

Katie felt another wave of despair, envelope her soul. Desperate, she felt she only had one chance left, to reach into his mind. She needed to find out where the strong emotions were coming from. Fighting the terror, that was trying to claw its way into her consciousness, she closed her eyes concentrating on Jackson's mind.

Images raced through her mind. At first, she didn't understand. Then she realized she was actually in Jackson's memories as he was on the verge of changing into animal form. She felt his fear as he struggled to figure out what was happening to him. Looking up, she heard Surgious's words as he forced him to make a decision to become a Seeker or die. She felt him bow down, and say a Seekers oath.

"I Jared Price, promise to become a Seeker. I give my rights up, as an individual which includes my free agency to choose my own destiny. I will use my gift for the cause of my leaders, for they are far greater than I. I make this covenant under no duress, and of my own free will and choice."

Katie listened intently and slowly, to the words Surgious made Jackson speak. She could hear a voice, echoing in his mind. *"You made a binding covenant to become a Seeker. "Do you honestly believe you can just walk away? You will always be bound to us…Always! Your loyalty is to us. We own you. We own your soul. You will never break free from the bonds that tie us together. Even in death, you will be bound to us."*

Katie felt the wave of despair hit her, sucking her energy and leaving her helpless. Struggling to stay in contact with his mind she reached out. "*Jackson, it's a lie. Do you hear me? The oath is a lie. You made it under duress. It was not of your own free will and choice."*

She could feel him reaching out, grasping her words, wanting to, but not believing. "*I believe in you. Candy is here, and she believes in you. Tyler and Lizzy are somewhere out there, risking their lives for you."*

Katie felt a blow to her head, knocking her down. Hitting the ground hard she opened her eyes, trying to get her bearings.

"HOW DARE YOU!" the woman screamed "Do you honestly think, you can save this pathetic piece of human tissue? He's not worth the scum on my shoe."

Katie slowly got back onto her knees, looking up at the woman.

"He's worth it," she said through clenched teeth. "His heart and soul are intact. He made the oath under duress."

She was hit again from behind, slamming her to the ground. Knowing she was probably going to die, she gave a small laugh as she slowly got back on her knees. "Don't want the others to hear, I see. Afraid they may start questioning the lies you've told?" Again, she was slammed to the ground.

"Katie, stop," Candy pleaded.

Katie looked over at her friend, a sadness enveloping her.

"I'm sorry, Candy. I wish I could have been a better friend." Getting back up on her knees, she reached out with one hand and grabbed Jackson's hand. Reaching with the other hand, she grabbed Candy's. She looked out over the crowd of Seekers.

"IT'S A LIE!" she screamed. **"YOU'RE NOT BOUND TO THEM!"**

She was hit so hard from behind, she momentarily blacked out. A sharp pain in her ribs awakened her, realizing she was being viciously kicked over and over again. She looked up, to see the shadow of a man kicking her. Rolling over, she tried to avoid the beating to no avail. Not able to do anything else, she eventually lay there unable to stop the assault.

The last kick was to her face. Seeing stars, she blinked a couple of times waiting for more. She lifted her head.

"*Katie, stay down, please, just stay down.*" She could hear Candy's heartbreak, and tears through her thoughts.

Katie spit out blood. The liquid threatened to choke her. Slowly, she lifted herself up and crawled back into place. Reaching out, she grabbed Jackson's hand, then floundering a little she found Candy's. Her eyes swelling shut she looked out over the crowd, lifting her head. She could barely see the Seeker's animal shapes Bracing herself for another beating, she took a deep breath. "They're lying to you," she croaked barely able to form the words. "It's a lie."

The woman laughed loudly. "Look at this poor helpless creature. See how desperate she is, for everyone to believe such a ridiculous notion. The oath a Seeker makes is binding. Once it is made, it cannot be undone."

Chapter 38
Forgiven

Katie shook her head slowly in defiance, looking out once again over the crowd. Her eyes caught a slight movement. Trying to focus, she latched on to a shadow, hope beating in her chest.

"Look" her thoughts rang out "*Look, Candy, do you see it*"

"I don't see anything."

"No, straight ahead of us, do you see it? "She was desperate for someone else to see The Great White Tiger as it walked towards her. She was so afraid it was a mirage. She heard Candy gasp, her hand tighten on hers.

"I see it, Katie."

Katie felt a wave of hope, as the spirit of The Great White Tiger walked through the crowd of Seekers, not seen by anyone but them.

"Jackson, do you see it?"

She felt a small squeeze of her hand. The first real response from him. The spirit ignored the woman, who was once again ranting to the crowd. It walked up to Katie purring loudly in her ear, it placed its forehead against hers. She felt a calmness envelop her soul, as hope became a reality. The pain in her body drained. Energy returned. She instinctively knew she would be able to change into wolf form once again.

The tiger stepped towards Candy, placing its forehead against hers. Withdrawing, it turned to Jackson. Katie watched his face, as he silently pleaded to the tiger to forgive him. The tiger took a few steps towards him and placed her forehead against his.

Katie could feel joy and acceptance replace the despair and self-hatred Jackson had been feeling. The tiger stepped back. Looking over its shoulder Katie could see a faint whisper of a black panther, as it walked up staring straight into Jackson's eyes for a moment. The panther stepped to the side, and positioned its body in the same position as Jackson, quickly entering his body. Katie turned back to face the tiger, only to see the last bit of her image disappear. All three of them bowed their heads, in a mock defeated posture.

"Get ready," Jackson thoughts rang out loud and clear. "There are three behind us, and two to the right that are the most dangerous. Katie, Surgious is directly behind you."

"He's mine," Katie communicated. She shivered, as she felt his hot breath against her neck. She tried to control the instinct to immediately change and fight.

Katie listened to the woman's ranting, as she eventually turned attention back to the three of them. She told the crowd what would happen to them, if they were not loyal to her. She stressed how she didn't want to kill them, but an example had to be made.

"Get ready," Jackson communicated.

The old woman faced them with a malicious smile. Katie could tell the next words out of her mouth were going to be, *Kill them*.

Jackson must have realized the same, because he lifted his head. *"NOW!"*

Katie felt as if it was just another practice day as they all jumped simultaneously in the air doing backward flips, changing in mid-air. She landed behind Surgious. Before he realized where she was, she jumped on his back, going in for the kill. Realizing she was there, he twisted clawing her stomach and chest with his sharp razor claws. She gave out a sharp yelp and quickly backed away.

Another oversight she mused. Playing fighting cats with their claws retracted was a lot different than fighting a cat with four sets of claws ready to rip your insides out. She circled the large bobcat, eyeing him wearily. Surprise rushed through her system, when the cat turned human.

Surgious gave her and evil smile, raising his hands and licking his fingers. "I knew a were-animal would be tasty."

Katie hardly registered the words, as shock rippled through her body. Unable to control the impulse she turned human, clothes automatically forming on her body.

"You!" She said pointing at the naked young man. "I know you!"

He was filthy, his hair was longer and greasy, but she recognized his features immediately.

Surgious smiled. "That's a nice trick you have learned. Too bad I have to kill you, before I can learn it from you."

"Steven Bends." The name exploding from her shocked system.

"That name no longer has any meaning to me."

Katie shook her head, trying to get control of her emotions "You were in the Black home, as much as I was. You are best friends, with Robbie Black."

Katie could picture him in the Black home, jockeying around with Robbie and David. The three of them were inseparable until Robbie and Steven had graduated. "How could you?"

"Are you planning on killing the guy, or just talking to him?" Jackson's thoughts slammed into her shocked system.

Katie ignored Jackson, staring at the face in front of her. "You loved the Blacks, and yet you killed Sam. WHY?"

Surgious stepped closer to her. "Samantha Black made her decision. She chose to die."

"You didn't have to kill her. You could have let her go," Katie tried to reason with him. "Do you have any idea the heartache you caused?"

"Why should I give her a break?" Steven's angry voice rose above the battle around them. "No one stepped forward to save me." He stepped closer.

"Do you need help killing him?" Jackson impatient thoughts rang out.

She automatically turned her head towards Jackson. She felt, rather than saw Steven change and attack. Jumping into the air she back flipped away from him, changing into her wolf form in midair. Landing ten feet from where she originally was, she once again jumped onto the cat's back. Using her weight as leverage, she wouldn't allow the cat to turn and claw her stomach and chest again.

Acting on instinct, she picked him up by the scruff of his neck and shook him violently. Lowering him, she repositioned her mouth ready to clamp down on his inner neck. The large cat took advantage of her letting go and clawed deeply into her face and neck. Letting out a yelp she didn't back away, but clamped down on his inner neck. She felt the large cat, struggle for breath. She could hear his heartbeat slow down, and eventually stop.

Allowing herself a few seconds to consider what she had just done, she silently mourned the young man she had once known. Looking up, she could see Candy backed up against a tree. Two large cats ready to attack her at once. In two strides she jumped on one of them, while Candy was able to attack the other. Using her strength and bulk as a weapon, she quickly used the same technique she learned with Surgious. She learned to protect her stomach, and chest from sharp claws.

She looked around and could see Jackson fighting three large cats at the same time. She headed in that direction when a huge jaguar jumped out of nowhere and landed on her back. As the large cat sunk its nails into her back, she jumped up in the air fell back onto her back hoping her weight would loosen the cats hold. She could tell, she had knocked the wind out of it. Taking advantage of the situation, she jumped up and whirled around, quickly causing the cat to fly off.

She was a little annoyed, when it landed perfectly on its feet. Jumping onto its back, she grabbed the back of its neck and shook viciously. Again taking advantage of a rattled cat, she went in for the kill. Looking up, she noticed Jackson didn't actually need any help at all. He had somehow taken care of the three, and was closing in on another cat.

She quickly glanced around for Candy, to find her sitting on her haunches watching Jackson fight. Taking a quick scan around, it was obvious the fighting was over. The large cats that were killed, were slowly turning back into human shapes. She tried not to look into their faces, afraid she would recognize someone else.

Katie glanced around, as she saw an African tiger direct a Seeker. The Seeker had given up standing in the center, where the other Seekers, didn't want to fight.

She caught a glimpse, of an old timber wolf. Keeping an eye on the wolf, she quickly looked around to make sure all of her friends were still alive. Filled with relief, she spotted all four as they quickly gathered up Seekers. They were herding them into the center. She spotted a black panther, he was looking down at something on the ground. Wondering what he was doing, she quickly ran towards him.

"You won't get away with this, I will be missed." The woman lay on the ground, her hands in the air. "You have no idea, what you are up against," she laughed. "What you have done, will not go unnoticed. They will come for you."

"We have legions. **LEGIONS!"** she screamed. "They will not allow, any of you to live."

Katie turned away, as Jackson went in for the kill. Facing the Seekers, she counted nine. She felt Jackson's presence next to her. "*How many is a legion*?"

"I don't know," Jackson uttered, *"more than five?"*

Katie nodded, "*more than fourteen*?"

Jackson looked towards the Seekers. "*Definitely."*

"*Just as long as we have a chance,*" Katie muttered.

Jackson changed into human form. His clothes immediately covering, where hair disappeared. Following his example, she changed also.

"I don't understand," he said softly. "It made no strategic sense, for you to come after me. Why? Why did you do it?

Trying to forget her indecision, Katie looked out over the meadow. "I don't understand what you're asking?"

Jackson let out a sigh, "I'm just a pawn, Katie, I'm expendable. If I disappeared, no one would care."

"You're wrong, Jackson. There are a lot of people who care about you, including your family." Katie looked down at the ground. "I felt the emotions, inside of you. You're the one who told me, those emotions will destroy the animal spirit inside of you. There you were, fighting worse demons than I."

He gave a derogatory laugh. "How do you think, I knew they were destroying you?"

Katie looked up, "No one's expendable on my team, Jackson. I don't think I'll call you a pawn, but if you are, you're just as valuable as any other player." She glanced out over the meadow again, seeing a gray timber wolf. "To hell with anyone who says strategy requires a sacrifice."

Jackson stepped closer, his eyes penetrating hers. "I felt your indecision, your fear of my becoming a Malus. You have been worried about it for weeks. What made you decide to come, and save me?"

Katie tried to hide the tears, simmering in her eyes. "There were a couple of reasons. I don't want to lose you. The thought of you dying..." She shook her head, unable to contemplate the emotions she felt. "It would be like losing Sam, all over again."

Jackson reached out and grabbed her hand. She looked down, watching his thumb rub her knuckle. "The second reason is Candy wouldn't allow it. She convinced me to save the guy we love today, not the one who made a grievous error yesterday. Or, the one who may become a monster tomorrow."

Jackson looked out over the meadow, watching the snow leopard for a moment before his gaze returned to her.

"If Candy hadn't noticed you missing..." She shuttered, not wanting to think about the consequences. "Not only would we have lost you, but we would never have known, if a Seeker can be repentant enough to return."

She stepped back, and gently pulled her hand away from his, giving him a weak smile. She walked towards the Seekers in custody, a snow leopard trotted towards her. She watched, as Candy changed into human form.

"Did you see a gray wolf, running around?"

"Yeah, Tyler said, When the fighting started, it came out of the woods and started helping. I'm not sure who it is." Candy shrugged, "I've tried to talk to it. It doesn't respond."

Katie turned back to Jackson, "Can you communicate with the gray wolf?"

Jackson walked towards them, his eye scanning the area. Seeing the wolf, his eyes narrowed shaking his head. "She's not responding."

Katie directed her thoughts towards the wolf. "*Who are you?"*

"*You must kill the Seekers, Katherine."*

Katie narrowed her eyes. There's only one person she knew, whoever called her by her whole first name. "*Who are you*?" she stressed.

"*If you must know, Miss Smith*."

Katie closed her eyes. She did not want to hear it. Looking back at her friends, she noticed them watching her intently. "Can you hear her?"

She could see Jackson, and Candace shaking their heads.

"*You must kill the Seekers, Katherine. They will never change, who they are.*"

Katie sighed, *I've already had this conversation, with Forrest. If the oath is made under duress, the Seeker can return.*

"*NO! There's no going back. That's how it's always been. It's too dangerous to let them go.*"

"*Go into my mind,*" she told Candy and Jackson. "*See if you can hear her.*" She could immediately feel their presence.

"*You made an oath, Katherine, to kill all Seekers, who enter into your domain.*"

Katie glanced at her friends, they both nodded letting her know they could hear. "*I've made no such oath.*"

"*Did you not go to the sacred ceremony, when you were of age?*"

"*Are you talking about the fire ceremony Old Elizabeth Hawk had all the women attend?*" Katie asked.

"*Yes, you made a promise. If you ever change into animal form, you will protect your people, and kill all Seekers who enter your domain.*"

Katie shook her head, "*I made no such promise.*"

"*I know my sister, Katherine, she never would have allowed you to leave the ceremony, without extracting a promise to all those who were there.*"

Katie looked up in surprise, her eyes catching those of her friends. "*You are Old Elizabeth Hawk's sister?*"

There was a pause. "*Yes, I'm her older sister.*"

"*Your last name is Smith.*"

"*I've had many names over the years. Smith is a name, that hides one's true identity well.*"

"*How did you know, we were fighting here?*"

A pause, Katie didn't think she was going to answer. "*David Black called me. He said you were all going to try and save a member of your team. He didn't explain to me, it was a Seeker.*"

Jackson raised his eyebrows covering his mouth, he gave a low chuckle.

"How did you know, I was a were-wolf?"

"*I followed you that day. I was not done talking to you. I saw you change in your wolf form, before jumping into the woods.*"

Katie smirked, at the word talking. If she remembered correctly, the teacher was screaming as she ran down the hall. Deciding not to change the conversation. "*How can I communicate with you, and no one else can?"*

"*We are wasting time, Katherine. We must kill the Seekers, before they decide to attack us.*"

"*I'm not killing anyone, and neither are you,*" Katie ordered.

Walking towards the circle of Seekers, Jackson and Candy followed closely behind.

"*I thought you guys were never going to come over,*" Tyler thoughts said wearily. "*I don't think they noticed, but we're still outnumbered.*"

"*They don't want to fight Tyler,*" Jackson answered.

Tyler changed into human form, his clothes automatically covering him. "I was hoping. I just wasn't sure." He turned to Katie. "It got pretty dicey there for a while, I didn't think you were going to make it."

Katie nodded, neither did she. Stopping in front of the Seekers, she at first didn't know what to say.

"*Katherine, you must kill them all.*"

Katie glanced towards the timber wolf, she gave a double take when she noticed a regular sized bobcat standing next to her. "*Forrest is that you?*"

The small cat gave her a quick nod.

"You seem small."

She heard Jackson and Candy give a small chuckle, as Forrest bristled from her comment. Wanting to point out Forrest to Lizzy, she looked around for her friend. She saw Lizzy walk up to Tyler, and grab his hand. He stiffly pulled his hand away from hers. Walking away he stood next to Jackson.

"*I wonder what that's all about,*" Candy mused quietly in her mind.

Katie nodded, turning back towards the Seekers. "Okay, the first thing I would like to ask, is there a Jackie Oaklin here?" Katie could feel Candy stiffen next to her.

A tiger stepped forward, cautiously.

Katie glanced towards Candy. "Would you like, to do the honors?"

Candy nodded slightly, "I would like to apologize to you, Jackie. I was aware you were about to change. I let our past grievances blind me. We tried to find you, but..." she shook her head, "I'm so sorry."

The tiger sat down, looking towards Candy.

Jackson cleared his throat. "She says, if you show her how to change while still wearing clothes, all is forgiven."

Katie couldn't help chuckling. This was going to turn out all right, she could tell.

"*Katherine, you must kill the Seekers. They will destroy everything we have fought for.*"

"Look, if you don't shut up. I'm going to tell the Seekers what *you* *want us to do to them."* Katie retaliated. She wasn't surprised, when the timber wolf and bobcat backed away and faded into the woods.

Katie looked back towards the Seekers. "It looks like you guys are all under new management," Katie smiled. "The first thing we need to discuss is accommodations. I recall the old management felt rather strongly, you needed to completely forsake your families. The first order of business, is for all of you to go home."

She felt Jackson stiffen, beside her. Looking his way she couldn't read his thoughts, nor did he give her any indication how he felt.

"I know you all have been told your families will be in danger. This may, or may not be the case." Katie looked down at her feet. Not knowing how, to put into words her feelings.

"We still don't know what to call the great evil that is out there." Katie said. "I just think, if it wants you away from your families, then we should do the exact opposite. So, go home. Tell your parents you ran away, or whatever story you want to come up with. Start up your lives again. Go to school, date your boyfriend, whatever you want to do. Come back next week to Candy's lodge, and we'll have some kind of plan formed."

The Seekers stood there, not moving. Katie cautiously glanced towards Jackson.

He shrugged giving her a twisted smile. "They think it's a trick."

Not understanding, she raised her eyebrow.

"They are used to the other management playing head games with them." Jackson tried to explain. "They believe the first person to start for home will be killed."

Katie quickly looked back, towards the Seekers. "I don't know how to convince you." She shook her head, giving a sigh. "I think action will speak louder than words." She turned around and started walking away from the group, all of her friends following. Turning back into animal form, they ran towards the lodge.

Chapter 39
Redemption

Arriving at the lodge, they observed the damage done to the place. Turning back into human form, Katie followed Jackson's lead. They started picking up overturned chairs and cleaning up broken glass. It became obvious, they couldn't do anything more until daylight. They sat down in the chairs. Katie noticed Tyler, sitting stiffly next to Jackson. Who was curiously looking, at a downtrodden Lizzy.

"*Trouble in paradise?*" she privately communicated to him referring to Tyler and Lizzy.

Jackson turned and winked at her. They shared a quiet smile.

Katie picked up her cell phone, and text David. "Everyone OK."

Candy stretched out, on one of the couches. "I wonder, how much of a dent, we made to the other side tonight."

Jackson laughed. "We're not going to hear about some poor camper, getting attacked by an animal."

"We could have missed somebody," Katie said cautiously.

Jackson shook his head "No way. They wanted to make an example of me. Everyone in the area, was required to attend. I hadn't even met half of the Seekers that were present." He shook his head, chuckling. "Not bad, for one night's work."

Katie frowned. “What do you think about Miss Smith, demanding we kill all the Seekers?”

“What?” Tyler and Lizzy said in unison.

Katie realized they were not a part of the conversation she had had with the English teacher. They didn't have any idea Jackson had received all of the Black Panther’s spirit heart back. Katie half listened, while Candy filled them in.

Katie got up and started pacing the room. “Old Elizabeth Hawk performed the ceremony intending on making everyone who might change into a were-animal promise to destroy all Seekers. She firmly believed there was no turning back, once the Seeker’s oath was made.”

Katie struggled, to put her thoughts into words. “She even came to me in a dream just before I changed, warning me I needed to have my mother perform the ceremony in her place.”

Candy sat up on the couch. “Once she was in the spirit world, wouldn’t she have realized she was wrong about Seekers?”

Katie shook her head, trying to figure it out in her mind.

Jackson cleared his throat. “Old Elizabeth Hawk had been living for more than 170 years. She firmly believed what she was doing was right. I can’t see her changing her mind in just a matter of months, regardless whether she was dead or not.”

“So what you’re saying,” Katie pointed out, “is that she would have the same beliefs and personality in the spirit world, as she had here on earth.”

“It sounds plausible,” Candy pointed out. “We will never know for sure.”

“Forrest told me Old Elizabeth Hawk was in love with a Seeker,” Katie said quietly. She looked up, as all eyes were on her. “He said there was no saving him. She asked the others to kill him, because she couldn't do it herself."

"We know that's not true," Candy interrupted, "because Jackson is no longer a Seeker."

Jackson got up and leaned against the wall with his arms folded. "Can you explain again, what happened at the ceremony?"

"There's nothing to tell," Lizzy piped up. "My grandma told us the story of The Great White Tiger. She was getting ready to tell us of some danger, when she had her stroke."

"The very moment, when she was going to tell about the Seekers, she had a stroke?" Jackson asked, his excitement showing.

"Probably," Lizzy watched Jackson carefully.

Jackson pushed off the wall. "My guess is, The Great White Tiger, was getting ready for the next generation of were-animals. She recognizes three potentials, in the ceremony. Not wanting them to make the deadly promise, she leaves Old Elizabeth Hawk's body, causing a stroke."

He started pacing the room, his excitement infectious. "The tiger watches the relationship, between Katie and me closely, but still allows us to become friends. She is probably hoping when the time comes, I will choose not to turn her into a Seeker."

He turned to Katie. "Remember I told you it took several weeks, for you to change? Four times longer, than anyone else I know. She wanted a friendship to develop."

Katie watched Jackson, finally understanding what The Great White Tiger was trying to do.

“Once Katie became a were-animal, it’s easier for others to follow,” Jackson said. “I go and screw everything up, by getting Sam killed.”

He sat down on the couch. “She’s not ready to give up on me,” he said with wonder. “When Katie gets in the car accident, she doesn’t go to any of you to save her. She comes to me. I follow her straight to Katie, which allows me to tell my story.”

He got up and started pacing the room again. “She has to rely on Katie having the personality to forgive, and have the heart to fight for a Seeker, a Seeker, who has the potential to become a monster.”

Katie felt uncomfortable, with the praise. Clearing her throat, “Jackson I already told you, I had reservations about saving you. Candy was the one, who convinced me.”

“I would never have given him a chance, if you didn’t explain the circumstances of how he became a Seeker,” Candy piped in. “I would have just assumed, he chose evil over good.”

“I wonder when Seekers first started appearing,” Katie said, changing the subject. “I mean, you think about it. It’s a diabolical plan. First,” she starts ticking off with her fingers. “The animal spirit recognize an evil, about to threaten the people they have chosen to protect. Second, they enter into the bodies of chosen vessels, to fight this evil. Only to have the evil, come up with a lie. Changing the chosen servants, into Seekers. Third, they are aware it’s all a lie at first, so they don’t trust the Seekers. They then use the Seekers, to create more Seekers. Fourth, the Seekers eventually, become just as evil as them and turn into Malus, who helps their cause.

The group sat in silence, contemplating over all the things they had learned. A small beep from Katie's cell phone, had everyone turning to watch her as she casually picked it up to receive a text.

"Where R U"

She quickly typed, "lodge," and then set the phone down.

Again the beep sounded, "Where R U"

She shook her head, a small grin acknowledging David's determination. Eventually, she typed in, "B home soon."

She looked up and saw Jackson watching her closely. She gave him an apologetic smile. "David's worried." She didn't understand her need to apologize, or give an explanation.

Trying to cover her confusion she got up and looked over the group. "There's something else I would like to discuss."

She looked around, all eyes on her. "David has talked to me several times, about how our families need to know the truth of what's going on." She could see the apprehension, in everyone's eyes.

"I know it's going to be hard, but I believe he's right. I tried to tell my mom once. It was disastrous." She smiled at the memory. "I think we should tell them all at once. Here at the lodge, where there can be no distractions." She waited patiently, for someone to agree with her.

The silence was deafening. She decided, she might as well get it all out. "The Black family needs to be here also."

She looked towards Jackson. "They need to know, what happened to Sam. Everything, the good, the bad..." She paused, before continuing. "Everything."

She kept looking around the silent group, wanting someone to agree. "We won't truly get past Sam's death, and the mistakes that were made until we face up to them." Her eyes now pleading, "any thoughts, or ideas?"

Still, no one said a word.

Jackson sighed, getting up he stood next to her. Turning around he faced the group, "I'm in."

Katie looked over and gave him an appreciative smile. "Thank you."

Jackson gave her a twisted smile. "I don't like the idea of facing the Blacks, but I miss my family." He nodded his head, "I want to go home."

Candy jumped up and gave Jackson a hug. "If you can face the Black's, I can face my mom."

Jackson smiled, shaking his head. "You're a lot stronger than I am," he said with a laugh.

Katie couldn't help grinning, as she watched them share a private joke. Turning back to the other two, she patiently waited.

"My foster parents," Tyler shook his head, "they are not my family."

Katie frowned. "Where are your parents?" she asked quietly.

"I never met my dad. My mom," he paused "she's in prison for vehicular manslaughter, while under the influence."

Stunned, Katie gave a quick glance towards Candy, who had a shocked expression on her face. "I'm sorry, I didn't know," she said inadequately.

"I have a brother and sister," Tyler inserted. "I haven't seen them, since I was twelve. I don't know where they are."

"You don't have to have your foster parents come," Katie said quickly.

"You have more family than that," Candy pointed out, "We're your family."

Tyler gave them a sheepish smile. He nodded quickly and looked down at his feet.

Katie looked towards her oldest friend, in the room. Lizzy was watching Tyler closely, a scared expression on her face. She glanced up and quickly masked her features. "Once again, I find myself the last one to agree to one of your schemes."

"I'm not going to force you to do anything you don't want to do," Katie said quickly.

Lizzy sighed. "Of course, you are."

Katie was a little taken back, "No, I'm not Lizzy. We just won't invite your parents to come."

"Your mother will be on the phone telling mine as soon as she gets home," Lizzy pointed out.

Katie stopped and took a deep breath. "This is the right thing to do Lizzy. We need our families."

Lizzy gave a derogatory laugh. "See? No choice."

Katie watched her friend closely, unable to gauge what was really going on. She finally, came to a decision.

"I'm not sure what you want me to do, Lizzy, so I'm just going to go ahead with the plan for telling our parents. I will leave it up to you, if your parents show up or not." Looking up at the clock, it was almost 2:00 am.

She rubbed her eyes in exhaustion. "Let's go home." Without waiting for anyone else, she headed for the Hummer.

Chapter 40
Another Beginning

Katie glanced over the railing and saw the parents congregating downstairs. The other were-animals on her team were milling around her, too nervous to speak. It had been two weeks, since Prom. Candy had asked to wait, until her dad could be in town. Katie liked the idea of waiting. They all could get through the distraction of finals, without having to deal with parents, having conniptions over what their kids had been doing for months.

School was out for the summer. It seemed like a perfect beginning. Looking over the crowd, she saw David leaning up against the back wall. He had a huge grin on his face. He looked up and gave her a small wave. Smiling at him, she waved back.

She shook her head remembering the small mishaps, when David and his parents first entered the Lodge. Candy had run up and embraced them like they were long lost, friends. Katie had to gently remind her, she had not officially met any of the Black family.

She knew everyone there, except for two couples who were dressed exceptionally well. They seemed ill at ease, of the camaraderie of the others around them. Forrest and Miss Smith were sitting in the back, frowns on their faces, which gave every indication they still were not pleased with the upcoming events.

She looked up at the clock. She would give Lizzy two more minutes to come with her parents, and then she was going to start without them. Looking back at Jackson he sat on a window seal, his face made of stone. He glanced her way. His eyes had such a hopeful, haunted look, her heart went out to him.

"It's going to be okay," she privately told him.

He nodded, his face returning to stone.

Glancing back at the clock, Katie decided it was time. Giving Candy a thumbs up, she walked down the steps with her following close behind. Standing in front, the parents immediately quieted.

"First," Katie began nervously, "I would like to thank you all for coming."

The front door opened. Katie turned to see her friend walk in, with her parents. She smiled, "Thank you for coming Lizzy."

Lizzy nodded and directed her parents where to sit. She then headed up the stairs, with the others.

Katie turned back to the parents. "There are some serious things, we need to discuss. I would like you to hold your comments and questions, until the end." She took a deep breath. "The first thing we would like to do is tell you all an old Indian legend. I know some of you have heard it before. Please allow all to hear." She turned to Candy.

Candy, her face red, stepped up and started to tell the story of The Great White Tiger, and the courageous woman who chose to stand and fight.

About The Author

My sister Dianna Kilpack, is an amazing woman. I admire and love her with all my heart and soul. Even though she is my younger sister, she has been a source I could always turn to for advice, without judgment. Like Katie in this book, she sees the good in everyone. She is very forgiving. When growing up, she always picked the person being bullied, to be her friend.

We grew up in West Bountiful Utah. We had a large family of twelve children. Six girls and six boys. Our youngest brother Jared, did not make it to mortality, but we still remember him and count him as one of us. Our brother Johnny has been with Jared since 2001. Our family moved to Missouri, when Dianna was thirteen.

Dianna is divorced now, has 4 children, and 3 grandchildren. Dianna's only son Mickey went to be with Johnny and Jared when he was only 10 weeks old. Our separation from these 3 courageous, fine young men, is only for a small moment. Johnny and Mickey are buried side-by-side, in our family cemetery. Even though we miss them, we believe and have the faith that we will be with them one day again. We know they are preparing a way for the rest of us, when we pass on. Until we meet again guys, love you!

Dianna now lives in Lake of the Ozarks Missouri, with her daughter. She has a bachelor's degree in Accounting, and MBA from Columbia College, Lake Ozark Campus.

Dianna has built her own business in commercial embroidery, and taught herself how to digitize any design. She has her own accounting business.

I am so proud of my sister Dianna, with all her accomplishments, and struggles. She is a beacon of light, that never fades. I hope you enjoy her books as I have. The message of hope and forgiveness throughout her books is a message we all need in our lives.

May God bless and protect you, Dianna, Always! Fly like the wind on eagles wings, way above the mountains, and know you have endured your journey well. I love you, more than life itself. God has blessed my life, having you in it. I am so grateful, God sent your special spirit to be my sister.

Love always, and Forever, Your Eternal Sister..... Forever!!
Cindy

www.ingramcontent.com/pod-product-compliance
Lightning Source LLC
Chambersburg PA
CBHW020605310726
48979CB00008B/1349/J

* 9 7 8 0 9 9 8 1 6 7 6 1 9 *